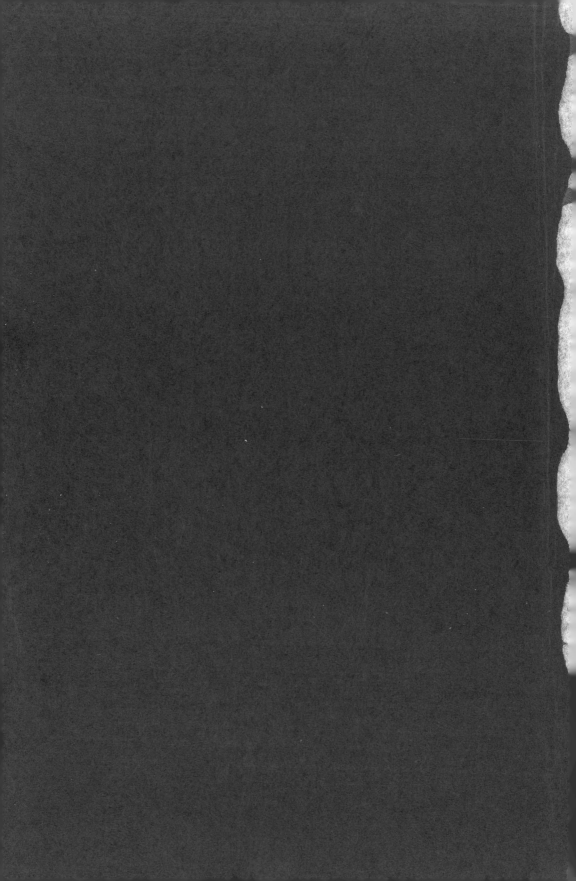

The Keeper

The Keeper

Meg O'Brien

A Perfect Crime Book

DOUBLEDAY

NEW YORK   LONDON   TORONTO   SYDNEY   AUCKLAND

A PERFECT CRIME BOOK
PUBLISHED BY DOUBLEDAY
a division of Bantam Doubleday Dell Publishing Group, Inc.
666 Fifth Avenue, New York, New York 10103
DOUBLEDAY is a trademark of Doubleday, a division
of Bantam Doubleday Dell Publishing Group, Inc.

BELLY UP TO THE BAR, BOYS from Meredith Willson's
"The Unsinkable Molly Brown" By Meredith Willson
© 1960 (Renewed) FRANK MUSIC CORP. and MEREDITH
WILLSON MUSIC
All Rights Reserved   Used By Permission

I AIN'T DOWN YET from Meredith Willson's "The Unsinkable
Molly Brown" By Meredith Willson
© 1960, 1961 (Renewed) FRANK MUSIC CORP. and
MEREDITH WILLSON MUSIC
All Rights Reserved   Used By Permission

I'LL NEVER SAY NO from Meredith Willson's "The
Unsinkable Molly Brown" By Meredith Willson
© 1960 (Renewed) FRANK MUSIC CORP. and MEREDITH
WILLSON MUSIC
All Rights Reserved   Used By Permission

BOOK DESIGN BY TASHA HALL

Library of Congress Cataloging-in-Publication Data

O'Brien, Meg.
The keeper / by Meg O'Brien.
p.   cm.
"A Perfect crime book."
I. Title.
PS3565.B718K44   1992
813'.54—dc20   92-12247
CIP

ISBN 0-385-42482-5

1   3   5   7   9   10   8   6   4   2

First Edition

For my agent,
Dominick Abel

With love and appreciation for his constant support,
excellent advice, and reassuring presence

The Keeper

Chapter 1

THE CHILD

THE KIDNAPPER TOOK CHARLY as she was climbing down from the back of a whale.

The sun was high and bright, the wooden dolphins arcing out of their tanks into a crystal white California sky. Charly was wearing the new dress her father gave her for her ninth birthday that morning. He was taking her to an early dinner at a special restaurant today. She couldn't wait.

Right now, though, she was at Universal Studios, in a blue-water tank on the back of a giant imitation whale, having her picture taken. A silvery spray hit her eyes and face. It splattered her dress. Charly didn't mind—she was having the time of her life. She laughed, closing her eyes briefly, thinking she could feel the whale leap through the cold blue waters off the Farallons, or one of the other places she had learned about in geography. Then she looked across to where her summer-school teacher, Mrs. Patterson, stood talking to a man. Mrs. Patterson waved. The smiling man next to her waved, too. Charly didn't know who he was, but she smiled back. Cameras clicked.

Too quickly the souvenir picture-taking was over. Charly was helped down from the whale by a studio employee in white shorts and a bright blue shirt.

She stumbled a little, and the attendant caught her with both arms. "Okay?" He laughed into her eyes as he held her aloft.

"Sure." He had curly blond hair, like hers (except that hers was long and pulled back in two ribbons) and he had eyes that matched his shirt. Charly thought he was the handsomest man she had ever seen. Her own eyes were a funny green with bits of brown, and she didn't like them much at all.

3

The attendant turned from Charly to help another child up onto the whale. Charly took a few steps back and nearly bumped into the man who had been talking with her teacher.

"Mrs. Patterson wants all the kids to meet in the parking lot for lunch," he said. "I'll walk you over there."

Charly decided he was one of the kids' fathers who had come along as a chaperon. Instead of buses, like during the school year, they had come, three or four together, in separate cars. And she knew it was time to break for lunch. Mrs. Patterson had said so. "Tailgate party in fifteen minutes!" she had called, just before Charly had left to have her picture taken on the whale.

Charly followed the man to the parking lot. There were hundreds of cars, and she couldn't remember where they had parked.

"I don't see the other kids," she said, slowing and looking around.

"They're over here, in the van." The man took her arm and pulled her toward a faded gray van with black windows.

"But that's not one of the cars we came in—"

The man gave a harder tug. "C'mon. Everybody's there, you'll see." He kept right on smiling, even though she was pulling back now, dragging her feet, and before Charly could stop him, or yell, or do anything, he was wrenching open the door of the van and shoving her, hard, inside. She fell, landing and scraping her knees on coils of rope and dirty rags.

By this time Charly knew what was happening, she had seen it on the news and on movies the police showed in school. Terrified, she opened her mouth to scream.

A hand clamped over her face. She was shoved flat onto the van's floor. The hand slipped.

"No!" she managed to cry, "no—!"

The man came down full-length on her back. Her chest and stomach burned. She could smell his breath, like spearmint gum. The man's weight ground her body into the metal floor. Something was shoved into her mouth. She gagged. Her arms were yanked behind her back, her wrists tied. Charly felt the ropes cut into her skin. She tried to kick, to squirm. The man swore. Her legs were shoved together, her ankles bound.

The man left her there. He moved quickly into the driver's seat and started the car, gunning the motor. Charly heard tires squeal as they sped from the parking lot, then they were going faster, faster, and the man began to sing, a *shaky, high-pitched tune that she knew somehow, and knew she had to remember, it was important, remember—*

Charly couldn't help it. She felt her bladder leak, warm-hot fluid wetting her new birthday dress. She squeezed her eyes tight, tears coming so fast they filled up her nose, and with the rag in her mouth she couldn't breathe—

The van lurched from side to side. Her head struck something sharp. It was the last thing Charly knew before she awakened in the room. Before she opened her eyes again, and the nightmare began in earnest.

Chapter 2
THE MOTHER

As Charly Hayes was being kidnapped in Southern California, her mother, Brooke, stood center-stage in a theater in San Francisco. She was tired but exhilarated, near the end of dress rehearsals for a show in which she was playing her first leading role.

The role was important in more ways than one. Brooke was on her way back up after hitting bottom the year before. She had a lot to prove —both to Charly and to herself.

In today's rehearsal Brooke had been tackled and pummeled, chased and yelled at, laughed at and scorned. She stood on a woodpile now, chin up, green eyes blazing. Her own shoulder-length blond hair was covered by a ragged, boyish, red-blond wig.

Brooke, not a great singer, but an Ethel Merman, belted out the words to "I Ain't Down Yet" with all the passionate hope of Molly Brown, the unschooled mountain girl whose role she played.

". . . so if you go from nowhere on the road to somewhere, and you meet anyone, ya know it's me . . ." The words pealed out over the theater, clear as cathedral bells. When the piece ended, there were tears in Brooke's eyes that had nothing to do with Molly Brown's search for respectability, and everything to do with her own. There was a long moment of silence, then the cast and crew began to applaud. As the cheers and clapping died down, Brooke laughed with embarrassment and rubbed at bruises on her arms.

"Not bad," grumbled Leo Walsh. He wore a black satin jacket

with *SuperDirector* emblazoned in yellow on its back. His red hair stood up in disarray, clashing with a luminescent orange tie. "It's getting there."

All within earshot groaned.

IN HER TINY CHANGING ROOM, Brooke sat at the antique dressing table that Sean—her feckless mountain "brother" in the play—had helped her lug up the hilly streets from a garage sale. At one point it had gotten away from them and careened, helter-skelter, down the street. She had watched it trundle over potholes and rocks, feeling horror: *Downhill, like my life,* she had thought. But Sean only laughed and went dashing off after the thing, and Brooke, after a moment, sprinted after him. They caught it and leaned together for a moment over its scarred mahogany surface, panting. Sean, his thick blond hair glinting in the sun like the straw on Molly's cabin roof, met her eyes.

"Not a scratch. It's tough. Sturdy and plain—like you, now."

He meant that she had sorted out the clutter. The weeds of guilt and confusion that had grown in her mind and made her crazy before.

The dressing table mirror was distorted, though. Funny how different mirrors can be, how they make you look. Fat, skinny, short, tall . . . Which of you is real? The one you see here, today, or that one, yesterday? Which is the person others see? (And which do you really want to be?)

She tugged off Molly's flannel shirt. Unbuckled the too-big leather belt and let it fall to the floor. Kicking off dusty brown boots, she wiggled her toes in their wool socks. She still wore Molly Brown's cheap cotton undershirt. Proudly, like a prize.

She wished Charly could see her in this play. She wanted her daughter to know there was a flip side to disaster. She wanted her back.

The song "Belly up to the Bar, Boys" began; the sound equipment being tested for the next day. ". . . Only drink by day or night or somewhere in between. . . ."

My old theme song, she thought, with a familiar flicker of shame.

For a solid year she had managed to drink by day, by night, and everywhere in between. At the end of it her marriage was over (although why people say that, escaped her, since they're always over long before), and Charly was gone. Nathan had full custody, while Brooke had one visiting day per month at Nathan's house—no longer hers—in Westwood.

She lifted a silver frame with three photos: one of Charly as an infant, one at the age of six, and another taken just last winter. She touched the latter, as if smoothing her daughter's long blond hair. Charly was beautiful at nine, she thought, and bright. More than that, she was good. A good soul. Charly had never, to Brooke's knowledge, done or wished anyone harm.

It was Charly who had saved her, finally. Charly, who—one day when Brooke came to the house in Westwood soused to the gills—had tape-recorded her insane babblings and played them back to her, cleverly waiting until Brooke was sober and fully conscious of what she heard.

Charly was eight, then, going on thirty-three.

Listening to that tape, Brooke had suffered humiliation, self-blame, and something more valuable than either one: a passionate, almost excruciating love for her daughter that was like no emotion she had ever known. From that moment on she hadn't touched a drop, and the pills that had become so addicting in those final months had been tapered off, then eliminated, under a dependency doctor's care.

It had been eight months since Charly made that tape. Six months since Brooke had become part of the Powell Repertory Group in San Francisco. The job had taken her away from Charly, but at the time it had seemed the only road back.

Jay Kramer, the lawyer to whom Leo had referred her last month, said that joint custody might be possible now. "You've cleaned up your life. You're straight, you're working. You've got friends here who can testify to your fitness, if it comes to that. Take the guy to court. Get joint custody."

"But Nathan is a lawyer, he has a lot of power."

"Lawyers don't have as much power as everybody thinks."

Jay Kramer probably didn't, Brooke surmised, looking around the shabby office on Green Street. He had been practicing only two years, working much of that time for other firms.

"I'm just not sure I can win," Brooke said.

Especially not with this attorney, she thought.

But it wasn't Nathan she was afraid of, so much as herself. Even after eight months, Brooke wasn't certain she would make it. She was sober today—had not had pills or booze today—nor any day in the past two hundred and forty-three. She wasn't all that sure about tomorrow.

Opening a jar of peach-tinted cream, she began to cleanse her face with cotton pads—humming softly to the still-playing bar song. Pretending to a happiness she did not yet feel. Happy wasn't something you could count on, Brooke knew. You had to make it happen. Like with *Molly Brown.*

When PRG decided to revive the musical, Brooke went after the lead with all the energy and tunnel vision her newly dry state had wrought. She worked at getting in shape with weights, exercise, running, gymnastics. You had to be strong for Molly; it was one of the most physically demanding roles ever written for a woman. Staying up nights, she rehearsed the songs to *Molly Brown.* She sang them mornings while making her bed and ran through dialogue while walking to work—ignoring bypassers who stared. Not that she blamed them. In faded jeans, no makeup, her hair covered over with a scarf, and mumbling, there wasn't much to distinguish Brooke Hayes from the average bag lady.

Before tryouts she had learned every word of the *Unsinkable* score, every nuance of expression. Molly Brown became the new addiction.

And up there on the boards, with spotlights blazing, it was as she had known it would be. She felt Molly's strength course through her veins. She became Molly, thought like her, fought like her. *As a man thinketh, so is he.*

"Think strong," a counselor had urged. "It will make you strong. Think sober. And think drug free."

All the things she needed to be, to get Charly back.

And that was the itinerary now—to get Charly.

"I'm well now," she would say when she saw Charly in a few days. "You can trust me now. I can care for you, love you. I'll never hurt you again." No more blackouts, no more mornings when she didn't know what she had done the night before. No more driving off the edge of the world, where you fall into a void so complete you might never come back.

The song now being tested over the sound system broke through the fog of memories. Johnny Brown's love song to Molly:

". . . I'll stay or I'll go . . . but I'll . . . never . . . say no."

That's right, baby, she thought. *I've got a plan. And from now on I'm never saying no. Not to you.*

That's what she would tell Charly when she saw her three days from now.

Chapter 3

The call came around eight that night, just after an argument with Leo.

He had been in her living room in North Beach, still fine-tuning the script—minor adaptations for PRG's cast, space, and scenery limitations. Brooke could hear him muttering.

"I think that tackle needs work," she called out. "Sean's holding off, probably because he's afraid of hurting me."

"Sean gets any tougher on you," he grumbled, "you won't be walking by opening night."

"C'mon, Leo. Talk to him, will you?"

A loud sigh. "You're a glutton for punishment, Brooke. You ever think of that?"

"Mm-hmm."

She was thinking it was fun to tumble and spar with the boys in the show. She had never had brothers, never gotten to play "boy" games as a kid growing up in the south. Learning to be a tomboy—even at thirty-one—wasn't all bad.

"That was a great scene yesterday," she said.

"You mean the cornstalks?"

"Mmm." She had been running through a "cornfield"—a dozen high clumps of cornstalks in pots that were weighted down with gravel. Sean tore through a row slightly ahead of her and stumbled, knocking

over a pot. The gravelly weight made it boomerang up. The stalks hit
Brooke in the face.

She turned without even thinking and took a swing at Sean. The
reaction was automatic, straight out of her role as the rough-and-tumble
Molly Brown. Sean ducked, though, laughing, and instead of connect-
ing with him, she struck another cornstalk—and the whole damn two
rows went falling down like dominoes, *thumpthumpthumpthumpthump-
thump*. . . .

The cast and crew doubled over. "Leave it!" Leo had yelled.
"We'll rig it, keep it in!"

It wouldn't be the original, untampered-with *Unsinkable Molly
Brown,* but then, nothing that Leo Walsh directed ever was. Nearly
every review of every show included mention of Leo's quirky personality—the main reason, that same review would admit, for PRG's phe-
nomenal success.

"Anyway, talk to him," Brooke said now. "Get him to stop holding back."

A grunt from the other room.

She took pasta from the stove, dumping it into a strainer. Wiping
steamy hands on her jeans, she tossed basil, fresh tomatoes, and sautéed
garlic through it with a fork. The windows above the sink were fogged
from the heat; she took a paper towel and dried a spot to look out. The
sky was a rose-yellow glow over a sliver of San Francisco Bay. Boats
skittered about in a stiff summer breeze. Leo read dialogue changes
aloud in the next room.

"That's pretty contemporary for Molly," Brooke yelled.

She heard a sound at the kitchen door, and, startled, she turned to
see Leo looking irritated, his red hair mussed, orange tie askew. He
tugged at a short, curly beard. *Like a crabby teddy bear,* she thought
fondly. *Afraid that if he smiles, his stuffing will fall out.*

"What's wrong with Molly being contemporary?"

"Nothing. In fact, Molly Tobin Brown was probably one of the
first libbers. But it doesn't fit, her saying things like, 'Oh, Johnny, I
can't commit to a life like that forever.' She sounds like nearly every
single man in America."

"You have some better idea, I suppose. You could, in fact, improve upon the original, never mind that Richard Morris was brilliant and wrote a million-dollar Broadway musical."

She ignored the sarcasm. "How about, 'I've got to think about it, Johnny.' Leave her an out, but without so hard an edge."

"Not very original."

He was staring at her, his expression smoothing out when she caught him, but not before she saw the flicker of anger. With a pang Brooke remembered that she had said exactly those words to Leo twice in the past three months.

She avoided his eyes, taking dishes from a cupboard and setting the square white table. The setting was high-tech, black on white. In the middle was one red silk rose—Sarah Rubin's decor, the woman she had sublet from. Brooke had added warmer, personal touches in the other rooms, so that Charly would be comfortable when she came here.

Bringing a third person—a man—into the life she was planning with Charly was impossible to contemplate now.

"You're in love with your daughter," Leo accused.

Brooke flushed. "You make me sound demented."

"It's true, though. All the energy most women put into a man, you put into thinking about that kid. You're obsessed."

She dropped silverware on the table with a thud. "Leo, I've *got* to be. It's better—" She sighed.

"Better than what?"

Facing him, she said, "Better than being drunk all the time. But I've got to *replace* that with something. If I want Charly, I have to make it happen, I can't be a victim anymore."

His laugh was bitter. "Is that really it? Or is it him, still? You're hoping that if you get her back, you'll get him too."

"Nathan? Please! And if you felt like this, why did you send me to that damned lawyer?"

"I was hoping he'd set you straight. You've only been sober eight months, no judge in California will give her to you this soon."

"I can give her a good life—"

"All the way up here? Away from her father and friends? In this cracker-box apartment, in the city?"

"Dammit, Leo! Why do you always do this to me?"

"Because I want you to see things the way they are, not the fairy-tale way you imagine them to be. I want you to stop sticking your neck out just to get it chopped off. The same way you do on stage, with Sean. Look!"

He grabbed her wrist, pushing up the wide sleeve of her cotton blouse to expose the mottled bruises from her onstage scuffles. "Every day they get worse. You wonder why Sean holds back? Look at them, Brooke, don't turn away. You get into a battle with Nathan Hayes over your daughter, and the bruises won't be so easy to cover up—"

She wrenched away. "No more, okay? Please. No . . . more."

Leo's angry gaze met hers a moment longer. Finally he sighed. "You're right. I'd better not tell you too many truths. We still have to work together."

"Leo—"

His voice grew cocky, an attempt to play it cool. His chin, which receded most of the time, jutted out in self-defense. "Don't say it. I know. You gotta do what you gotta do."

She didn't answer.

"So. I guess I'll just take up my script and go."

Brooke drew fingers through her thick, sun-woven hair. "You don't have to leave."

"Right." He picked up a shiny black plate, held it up to his soft round face like a mirror, made a grimace, and slammed it down. "Funny. I keep thinking it'll be okay. I can come over, be around you, just like before. But I'm always wrong. I can't be around you anymore."

He crossed to the kitchen door. "Seven A.M.," he said curtly. "Tomorrow. Onstage."

"Right."

He shook his head morosely. "Christ, Brooke. You're letting this fixation fuck everything up."

She heard the apartment door slam behind him. Heard his angry footsteps on the stairs. Around her rose the scent of basil and garlic. Brooke sank into the nearest chair.

Damn. If only she could make Leo understand.

Or was the failing in her? Was Leo right, about her being obsessed? Maybe. A little. But there was also the reality of Nathan. More than anything, Charly needed to grow up with more than just Nathan's power-hungry view of the world.

I could do that for her. I could.

She thought of how good it had been, when Charly was first born. The milky breath against her neck. The soft, shuddery burps. Charly saying *mama* the first time, with sticky raspberry on her lips from an icy Popsicle on a hot summer day . . . Charly taking her first steps, unable to stop the momentum, her chubby legs rushing headlong into a chair.

Oh, dear God! Nothing—not even Nathan—had been so bad that she'd had to drink. She, who had never even touched a beer, never taken anything stronger than aspirin, until three years ago. . . .

She had thrown it all away.

Brooke didn't know how long she sat like that. When she looked up again, it was near dusk outside. The steam had gone from the windows. And the phone was ringing. That was what had roused her—the phone.

Brooke turned wearily in the chair and reached for Sarah's neon receiver. "Yes?"

"Mommy . . ." The voice was distant, eerie. A whisper. There were a few words that Brooke couldn't understand. They were too hurried, running together.

"Charly? Charly, is that you?"

"The man—" Her daughter began to cry. Brooke's limbs turned to ice. "Say no, Mommy, *say no, say NO . . . !*"

"Charly, slow down! What's wrong? Where *are* you?"

"I don't know, Mommy, the man—"

There was a choked sound, not a scream, but a cry of distress. Then the line went dead.

"Charly? *Charly!*" Brooke's thoughts were a jumbled mess. She stared at the phone, then jiggled the hook—things that she knew made no sense but that must have been built into mothers at birth. When none of them worked, not even the screaming of her daughter's name into the dead phone, she was nearly paralyzed with fear.

She dialed the number of the house in Los Angeles, her fingers shaking so much she got it wrong on the first try. A recorded message came on, saying to try the number again. Brooke did, forcing her stiff fingers to slow down. The line was busy—and again, still busy. *Fuck! Oh fuck, oh fuck, oh fuck! What in the name of God am I thinking of?* She punched numbers frantically, getting an operator and demanding that she break into Nathan's line. The woman wasted precious time asking questions.

"What the hell is the *problem?*" Brooke finally yelled. "This is an emergency, for Christ's sake, just do it!"

The woman left the line, then Brook heard the click of connection, and after several moments, Nathan's guarded voice. "Hello?"

"Where's Charly?" she demanded.

A pause. "She's here. She's right here, Brooke. What's wrong with you?"

"Nathan, don't lie to me. Something's wrong. Charly just called me, she's in trouble, she was crying—"

As her voice rose, Nathan's became colder and more distant. "You're imagining things as always, Brooke. Calm down. I tell you Charly is right here."

"Check her room! God, Nathan, for once, will you listen to me? There's something wrong!"

"Brooke, Charly is fine. She's sitting across from me. We're having dinner. For God's sake, take a pill, go to sleep."

"Let me talk to her, Nathan—"

For the second time in ten minutes, the phone went dead.

Chapter 4

THE FATHER

NATHAN HAYES SAT AT HIS DESK in his study in Westwood. The room was well appointed with dark woods and Oriental tapestry, but cold—reflecting nothing of family, and only a little of Nathan's work: three diplomas from top-notch law schools across the country, two of which were honorary, and framed news clippings of Nathan Rusherton Hayes with politicians, bank presidents, business leaders.

Nathan himself looked cold. Not an unattractive man, he had recently taken to brushing his thin blond hair flat over his scalp. He wore a gray banker's suit with a stiff-collared white shirt. His back was ramrod straight, his eyes like chips of ice.

His hand rested on the receiver of the phone. He had just hung up from talking with Brooke. He rubbed his face, resting it on his palms, elbows on the desk. Then he straightened. Sighing, he pulled from a drawer a silver-framed photo of the three of them together: Charly, Nathan, and Brooke.

"Damn her! Damn her to *hell!*" He set the picture face down with a thud.

He had met Brooke when she was twenty, playing a small part in *As You Like It* at the Greek Theatre. He had been taken in by the cool, Shakespearean demeanor of the woman whose part she played, the ladylike way she held her head and moved. He had asked to meet her after the show—one of the worst mistakes of his life. The two of them couldn't be less alike.

Brooke, in person, was headstrong, high-spirited—not always be-having in a balanced way. Nathan, at forty, was quiet, determined, cautious. The one time in his life he had done anything on impulse was a few months later, when, after an ill-conceived weekend with Brooke in Cabo San Lucas, he had asked her to marry him. He'd regretted that decision ever since.

He picked up the phone and dialed another number in Westwood. A male voice answered.

"Her mother is going to be a problem," Nathan said. "I'm not sure I can handle her."

"You'll have to figure it out," the voice replied. "You knew it wouldn't be easy this way."

"You just do your part. If anything goes wrong—"

"Don't worry," the voice said. "I've got it covered."

Nathan hung up. He sat for several minutes, looking at the facedown picture. Tapping with a black onyx pen on his desk.

Chapter 5

BROOKE'S NEXT THOUGHT was to call Sean. He was like a brother; he had been there for her from the first, even from the old days in LA. Sean had moved to San Francisco last year, and no sooner landed a part with the Powell Repertory Group than he'd gotten Brooke an audition too.

He knew about Nathan, and how it had been. He would help her clear her thoughts, figure out what to do.

But Sean was out of town.

"An emergency," his roommate, Brent, said. "He'll be back in time for rehearsals tomorrow."

"What kind of emergency?"

"I'm sure I don't know. Something about the mountains . . . he rushed off without even saying good-bye."

Brent was little help; he was jealous of her friendship with Sean. Christ, did gay men really think their boyfriends fooled around with all the women they knew?

Brooke left no message, uncertain what she would do.

Again, she dialed Nathan's number in Westwood, hoping to get the housekeeper. Mrs. Stinson loved Charly; she would tell her honestly if Charly was there. If not—

If Nathan answered, she would demand again, to speak to her daughter.

But this time there was no answer at the Westwood house. And the message machine was off.

She called Leo. Pacing all the while. Pacing, and scrabbling in drawers. She drew in a harsh breath as her fingers, in the deep cluttered drawer, felt the blade of a knife. She drew out her hand. It was bloody. A cut on the index finger. Bright red droplets oozed, and Brooke wiped the finger on her jeans.

It was a minute before she realized what she had been looking for. Pills. Valium. She used to keep a bottle here—there had to be some left! Dammit! *One stupid five-milligram yellow pill!*

But she had thrown every one out, she remembered now, in a foolhardy blaze of courage months before.

Leo answered sleepily, and Brooke told him what had happened, and that she was leaving right away for the airport. "There's a shuttle every hour. I'll wait standby if I have to."

"Brooke, slow down. Take a breath. You don't really know anything yet. Get some facts first, then decide what to do."

"I can't get facts from here," she argued, her voice rising. "Nathan won't talk to me, and I don't know any of Charly's friends this year. I can't even reach the housekeeper."

"Look, what if it wasn't Charly? Maybe it was some kid with too much time on his hands, playing a practical joke."

"It was *Charly*. I know it was her."

"If her father says she's all right . . ."

"Her father can't be trusted."

"Oh, come on, Brooke. Nathan took care of her when you were too stoned to know your own name. What do you think, he's hurt the kid now or something? Become some monster overnight? You're getting paranoid, with all this custody stuff coming up. And what about the show? We're opening in less than two weeks, you can't bail on us now!"

"I know that show better than my own hand. Vicky can stand in for me. I'll be back in a couple of days."

When I get there, I'll find out he's right, she thought desperately. *I am going crazy, getting paranoid again. Nothing's wrong with Charly. It was all a silly game.*

·   ·   ·

THE 737 DIPPED ITS WING, turning north into the LAX corridor. Brooke glanced out the cabin window and saw the flat sprawl, the smog, the traffic jams.

Driving into LA fourteen years ago, at seventeen—with her sputtering old yellow VW dragging its tailpipe—she had known immediately that this wasn't the Hollywood of her dreams. It was a hard city. Not tinsel but ice. It could break the best of them, and if she wasn't careful, it would get her too.

But there was no turning back. Her mother, Livvy, had given her a mission just before she died in the big white house in Georgia that summer. Brooke was to live out Livvy's dreams. That Livvy's dreams of stardom and Hollywood glory sprang primarily from the bottom of a bottle of scotch, was not a consideration. (And such—Brooke often thought with some bitterness in latter days—is the power of mother-daughter love.)

She got a job at Paramount, filing, in an office. A way to get your toe in, a girl she roomed with had advised. And despite the boredom, it was. By the time Brooke was twenty, she had months of study behind her and was getting bit parts in films. The stage, though, had become her real love. She did *As You Like It* at the Greek Theatre her twentieth summer, and it was that same year that she met and married Nathan. A Red Letter Year, she had called it at the time—everything good happening all at once.

Nathan was forty; he had already made it. He had a booming law practice in Westwood, with politicians and movie producers as clients. He was tall and handsome, in a pale, blond, William Hurt way. Bill Hurt had done *Body Heat* with Kathleen Turner by then, and he was all the rage. What girl wouldn't want a man who looked like him?

"Arrogant," her friend Denise had said. "Nathan Hayes is arrogant and domineering. That man treats you like he's your father."

But Brooke was drawn to Nathan's poise and self-assurance, as she saw it then. She hadn't had anyone that strong in her life since grade school, when her father ran off with the Orange Bimbo—a twit, according to Livvy, with red hair and a penchant for Sunkist jumpsuits.

Brooke knew, that first year of marriage, that she didn't love Nathan—that he didn't love her—that they shouldn't have married. If they hadn't been caught up in the romance of a weekend in Mexico, the strumming of guitars, too many margaritas, and the sound of a softly rippling surf beneath their room . . .

Nathan was critical, nit-picking. Brooke was casual. ("Define *casual,* Brooke—why not admit it, you're sloppy.") The kinds of things that don't show up in courtship took on mammoth proportions within the narrowly defined limits of marriage with Nathan Hayes. Nathan's calm maturity became indifference, his strength, rigidity. Brooke's liveliness was seen as volatility, her passion as far too mercurial for a successful lawyer's wife.

Their marriage became a Tracy and Hepburn movie, without the laughs.

Oh, it wasn't just Nathan Brooke was quick enough to admit it. She had given her share of grief. First, there were all those creative but flaky friends she had brought to her marriage—like a dowry, hoping they'd be a gift. And the late hours her profession demanded. Often she would tumble in at two A.M., traces of greasepaint still clinging to her face, and her hair in bobby pins but without the stage wig. Brooke could imagine Nathan waking up in the morning, seeing this, then grabbing his head and moaning, "Oh my God, what have I done?"

The Playboy's Lament, made permanent and continuous by marriage.

That first year she wanted to cut her losses and run. She steeled herself to face the inevitable, to tell Nathan and set them both free. But the week she planned to leave, she learned she was pregnant. Her passion for—and protection of—the unborn child was all that mattered then. She stayed.

But if Nathan had been difficult up to then, his faultfinding now rose to an all-time high. Brooke's body became a project—something to study and observe—to judge. She was expected to be in every night by seven. To read all the "right" books, listen to only the "right" music. To gain no more than fifteen pounds, to have her urine tested even more frequently than her doctor advised. Nothing must go wrong with this child.

In her new role as Carrier of the Seed, Brooke had to learn her lines with perfection, or face a review more cutting, more sarcastic, than Frank Rich's—or even Rex Reed's.

The first things to go were her friends. They were dispatched willy-nilly, like the old VW, and her career, in due time, too. When Charly was born (a feat, a triumph, a boon), Brooke half expected Nathan to be disappointed that she wasn't a son. Nathan, however, was as crazy for Charly (named for his father, Charles Rusherton Hayes) as she. He would come home late at night after meetings and walk Charly when she cried, his spare blond hair falling over the high forehead, his straight blueblood nose nudging the downy cheek. He would murmur and sing lullabies, a diaper over his shoulder to keep spit-ups from souring the pin-striped suit he had worn in court that day.

For a time it seemed things might be all right. Brooke was content, for a while, to give up the embryo career in favor of the living, flourishing child. As Charly grew, however, Nathan became more and more involved in the politics of the city. He was moving up, not just as a lawyer, but as a figure of power. He had little personal time to spend; his interest focused on Charly's schools, music lessons, summer camps. He was like a kid at Christmas, when the wrapping becomes more fun than the toy.

Friends were chosen like fine china. They had to match. Economic background, IQ scores, native intelligence all in order? Fine. Step right up, folks, get your piece of Charly Hayes.

The drinking began because of that . . . Brooke thought . . . because of the control, both of her and her daughter. But was it something that would have happened anyway, given the genes of Livvy Leeds?

Brooke's drinking had started three years ago, when Charly was six. When she went to school, when Nathan began to monitor Charly's grades and posture with equal fervor, as if straight A's and a straight spine were the answer to everything. At the same time it became clear that if Nathan had his way, Brooke's life would forever be dedicated to the Keeping of the Home, the Evolvement of the Child, the Management of Social Assemblage—

While fighting, every step of the way, Nathan's need to control.

And which came first, cart or horse? Control, or the necessity for it? For by then, Brooke was clearly on a downward slide.

Well, it was all a mishmash now. Never to be sorted out, her therapist had said. Forget. Go on from here.

Brooke had tried. She had worked at getting straight, but growing up was something else. She knew she still made mistakes, that she didn't always think clearly or plan things well. Now and then she even blanked out painful events that had happened. And Leo was right, she looked for punishment still.

Was that why she had told Charly so soon about the custody plan? Hoping at some level that Nathan would interfere, and she could go on feeling pain?

Damn therapy. It gave reasons for her actions, yet opened the wound of memory to show that in the final analysis, only she, Brooke, was to blame.

The flight attendant was gathering drink glasses in preparation for landing, and Brooke leaned across the other two seats to hand over her own, with its traces of orange juice, plain. No rum, no gin, no tequila—

Hold on, kid. But her hands shook, and her mouth was dry. Her stomach almost didn't make it as the 737 rumbled over the runway and touched down.

Chapter 6
THE DETECTIVE

LIEUTENANT MARTIN DE PORRES of the West LA Division, LAPD, was closing in gracefully on fifty. He was tall and slender, with only a slight paunch; he had a mellifluous voice, a lean, bronze face, and luminous eyes. He looked, in fact, much like the saint for whom he was named.

That had never stopped him, as a young hot dog thirty years ago, from indiscriminately whacking suspects over the head with his billy club. Despite the altar-boy appearance, Marty was a worker cop, just as the original Martin de Porres was a worker saint. The fact that he was black kept the original Martin from getting canonized for a long time—until after the sixties, in fact, when civil rights came about.

Well, God bless affirmative action. It worked for saints and sinners alike. Got Marty his job, and Martin his heavenly crown.

Middle age had tamed Marty a bit; there was that thickening at the waist from too many beers and pastrami sandwiches, which was one problem, he guessed, that saints didn't have. And he worked the slower evening shifts now, four to midnight behind a desk, ever since the doc had caught that little off-beat rumble in his chest. But they hadn't been able to make him stop smoking. Marty was a sensual man. He liked the feel of a cigarette between his fingers, the dangerous bite of smoke sliding along the soft, moist tissue of his lungs. He was a young man, as he saw it. Still in his twenties, still a hot dog—if only at heart.

He had even kept his hair. Often, throughout the long slow evenings, Marty would smooth it proudly, feeling the springy, gray-black

25

curls rebound with health and vigor. He pictured himself on a Kona beach a year from now, retired from the force and surrounded by a bevy of island girls just dying for the chance to decorate his still eager dick with leis and mango cream.

In the meantime, Marty kept the old billy club hanging behind his desk, on the wall, to remind him of the good old days—and when things weren't going well, he'd take Old Billy down and heft the ebony weight, slide his long brown fingers over the sweet ebony smoothness, and dream of shoving Old Billy up some goddamn pervert's ass.

Marty hated perverts. It was perverts who had raped him, back home in the islands, when he was twelve. There was no record of the attack. Marty never reported it to the authorities there. Instead, he bided his time, waiting for revenge. Moving out to this gay mecca of Los Angeles had been part of the plan. Becoming a cop here was another. Marty figured he just might get a chance to bust a few queenly heads.

Funny thing was, after he'd been around the scene a while, he learned that it wasn't gay men, usually, who raped little boys. It was the heterosexuals—the bane of the world, as he saw it now. Straight men began and fought the wars. They were the ones who beat up the women and raped and murdered the children. They were the ones, for the most part, who committed the violent crimes. Marty, with the coming of age and wisdom, found himself in the position of trading in his Holy Grail for a new, less certain (and far less comfortable) view of life.

It still rankled. He still wanted to bust heads. He just wasn't all that sure which heads to bust anymore.

Oh, he supposed he was too old for that sort of thing anyway. Ten months from retirement, and pretty soon now he'd be sucking up drinks from a coconut in that grass-hut Hawaiian bar. Meanwhile, Marty slogged home to his boxlike apartment in Culver City every night, watched *Magnum, P.I.* reruns, tossed down the usual two or three beers, and nodded off to sleep. When he could get some sleep. When he wasn't constantly having to solve political problems for the captain, like this one now.

Christ, he thought he'd gotten rid of the Hayes woman months ago. And now here she was again—sober this time, according to Jilly out at the front desk, but wired. Nothing new; Brooke Hayes had been trouble with a capital *T* until six, eight months ago, when all of a sudden, the stories went, she sobered up and left town.

What the hell was she back for now? And why had that uptown lawyer husband of hers called a couple of hours ago to put the heat on —yet again—to keep her out of his hair?

Worse . . . why did the captain burden *him* with such things, when all he'd wanted to do was go home at midnight, put his feet up, and dream about those girls with their leis, and the sweet wind sighing softly through gently swaying palms?

Marty sighed. He took one last deep drag, coughed, and stubbed out his cigarette. Swiveled in his chair. Shouldering the phone, he took Old Billy off the wall and fingered him morosely. "Show her in, Jilly," he said, with only a hint of his old Caribbean lilt. "And get me Gibbs and Lloyd."

Chapter 7

IT WAS A FEW MINUTES AFTER MIDNIGHT. Brooke stood in a glass cubicle office at the West LA Division police station. It was an upscale station for an upscale area, but she supposed cops were the same everywhere. The desk she paced before was piled high with well-thumbed manila folders, sandwich wrappers with leafy remains, and stained coffee mugs filled with sodden cigarette butts. She looked at the plainclothes cop behind the desk, wondering if she had ever seen him before. A possibility, since she'd spent considerable time locked up in this very station last year. She wouldn't remember anyone, of course—she had been drunk out of her mind every time.

The cop was well-dressed, tall and slender. His face was black and unlined, the eyes large and polished, the expression closed—at least, to her. *Lieutenant Martin de Porres,* according to the wooden sign on his desk. He smoked like someone on death row, savoring every drag, and in between stroking the smooth white cylinder with his thumb. Over the room drifted a blue haze; it permeated Brooke's skin, her clothes, her hair. De Porres rose and brushed a hand unnecessarily over spotless, well-cut gray slacks. He crossed to a coffeepot on a cabinet along the wall and poured himself a cup, then raised the pot in her direction.

She shook her head. De Porres took the opportunity, while setting the pot back, to examine her once more. Brooke tried to remain calm.

"You don't understand," she said quietly, shoving her hands into her jean pockets to stop herself from wrapping them around his neck and yelling, *Listen to me, will you? Will you listen?* "I got a call from my daughter. She was crying, she needed my help. I called my ex-husband in Westwood, and he said she was right there with him—but I know he was lying, because Charly would never have called me like that if she was all right. And when I went to the house a little while ago, it was dark. Nathan didn't answer the door. He won't answer the phone. And even the housekeeper was gone."

"You say your husband *won't* answer the phone. Any reason to believe he's not talking to you on purpose?"

"Good God, I don't know! I don't know what to think. Maybe somebody broke in, and Nathan *couldn't* talk to me. Maybe something awful has happened. Can't you just send a car out there, look inside the house?"

"What else did your daughter say?"

"Something about a man. 'The man,' I think. And that she didn't know where she was—"

"Like that? 'I don't know where I am'?"

"No, it was when I asked her where she was, Charly answered, 'I don't know—' " She shook her head. "Look, what does it matter? Something's happened to my daughter. Why aren't you *doing* anything?"

Brooke pulled out her hands and wiped them, shaking, against her hips. She knew she wasn't making a good impression, that she had to calm down, not act hysterical in front of this cop who had just been looking at black-and-white, incontrovertible evidence of the old unstable Brooke.

When she'd first come into the station and told her story to the officer at the front desk, he had clearly recognized Nathan's name, or hers, and pulled a file from a long row of cabinets against a wall. As she waited with mounting panic, he had taken the thick folder to de Porres, who had studied it thoughtfully. He had glanced up at her, finally, and made a phone call, after which the desk cop took her back there and ushered her in. While de Porres asked preliminary questions, Brooke had rubbed at her arms, accidentally revealing the bruises from *Molly Brown*. De Porres' sharp, suspicious look told her he had seen them, and that she had failed at portraying the rational, respectable woman she had promised herself she would be.

"Look, Mrs. Hayes . . ." De Porres sat behind his desk. Before him was a burnished black nightstick, a billy club. He set it gently aside and folded his arms. "I don't know what you're hoping to get out of this . . . but you're not helping anything."

Brooke stopped pacing. Her green eyes narrowed. "What the hell does that mean?"

"I mean your husband called a couple of hours ago. He said you might try to cause trouble of some kind. Maybe you should just go on home, now, before you make things worse."

Brooke hugged her arms, which were shaking. *Nathan. Pulling his power trips, the one thing he was good at and knew how to do.* She leaned over the lieutenant's desk, flattening her hands on the sandwich wrappers and knocking a cupful of butts aside. "I know all about Nathan. I know he's a big-time lawyer, and that you know him pretty well around here, and that you know me pretty well too. But let me tell you, de Porres, that's all old business, it has nothing to do with Charly, and if you don't listen to me now and pay attention to what I have to say—"

Two other men slipped quietly into the room. Brooke sensed their presence. There was a tense silence as she continued to face de Porres down, and then she pulled back. *Oh, God. What am I doing? They'll lock me up. I won't be able to help Charly.* She turned slowly and looked at the other men.

One wore a dark blue baseball-type cap with the name GIBBS in white letters across it. It was pulled low enough so that she couldn't read his eyes, except to know that they were fixed, unmoving, on her. A yellow T-shirt was visible beneath a faded denim jacket. His wiry arms were folded. He leaned against the wall, legs crossed at the ankle.

The other man was of medium height, with stubby gray hair. He was dressed in a rumpled powder blue suit, from which he pulled a handkerchief just in time to catch a sneeze. "Please put that out," he complained to de Porres, who had lit up again. "My allergies . . ."

De Porres sighed and ground the cigarette into a lettuce leaf on one of the sandwich wrappers.

The man in the suit took a chair. He snuffled delicately against a finger. "Mrs. Hayes, at Lieutenant de Porres' request, I called your ex-husband's house a few minutes ago. He's there. He answered the phone, and everything is all right."

"Nathan's there?"

"Yes."

"I don't—" Brooke stumbled over her confusion. "He didn't answer when I called— Who are you?"

"Raymond Lloyd. I work in Children's Services."

"Are you saying you talked to my daughter?" *Hope. Relief. All those things at once.*

"Not exactly."

"Then I don't understand. How do you know she's all right if you haven't talked to her? You've got to hear her voice!"

"Mrs. Hayes, please calm down." Lloyd looked pointedly from her to the lieutenant. The first man, Gibbs, was still watching Brooke impassively.

Her heart sank. Lloyd was Children's Services. The other one was probably a witness. Her attitude, condition, would go into a report that would be seen by a judge in these courts when she sued for joint custody of Charly.

If it was true that Charly was all right. If—

Brooke forced herself to think calmly, to appear reasonable, an ordinary mother concerned in an ordinary way about her child. Doing the sensible thing.

"You say you talked to Nathan."

"Mr. Hayes told me that your daughter left a few hours ago on a camping trip. It's been scheduled for several weeks."

"A camping trip? But that's not possible, Charly never told me—"

"Perhaps she didn't want you to know." Lloyd shifted in his seat, tracing the creases in his rumpled pants, then fixing Brooke with a tired, allergy-reddened gaze. "Mrs. Hayes, according to police records, before you were divorced, you caused certain problems for your husband and child. Do you think . . . just possibly . . . that Charly might be afraid of you?"

"No! That's ridiculous! Charly and I are fine, I was coming to see her in a few days for her birthday—" Was that what Nathan had told him? That Charly was afraid of her? "Wait a minute. This camping trip. Who did Nathan say she went with?"

"A friend, and her family."

"Did you call them?"

The man sighed. "Mrs. Hayes, they're on the road. On their way to the Grand Canyon."

"Can't you find them? Send the highway patrol?" Her voice was rising again. But every time she tried to be rational, they said something that made her crazy.

"We have no reason to do that." Now Lloyd sounded irritable. "Your daughter's father has full custody, and he's known to all of us here in Westwood. He has an excellent reputation. If Mr. Hayes says the child is all right, we have to believe him. Why would he lie?"

Brooke didn't know. But the only alternative was that she had imagined the call from Charly. Was that possible? Worse things had happened . . . when she was drinking.

And each of the men in this office knew that. They knew all about her. About the midnight runs for booze, the drunk driving, the disorderly in public—

The times she had left Charly alone.

Their judgment hovered in the room like a noxious cloud, tainting everything. And de Porres was right. She wasn't helping anything.

The lieutenant cleared his throat, glanced at the other two men, then surprised Brooke by speaking gently. "Tell you what. When the family your daughter is with gets to the Grand Canyon, we'll locate them. We'll get them to put your daughter on the phone, so you'll know for sure."

"I . . . When will that be?"

"A couple of days, probably."

"No, that's too long!"

He shrugged and stood. "It's all we can do. Look, you wouldn't really want us to send the CHP after your little girl, frighten her like that? Besides, it doesn't look good—"

That again. "Jesus Christ! *Look* good? For *who?* For Nathan? For Charly? What if she's hurt? That's not going to look good for your goddamn police department, is it?"

"Mrs. Hayes—"

"Never mind!" *Fuck* them! Fuck them all. She would find Charly herself.

Without looking at any of the men again, she fled the room. Striding angrily through the larger area of cluttered desks with ringing telephones, she ignored the curious eyes of a handful of bored cops as she swept by.

Outside at the curb she rummaged for the keys to the rental car she had picked up at the airport. A voice spoke behind her. "Mrs. Hayes?" She turned. It was the man who hadn't said anything. Gibbs. He reached inside his denim jacket and brought out a slip of paper. She saw that his T-shirt had kangaroos on it, and the words, SAVE THE ROOS.

Brooke looked at the paper. On it was written one word—*Keeper* —and an address at the beach, in Venice.

"Talk to him," Gibbs said. "Can't hurt."

"Who is he?"

"A friend."

"A friend of yours?"

"And yours too, maybe."

"But why—"

It was too late. He was gone—a tight bundle of energy, slamming back through the station doors again and leaving them flapping.

Chapter 8

THE KEEPER

JOHN CREED RAN until sweat popped from every pore—until his shoulder-length black hair was soaked and plastered to his forehead, despite the black headband he wore. He ran until his lungs were hot and stinging, until he felt that another breath might close the ventricles down, make them bloom, and finally, permanently, take the rest of his pain away. He did this several times a week—night or day, depending on how things went.

Every time, he drove at random to a different neighborhood in Los Angeles County. He would park the jeep, get out, and run. Combining exercise with exorcism.

Along the way Creed would search the faces. During the day it was the kids in the neighborhoods, on the way to school. At night he'd check out the hookers, the street people, the children of all ages who had no homes. In his head he carried pictures of missing children, photographs from his wall at home. The ones still not found. Primarily, though, he looked for a complexion that was darker than some, for thick black hair, serene gray eyes, and an angelic grin . . . although he knew that if he found that face on these streets, the grin by this time would be gone and the eyes would be flat. There wasn't much humor down here, and five years was too long to maintain innocence.

After five years Creed was still looking for his son.

He knew it made no sense. He knew, because he worked as what some in the LAPD called The Keeper. Keeper of files, keeper of the faith—you pick the translation, somebody had used it at one time or another. The name originated because he had gathered more files in his house alone, on dead and missing kids, than any single police department in the state. It wasn't a difficult accomplishment; you just had to be obsessed. Creed knew the name they called him, and had scorned it at first. Later he had decided it might be okay. Like any title, it set him apart from the people he worked with—the mothers and fathers of missing kids. Put a cushion between himself and their pain.

At thirty-nine, Creed no longer worked for the department, but solo, with unofficial help from the police commissioner's office now and then. Four interminable years ago, the commissioner had called Creed to his home, and the two men sat opposite each other beside a well-kept but unused pool, on a wide terrace that looked across to, but wasn't a part of, Beverly Hills. Creed was nervous to be singled out this way, and because it had been a personally traumatic year, he was strained, his face drawn. The commissioner was in a wheelchair; the many years of walking a beat in his early career had caught up, leaving him with ruptured veins and gout. On top of that he battled emphysema. It wouldn't be long, went the rumors, before the old man was out.

This meeting followed the occurrence in Los Angeles of the most widely publicized, and most gruesome, kidnapping in the country. Poor investigative procedures had hung the case up, giving Andrew Laskov, the DA—who was busy being courted by the Republican party as their next candidate for state's attorney general—just the excuse he needed to procrastinate over bringing the offender to trial. Nothing like a messy trial to jinx a man's political hopes. The public wasn't happy about the delay, though. They raised a furor. The DA laid the blame—expediently, and even justifiably—at the police commissioner's door.

"I've heard about your tarnished halo, boy." The commissioner fingered a thick, earmarked file in his lap. "The DA wants your ass. He wants it bad. You know why?"

"I know." Creed's heart sank. He was dismayed to learn that the commissioner knew, and struggled not to show it.

"Well, don't feel bad. He wants mine too." The commissioner laughed, but it came out "hee-hee-hee," like a wheeze. Sun glinted from the long blue pool. A traffic helicopter buzzed a mile off, and a thin Mexican maid came onto the terrace, bearing iced tea. Creed took the tall, frosted glass as if it were a snake. Everything was suspect here today.

The commissioner shifted his bulk in the metal wheelchair. His feet, poking out from beneath a red plaid blanket, were the size of young tree stumps. He gazed at them gloomily and continued. "I'm just as determined as Laskov, John, but our agendas are different. He's still in the game, still has a few rules to follow. Me? I'm just about out of it, and I say, the rules be hanged. Right, boy? You know a thing or two about that—don't you?"

John Creed choked down a piece of ice. "Yes, sir."

There weren't many people anymore who commanded his respect. The commissioner was one exception. John knew the old man had come up through the ranks, and not entirely by benefit of cronyism. He was known for outstanding investigative work early on, and then for his humane way of dealing with the younger up-and-coming cops on the force. When Jason first disappeared, the commissioner had come to Creed's house, arriving in the big black van with the letters PC on its rear. An aide had wheeled him to the door, and he had stayed long enough to talk awhile, extending his sympathies and then offering his personal assistance and that of his staff.

It was no wonder the DA didn't like the commissioner. Laskov hated cops. His hatred for Creed was stronger, though. And his reason for it more personal.

Jason. It had all begun with Jason. And would it never end?

The commissioner was speaking, and Creed drew his eyes back to the scene at hand: the man in the wheelchair, the still blue pool, the not luxurious but large house, bought by the old man, he knew, a long time ago—when prices here were still within a cop's budget.

"I want this business of missing children cleaned up before I retire," the commissioner said softly. "There's too damn much of it going on in this county these last few years. Too many drugged-out sickos, too many perverts. Something's got to be done to stop it."

"I agree, sir." Creed waited patiently, sensing the point was near to coming. He was right.

"I figure you're the person to help me do it," the old man said. "Nobody's worked harder than you this year, looking for your son. You know things—not just facts and figures, but motivations—you've got an instinct, boy."

He waved a heavy, bloated hand to halt Creed's protest.

"I know, I know. None of that's helped you find your son. And I'm sorry about that, John, truly sorry, believe me. But I've watched you go about your work over the years. You *care*. Goddammit, boy, too many cops these days are clerks. They do their eight hours and take their pay. Only a handful really care."

Creed had no answer to that.

"It's true, boy, take my word. When you look at the reports from this end, you know it. And one thing about you"—he tapped the heavy folder—"you don't spare yourself. Anything you've ever done, you've done all the way."

Creed winced. All the way, true . . . but very seldom by the book. What exactly did the old man want from him? Not accepted methods, that was clear. More likely the kind that had gotten him that "tarnished halo" the commissioner had mentioned.

Then the thunderbolt struck.

"I want you to take a leave of absence, boy."

Creed flushed. *A leave of absence.* Anger, humiliation, a ferment of conflicting emotions landed in his gut. He hadn't expected this. Had he fucked up so bad?

"Three months," the commissioner continued, eyes on Creed. "Let's try three months. Then we'll see. In the meantime, I want you to go home, and I want you to sit down awhile, and I want you to think."

Creed finally found his voice. It wasn't too steady. "Think, sir?"

"About where you're going. It's been eight months since your boy disappeared. How many narcotics arrests have you made in that time?"

Creed didn't answer. The old man already knew.

"Your heart isn't in it anymore, John. You know where it's at?"

"I . . ." It was out there, finding Jason. The need had consumed him, day and night. Even down in Venice—on the streets, along the beach, in the crack houses, he was no longer looking for dealers, but Jason.

The commissioner continued. "Now, while you're sitting there at home thinking, boy, I want you to do one other thing. I want you to figure out how you can better put to work all these skills you've acquired the last eight months looking for your boy."

Creed's mind was still whirling. "I don't understand, sir. Are you talking about a transfer? To Missing Persons?"

The sound the commissioner made was contemptuous. "Oh, not that there aren't some good men in those units. But they're spread too thin, and they're up to their noses in runaways—all these abuses going on, and this goddamned drug culture we've got out there—"

"Then I don't—"

"Boy, let's say that after you think awhile, you realize your life's taking a different course. It happens, you know. People have some bad thing happen, they find themselves on a different road." The commissioner's smile was placid, his expression bland. "And let's say you decide that where your talents now lie is in looking for missing kids. Let's say, too, that you've got none of the restrictions and distractions Missing Persons has to contend with."

Creed's tone was cautious, but laced with anger. "Let's say you just tell me what you've got in mind, sir."

The commissioner gave a nod of satisfaction. "What I have in mind is that you might just work alone from now on—out of your home, say. Set up one of those clearing centers they've got around the country to find missing kids. Computers, faxes . . . you've seen how it's done firsthand, and you've worked with it. John, we need somebody like that here in LA. Somebody working close to the department, but not part of it. Not bogged down by certain . . . details."

"Not part of the department." Creed couldn't believe it. Was he being *terminated?* Was that what it amounted to?

"You want me to resign the force?" he asked flatly.

"Oh, not right away. Not until after you've thought about it awhile and made up your own mind. Hell, I want you on my side, boy. I want you finding these kids, the ones who've been snatched, before it's too late. I want you coming up with proof—enough so the DA is forced to prosecute. One way or another—you'd get proof. Right, boy?"

One way or another. Creed blinked. He nodded. "If you say so, sir." The idea was frightening and yet strangely appealing. The old man was right; his heart hadn't been in Narcotics for a long time now. But to give up working for the Department? It had been an anchor, holding his life together—

Anchors can have an adverse effect as well. There had been too many restrictions lately—too much holding down.

The commissioner slapped his bloated leg. It must have been painful, but he didn't flinch. "You know what I've hated about my job, really hated all these years? The stinking, goddamned, pig-in-a-poke justice system. Gets in the way every time, you know. And it's not just the courts, the lawyers, the judges. Not that they're lily-white. But you know what the main problem is? Too many times we don't nail them. We make mistakes. Sloppy investigative techniques, the public's right about that. Too many clerks . . ."

His raspy voice trailed off, and he stared at the thick layer of smog that began, that day, only a mile or so to the east. "And not enough fresh air." After a moment he roused himself. "Especially in the DA's office."

Creed felt he had to say something. "In all fairness, sir, I think Andy Laskov would *like* to prosecute kidnappers and child abusers."

"If it's politically expedient," the old man rumbled. *"If* the possibility of losing a high-profile case doesn't come in an election year." He cleared his throat, drawing the phlegm up and swallowing it loudly, smacking his lips. "I'd like a nickel for all the ifs that have to be answered before Andy Laskov will move his ass off the ground." He took up his tea and drank it greedily.

"Now, boy, tell me you'll help me out here—request the leave of absence yourself. There won't be a black mark on your record that way."

"And if I don't?"

The old man's expression was shrewd. "I'll put one through myself. I'll say you're burnt out, no longer performing to department standards, a danger to your fellow officers . . ."

Creed stared. *Shit.* His career, his future, his whole damned life, was being manipulated by one fat, pushy man in a wheelchair who was on his way out.

He was silent, torn between anger and strange new feelings of hope.

"You have enough money to tide you over?" The commissioner smeared the frost on his glass with his thumb. He didn't look up.

Creed decided to push back, wondering just how far the old man would go to get his own way. "You offering to float me a loan?"

A grin. "If I have to."

"And say I decide to do this? I'll need equipment."

"There are foundations," the commissioner said smoothly. "I'll see about getting some funding for you. Seed money, to get you started."

Creed studied a loose thread on the new jeans he'd bought to replace the usual hole-in-the-knees variety: a small show of deference to the commissioner's generation. Finally he said, "I'll take the leave, sir. I'll think about it. I can't promise any more than that."

The commissioner smiled slyly from under his thick shelf of a brow. "Fair enough. And naturally, my involvement will be on the q.t. It wouldn't do to have missing-persons units around the city know that this came from me. They might even get the idea I didn't trust them to do their jobs."

ALL THAT HAD HAPPENED four years ago, Creed remembered as he continued his run, heading for Sunset. The three-month leave had turned into six, and finally into permanent retirement from the force. It took a while to admit that the old man had been right all along. He was better off doing what he did now, and he was glad he'd been forced into it. He might never have otherwise swallowed what, at the time, seemed a bitter pill.

In the meantime, the "old man" went on and on—defying every rumor of his imminent departure from both the department and the world. He still kicked ass—and Creed was now and then his fall guy in the press, when a missing child wasn't found in time.

Which happened all too often. Most kidnapping cases were either for sexual purposes, or ego driven, or both. A kidnapped child might be abused and held prisoner for years, then released when the kidnapper was no longer able to contain him. When this happened, kids were often too afraid, or too ashamed, to go home. They might wind up in one of the many formal or informal underground networks now in existence for runaway kids, along with children who had deliberately left home because of abuse. That was one scenario.

The one that occurred more often, however, was that a pervert, using a child for quick gratification, would kill the child within hours of his or her disappearance. The child would never be found—or would turn up dead.

So, Creed thought, picking up speed—to believe that his son Jason, who would be ten now, was still alive—to believe that he'd see him on a street somewhere, just from running along like this—was insane. Any psychologist could tell you that. A psychologist would say (and more than one had) that Creed hadn't dealt with his grief, that he needed to let go. Creed knew all this. He could have taught the psychologist a few things.

Even so, he hoped. You couldn't stop hoping. Except on those days like the one last week, when they'd found that little girl in a filthy, dark flat on Cahuenga. The things that had been done to her, the revolting, animal savagery, had left her parents with little hope—either for the child's recovery, or theirs. In instances like these, he always wanted to say, "It'll be all right." But it would never be all right. Those parents would carry a rage for the rest of their lives that would change them and everyone they touched. John Creed knew this as well as most. He had nurtured a similar rage, founded on loss, since the age of seventeen.

He rounded a corner onto Sunset, scanning the curb without much interest. They cleaned up Sunset all the time—but the hookers and druggies kept coming back, and it was always the same scene. He knew most of the girls by name, the girls in their short leather skirts and sweaters with fake fur on the shoulders. He knew their sequins and cheap gaudy earrings, their forced patter whenever a car slowed, looking for a quick hand job from a little girl who might, just the week before, have been drying dishes in her mother's cookie-scented kitchen in Compton.

He passed by at a trot, acknowledging the sly grins and winks with a brief, not unfriendly, gesture. The hookers knew he'd been a cop. They also knew he wasn't here to arrest kids anymore, but to find them. They delighted in giving him a brazen up-and-down.

Not once did Creed think there was anything personal in the girls' lewd appraisal. He would never describe himself as good-looking. His eyes were as gray and fierce as the North Dakota sky he first looked into at birth, his hair black like his father's, his features angular and hard. The fact that this off-beat look seemed perversely attractive to women seldom entered his mind, obsessed as he was by his work. Flirtations took up valuable time. They would only get in his way.

As he ran, Creed paid special attention to the boy-kids, the punks, the purple-haired freaks with black daggers and swastikas hanging from their ears. He looked into their eyes for some fragment of the five-year-old that Jason had once been. Some flicker of recognition. Instead he met faces that were skinny from drugs and malnutrition, eyes that were sharp and hungry, darting from left to right, scoping out the next score.

Most were dead. *DeadEyes*. It didn't matter if they were out here walking around or on a slab downtown; most of these kids were already gone.

So why did he bother?

Once in a while Creed thought he knew the answer to that. He bothered because there was nothing else he could do. And with that thought came the anger he worked so hard every day to run off. Anger at being powerless. As powerless now as he had been all those years ago, at seventeen.

Even today Creed remembered that year with all the panic and terror of his first real fuck, which occurred around that time too.

He was born in a small farming community, the only son of Matthew and Marie, who taught English and American history at the University of North Dakota. His parents were peacemakers, pacifists, who prayed on their knees every night that the harsh Dakota winters would leave them with one honest, substantial, mortgage-paying crop.

So it wasn't upbringing that rose to Creed's defense twenty-two years ago, when all hell broke loose. Instead, he guessed, it must have been the genes of his outlaw grandfather, Nicholas Alessandro Cristofaro. Cristofaro was a massive man, with dark good looks and a booming voice. An Italian immigrant, he had hightailed it out of Chicago the winter of 1910—on the lam from what passed back then as the Chicago mob. He ended up in North Dakota by way of a blinding, face- and foot-numbing blizzard and was taken in by the Sioux. It

wasn't long before he ran afoul of missionaries. Grandpa Nick, despite himself, was saved. He married an Indian woman, bought a farm with stolen mob money, and changed his name to Creed.

Things were pretty quiet after that. A son, Matthew, was born and grew up peacefully, and he and his wife Marie begat John—an amiable boy with straight A's most of his life, and a bright future. Creed was set to go off to college on a scholarship in the fall of that year—a year when he looked into the belly of Hell and found the Devil safe and well, despite the fact that God, according to all reports, was dead.

He had fallen asleep one night in the sprawling white farmhouse, studying in bed one minute and dreaming about Princeton the next. Princeton—and Betsy Leaming, who was a year behind him in school but had been the only girl to look his way since eighth grade. Betsy . . . with hair like a cloud and eyes like a warm summer day.

"Don't go away to school," Betsy had pleaded that previous Friday night. They had been on their way back from a school dance, driving John's battered pickup, when Betsy's hand did one of those light-as-a-bird numbers in his lap. He had pulled over to the side of the clean-scented country road, where the trees were as straight and tall as the erection Betsy was so wonderfully ministering to, and taken her in his arms. Sticking his raw, adolescent tongue in her mouth, his anxious hand fumbled between her thighs. "Stay here, Johnny," she whispered, arching her strong young body against his touch. "Your mom and dad would love it"—she sucked on his ear until he thought he'd go through the roof—"and so would I."

John Creed, remembering Betsy Leaming a few nights later with a tug at his groin, had rolled over in bed. It was a mountain of down, and the sheets smelled like fresh-cut hay. He wondered what softener his mom was using on the sheets now. Some new free sample, probably, saving money the way she did.

His books, which were always piled high beside him, slid to the floor. He threw a leg over the extra pillow, rubbing his cheek on its smooth, silky whiteness and, by proxy, Betsy Leaming.

Some time later he awoke, uneasy. Thinking he had heard an alien sound. He glanced at the alarm clock on his night table, saw it was still before twelve, and relaxed. His mother and father graded papers at night, after which they drew up lessons plans and tests. Their days, because of this, were long—sometimes not ending until way past midnight. So the sound John had heard was probably his father, he thought, getting up to shut the window in case it snowed. By now he would be turning off the lights to sleep.

The shots that resounded throughout the farmhouse seconds later might as well have gone into Creed's heart, for all the life they left him with. He lay rigid at first, unable to move. Then he leapt from the bed, dragging sheets, books, papers, behind him.

For interminable moments he stood there, numb. Finally he realized he was naked, that the room was icy, and that the shots had come from his parents' room.

There was absolutely no doubt in Creed's mind that his parents were dead.

He didn't question how he knew, without any logical sequence of thought, that this was what had happened. It was like waking to find that a nightmare you've had since childhood has come true. That it wasn't a nightmare after all, but a vision of terror to come.

He shivered and clamped down on his chattering teeth. Pulling a sheet around his frozen limbs, he stumbled ahead, then halted, afraid to go out there and look. He had heard no other sounds. No voices from his parents' room. No running feet. If he didn't look, didn't see—

He never could remember, later, how long it took him to move. It seemed like hours but could only have been minutes, given the time that his call to the sheriff was logged in.

He did remember that when he finally stumbled to the big master bedroom at the far end of the hall, there was no sign of an intruder. He stood at the door with one last, brief, foolish hope that he had dreamed the shots, after all. His mother lay on her side as if sleeping, one soft pink hand curled under her cheek, a knee drawn up toward her waist. But the exposed side of her face wasn't where it belonged. Blood and tissue stained the flowered wallpaper, the ceiling, the bed. Twisted into it were strands of his mother's long blond hair.

Creed took in the awful scene as if it were a movie—stopping and rerunning it, making it come out differently every time. Then tears began to roll from his eyes, soaking the sheet he pulled from his body, to cover—with icy hands, smoothing it tenderly—the remains of his mother's head.

How long was it before he found his father's body on the floor, on the other side of the bed? Creed didn't know. It might not have been until much later. Somewhere in all that horrible, slow-motion space of time, he had picked up the phone that was coated with pieces of his mother's flesh and called the sheriff's station.

The case never went anywhere. It was made to look as if some crazy had broken in, some itinerant. "Halfway to hell and back by now," Arne Pedderson, the sheriff, said. But John Creed knew why his parents had died.

For months there had been big-city developers hanging around. They'd already bought off half the surrounding countryside, and you'd have thought that was enough. The county, however, wouldn't let any building begin until the developers provided highway access . . . and the closest, cheapest access ran right through the Creed farm. The Creeds had refused to sell.

Their son didn't have to look far to see who had emptied the bullets into his parents that night. Having left no will, and with no other living relatives but him—a minor—the farm would be administered by the state. From that point on, with a few payoffs here and there, it was only a matter of paperwork.

Creed discovered, however, that he was powerless to prove it.

He talked to Arne Pedderson, in the log cabin that served as a seat of law in their rural county. He pleaded for an investigation. Creed might as well have been talking to one of the Grand Buttes. Arne listened, but he was over sixty, cautious about hearing what John had to say. It was only later that Creed realized Pedderson had been afraid.

"Go home, son. Forget it. Put your life together. Go off to college, join the army. Just don't stick around here. And don't say anything about this to anyone else, you hear?"

Creed couldn't forget it, but he did move away. He drifted at first, unable to shake his grief—working here and there as a farmhand, for meals. Dusty and bone weary at night, he would dream weird dreams: of Betsy Leaming in his arms in a big soft bed, her pale thighs spread, and then, when she turned . . . with half her face gone.

In the fall Creed landed in Los Angeles. LA twenty years ago was a lonely town. It was an era of protest marches, draft-card burnings, political paranoia, and drugs. Most of the people his age were turned off, tuned out. Creed shared a beach apartment with some of them in Venice. He got to know them, the users and dealers, the kids on the streets. It was an education that would pay off, later on, better than any college.

He had experimented with drugs for a while—with anything, in fact, that felt good. Then, on one of those glass-clear, sunshiny days that LA used to be known for and hardly ever had anymore, he lay on the beach below the apartment, wiggled his toes in the hot sand, and opened up his mail—to find a letter from Uncle Sam.

He thought about Canada. His mother had talked about friends up there. But the drugs had neutralized his resistance; combined with them, his parents' death had taken away his will to protest. Creed drifted into Nam the way he was drifting everywhere else those days.

His anger at his parents' brutal murder, however, came back full force when he saw the senseless killing over there. Creed's frustration grew. An understandable response might have been to refuse to fight, to run. That would have been okay, Creed thought. But something else happened to him. The genes that had skipped a generation—the ones belonging to Nicholas Alessandro Cristofaro, late of Chicago and other outlaw environs, rose and demanded to be heard. A rage like none he had ever known settled inside him. At first it shocked him, but then, like bad companions everywhere, the alien thing became salutary . . . a standard by which all other experience was perceived.

From that moment on, Creed won medals for heroism that had nothing to do with Nam and everything to do with North Dakota and his parents' death. Fortunately, the government didn't discriminate about such things. What might have been called murder (and in fact, by an aware country, was) gave John Creed the credentials to move up fast in the after-Nam civilian world.

He was wounded and sent home. In Los Angeles once more, in a VA hospital, John Creed took stock. What, he asked himself, does a twenty-two-year-old with a boxful of medals and no talent for anything besides killing do?

He became a cop.

At the Los Angeles Police Academy, he graduated with honors. He distinguished himself as a rookie, then a patrolman, and sooner than

most got promoted to detective first and assigned to duty as an under-
cover narcotics cop. With money saved while in the army, he bought a
fixer-upper cottage on the beach in Venice, moved in, and renewed his
connections with the users and dealers there. He worked his way up
through the drug world, and then, from behind the scenes, tore through
the criminal infrastructure in Los Angeles County the same way he had
torn through Nam. Before long Creed had more arrests under his belt
than any cop in LA. And he had a reputation as bad news. He would do
anything for a bust.

The Department didn't care; they gave him a promotion to detective third.

As for a personal life, that was slower going. If Creed had thought
himself less than good-looking at seventeen, what Nam did to his face
(never mind his body, a goddamned, but temporary, mess) was the final
blow. His nose had been broken several times and never set right, there
was a slash through one eyebrow where the hair would never grow
back, and his chin had a scar an inch long, from the bottom lip down.
Add to that a disposition that would freeze steel, and Creed didn't have
much hope that he'd ever meet a woman who liked him—much less
one to share a marriage bed. Until he met Karen.

Karen was an artist. The most gentle woman he had ever known,
somehow she looked beyond the anger and found something hidden
there—a tenderness Creed's mother and father had planted in boyhood
but that had lain fallow, waiting for rich enough soil to grow.

At Karen's subtle probing, Creed remembered helping with the
birth of a calf one year, when he was seven. He remembered his tears
when the head presented, and the tender way he had helped the calf to
stand. How he had always been a sucker for holidays, for Christmas, and
children.

He had buried all that with his parents. Karen, with her shiny
brown hair, her gentle whispers, and her warm accepting body, had
miraculously found it. The first time they made love, it was like being
born, like exploding from a womb.

There never was any question they would be together all their
lives. They married almost immediately. Creed bought a house with a
yard in Santa Monica, and Jason was born within ten months of the day

of the wedding. He was eight pounds, three ounces, with a mop of black hair and eyes that were pale like his father's. He had Karen's nose, however, so Creed thought he'd be okay.

Okay. The word rose like a caustic substance as he ran, to burn his throat.

When he was five years old, Jason had disappeared from the backyard of the small white house Creed had bought for his family in Santa Monica. One minute the small boy with the serene gray eyes and angelic grin was playing on his swings; the next he was gone. He was never seen again.

Chapter 9

BROOKE FELT AS IF she were in one of those frightening computerlike dreams where a word or phrase gets into your mind and keeps repeating itself over and over, until you have to wake yourself up because you can't stand it anymore.

Charly's gone, Charly's gone, Charly's gone, was this night's information. But when she had awakened, somewhere between the call in San Francisco, and here—when she came out of the initial shock—there was no one around to listen. That was the downside of living alone; sometimes there was no one to listen.

She pulled the beige rental car over to the Venice curb and rolled down the driver's window, peering through darkness and fog at street signs. Barcelona and Firth. Before starting out she had found a map in the glove compartment but had remembered enough of Venice to get this far without it. She had visited friends here, other actors, over the years.

She flattened the map, now, over the steering wheel, and peered at it in the car's dim interior light. There . . . Pacific and Venice. The address she wanted was only a few blocks away. She placed the map beside her on the seat and drove, turning right, finally, toward the ocean.

A glance at the dashboard clock told her it was after two A.M. She was startled to see how late it was. The streets were dark and silent, the fog so thick she had to turn on the wipers. Brooke wondered what she was getting into. There was a lot of crime in Venice now. Houses with barred windows were smack against clothing shops, grocery stores, delis. Gangs of kids hung out in doorways and on corners, blatantly dealing as cars drove by.

If she lived here, she would never let a stranger in. Would the person on this piece of paper—whoever the hell he was—even see her at this hour? Would he think she was crazy, the way the Westwood police had, and send her away? She should have called ahead.

But she couldn't have called; the man named Gibbs hadn't given her a number. Or a proper name.

For one sickening moment Brooke wondered if this was a trap. How did she know who Gibbs was? Maybe he didn't believe her any more than the other two cops. Maybe . . .

Maybe he was on Nathan's side.

Stop it. Paranoia leads to madness. She had already been there and learned its lessons; the road didn't need to be traveled again. It *mustn't* be traveled again.

Her hands trembled on the wheel, but she found the street, the last one before the beach, and turned right. It was no more than an alley, empty but for a few parked cars. A neighborhood where the houses and apartments are piled one on top of another, with little breathing space between. You couldn't see the fronts of the buildings; they were behind fences, facing the beach.

A little more than halfway down the block was a gate with the address Gibbs had given her. She pulled alongside a high picket fence on the opposite side of the alley and cut the motor. After a moment she slid from the car. Animal sounds issued from behind the fence—dogs sniffing, then barking, after her scent. You could actually hear the humidity dripping from rain pipes, see it glistening on gray cement walls. Brooke shivered. She was losing heart.

But what were the alternatives? She didn't have friends anymore down here; she had worn them all out while drinking. Fed up with requests for loans, and rampaging late-night phone calls, they had tiredly drifted away. So . . . find a motel, lie sleepless on a strange bed, and agonize about Charly until morning? No. She had to keep moving. Even drunk, she had always had to be doing something, even if it was something crazy. Nothing had changed. That's the thing about getting sober. All your manic habits are still there; you just aren't drunk enough not to be irritated or embarrassed by them anymore.

She approached the tall wooden gate with its aluminum number plate: 431. The plate was pitted from the sea weather, and one edge had come loose. It hung slightly crooked. A mailbox tilted too, and Brooke found herself thinking nervously of an old children's song . . . *There was a crooked man, and he had a crooked mouse, and they all lived together in a little crooked house.* She used to wonder if the author had been an embittered wife.

In the murky illumination of a streetlight, she looked for a bell and found none. She tried the gate. The latch was loose and slippery from the damp, but it wasn't locked. She pushed the gate inward, expecting it to squeak. It did.

There were stairs going up alongside the house, which she saw was brown-shingled and weathered. It was two-storied but not large or ostentatious, one of the older cottages of Venice—built, probably, in the forties, long before prices had shot up. A new owner might have paid under twenty thousand dollars for it in the fifties.

At the top of the stairs, the ocean sounds were louder. A spotlight attached to the deck railing drew a moon-circle on the sand and the strip of concrete boardwalk below. There were huddled figures out on the beach; homeless people, she knew. The homeless had their own community out there. Some slept in the cabanas, like Arabs in tents, some right out on the sand. During the day there would be bicycles, street entertainers, roller skaters, hot-dog stands. Now, in the dark, no one walked on the boardwalk alone.

The deck where she stood was in shadows. It was huge, with a round umbrella table, some scattered chairs. Brooke's attention was caught by a lighted room at one end of the deck. Its windows wrapped around on three sides. On the inside wall were shelves with books, a fireplace, and a large cork board with snapshots attached. Below them, a desk with a computer, file cabinets, stacks of manila folders, and scattered newspapers.

At one side of the deck was a sliding glass door. Brooke crossed to it and knocked softly. She waited. No answer. She knocked again—and again—more loudly each time.

The only response was the sound of foghorns and the steady *tick-tick-tick* of ocean damp.

She stood there, hunched against the chill, wondering what to do. Was this person . . . Keeper . . . out on some quick errand? Would he come back?

Something rustled, and she jumped, then saw that it was bougainvillea against the solid wall of a house next door. Dry and papery, it rattled in a desultory wind. Brooke shivered. She walked nervously back and forth on the deck, hugging herself to keep warm. A gull that had been sleeping on the railing woke and flapped its wings, scaring her half to death. It flew off into a white wall of fog. The foghorn wailed again, like a child lost in a well.

Like Charly, on the phone.

You're tired, Brooke—overreacting. Charly is all right, she has to be. How could anyone hurt a child as innocent, as beautiful, as Charly?

Yet she knew that people hurt beautiful children all the time.

Oh, God. Where was this person that Gibbs had sent her to?

More important, *who* was he?

Looking through the lighted windows, it was hard to get a fix on the man who lived here. There was a strange mixture of objects scattered around on shelves, tabletops, a fireplace mantel. A stuffed dog; a garishly painted porcelain angel; some sort of Indian object, a totem—and on the sofa, a square satin pillow embroidered with the words WHEELING WEST VIRGINIA.

Then there were all those businesslike books and files. The desk and computer. Was Keeper a scholar, a professor? And why did she keep thinking he was a man? Gibbs hadn't said that, had he? Perhaps Keeper was a woman. *Ms.* Keeper, a middle-aged woman, a teacher, who traveled every summer and brought home knickknacks and souvenirs.

Her mind was rattling on and on, making illogical leaps and jumps, in the manner of a child who walks past shadowed trees on a country road and whistles in the dark. She knew she was not thinking rationally. She was close to losing it—and astounded at how quickly she had gotten this way. After months of healing, months of sobriety and sane thinking, how could she have reached the edge again so quickly? It was as if that entire struggle had never taken place, as if she had been picked up and transported instantly back to the bad, sick times.

She wished she had a pill.

Brooke sank down on one of the deck chairs, hardly noticing that dampness soaked through her jeans. It didn't matter. Nothing mattered now, except Charly. Even *Molly Brown* seemed years away. Molly's strength, which she thought she had absorbed—was it all an illusion? A mirage?

Nathan would say that. He would say, as he had so often, that she had inherited her mother's instability.

He would be right.

Brooke glanced up at a small noise. But there was no one here. Probably just the bougainvillea. She'd have seen—

A hand touched her shoulder.

She jumped to her feet, whirling about so fast, she knocked the light metal chair over. Fear tightened her throat, a pulse in her forehead pounded.

There stood before her a frightening apparition with straight, collar-length black hair held back by a rolled headband. In the half-dark, the eyes of the apparition looked enraged. He was taller than she, but under six feet, she thought—and just as quickly wondered how she could still think. He wore dark sweatpants and shirt; his angular face was slick with sweat, although the night was cold.

"Who are you?" He rapped it out, as if he might strike her, were she to answer the wrong way. He took a forward step.

A madman. A street person, come wandering up here, or a drug dealer—

Brooke turned to run, but he caught her arm.

"Who are you?" he repeated. There was a midwestern tang to the harsh query.

"I . . . I . . . Brooke Hayes. I'm waiting . . . waiting for someone."

"Who? Who are you waiting for?"

"Keeper. Someone named Keeper."

"What do you want with him?"

She didn't know why she answered, except that it would have been impossible not to. "My little girl is missing. A man named Gibbs, at the police station, sent me to talk to this person—this Keeper."

"Talk, then," the man said.

Chapter 10

THE WOMAN OPENED HER MOUTH, then closed it. With an abrupt motion, Creed pulled her into the light from the windows. His eyes swept over her intently—looking, among other things, for signs of guilt. *My little girl is missing,* she had said. Parents were sometimes the culprits in these things, pretending sorrow over a child they had in recent hours injured or killed. It wasn't a pleasant fact. It was one he had learned to live with.

Brooke Hayes was around thirty, he guessed. About five seven or eight. Light brown hair streaked with blond. He thought that when she fixed it to go out, it would be in that stylish way women do, wavy and full. It would fall to her shoulders the way Karen's had—

For one brief moment, when he came up the stairs and saw her sitting there in the dark, he had thought, in fact, that Karen had come home.

But that wasn't possible. And knowing it had made him illogically angry.

The woman's hair was pulled back now and simply tied, as if she had been too distraught, or hurried, to do more. Her face revealed signs of difficult times: fine lines about the eyes and mouth that didn't come from lazy hours beneath a California sun. Her complexion was too soft, too pale for that. The color of the eyes was hard to tell. They were darker than usual now, he guessed, because of the defensiveness he saw there. She tried to hide it, but her chin jutted up a fraction of an inch

54

too far—a giveaway. Her mouth was a white slash, her figure that of a young girl, slim-hipped in tight jeans. A small waist. Simple cotton shirt. Long, slender legs.

The legs trembled. He could see them shake through the faded jeans. There was something wrong with this woman, something more than the missing child, or even fear over the way he'd approached her. His perusal ended abruptly.

"Come inside," Creed said.

"I . . ."

"Inside." He pulled keys from a pocket and unlocked the sliding doors.

She followed. Stumbling a little over the aluminum track.

"Here." Creed motioned to an armchair.

The woman sat. Some of the defensiveness left her eyes and was replaced with questions.

He wasn't what she had expected, he knew. Her mind was struggling for the words that would beg this sullen stranger, whom she knew nothing about, to help her.

Creed saw this, and hated it. He hated the fragile ones. They brought out his own fear. Damn Gibbs, why was he always sending him this kind?

He planted himself across from her, arms folded. "How old is your child?"

"I . . . Nine. Charly is nine."

"How long has she been gone?"

"I . . . I don't know. . . . I got a call from her around eight tonight—"

"She called you?"

"I live in San Francisco," she explained. She was choosing her words carefully, as if they might shatter. "Charly called me there. She . . . was crying, and she said, 'Mommy, the man.' I asked what was wrong, and she said she didn't know where she was. It was . . . awful. She sounded hollow, kind of, like a . . . a . . ."

"Ghost."

She looked startled. "Yes. Like a ghost."

"She was frightened," Creed said, gentle for the first time. He thought of Jason, and the voice he still heard calling to him, in nightmares. "No one knows where she is. No one who loves her can see her."

The woman's eyes blurred with tears. "Please don't say that, I can't bear it."

"You'll have to bear it." He was instantly hard again. "If your daughter is missing, it will get worse, not better."

She needed to know that. It didn't help to soften things.

HE SHOWERED WHILE BROOKE WAITED, frantic, gulping down coffee. He had brought a thermos from a downstairs kitchen.

"You're going to shower *now?*" she had said. Angry. Feeling the pressure of passing time, time wasted, time without Charly.

He had paused at the door he was already halfway through. His voice was without expression, to match his face. "I know that finding your daughter is the only thing that matters. And I know that it has to be done quickly. I'll be making phone calls while I'm down there."

"But I can't just stand around, while Charly—"

"Would you like to search the streets?" He asked it as if it were a crazy idea, but not impossible. "There are over sixty-four square miles in the West LA District alone, but if you'd like, we can do that later."

Then he was gone.

Brooke had to admit, in this darkest of moments, that if there had been a bottle of liquor in sight, she'd have had a drink. Several. She might never have stopped.

She didn't know what she was doing here. She had dashed off in a panic, running for help from any quarter when it seemed there was none to be had from the police . . . and yet, what did she know about this man?

Nothing. Except that he was curt, to the point of rude. Abrupt. Odd.

It was a sign of ongoing madness, something she thought she had conquered over the past eight months, that she was still here at all.

Rubbing her arms for warmth, she studied the photos on the wall by the bookshelves. Most were of children, candid snapshots, of the type from family albums. But there were adults, too, several men, and a couple of women. Some were mug shots, straight front and then sides, with identification numbers across their chests. Others were drawings, the kind made by a police artist from a description.

What would inhabitants of a future world think, if they stumbled onto something like this? "Art of the nineties, Neptune Elyse . . . a horrible, dark era, when children were stolen, and maimed, and killed." The mother in the future world museum might then tuck an arm around her little girl's shoulder and draw her close, grateful that things weren't like that anymore.

A nerve twitched in her cheek, and Brooke raised a finger to still it.

When Creed returned in jeans and maroon sweater with his black hair damp and brushed behind the ears, the room seemed to shrink. He looked, she thought now, solid. Capable. More professional than fierce. Wire-rimmed glasses softened the hard eyes.

"I've called a few people," he said, pouring coffee into a mug for himself.

"What people?"

"Gibbs. And others."

She couldn't keep the hostility from her voice. "You mean Lieutenant de Porres? And the man from Children's Services?"

"Yes."

"You know things about me, then."

"Right."

Her mouth twisted. He knew. All the things the others knew, about her past. "What did you think?"

Creed glanced her way. "Will you please sit down?"

She had been striding back and forth, picking up objects and putting them down. The painted angel on the mantel, the pillow from Wheeling, West Virginia. "I can't. I feel like I'm strung with wires from head to toe." She looked down at her hand, holding the angel, and realized for the first time what she was doing. "What are these, anyway? All these things? They look . . ." She didn't say it. Bizarre, for a man like him. Out of place.

"They're from parents whose children I've found."

"Oh. That plaque, too?" It was on a bookshelf, a ray of light surrounding an outstretched palm. Above the palm was a quote from Isaiah: *See, I will not forget you . . . I have carved you on the palm of my hand.*

"No. My wife . . ."

That was all. "My wife." He looked away, for the first time seeming awkward. Removing his glasses, he ran a hand over his eyes. Then he got up and crossed to the fireplace, lighting a prebuilt fire. The kindling blazed. Brooke noted its warmth but wasn't comforted. She could only think of Charly. And the fact that nothing was being done.

She stood above him as he knelt, warming his hands at the flames. The angel thunked on the mantel as she slammed it down. "Look, I don't even know your name."

He rose and faced her, his gray eyes weary. "My name is John Creed."

"*What* are you? Why am I here? Why did Gibbs send me here?"

"I guess because he believed what you had to say."

"He said that? When you called him?"

"Yes."

"Then why didn't he speak up? Why didn't he say he believed me?"

"A wise man doesn't spit in the wind."

"A . . ."

She fell silent, and he gave her time to think about it, watching her face. She wondered if he could read her thoughts.

What *were* her thoughts? Primarily, that she didn't know where else to go.

"Gibbs called you Keeper."

He grimaced. "Gibbs would."

"What does it mean?"

"Those files," he said, reaching for his glasses again and gesturing to a bank of metal cabinets at the far end of the wall, "are only the tip of the iceberg. I've got thousands more downstairs, in a storage room. Almost all of those are on computer now. That, and other equipment, came from various foundations over the years."

"Are you a cop?"

He listed his credentials simply, as if they held no interest for him, yet knowing it had to be done. "I was a cop. For the past four years, I've been running a kind of independent clearing house—small scale, really, compared to most—for finding missing kids. I've got a bad reputation with some on the LAPD, but a good one for getting things done."

She frowned. "Why do you have a bad reputation with some?"

"I don't know. It's something I've never figured out . . . why people resent getting the job done, no matter who does it."

Professional jealousy, Brooke thought. She ran up against it all the time. Her gait, as she paced the room from one window to another, was driven by nerves.

"Can you find my daughter?"

"My success rate at finding children is higher than most. That doesn't mean I find every child I look for. Some have disappeared on purpose, because they were brutalized at home. Some are dead—"

She didn't want to hear about the ones who were dead. "The children in those pictures." She motioned toward the wall of photos. "Are they all missing?"

"Yes."

"You've been looking for them and haven't found them?"

"That's right."

Dear God. So many. "Are they all from around here?"

"No, different parts of the country. I sometimes take those on a private basis, for personal reasons."

"How do people hear about you?"

"Word gets around."

"Why didn't the police send me to you? The others, I mean, not just Gibbs?"

"Like I said . . . word gets around."

They don't like him. Any more than they like me.

It was the best credential he could have given Brooke.

"Will you help me?" she asked.

"I don't know. We can talk. I'll try."

WHILE SHE CONTINUED to circle the room nervously, Creed asked questions, one after another. Brooke answered without embellishment. If she had thought, for any reason, to lie about anything, she discarded that idea as well. She told Creed everything that had happened, starting with the call from Charly, and ending with what had happened at the police station.

"You don't believe your ex-husband's story about this camping trip?"

"It just doesn't make sense. He told me she was with him, right after Charly called me, crying, and saying she didn't know where she was. Now he's telling the police she's on this damned trip—when Charly had told me all along she'd be here when I came this weekend."

"Do you think he would hurt Charly? Put her in danger?"

"I don't know. . . . I guess I don't really think so."

He asked for a picture of Charly, and she found one in her purse, a class picture that Charly had given her the previous month. He adjusted his glasses and studied it for several moments, as if committing it to memory, then put it on his desk next to a fax machine. He asked her about Charly's home life, her possible state of mind. Brooke had to admit that she wasn't sure.

"When I left Nathan, there were people and things I needed to get away from here. I moved to San Francisco. That was eight months ago."

"It didn't bother you, leaving your daughter behind?"

"Of course it bothered me! It killed me. But I thought that if I got my life in order, that would help Charly more than anything. At first I flew down here once a month for the visiting weekends allowed by the court. But every time, Nathan had something else planned for Charly to do. I finally stopped coming down. I did write to her, every day for a while, but she didn't answer. Last month I found out that Nathan had kept my letters from her. I flew down and insisted on having lunch with Charly. I just wouldn't leave. Since then we've been talking to each other several times a week."

"She calls you?"

"Yes." Her voice shook as she remembered how good it had been to get those calls. She swallowed, to steady it. "I call her too. I think we're as close as possible, under the circumstances. I sent her a rehearsal tape from the show I'm in—*The Unsinkable Molly Brown*. She sends me her drawings from school, and stories she's written."

"And you say you're going for joint custody now?"

"Yes."

"Have you talked to Charly about this?"

"Yes, last month. I wanted to know how she felt about it before I went ahead."

"And?"

"She was excited. Joint custody would mean that she could spend half the year with me in San Francisco. She said she would like that."

He removed his glasses and crossed to the windows, seeming to stare out at the white wall of fog. But she could feel him watching her reflection.

"According to Gibbs, you were drinking heavily for at least a year before your divorce. You took pills. There were several arrests for DWI, and drunk and disorderly. You were eighty-sixed from bars and you caused scenes in just about every restaurant, clothing, and grocery store —you name it—in upscale LA."

"That Gibbs. What a guy."

He faced her. "Was he wrong?"

"No . . . he wasn't wrong."

"Apparently people in Westwood haven't forgotten."

"I never supposed they would."

"You mean because your ex-husband has influence? Do you think he's responsible for their not having forgotten?"

"Possibly." Brooke shrugged. "Probably. He seems to need to paint me black, so he comes out white." *Like a photographic negative. Opposite aspects of the same scene.*

"He may be jealous of you and Charly."

"Nathan?" *Nathan, who has it all?* "I can't believe that."

"No? Who did Charly call yesterday when she had the chance? Him?"

"I . . . I don't know."

He returned to gaze at the photos on the wall, clicking the stem of his glasses against his teeth. "She couldn't have had time for more than one call," he mused. "She made it to you."

"But Charly adores her father."

"Sometimes children know things . . . without knowing." He paused a moment, thinking. "On the other hand, there are other possibilities. Let's say your daughter really did go on this camping trip, and something happened to her along the way."

"But Charly wouldn't have gone off like that without telling me.

Today—yesterday, now, I guess—was her birthday. This Saturday is a court-scheduled visiting day, and I was flying down to see her. She was looking forward to it. Besides, that brings us right back to Nathan, and why he lied about her being with him, right after I got her phone call."

"Well, let's assume the worst—that your daughter has been kidnapped. He may have had a ransom call, warning him not to tell the police, or you."

He waited patiently, letting her think it through.

She dropped heavily to the armchair, closing her eyes and leaning her head back. "I just don't know. My mind won't work."

He pulled a yellow legal pad from his desk and wrote something, leaning against a file cabinet. "We need to talk to your ex-husband. I'll get Gibbs on it, looking for him."

She opened her eyes. "You'll help me? You do believe me, then, that something is wrong?"

"Let's say I'd rather not disbelieve. The stakes are too high to waste time at the beginning of these things."

"But then why didn't the police see it that way?"

"Maybe my agenda is different from theirs."

"You mean they don't want to find Charly?"

"I mean they don't know yet that they want to. Right now they think they want to keep things nice and peaceful in their pond. Did you know your ex-husband is a good friend of the captain there, and the DA?"

"No . . . no, I didn't, not really. But I guess it doesn't surprise me. How do you know that?"

"Gibbs mentioned it. I think what they need over there is for someone to come along and skip a few stones in that pond, ruffle the water a bit."

"And you'll do that?"

"It will be my pleasure."

Creed sat at his desk once more, toying with the keyboard of the turned-off computer. Behind the stone black eyes was the anger Brooke had glimpsed earlier. It didn't frighten her now, the way Nathan's cold anger always had; she was simply glad it was there. Almost as if, seeing Creed's, she was able to release her own. The fire crackled, and finally she felt its warmth.

"How has Charly been since the divorce?" Creed asked.

"At first she had nightmares. Nathan sent her to a psychologist. He didn't go with her, like to family counseling." *He sent her to be fixed—like sending the Mercedes out for repairs.*

"How did the therapy go?"

"Have you ever been to a psychologist?"

"Yes."

"How do *you* think it went?"

"I think the guy asked her a lot of questions, made her figure things out little by little, bit by bit, week after week. I haven't got much patience for it."

She narrowed her eyes. "You haven't got much patience for anything, have you?"

"No. I believe in moving things along."

Brooke studied the flames.

"Woman," she said.

"Huh?"

"The psychologist was a woman. And you're right. It didn't help much. Charly's too smart, she understands mind games. She was always way ahead."

"Children usually are."

THE FIRE GREW COLD. Brooke sipped at her coffee, and Creed made phone calls—in her presence this time, from a cordless phone. One was to Gibbs, a patch through the LAPD dispatcher.

"Talk to the father, see if you can get a name and address for the people he says took Charly on this trip, and a description of the car. If there's even a chance she's actually on her way to the Grand Canyon, I want to know it. Talk to the phone company, too. See if they can come up with anything on calls to and from Hayes' phone in the last twenty-four hours." He asked Brooke for her phone number in San Francisco and passed it along to Gibbs. "See if you can find out where the call from Charly to this number came from. Yeah, I know, not much chance, but try. Also, get some help if you need it, but I want a tail on the father. The usual."

He listened, then spoke again. "Well, you know how these things

go. He could be involved. But we can't overlook that she might have
been snatched. Either way, given the SOS to her mother, the kid's in
trouble."

Brooke felt a wave of pain, hearing him say it. There was an actual,
physical ache in her body. She watched as Creed moved again to the
window and looked through the darkness and fog in the direction of the
water, his back to her. He nodded. His words faded in and out.

". . . her school . . . yeah . . . I'll do that . . . and the
computer. You take the neighbors . . . call me as soon as you know."

He hung up and turned to Brooke, checking his watch. "It's almost four. In a few hours, we'll talk to people at Charly's summer
school. Gibbs will be back to me with answers on other things. You
might like to know that I reached him on his car radio, outside your
daughter's house. He's been keeping an eye out. If there's any sign of
Charly, he'll let us know."

She was surprised at how swiftly things were moving, suddenly.
"Why is Gibbs doing this?"

Creed shrugged. "He helps me out sometimes."

"He works for you?"

"Unofficially. Now and then."

She sighed. Nathan had always told her: "It's not money that
counts, but power. With it, things get done." For the first time she was
grateful rather than scornful of it. "Thank you," she said.

Creed took the coffee cup she was still holding. "I'll have more
questions for you later. Right now you need sleep."

She opened her mouth to argue, and he said, "There isn't anything
more you can do right now. This isn't the kind of case where there's a
ransom note, or someone has seen the child being snatched. Until we
know more, it would be counterproductive to run door-to-door or
drive up and down streets. You need to rest, for later."

She nodded, finally, and stood. Swaying. "I have to find a hotel."

"No hotel. There's a room downstairs you can use. I'll wake you
in three hours, and we'll begin again."

"I . . ."

"Please don't argue," he said irritably. "You'll be helping your
daughter best this way."

She hesitated again, then nodded. "What happens in three hours?"

"If Gibbs or I haven't turned up Charly by then, we'll work together on it. I'll want you available twenty-four hours a day. This is your child, you know her better than anyone, and it's as much your job to find her as mine." The edge in his voice increased. "Further, I am not a hero and I will not hold your hand. So far, you've been reasonably tough. I hope that continues. I can't stand weeping."

Brooke answered with an edge. "Just what I needed. Mother Teresa's drill sergeant."

"It's better that people know what they're getting into. So . . . do you stay?"

"Show me where I sleep," Brooke said.

HE TOOK HER DOWNSTAIRS and showed her the kitchen first, which was below the living room, with a wide brace of double-hung windows facing the beach. There was a bathroom in the hall, and one connected to the second bedroom, where she was to sleep.

It was a Spartan room, clean and neat, painted white, with few pieces of furniture. A double bed with a dark blue comforter. A red architect's lamp with a swinging arm, attached to a square oak night table. A simple, double-hung window with red Levolor blinds.

Creed brought clean sheets from a closet in the hall, and together they made the bed. He made his side the way he talked, methodically, squaring the corners and leaving no valleys. Then he left her there.

"I'll wake you in three hours," he said.

Brooke was too tired to shower. She slipped off her shoes and socks, and turned out the light. Fully dressed, she crawled between the plain white sheets, turning on her side and pulling her knees to her chest.

Was it only a few hours ago, she thought bleakly, that I was on stage playing a brazen seventeen-year-old? That the only major question in my life was whether I would be able to have Charly live with me, while now . . .

It was a strange bed, a strange house, with strange noises. Brooke thought she wouldn't sleep, but she did. As she was drifting off, she wondered at the fact that she was feeling safe enough to do so, under the same roof with that strange, abrupt man.

Chapter 11

HE WOKE HER AS PROMISED, with a rap on the open door. In the first few moments of waking, Brooke forgot where she was and what had happened. But it all flooded back, and she jerked up and out of bed, her bare feet slapping the unfamiliar floor. Her heart started to hammer, the way it had on exam days as a kid, then, later, on opening nights—only this was much worse. It was like a door to evil fell off its hinges, revealing a scene so horrible, she couldn't bear to look. She actually shifted her eyes, searching for other, happier images, and found none. Only bare white walls, and cold gray light outside.

She saw that Creed was gone, but that her small suitcase had been carried in from the rental car. It rested just inside the bedroom door. The car keys—which she had forgotten, upstairs, on a table—were on a dresser by the door.

Brooke lugged the suitcase onto the bed and took out a pair of white jeans and a red cotton shirt. The mixture of clothes she had thrown in before rushing to the airport would have been funny at any other time. A suit that was rumpled and dirty. No matching blouse. Jeans, but no extra underclothes, toothbrush, or shampoo.

She worked at orientation as she showered, reliving painfully everything that had happened the night before. She scrubbed mechanically at her arms, breasts, abdomen, thighs, genitals . . . a chore, no more than a whore's bath, something that needed to be done. Could she scrub her past mistakes away? In the light of day it seemed certain that her sins had caught up, not with her, but with her daughter. She prayed under the coarse, hot spray: *God help her. I'd rather find that I am paranoid, crazy, than that something has happened to Charly. Even if it turns out that Nathan—*

Oh, Nathan. What game are you playing now?

A master gamesman, Nathan Hayes—a player, as surely as she. Had she seen their similarity, back in those crucial days of first-meeting, and mistaken its importance to love?

And just how much of that went back to her own mother—Livvy?

After the knock-down-drag-out custody fight a year before, after Brooke had heard the decision and cried all the tears she thought were left, she had thought about Livvy. She sat in a borrowed, rent-controlled cottage in Santa Monica, playing old Sinatra records, and watching the sun turn pink over the sea. Her thoughts were a bit scattered, perhaps, by the bottle of Tequila Gold cuddled against her terry-cloth robe, and the fact that she was weeping again, into the one unbroken crystal tumbler left from her mother's things.

Her mother . . . Olivia Tucker Leeds. A broken bird if there ever was one.

Livvy had grown up in the red clay country of Georgia, a bare breath of a woman who never in her life wore anything but a dress. She was Catholic to the point of madness, and just as Irish. More often than not, Brooke would come home from school at three in the afternoon to find Livvy Leeds sitting at their lace-covered kitchen table, pasting holy cards into a scrapbook while drinking scotch from a cut crystal glass. On every surface—counters, sink, stove, fridge—candles flickered. Votive lights in tiny glass holders of varied colors: sapphire, ruby, emerald, gold . . .

It was like coming home every day to High Mass.

Livvy liked to work with her hands. Once, she had whittled a statue of Jesus from a bar of Coast deodorant soap. When Brooke told her it was "Great, Mom, really great," Livvy carved Mary out of pink Camay.

On Saturday mornings Loony Livvy (as she came to be called by neighbors) would experiment with her daughter's hair, trying to make her look like someone from the movies: Debbie Reynolds, or sometimes Sandra Dee. Thus Brooke learned at an early age the fine art of looking and acting like someone other than who she was.

It was during one of these times, while Livvy was rolling Brooke's hair in orange-juice cans to make it more bouffant "like Jackie's used to be," that she said, "We're related to Frank Sinatra, you know."

Brooke said, "Yeah?" She hadn't noticed it made any difference. Uncle Frank never came around when the rent was due.

"Don't say 'yeah,' that way." Livvy had sprayed them both with Coty's L'aimant—a fragrance they had given each other at Christmas for years. "Someday we're going out to Hollywood, and I'll figure out a way to meet him . . . maybe run out of gas outside his house, or something. Then all our troubles will be over. You'll see."

At times like these, her mother would be playing Sinatra records on the tinny hi-fi, and she'd be singing along, knowing all the words. Brooke would look into the mirror above her dressing table and see her mother's face . . . young, and alive with hope. She didn't have the heart to question her mother's dream. Some instinct told her that the dream might be all that was keeping Olivia Leeds alive. And it might have done that, too, except that Livvy only dreamed like that on Saturdays. The rest of the week was devoted to drinking herself to death.

Brooke left the decaying white house in Georgia at seventeen. She stored the few larger ancestral belongings Livvy had willed her a few months before—having sold most over the years to pay the mortgage—and squeezed the smaller ones into the trunk of a beat-up yellow Volkswagen car. Livvy had hated dying, hated letting go, and her things (and spirit) had followed Brooke around the country for years, like the shell of a turtle that won't be left behind.

Heading for Hollywood, Brooke had hoped to live out Livvy's dreams. But like Molly Brown, who aimed for Paris and at first made it only to Leadville, Brooke had learned that most people don't make it to the place where they expect their dreams to come true. Sometimes they make it somewhere else, finding their dreams—or nightmares—along the way.

So, she thought, rinsing off— Just how much of all that had happened could she blame on Livvy Leeds? Mothers were always to blame, weren't they? For hundreds of generations, perhaps thousands, mothers had born the brunt of that premise . . . *through my fault, through my most grievous fault.* No wonder more women drank today than ever before. Guilt was almost certain to be found one day to be cumulative, passed along the mother genes.

Mechanically Brooke stepped from the blue stall shower and stood naked at the sink, brushing her teeth with toothpaste from the medicine cabinet, dabbed on a finger. She fastened her hair into a ponytail with the same rubber band, drew on the jeans and red shirt, and went upstairs to the smell of hot coffee and fresh-squeezed orange juice. Creed was outside on the deck, striding back and forth as he talked on the cordless phone. He wore a pale yellow shirt with faded jeans and running shoes. Even through the windows, she could tell that he was wired. His back was tense, the narrow planes of his face made sharper still by the harsh morning light. Now and then he would bump into a chair, forgetting it was there. A kick would shove it aside. As he paced erratically, a silver medallion glinted against his chest. Like him, it was large and primitive looking, in a way that Brooke found reassuring. A few hours ago she had been put off by Creed's rough edges. Now she was glad to have someone with less than civilized instincts helping her with Charly.

She wondered what time it was and checked the clock on his desk. Seven thirty-four. The computer was already on. A fax spewed reams of paper. She noted that one of the handles on the wooden desk hung crookedly, having come unscrewed—like the mailbox, and the number at the gate. Not much attention was being given to inanimate objects around here. Yet the computer setup was extensive; it must have cost a small fortune. This, too, she found reassuring.

A scarred sideboard next to the sliding doors held a pitcher of orange juice, several blue-and-white mugs, and a couple of tall slim glasses. Outside, on the metal deck table, was a glass pot of coffee. Brooke poured orange juice and took it out there, standing at the rail. As Creed continued on the phone, she looked down on the boardwalk and beach. The sun was coming in from the east; it cast a dull red glow over the sky, reflecting color down to a gray morning sea. The air was chill.

Was Charly cold? Did she have a sweater with her? Wherever she was, was she safe?

Brooke's throat filled. She started to say something to Creed, but he was still on the phone. She paced from one end of the deck to the other.

Down the beach to the left, she could see Venice Pier. To the right, the curve of Santa Monica's hills. Packed along the beach in between were a few houses of the same era and condition as Creed's, but most were high-rise apartments, condominiums, hotels. From surrounding coffee shops and cafés came the scent of bacon cooking.

Brooke remembered how it used to be, here, with beaches where you could take a child—if you chose your spot well. Now there were street gangs, and crumbling buildings with barred windows right next to movie stars' homes. The beaches were topless in some places, gay in others. She didn't mind that personally but had never felt she could bring Charly here—

Dammit, what was taking so long? And what time was it now? She went back inside, saw that only four minutes had passed. She looked at the computer screen. Addresses from all across the country were scrolling alphabetically, below numbers that seemed to be a code. South Carolina, South Dakota, Tennessee . . .

Creed was setting down the phone. She went back out.

"I roused the principal of Charly's school," he said, pouring more coffee. "We have an appointment with her at ten o'clock. But it's a small, private school, and she remembered that Charly was on a field trip yesterday at Universal Studios. She left there early—with her father, the principal says."

"With Nathan? What time?"

"Noon—a little after."

"But why would Nathan take her from her field trip?"

"He said they were going somewhere for an early dinner. For her birthday."

"Her birthday . . ." Brooke's eyes closed.

"What?"

She shook her head. "It's just . . . I bought her a doll for her birthday. I didn't think to bring it with me."

"We can get something here, if you like. You can give it to her when we find her."

Brooke ignored the other, awful possibility—that Charly might never be found.

"The principal also says Charly left last night on a camping trip."

"That, again? That's bullshit! Why wouldn't Charly have told me, if that were true? You can't believe—"

"I didn't say I believed it," he interrupted quietly. "Did I?"

She stared into the pulpy juice in her glass.

"It's what your ex-husband told her," Creed said calmly. "Don't try to work it out, we're just gathering information now. The time will come, soon enough, to put it all together."

He pulled out a deck chair for her, brushing away dry leaves. They had been carried on the wind from a neglected ficus tree in a cracked Mexican pot.

She waved away the chair. "I can't sit. Look, I've got to go look for Charly, I've already wasted too much time. What if she's hurt? What if she's lost in some awful place and crying, right now, wondering why I haven't come for her?"

Creed's eyes were tired, with a network of lines. There was a healed gash, Brooke noted for the first time, in one eyebrow. A fine scar ran down from his bottom lip, along the chin.

"Where would you like to go?" he asked.

"I . . . to the house, in Westwood. You said so yourself, we've got to talk to Nathan."

"Your husband isn't there. He didn't return during the night, and there's been no discernible movement inside the house."

"How do you know that?"

"Gibbs. He watched the place all night."

She ran a hand impatiently through her still-damp hair. "Okay, so Gibbs has been busy. I'm impressed. But I still want to go there. I want to go in and make sure Charly isn't in there, that he's not just keeping her from talking to me—"

"Charly's not there."

"You can't know that—"

"I can."

"How?"

"Trust me. Charly is not in the house."

She realized, then, what he was saying. "You don't mean that Gibbs—"

He leaned against the rail. "Don't ask." His smile was pained. "Just don't ask."

"Oh." She stared, then glanced away, hiding a small flutter of excitement.

It was more than she could have hoped for. Gibbs had been in the house. Without a search warrant, apparently. He'd gone in and looked for Charly there. *Broken* in? To Nathan's home, his castle? In the night?

A felonious knight-errant, breaching the moat to rescue fair maid.

The day seemed brighter suddenly. Filled with possibilities.

"I'm trusting you not to mention this to anyone else," Creed said.

"Of course not," Brooke agreed quickly. "But then, what about Nathan's office? Can we go there?"

"Gibbs is there now. Your husband hasn't shown yet."

"*Ex*-husband. Call him Nathan, please. And Christ, Gibbs is everywhere!"

Creed's mouth twitched. "He does have that tendency."

"Why is he working so hard on this? Because he's your friend?"

"That's part of it. But Gibbs is a saver."

"A saver?"

"He has to be saving things."

She remembered. SAVE THE ROOS.

"Ask him about the redwoods sometime," Creed said.

Brooke put her glass on the table and forced herself to sit. "Have you ever had a parent fall apart on you?"

"Yes." He leaned against the railing, drinking coffee. *Several. But Karen was the first.*

"How do you stand it?"

"It's part of the job."

"Then why do you do it?"

He didn't answer, and for some reason she didn't push. "What have you been doing on the computer?" she asked.

"There are networks all over the country, people who help look for missing kids."

"Police departments?"

He returned to the table and sat with his feet up, fingering the cordless phone as if willing it to ring. "Some. But the problem is too vast now for most police departments. There's a National Center for Missing and Exploited Children, and there are other smaller agencies and groups—the kind of thing I do. Many have hotlines, and we all have computers. We send and receive information about missing kids twenty-four hours a day. Just to be on the safe side, I sent Charly's picture—the one you gave me last night—over the fax, to several of these centers. That, and her description, are all around the country by now."

She picked blindly at a chip of white paint on the metal table. "That makes it pretty official," she said in a small voice.

"It's only a beginning. It's important, early on, to cover all bases. But as to what's really happening, I'm not sure. My first guess is that her father's got her, given the fact that he lied to you about her being okay right after her phone call. What I can't figure yet is *why* she called. It would seem he's put her in some kind of dangerous, or at least frightening, situation. Are you sure he wouldn't do anything to hurt Charly?"

Her hands shook, and she shoved them together, lacing the fingers. "Emotionally, yes—he might. Nathan's the coldest man I've ever known. But hurt her physically, deliberately? No. I just can't believe it."

"So the way it is, we're working in the dark. There's been no ransom call that we know of, no good-bye note saying she's run. No witness to say somebody grabbed her. And children seldom just disappear." *Except for Jason. He disappeared.*

"On the other hand, it's been less than twelve hours since you got Charly's call—"

At her startled expression, he said, "I know. It seems longer. And I'm not minimizing your worry or the harm that could come to Charly with each additional hour that passes. But the way these things work, it's early still. There could be a request for ransom today. Or Charly could just show up— By the way, did you make arrangements before you left San Francisco to have someone cover your phone? In case she calls again?"

"My God. No." Brooke leaned forward anxiously. "Should I have? Do you think she might have tried to call again—" Of course she might have! *What was I thinking?* "I could get someone now, a friend, to go over there—" She saw his expression. "You think it's too late."

"Not necessarily."

"But you do think that!"

"No, what I think is that you should stop looking for things to blame yourself for."

Her eyes closed. "I just—I just thought I was doing okay . . . up to now."

"It's understandable. Don't ask too much of yourself."

She looked at him. "But I've been acting crazy. When I got here last night . . . I didn't know what to do, which way to go . . ."

She realized something else. "You never had any intention of taking me out on the streets to look for Charly, did you?"

He shrugged. "It's too soon. If she's been kidnapped, the chances that she'd surface this early are slim. If her father's got her, she won't be on the streets."

"So you were placating me, when you said we could look."

"Appeasing might be a better word. I knew you needed to hear it. It's hard, not doing anything."

She sighed. "It's rotten."

He rocked back and forth on the light metal chair, using the power of his legs to keep it in balance. "What about the housekeeper—at the house in Westwood. Did you get along with her?"

"Mrs. Stinson? Yes, we got along. She was Charly's nurse from the time Charly was born. She loves her."

"If Nathan has spirited Charly off somewhere, do you think she knows and has gone along with it?"

Brooke hadn't thought of that. "I doubt it. She's pretty straight."

"Do you have a picture of Nathan?"

"I think so, in my purse. A picture of Charly, really, but he's in it." She laughed shortly and brushed her hair back from her face with a shaky hand. "I suppose I could have cut him out. Women do."

"Do they?"

"After a divorce? All the time."

"Why haven't you?"

"You mean, do I still care about Nathan? I despise him. But cutting his picture out would be like saying he mattered. You know?"

"I know."

"Do you think that's dumb?"

"Does it matter what I think?"

"Not much." She found herself smiling.

"Well, that's encouraging."

She laughed. This time it sounded almost right.

The phone rang. Creed answered and swung to his feet, as if he couldn't talk without striding back and forth. "Yeah. Uh-huh. Okay, we'll be right there. Why don't you go home now? Get some rest, I'll see you later."

"Gibbs," he said, hanging up. "Nathan just arrived at his office."

They went inside, and Brooke ran downstairs to make sure the windows were locked, at Creed's request. When she came back up, he was putting on the answer machine. He left the computer running but locked the sliding doors carefully as they went out. She raised a brow at his thoroughness.

"The people," he explained, "from the beach. They come in where they can, for food, a roof, a toilet. It's one of the dichotomies of my life—to expound upon the plight of the homeless, while locking my home against them."

At the bottom of the stairs, he reached into the mailbox, which opened on both sides of the fence. There were several letters, still sitting there from the day before—one of which he kept apart from the pile and read as he was warming the jeep in the garage. He scowled as he finished and shoved it inside the glove compartment. Jamming the gear into reverse, he leaned hard on the gas pedal, jolting them out into the alley. A bunch of cassette tapes slid from the dash to the floor. Brooke picked them up, then wondered what to do with them. Finally she opted to hold them.

"Everything okay?" she asked when he still hadn't spoken ten minutes later.

"No."

It was like that all the way to Westwood. Where matters grew worse.

Chapter 12

THE MORNING COMMUTE WAS STILL ON. Traffic was heavy. Creed drove
the dusty red Willys jeep like a tank, plowing through traffic as if part-
ing the waters, seldom letting up on the accelerator. The wind tore
through the old canvas top. Brooke didn't know which was worse—the
prospect of seeing Nathan soon, or the ride to his office.

The office was in a rose-brick, white-shuttered building in Westwood. It was nestled in a courtyard on a street that was lined with trees
and boutiques. Not a glitzy high rise, like those in nearby Century City,
where many of Westwood's movers and shakers did their wheeling and
dealing, but more upper crust. Nathan was old money. His father had
been an early trustee of UCLA, in the days when Peter Lawford and
June Allyson pranced around college campuses in movies like *Good
News*. Those were the days of raccoon coats, of cars with running
boards and rumble seats. Villains came in the form of a gorgeous Liz
Taylor, who stole boyfriends from the fresh-faced ingenue, while whole
crowds of extras (boys and girls who worked for scale and drank beer in
convertibles at night) sang "The Best Things in Life Are Free." And
believed it.

The house that Nathan had inherited from his father, the house
where Nathan and Charly lived, was near the campus. It was large
and sprawling, a three-story stucco, with palm trees, jacarandas, and
live oaks. There were gardens with wild orchids, roses, camellias,
and rhododendrons. No pool. Pools were too nouveau, accord-

ing to Nathan. Nevertheless, it was a perfect home for a child to grow up in, Brooke had thought. She wanted Charly to have that kind of life.

It was a life she had always yearned for herself. Not the money, but the security. It occurred to her now, with some bitterness, that even she —with Loony Livvy as a mother, and with the crumbling house in Georgia—had been safer than Charly.

They parked in a tree-shaded lot across the street and entered the cool, flower-scented lobby, their footsteps breaking the silence on a highly polished parquet floor. From there they took a well-oiled elevator to the third floor. A carpet of soft rose muffled their steps down a long corridor and through double chrome-and-glass doors. A receptionist, someone Brooke had never met, sat at an ornate desk with a bank of phones, a typewriter, and a vase of steel gray roses. She passed them through without any problems (were they expected? Brooke wondered), and they followed another hushed corridor lined with windows that overlooked a lavish back terrace and more trees. The windows opposite looked out over Westwood and Wilshire Boulevard—a million-dollar view.

"More like Hollywood than Hollywood," Creed muttered.

His black hair had been blown about as they drove here, and he hadn't bothered to smooth it. His eyes swept side to side, while his hands were jammed into the pockets of his jeans. He was frowning.

Alix MacEnroe, Nathan's assistant, was already standing as they came through the door. She was in her thirties, an attractive woman— but with dark hair pulled so tightly into a twist, it seemed to drag her high, sloping forehead with it. Her lips were red and full; she continually wet them as she talked.

Her eyes gave away tension, and Brooke wasn't surprised. She supposed that Alix had plenty of reason to be unfriendly. There had been offenses in that last awful year . . . like the time Brooke had staggered in here in filthy jeans, her shirttail hanging half out, screeching for Nathan—accusing him of things that she knew, now, weren't true. She could still see Alix's appalled look and that of the clients in the reception room.

There would be other things that Alix would never forget, and that

Brooke, due to her drunken state at the time, would probably never remember.

"Nathan isn't in today," Alix said crisply. She placed herself a few feet before Nathan's inner door, a tall, slim, barrier. "He's taken a few days off."

"We know he's here," Brooke argued. "He was seen here, just a few minutes ago."

Creed ambled casually off to the side, letting Brooke do the talking.

"He's left," Alix answered. "He had business out of town." She broke off. "What are you doing?"

Creed was behind her, wrenching open Nathan's door.

"Empty," he said a moment later, with a shrug to Brooke.

"Now, just a minute—"

"You must know where to reach him, Alix."

"I don't. Nathan didn't tell me where he was going."

"Isn't that unusual?"

The woman leveled a cool gaze at her. "How could you possibly know?"

Brooke moved a step closer. "Do you know where my daughter is, Alix?"

"Charly? Why on earth—"

Creed broke in. "Just answer the question."

"Who *are* you?" Alix demanded.

He was glowering at the woman. The way he stood scowling, with hands on hips, feet spread in a fighting stance, he looked as if he might blow the place apart.

Instead, he pulled out a police ID, flipping it open irritably. "Creed. I'm working for Mrs. Hayes."

Alix took his hand, holding the ID with slender red-tipped fingers as she gave it a careful look. Office of the Commissioner. She raised a delicate brow, turning her searching gaze on Brooke.

"Charly left last night on a camping trip."

"Did you see her go?"

"Certainly not. I work here in this office, Brooke, I have no reason to spend time at Nathan's home."

There had been rumors. Brooke had believed them, off and on, generally when looking for grievances to air. When sober, she had given the matter more thought and decided that the rumors of their affair probably weren't true. Nathan didn't have all that many emotions to spread around.

Creed said, "You only have Hayes' word, then, that his daughter actually went on this trip?"

"I've never had reason to doubt Nathan's word," Alix replied. Her tone said there was every reason to doubt Brooke's.

Several more questions were asked—of Alix, the receptionist, and two word processors who worked in a small back office without a view. They led nowhere.

WITHIN FIFTEEN MINUTES they were at Charly's summer school. It was a small private school of Spanish design in a Westwood neighborhood of million-dollar homes. Nathan had chosen it so that Charly would "associate with the right people." Brooke expected that the people who ran it would think along the same lines: that there was an important difference between the "right" and "wrong" nine-year-olds.

Instead she found the principal, Roberta Shell, a blunt, no-nonsense older woman with short, straight, salt-and-pepper hair. She offered them both a chair in her office, before a desk piled high with open books and lined yellow pads. Brooke accepted the chair, while Creed prowled. The principal removed her rimless glasses and answered his questions without hesitation.

"As I told you earlier on the phone, Mr. Hayes called yesterday morning and said he was taking Charly out to a special dinner for her birthday. He said that he wanted her to have at least the morning at Universal, but would pick her up when we broke for lunch, rather than have us bring her back to the school."

"Did you talk to him yourself?"

"No, one of the secretaries took the call. She followed the usual procedure, asking for personal information—Charly's home address and phone number, her mother's social security number—"

Brooke interrupted. "He knew my social security number?" It was something Nathan never remembered. He'd always had to ask her, before calling the bank for a balance.

"Absolutely," the principal said. "The secretary okayed the call and passed the message along to Charly's teacher. . . ." She glanced at Brooke warily. "I don't understand. According to our records, the father has custody. What's the problem here?"

Creed answered. "We think something may have happened to Charly," he said.

"Have you talked to her father?"

"He claims she's on a camping trip."

"Well, that is what he told the office when he called this morning. A last-minute opportunity, apparently, for Charly to go with friends to the Grand Canyon."

"Do you know who she might have gone with? Is there another child here on a trip to the Grand Canyon?"

"If so, I haven't heard about it. We can check, of course, to see if anyone else in her class is out today."

"You say that Charly's father picked her up at Universal Studios yesterday?" Creed asked.

"Yes. I've talked with Ms. Patterson, Charly's teacher, and she's confirmed it."

"She actually saw Mr. Hayes?"

"Of course. She wouldn't have let Charly leave, otherwise."

Brooke leaned forward earnestly. "I got a call from Charly last night. She sounded afraid, and she told me she didn't know where she was. She said something about a man. She was crying."

Roberta Shell sat back, looking first at Brooke, then Creed. With a decisive motion, she pushed both hands against the desk and stood. "What would you like me to do? I'll help any way I can."

"First, we need to talk to the teacher," Creed said. "And I'd like a list of all of Charly's classmates. Their names, addresses, phone numbers."

The principal nodded and spoke briefly over her phone.

"The list will be ready before you leave," she said.

THE TEACHER'S NAME was Linda Patterson. She was young and soft-spoken, with freckles and short red curls. Around her neck was a small gold cross. She had a class of fifteen and seemed well in charge of it. Some children were reading, while others, in groups, worked at art projects. Brooke stood at a blackboard, looking at drawings taped above it in a row. One was Charly's, a palomino pony galloping across a sea of tall grass. Its haunches glistened; you could see the strain of muscle and almost hear the pounding of its hooves.

Charly had signed the picture in the painstaking cursive she was so proud of. "I've got the best handwriting in my class," she had told Brooke last month, at lunch. Her eyes had been bright, her smile wide, and Brooke had reached over with a fingertip and gently removed a piece of cake from her chin.

She pulled away from the drawing, feeling her throat tighten. Charly's teacher was with Creed, at a distance from the children, talking.

"I've only been here a couple of weeks," the teacher told them quietly, "but I was struck by Charly immediately. She's a beautiful child. I'm sure she's just fine, she's very bright—"

Creed hated these interviews. They were necessary, but he had no patience for them, no tolerance for the rambling answers that kept him from getting on with things. "Mrs. Patterson—"

"Please, call me Linda. The children do."

"Do you know who Charly might have gone to the Grand Canyon with? Someone in this class?"

"Why, no . . . everyone is here today."

"Would you ask the children, please?"

She did as he asked, making it sound like an ordinary occurrence that Charly's mother was here asking questions. Despite their bright, curious gazes, no one knew anything about Charly having planned a camping trip.

"Does she have friends in the other grades?" Creed asked the teacher.

"I think so . . . certainly, a few."

"I'll want to talk to them." He was gazing thoughtfully toward the far end of the room, at the children. Turning back abruptly, he said, "How do you know Charly's father picked her up at Universal yesterday?"

The teacher seemed confused. "How do I know?"

"Yes. You said you've only been here a couple of weeks. Did you recognize Mr. Hayes? From visits to the school?"

"Well, no, I hadn't met him before. . . ."

Brooke moved in closer. "Are you telling us you let Charly go off with her father, without making sure he *was* her father?"

"Certainly not. He called the office first to say he'd pick Charly up at Universal, and when he got there, he introduced him-self. . . ." Linda Patterson's voice trailed off. She wasn't a stupid woman, and uneasiness crept into her eyes as the implication took root.

Creed took out the snapshot of Nathan that Brooke had given him earlier. "Is this the man who said he was Charly's father? The man who took her from Universal?"

Linda Patterson stared at the photo, her face paling beneath the freckles. "No," she said shakily. "No, it isn't."

Brooke's eyes flew to Creed's.

"I . . . but it all made sense," the teacher said. "I mean, he *waved* to her, and he seemed so proud! And Charly smiled back. They have that new exhibit, you know, with the whales and dolphins, and she was up there on the whale, and then he went and got her . . . she took his hand. . . ." The teacher's eyes widened with horror. Her fingers closed over the cross at her neck. "Oh dear Christ, what have I done?"

John Creed's anger was beyond words. He stood with his hands jammed into his pockets and turned his back to the woman. Then, his frustration so great, he swept an arm against an easel, knocking it over. Chalk went clattering to the floor in an angry kaleidoscope of colors. "What kind of system is it, when something like this can happen? Why do we make it so damned *easy?*"

Brooke began to shake. "We turn our children over to you," she said in a low, harsh voice. "We trust you to take care of them, see that they're safe."

The other woman wiped back tears. "We can't do it all," she said just as angrily. Her face twisted. "For God's sake . . . where the hell were *you?*"

. . .

FROM THE PRINCIPAL'S PHONE, Creed spoke to Missing Persons, and to both the Hollywood and West LA stations. He now had both divisions' complete support. That Charly had left Universal Studios with a stranger purporting to be her father meant that her phone call to Brooke could no longer be ignored.

Who that stranger was, and whether a kidnapping had actually taken place, was still uncertain. Missing Persons began to move, and officers were detailed to find Nathan, to get his version of what was going on. In the meantime Creed proceeded on the premise that the first, early hours of a kidnapping are always the most crucial. Better to be ahead of the game than to find out later that you were way too far behind.

The teacher gave descriptions of everyone she remembered Charly having contact with just before leaving Universal. The studio employee who had helped Charly down from the whale was questioned. Between him and the teacher, a police artist was able to come up with a computer sketch of the short, light-haired man who had claimed to be Charly's father, the man she was seen to leave Universal with. Each of the children who had been with her at Universal was questioned, as well as the parents who had served as chaperones.

One missing link was the souvenir Polaroid photo of Charly on the whale. It was nowhere to be found. Creed interviewed the studio photographer, Michael Arnott, in his office at Universal. It was no more than a broom closet, stuffed with film, equipment, a metal file cabinet —the walls layered with photos of children. The photographer didn't remember Charly in particular.

"But sometimes the kids go off without their pics," he said. His nose was peeling from sunburn; he scratched at it with a fingernail. "In their excitement, they forget. Usually the parents come back for it."

"If she didn't take it, and no one came back for it, would you still have it somewhere?" Creed asked.

"Probably." Arnott's thick fingers rummaged through a box of Polaroids. "I don't know," he said, "I don't see it. Let me ask Felipe."

Felipe, his young assistant, had poked a head in earlier as they talked. Arnott opened the door now and looked up and down the hall. "Hey, Felipe!"

"He's seventeen," Arnott said while they waited. "And jumpy. Probably illegal. Don't guess I should be telling you that."

Creed shrugged.

"I hired him to gofer. There are all kinds of odds and ends, and it saves me legwork. . . ." Arnott moved his wide, bearish shoulders back through the door as the boy approached. "Kid doesn't do much . . . but then, I don't pay him much."

Felipe appeared. "The veedeo company say the tape be done tomorrow." Liquid brown eyes shifted nervously from Brooke to Creed.

"Great."

Arnott explained. "I have the Polaroids put on tape sometimes for the parents. We do a kind of video album, a collage, along with school and vacation snaps. It's a good side business in the summer. But I'm wondering if that Polaroid you're looking for might have gotten mixed up with that last order."

He showed the boy the photo of Charly that Creed had at first handed him. "Have you seen a souvenir shot of this little girl? One of the ones I take on the whale?"

Felipe glanced at the photo. He looked at Brooke and Creed, then back at the image of Charly again. "I don't theenk so." He stared at his feet, at Jordan Air running shoes that looked too new, too white, beneath tattered blue jeans. There were stains on his lime green T-shirt.

"You sure it didn't slip into that batch you took to be put on video?"

The boy shrugged.

Arnott sighed. "Tell you what," he said to Creed, checking his watch. "I have to go over there myself in about an hour. Sunset Video Creations. If the Polaroid's fallen in with that batch, I'll let you know."

Creed considered going for the photo himself. He wanted that Polaroid; the man who had taken Charly just might be somewhere in the background. But he knew Sunset Video Creations. It was north of here, on the eastern edge of the Valley.

In the end he decided it was more urgent to get back to the beach.

"I'll call you at Sunset in one hour exactly," he told Arnott. "You'll be there? This is important."

"Sure," Arnott said. "No problem. I've got a kid myself. A little boy." He gave Brooke a sympathetic glance—the first time he'd looked her in the eye since they entered the office. "Sorry for your trouble," he said awkwardly.

It's like when someone dies, Brooke thought. *You can't fix it, and you don't know what to say.*

"Just hang on," Creed said. "We don't really know yet what it's all about. Until we do, you can't get crazy on me."

They were in the jeep, driving back to the beach. Gibbs was to meet them there.

"She's gone," Brooke said, the words barely coming out. "It wasn't Nathan at all. Somebody's got her."

"Don't jump to conclusions. There's still a matter of how the person who called the school office knew your social security number."

"You think he was working for Nathan?"

"It's a possibility, one we have to consider."

"But anyone can get social security numbers now. You can get them lots of ways."

"True. And yet . . ."

"What?"

"It would almost have to be someone who knew you, or Charlie. To plan it out that far ahead, calling the school . . . to know about the trip to Universal, and that it was Charly's birthday. . . ."

Brooke suddenly felt cold in spite of the palm trees along the streets and the muggy eighty-degree weather. "You were so angry back there. It frightened me. I frightened myself. And that poor teacher . . ."

His hands gripped the wheel of the jeep. It picked up speed. Anger could well be the least of their problems now.

A few years ago there had been a case—a seven-year-old boy, abducted while riding his bike. The kidnapper left him for dead, but not until he'd been raped and his penis hacked off. When they found the kid—Creed remembered all too painfully—he was worried because he had lost his bike. The mutilation was too much to contemplate, so he focused on the goddamned bike.

They caught the guy, eventually. He spent fifty-three days in jail, during which time he said that when he got out, he would do it again. They had released him anyway.

Creed swerved violently, just missing another car. There were people who thought that rapists should be castrated. Others said that that wouldn't do any good, because rape isn't a sexual crime, but one of violence. Personally, he thought they should cut off a rapist's thumb, middle, and little fingers of one hand. After all, cutting off their balls doesn't tell anybody a thing. You can't even see it. But if some sick weirdo walks up to a little kid, and his thumb, middle, and little fingers are missing, and everybody in America knows what that means, the kid's going to ask questions. He might even have time to run.

He slowed the jeep, realizing suddenly that he was thirty-five miles over the speed limit—and that Brooke was huddled miserably against the far door, her face turned away.

"Don't worry," he said softly, stretching out a hand to grip her arm. "We'll find her. I promise you, we'll find her."

BACK IN VENICE, Gibbs arrived, wearing a Greenpeace T-shirt and carrying two white paper bags. He set them on the coffee table in front of the couch. "I brought food."

He tossed his leather jacket onto a chair and his hat over the gaudy angel on the mantel. "Thing gives me the willies," he complained. His hairline began halfway back, where it fringed into thick brown curls that grazed his neck. His jaw was hard, the eyes blue and deceptively mild.

"Deli stuff. Sandwiches, potato salad, cold drinks . . ." He began unloading the bags. "You stick around here long enough, Ms. Hayes, you'll starve. And be jumpy as hell, all the coffee this damned fool drinks."

He shoved a thick wrapped sandwich into Brooke's hand. Grease leaked from it. The scent of corned beef rose to her nostrils. She hadn't realized she was hungry.

"Sorry about losing Hayes this morning, Keep. I figured the time you'd probably get there, and I left right before. I had to get over to the phone company."

"You did just fine, Gibby, relax. We'll find him."

Gibbs cracked his knuckles.

Brooke winced.

"Sorry. You want a Coke? Here." He shoved a cold, sweaty can into her other hand. "Eat. You look pale, you don't mind me saying so, Ms. Hayes."

Brooke attempted a smile. "Call me Brooke, okay? I appreciate what you've been doing, Gibbs." She sat on the couch and unwrapped the sandwich, taking a bite. It sank like lead in her empty stomach, but almost immediately she felt the comforting sensation of adrenaline rising to digest it. She took a sip of Coke.

"Food, Keep?" Gibbs was rocking up and down on his toes, his glance darting around the room as he spoke.

Creed was at the computer, checking incoming messages. He didn't seem to hear. Gibbs sighed. He carried a sandwich over and put it next to him, pouring a cup of coffee from the ever-present thermos on top of a file cabinet. He thunked that down next to the sandwich.

"Sometimes I feel like a Jewish mother. Or an Irish mother, or an Italian mother . . ."

Eating from a plastic container of potato salad, Gibbs took up a thick stack of paperwork and settled impatiently at the other end of the couch from Brooke.

After a while Creed glanced up and spoke to Brooke. "I've got several people arriving in the morning to help. Some are from volunteer agencies, and some are friends and off-duty police who've assisted in other cases."

There were four extra phones, he told her, in a cupboard beneath the bookshelves. They would be brought out and connected to existing modules along the wall. Folding tables and computer terminals would be brought from downstairs. The small living room—already crowded—would look like a campaign office the week before election day.

"All leads have to be followed up. There will be erroneous sightings along with crank calls once the story hits the papers. The phones, fax, and computer need to be covered twenty-four hours a day."

Brooke finished her sandwich quickly and pitched in, feeling self-indulgent for having taken the time to eat.

BY FOUR IN THE AFTERNOON, everything that could be done was being—or had been—done. A news release had gone out, and officers were talking to Nathan's neighbors in Westwood. He had no living family other than Charly, but friends and business associates were being questioned—their names provided grudgingly by Alix MacEnroe. Lieutenant de Porres had called from West LA Division to say they had a lead on Nathan's possible whereabouts and would check it out. De Porres had agreed, as well, to pass along information to Creed, from officers in the field.

This was the bad time, the time of waiting, when nothing seemed to happen fast enough. A child disappeared, there was a flurry of fear and activity, people were notified—and then everything slowed down while the complex machinery of law and communications took over. Later all hell might break loose. But now? It drove Creed nuts. He had to sit—or wear out the deck.

He sat in the sun, going through mug shots culled from a computer search, matching general descriptions to coded sets of files. It was a tedious task, trying to find someone who came close to a police artist's computer sketch—which, by definition, was vague. Brooke and Gibbs had taken turns at it earlier, while Creed sent new information over the fax and computer. There wasn't much. They still had far too little, in the way of hard facts, to go on.

Creed found his mind wandering. Something bothered him, but he didn't know what it was. He became peripherally aware of the scene below on the beach. Far down at the water's edge, he saw a child lift a yellow pail and tilt it. A diamond spray of salty foam glittered through sunlight. A wave sneaked up behind the child and whomped him on the back. The little boy stumbled and fell, but laughed and hung in, playing in the miniwaves that rolled over his legs.

"Danny!" His mother—possibly—stood nearby in a pink-and-white polka-dot swimsuit. She called out and smiled, snapping a picture.

A beach bunny sauntered into a gaggle of sunbathing surfers. One, a boy with platinum hair and a sunburned nose, plastered a bumper sticker on her bikini bottom, playfully. Plastered across it were the words: IF IT SWELLS, RIDE IT. The girl tossed her long wet hair, stretching her neck to look behind her. She grabbed the sticker off and giggled.

Creed went back to work.

A short time later Gibbs came out. He sat at the table and yawned. So did Creed. "Where is she?" he asked, looking up suddenly.

"Downstairs. She had to be doing something. She's making coffee."

"What is that awful smell?" Creed wiggled his nose. "Like metal."

"She burnt the pot."

He stared.

"She's tougher than you think," Gibbs said.

"I know."

"She's not like Karen."

Creed sighed. "No."

The mug shots became a blur, and he slid the pile over for Gibbs to take a turn. Leaning back, he stretched his arms and worked his neck in circles, hearing it crunch. From the boardwalk below came the noise of kids on roller skates, and a street entertainer playing a sax. There were smells of garlic, hot dogs, and french fries. The air was hot and humid, the ocean calm beneath a late afternoon sun. Not much surf, and the boards had mostly all been turned in at the rental place up the beach. He could see them behind the chain-link fence, twentieth-century monoliths standing at attention, keeping watch over the sea like the ancient rocks on Easter Island.

Karen used to surf.

He closed his eyes.

Last night in the dark, Creed's first impression was that Brooke reminded him of his wife. But Gibbs was right, she was actually much

sturdier—more durable, he thought now. Even before Jason disappeared, Karen wasn't strong. There were months of postpartum depression after Jason was born, months when she couldn't cope with things,
including the fact that her husband was a cop—and the dangers he faced
every day. Even his hours became a source of constant tension.

It wasn't that different from most cops' marriages. Maybe that was
why he hadn't noticed how bad it was getting. Or maybe—as Karen
had often complained—he just wasn't paying attention.

When Jason disappeared, it was the final blow from a weapon both
invisible and unexplained. Karen wouldn't talk about it but sat for hours
at a time, rocking in the chair in Jason's room, her gray eyes hollow and
empty.

This morning's mail had brought the usual frustrating letter of
progress (No Progress) from his wife's doctor in Santa Maria. She would
come out of it once every few weeks and talk, then fade away again.
Her talk would consist of vague recollections from her past, told in third
person, like scenes from someone else's life. "She had the most beautiful
long brown hair," Karen might say, "and a black-and-white cat, named
Hilda. She had a brother, too, but he died."

The "she" would be Karen herself . . . the "brother who died"
would be Jason, their son.

Creed's visits had become more painful and less frequent the past
couple of years, dwindling to once every other month, or less.

He would have to go up there again soon.

Sometimes Creed wondered if marriage—love—all of it—had
a built-in life span, like an electric bulb. Designed by a greedy manufacturer to burn bright for a preset period of time, then flicker and go
out.

When he had first left Karen in that safe, alternate world in the
gentle hills of Santa Maria, it had taken every ounce of strength to drive
away. As each mile passed, the anguish grew worse, and Creed had
come close, several times, to turning back—to grabbing her up and
fleeing with her, back to their home. They would just sit together, he
thought, for the rest of life, in that cold, dark, empty house, letting the
world dissolve away.

Anything, to keep Karen by his side.

But she wasn't really Karen anymore. She was a shell, whose occupant had ossified—had drawn up into a tight, hard ball without discernible thoughts, feelings, or life energy. Creed remembered, as a child, being on vacation at a beach somewhere, and prodding a shell with a stick to force its snail-like creature out. Finally, the need to expose the contents of that shell was so great, he ended up breaking it—only to find a dry, lifeless lump inside.

Some instinct told Creed that even if the doctors were able to break Karen's shell some day, the disappointment would be much the same. She would no longer be alive inside.

A few weeks after that first trip to Santa Maria, four years ago, he had sold the house in Santa Monica and moved back down here to the beach. The tenants he'd had here for years were retiring and moving back east—made nervous by the recent rash of earthquakes. Creed was glad that he'd hung onto the cottage, even when real estate soared and he could have made a small fortune selling. It was a simple existence here. There was funding for the work, and personal expenses were covered by money invested from the sale of the Santa Monica house. As long as he was careful, he didn't have to think about too many external things.

Brooke came out onto the deck with a tray of coffee and cups. "I had to make instant," she said, looking embarrassed.

"Smells great," Gibbs enthused, jumping up and taking the tray.

Creed didn't seem to hear.

THEY PUT ASIDE the endless paperwork for a while and sat quietly at the round metal table. Brooke was lost in thought, her face reflecting inner misery. The sun was low, and 1940s dance music could be heard from a neighboring apartment house. A hundred or more yards away, on the sand to the left, the homeless were gathering in their possessions for the night, smoothing out beds of sand beneath cardboard boxes. A mother was fixing hot dogs on a small round grill, for three children. Nobody there was dancing, Creed noted. The mood was one of dejection. Men —and women too—would have been panhandling all day. A few would have gone out to look for work—a fruitless task, for the most part, when you don't have a phone number to put on an application, or a place to wash your clothes. Food would be in short supply, and children would be cranky.

"They aren't happy campers," Brooke said, as if reading his thoughts.

"No. Someone has said that the test of every civilization is the point below which the weakest and most unfortunate are allowed to fall. The weakest in our society are the children, the elderly, the homeless. All of them abused—if only by the system."

"I can't believe how bad it's gotten here."

He nodded, leaning his chin against a fist. "It used to be, if you lived at the beach, you could relax, gaze out to sea and contemplate life in a positive vein. Now we're faced with daily proof that life is going bad. Sure, there are people down there who don't want to work, who choose to live like that. But what weakness in our society led them to end up that way? And it's supposed to be cold tonight. What do people without homes feel, when they look up at our lighted windows, knowing we're inside where it's warm, where we can sleep in a bed? Do any of us, the three of us, know how it feels to go an extended time without a roof over our heads?"

Gibbs, who had finally begun to relax with his face to the sun, pulled his cap down over his eyes. He cracked his knuckles. "Sure glad I stopped by, Keep. I needed cheering up."

Brooke could only think of Charly, possibly without shelter now. Left in a ravine—stripped—even dead? All the images you see on the news: a mother's worst nightmare. She began to feel ill.

"Well, we aren't all that far from barbarianism," Creed went on, oblivious. "Not here, or anywhere. In Britain they used to put young girls in wicker baskets and run swords through them, thinking they could tell, from the way the blood flowed, the will of the gods. In the fourth century the Scots in Britain ate human flesh, even though they had plenty of cattle and sheep. The thigh of a herdsman or a slice of the female breast was considered a delicacy."

He grimaced. "They say it took six and a half hours to hack Anne Boleyn's head off. Blunted several axes in the process. It's no wonder people—children—are so little valued, even now."

Brooke's face was now as white as the metal table, glaring under the harsh sun. Gibbs made a sound, a warning note, but Creed didn't hear. He had crossed to the railing and was staring at the people on the beach. Thinking how they never changed. Oh, the bodies were different. Some moved on, some died. But they were replaced with nameless, faceless people who looked exactly like themselves.

Brooke slipped down the outside stairs. He saw her as she crossed the boardwalk and walked down the sand to where the water began. She trudged through the tide, barefoot, then headed north—a slight figure in red shirt, hands in the pockets of her white jeans. She walked as if it were a duty—with a hard, quick stride, not looking to either side, but down, dark blond hair falling over the sides of her face.

Gibbs spoke softly. "You seen Karen lately?"

"No. Why?"

"You're getting in one of those black moods, Keep."

"I am?"

"You just scared the shit out of your houseguest. Funny you didn't notice."

"She's getting ready to break," Creed said.

"She's already broken, Keep. You took care of that."

He looked after her. Brooke was running—a dot-figure now, way down the beach.

After a moment Creed went inside. He put the answer machine on, slipped into shorts and a T-shirt. When he came out, he said, "Lock up when you leave, okay?"

Gibbs stretched. "I'm leaving? And I was having such a wonderful time."

Creed followed her footprints along the moist sand, trotting past volleyball nets and young, tan boys and girls who didn't have much to do but make out at sunset on beaches . . . who didn't have a clue to what might lie ahead in a world of pollution, poverty, lost jobs, stolen children—

Maybe the homeless had it better. For them, it couldn't get much worse.

They were prepared.

When he caught up with Brooke, she was crying. Tears ran unchecked down her face, and her lips were contorted with the effort of gulping back sobs. Creed ran alongside, matching her strides in a body language of comfort.

"You could have done this in front of me."

Her pace never slowed. "No, I couldn't. You told me—no weeping."

"Pain is allowed now," he said.

Chapter 13

ALONG THE CALIFORNIA COAST, about midway between Los Angeles and San Francisco, is a town built on the sea. Rocks rise up out of the foam like black icebergs, sharp and jagged. The ocean shimmers green with daylight, a hard, cold silver at night. In summer there is nearly always fog offshore.

So you can't see "clear to China" when looking out a window over this blustery coast.

That, at least, was what Charly thought.

She was allowed to sit by a window, looking out. Her hands weren't tied, but her ankles had something around them that fastened with a lock—a plastic cable. She had tried everything in the room but couldn't cut through the cable. The soft plastic had steel inside, like a bicycle chain.

Her legs hurt from keeping them this way. They weren't tight together, but cramping. She wanted to move them apart, but couldn't.

It was her own fault. That's what the man said. If she hadn't tried to run . . .

A long way below were the pointed rocks, and nothing from there on out but ocean, with one narrow strip of sand. A sandbar, she thought it was called. Once she had seen a man out there, walking, or at least a figure in pants. She tried hitting the window with her fists, but he didn't hear. The wind was too loud.

The wind made her afraid. It never stopped. It was so strong that a gull, flying against it, stayed in one place, like a helicopter, like he was hanging from a string.

When she had first got here, the door to this room was locked, but Charly wasn't tied at all. She could walk around and look at things, like the dolls on the big, soft bed, and the paintings. The bedroom was large, twice as large as her own room in Westwood, but with these pointed windows across it, like in an attic.

Most of the time Charly sat on one of the window seats, looking out. It made her feel almost free . . . like she could open the window any minute, stand on the ledge, and fly away.

The wooden frame was nailed down, though. It wouldn't budge. All the others were too. And she hadn't been able to break the glass. It was thick and sounded dull when you struck it. Not like glass at all.

There weren't any other houses around that Charly could see. Instead, huge trees stood on either side, with those flat branches that stick out like arms, waving, and bob up and down . . . the kind you hang Christmas ornaments on, and they don't hang crooked, but straight, in the open space.

On a hill way off to the right, where the coastline curved, Charly could see cars winding along a mountain road. They were far away, like little dots, and she knew they were there only because of the moving reflection of the sun—or at night, from their headlights.

At first she had thought she might flash a message somehow, the way she had seen it done on television, like in those old reruns of the Hardy Boys. But even if she could think how to do that, how to say she needed help, there was nothing to flash with.

He must have thought of that. There were no lamps you could move, and he had taken all the mirrors away.

Sometimes Charly tried jumping up and down to attract attention, even though she knew that if the cars were almost impossible for her to see, she would be invisible too.

She tired of that after a while. Then she would sit, just listening, and think about things.

She could hear the sound of music playing every now and then. Not the kind her mother liked, but the kind her father played. Classical? She hadn't heard many other sounds. Once, a telephone.

The meals the man brought her weren't bad. Always meat, potatoes, a vegetable, and dessert.

And there was a photograph of her mother on the wall.

It was big, like a poster. Her mother was beautiful in the photograph, her blond hair full and curly, just touching her bare shoulders, her eyes green as emeralds, her mouth red and smiling. Charly had a picture just like it, at home in her room. "It's a publicity photo," Brooke had said when she sent it. "I'm sorry it's not smaller, Charly. I'll get you a wallet size when I can."

Charly didn't understand why she was here, or why her mother's picture was on the wall. The only thing she knew, the one thing she could cling to, was that her father would come for her. Her father was a lawyer—an important man. People trusted him, and sometimes they were even afraid of him. Charly had known that from the time she was small.

So her father would find her and come for her, and everything would be all right.

Charly had to believe that. When she forgot it, her mind would go all funny. She'd feel crazy, like the man who had kidnapped her. When he looked at her, even if he was smiling, it made her afraid. It was like the time she had gone downtown with her father to shop. There had been a bum shuffling by on the street, talking to himself, his eyes kind of jumpy and wild. When nobody paid attention, he began shouting like he couldn't stand it that nobody saw him or listened to what he said.

And that's the way Charly felt every now and then, when she'd start to think that maybe her father wouldn't find her after all. Her mind would get all loose and crazy like that bum's, and she'd start to cry, and in her throat she would be screaming for somebody to help, to pay attention, but only in her throat, because the rag was nearly always stuffed in her mouth, and no sound came out.

Charly lay on her side on the window seat, the rag in her mouth and her legs tied. She wanted to pull the rag from her mouth, and she could, she could do it easily, nothing was stopping her, was it? Her hands weren't tied. But the man had told her she wasn't allowed. When she had taken the rag out the first time, and he came in and saw, he had hurt her. She was too afraid now to take it out again. He might come in anytime.

"How can I ever trust you," he had said, "if you don't learn to mind?"

Charly tried to think about her mother, to keep her mind off things. She thought about the sound of her mother's voice yesterday . . . or two days ago. When was it? She wasn't sure anymore. She had been in the van a long time, and he had stopped once and stuck a needle in her arm, she remembered that. But nothing after, until she woke up here.

*Charly remembered that when she got here, it was dark outside, and she
had thought it was only one night since then. But now she knew that her mind
was playing tricks on her all the time, so maybe it was a lot of nights.*

But somewhere in between, she had managed to call her mother.

*Right after he brought her here, the man had sat her on the bed and taken
the rag out. Then he took a picture with one of those cameras—a Polaroid, she
guessed, the kind that shows you the picture right away.*

*He made her drink a glass of water. "Children need water," he said, as if
he were the kindest person in the world. But then he started singing that song in
a weird funny voice as she drank it down.*

"I'll never say no . . ."

*Charly recognized it then, even though the tune was off-key and didn't
sound like a love song when he sang it, which it was supposed to be. It was from
the play her mother was in,* The Unsinkable Molly Brown. *Brooke had sent
her a rehearsal tape last month, and Charly had played it a hundred times.*

*She didn't have the strength to think about that. She was terribly thirsty.
She had taken deep gulps of the water, grateful because her mouth, from the
funny-tasting rag, was so dry. "I . . . I have to go to the bathroom," she had
said after she finished.*

*The man untied her wrists and unlocked the thing on her ankles. He took
her to the bathroom that was connected to this room. She had gotten a glimpse of
gold fixtures and marble, a giant sunken tub.*

*But she didn't just quietly go in there, the way the man expected. She was
afraid, scared to death, but she had been waiting for a chance like this ever since
the moment he had pushed her into that van. She and her girlfriend Becky had
talked about it one day, after seeing a movie on kidnapping at school.*

*"I'd scream," Becky had said. "At the top of my lungs. After all, once
they get you, it's too late. You've got to kick and scream and get away."*

*"But what if you can't? What if nobody hears you scream? And what if
he's too strong?"*

*"You've got to try. And if he does get you, you've got to make trouble.
You can't just sit around and take it."*

*Charly, munching on an apple and counting up New Kids on the Block
stickers, had agreed—never thinking it would happen to her one day. It only
happened to children on the news.*

*But she remembered what Becky had said. And just as she and the man
got to the bathroom door, with him right close behind her, Charly slammed the*

door back against him, screaming as loud as she could. She nearly knocked him off his feet, and her heart felt like it would burst right out of her chest when she heard him shout with anger, but she ran. She tore out of the bedroom, falling and tripping on the stairs, grabbing the slick banister for balance, tripping some more, and then finally falling hard against the wide front door—

It was locked. She couldn't get it open. She shoved the bolt back and forth with shaking fingers, then the knob, pushing, shoving, banging, yelling, but the door wouldn't budge. She could hear him up there, hear him coming along the hall toward the stairs, but taking his time. Singing: ". . . say no . . ."

Charly began to cry. She leaned her back against the door, so weak she almost fell. But then she saw that down the hall was a kitchen. Maybe . . .

She ran there, and yes, ohthankGod! there it was, on the wall, a phone. She ran through the huge, shiny kitchen, past a butcher block table with copper pots and hanging pans, with spoons and ladles and forks and knives, and she grabbed up the phone and punched out the first number that came to her mind. Not 911, but her mother in San Francisco, the number she had been calling every other night for the past few weeks. Charly had memorized it, as if by doing so, Mom was that much closer—she could reach her anytime. Her fingers, wet from fear, slid on the keypad, but she got it right on the first try. The phone rang and rang, and then her mother's voice answered. Charly started to cry and talk at the same time, hearing footsteps on the stairs, and coming toward her through the hall. Her mouth was rigid with fear—"Mommy . . . the man!"

And then the man was there, grabbing a knife from the counter, and cutting the cord of the phone.

"That wasn't nice, Charly," he murmured. "Bad girl."

The man had taken her upstairs and pulled down her panties and whipped her with his hand, hard. It stung, but that didn't frighten her nearly as much as when he'd stroked her afterwards, to "take the sting away." Charly shut that moment out of her mind. Instead, she stared at the carved bedroom ceiling and thought of her mother, and how close she had come to telling her how she missed her, how she'd give anything now to be with her.

She had only seen her mother once in all the past eight months since she had left for San Francisco. Lunch, last month, in Los Angeles . . . with her father dropping Charly off at the restaurant, and picking her up. When he left them together, he'd had that watchful look in his eyes that Charly had seen so much of before her mother had moved away.

Brooke was an actress, and she had a good job now in San Francisco, but Daddy didn't like to talk about her much. Her mother had been pretty sick last year, she knew. But she was better now. When Charly saw her at lunch last month, her mom had talked about Charly coming to live with her part of the year.

When Daddy heard about that later, he had been so mad at her—Charly —for even mentioning it, he wouldn't talk to her for a week.

It wasn't the first time.

Like last year. They thought she didn't know what was going on, but she did. From the time she was little she had learned a lot of things—from books, and school, and from watching television. Watching TV was all there had been to do some nights when her father and mother worked late. They didn't like her watching at night, but she had gotten hooked, and Mrs. Stinson never told. Charly had watched movies, talk shows, comedies, and sometimes even the serious stuff on PBS. She would turn the television off real quick when she heard her mother or father's car drive up, pretending to be asleep before they came up the stairs.

But from television she had learned a lot. She knew, for instance, that her mother was taking pills and drinking too much before she and Daddy were divorced last year. And she knew something else.

That her father was glad.

He used to go to the drugstore and buy the pills for her mother. He'd even call the doctor to get the prescription filled. Then he'd bring the pills home, and when Mommy got upset at something and started yelling or crying, he'd say, "Brooke, calm down. Take a pill." He would hand her a glass of water, along with a handful of shiny blue capsules. And there would be something in his eyes.

Something glad.

Charly had asked him once: "Why do you give Mommy those things? They only make her sleepy, and I heard on Oprah—"

After that, he hadn't talked to her for a long time.

The bedroom door opened. The man came into the room. He smiled, the way he always did. Like he was a good friend, and they were just playing at some silly game that she was supposed to understand.

"I've got something for you," he said. Both hands were behind his back. He brought one out, holding a doll. It was a large doll, the porcelain kind she had always liked, dressed in a velvety blue outfit and hat. The doll's face and hands were pale, the lips and fingernails painted pink.

"She looks like you," the man said. He put the doll on the window seat next to her. One hand was still behind his back.

Charly sat up, with him helping her. She looked at the gift feeling weary and cautious, a hundred years old now. The doll did have blond hair with long curls and greenish eyes, she thought. And the eyes didn't have the brown she hated so much in her own. That was nice. Charly stuck out her hand . . . hesitating . . . and finally she touched the doll. She stroked the blue velvet, for a moment like that little girl again.

"That's right," the man said shakily. "See? Even her fingers are like yours."

Charly let her hand rest next to the doll's. Hers was much larger, of course. The man reached down. He stroked the doll's fingers . . . and then his hand slid over to stroke hers. Charly started to snatch it away, but he whispered, "No, don't . . . see how good it feels?" In some horrible way, it almost did. She stared at his hand, the short stubby fingers with strange orange stains on them. She stared at the finger that stroked hers, spreading them slowly, evenly, apart. Not daring to move. Then she heard a sound like a whimper come from the man's throat. "Now you have to give me something," he said.

She felt movement from his other arm.

Charly looked up. He was holding above his head something shiny, with a sharp glittering edge—one of those things that butchers—

Charly screamed into the gag. OH GOD, OH GOD, OH GOD—!

The hand slashed down.

Chapter 14

A FEW HOURS LATER Nathan stood at his kitchen counter in Westwood—dragging off his suit jacket, pulling loose the tie, turning the faucet on for a drink of water. It had been a long, weary drive up north, an endless night and day.

A small, unopened box lay before him. It was silver, tied with a violet ribbon—Brooke's favorite colors. The silver tag on it read: *To Nathan from Brooke.*

He had picked it up at the door on his way in, and now he pushed the box away in irritation. What in the world was she up to?

He sighed, opening a utility drawer and searching for the scissors that were always there. He found them, drew them out and wearily pulled the box toward him once more, snipping the string. He wiggled the lid off and set it down.

Inside was red-stained tissue, folded over something oblong—

Nathan unfolded the tissue and stared in horror. He paled. Retched. The room rose and fell, revolving, turning in circles. . . . Nathan felt his chest constrict. He began to fall.

clever she can be! Some of the appalling things she's done—and she doesn't even remember half of it!"

"I was drinking then, Nathan. People change."

"And you're not drinking now? Or on pills?" He turned to Creed. "Have you been with her every minute? Just look at her!"

Brooke shrank from the judgmental eyes that involuntarily turned her way. She was rumpled, unkempt, she knew it. The call from Gibbs had shaken her to the core, and she hadn't taken time to change after the run on the beach. She made a sound like a whimper and was immediately humiliated at having allowed Nathan to do this to her so quickly. "Nathan, stop it, please. For Christ's sake, *think!* Some madman has got our *daughter!"*

Nathan's eyes flicked to the box. "You know what that is, don't you?" He said it harshly, to the room at large. "It's her demented way of saying that if I don't give in to her demands about Charly, this will be real next time."

Brooke moaned and covered her mouth with a hand.

There was activity at the door, and Gibbs hurried in. "I talked to the manager at the messenger service. Somebody dropped the box off during the lunch hour when they were short-staffed. It was left on the counter, with cash."

"Brooke could have had anyone drop it off," Nathan said. "Any of her old friends. They were scum, every single one of them, actors, always drinking, on drugs—"

"On the other hand," Creed said quietly, "where exactly have you been since last night?"

Nathan focused on Creed, his expression one of distaste. "What are you saying?"

"I'm saying it wouldn't be the first time a man went out of his way to make his ex-wife look bad."

"Well, I wouldn't have to go far. Brooke does that quite well on her own."

De Porres broke in. "Can we leave the infighting out of this? We've got a situation here."

But Creed was spoiling for a fight. He was already fed up with Nathan Hayes. The man was a pompous ass. "Just what is the situation, Marty? Why are you even listening to this jerk?"

Chapter 15

THEY GOT THE CALL from Gibbs at eight forty-five, and were at the West LA Division by nine. Lieutenant Martin de Porres hunkered over his desk as before, but the coffee cups and sandwich wrappers had been shoved aside to make room for one object: a silver box. Brooke sat in the chair across from de Porres, pale and silent, while Nathan stalked the room. His face was stained a bright, angry pink. He had traces of soap on his cheek, below the left sideburn. His suit was uncreased, the tie gray on gray. Brooke remembered giving it to him many years ago. Nathan had a passion for gray on gray.

Creed leaned over de Porres' desk, taking up the box.

"It does look real," he noted, picking delicately through the red-stained tissue with a tweezer-like instrument. "Small, of course. Porcelain—a doll's hand. Might be possible to find where it was bought."

"The lab says the stain isn't blood," de Porres said. "Mercurochrome. They won't know if the lock of hair is hers until they've run tests on samples from the child's brush and comb."

Nathan made a move toward Brooke, lifting a hand as if to strike her. "How could you do this? Just how far will you go?"

Creed straightened and moved casually between them. "Mrs. Hayes has been with me almost since she arrived in Los Angeles last night. She couldn't have done this."

"She had someone else do it, then. Oh, you have no idea how

103

"A better question—" a new voice said, "might be why is he listening to you?"

A man in a dark pin-striped suit had entered the room. He was tall and heavily built, with thinning silver hair.

Creed turned to the newcomer, his tone cool. "Well, well, well . . . Captain Dunwalt. What brings you down to peasant level at this hour of night?"

"You can leave, now, Creed. We're holding Mrs. Hayes for questioning. There's nothing more for you to do here tonight."

"Like hell you're holding her. On what charge?"

"That package, to begin with. Harassment."

"Harassment? We've got a kidnapping here, and you're talking *harassment?"*

"There *is* no kidnapping. Mr. Hayes has explained everything. It was all a mistake. The man who picked his daughter up at Universal Studios was a friend, he was taking her on a camping trip. Mrs. Hayes, on the other hand, has been up to her old tricks, it would seem."

"Dunwalt—Goddamn! She didn't send that package. And *what* friend? I don't believe it. What the hell's going on here?"

"What's going on is that she can't do this sort of thing and get away with it, not anymore. We're holding her pending—"

"Like hell! I need Brooke Hayes to help find her daughter. I will not let you detain her here."

"Let me?" Dunwalt laughed.

Creed took a step toward the captain of police, who backed up warily.

"The mother did not do this," Creed said.

"We can't be sure of that. And the evidence—"

"Name it."

"The box, sent by her. The fact that she's instituting a custody suit and is playing a war of nerves with this threat: either joint custody, or she'll hurt the child. Her reputation—"

"The child has been *kidnapped."*

Brooke interrupted. "How do you know about the custody suit?" She looked at Creed. "Charly must have told Nathan. He couldn't know, otherwise. And if Nathan knew—"

Creed picked up on it. "Exactly. The same motivation for harassment applies to Hayes. You're not holding the mother unless you hold the father.''

"Oh, really, John. Nathan Hayes grew up in this neighborhood. He and I went to school together, I know him like my own hand.''

"Which is busy scratching his goddamned back!''

Dunwalt flushed. "I don't need to listen to this. Book her.'' He headed out of the room.

"You do, and I'll raise a stink in the media,'' Creed warned. "Powerful attorney, struggling young mother making a new life for herself, child as pawn—''

"Stop it!'' Brooke was on her feet, her eyes flashing angrily. "For Christ's sake, will you all stop the goddamned arguing? Doesn't anybody care about *Charly?*''

De Porres spoke from behind his desk. He tapped twice with Old Billy against a metal lamp and cleared his throat, calling order the way a judge might with a gavel. "We could hold off another twenty-four hours, Captain,'' he said peaceably. "Long as Creed takes responsibility. We can pick Ms. Hayes up anytime.''

Dunwalt was shaking his head. "Absolutely not.''

Creed swung to Brooke and said smoothly, "Didn't you tell me this is your visiting weekend?''

Her eyes locked on his. "Yes.''

"Well, the custodial parent has to produce the child on visiting weekends. Where's the kid, Hayes?''

"I told you—''

"Yeah, you told us. She's on a camping trip when she should be here, available to her mother. Brooke? You want to bring charges against this jerk? Contempt of court?''

"Yes,'' Brooke said firmly, turning to de Porres. "I do.''

"Now wait just a minute—'' Nathan purpled.

"You're out of line, John.'' That from Dunwalt.

Creed went on reasonably, "As an alternative, Hayes, you could cooperate. First of all, who is this so-called friend who picked Charly up at Universal? And why would you let him pretend he was you? Why didn't he just say who he was?''

"And why,'' Brooke added, "did you tell me she was right there with you at eight o'clock last night, when she had just called me, crying, and didn't even know where she was?"

Nathan sent a pained look to the captain and de Porres. "In the first place, Brooke, we have only your story about a phone call from Charly. I'm sure there never was one." His cold eyes swept from her to Creed. "My ex-wife imagines things, you know."

"Damn you—"

"The camping trip," Creed reminded him. "What about that?"

"It's absolutely true. I let Charly go to the Grand Canyon with her friend, and her friend's parents, and I didn't want to have to deal with Brooke about it last night, so I lied. She's been obsessive lately about Charly. I thought I'd just call her tonight and tell her about it before she could come down on Saturday."

"And this man who picked Charly up at Universal," Creed said. "Who was he?"

"The father, of course. I've already told everyone that."

"What father?"

"Of . . . of Charly's friend, the one she went camping with. I was too busy to pick her up myself, and I sent him instead. I gave him the information he needed."

"And he lied to her teacher about being you? Put on an act? You let your daughter go off with someone like that?"

Nathan was silent.

"What's the man's name?" Creed demanded.

"I . . . Hutchins."

"Hutchins. Uh-huh. He have a first name?"

"William. William Hutchins."

Creed pulled a notepad from his pocket. "Address?"

"I certainly don't have it with me," Nathan said irritably. Deep lines formed above his eyes, and his blond hair fell forward over his brow. He pushed it back, and it fell forward again. He ignored it.

"Phone number, then."

Nathan shrugged and shook his head.

"What is Charly's friend's name? Hutchins' daughter?"

". . . Jennifer."

"What school does this *Jennifer* go to?"

"I don't believe I remember. Charly met her at the country club, during swimming lessons."

"So you don't know anything about this kid, you don't have her parents' address or phone number, yet you let your daughter go away with these people? All the way to Arizona?"

Nathan didn't answer.

Creed flung an arm out angrily. "Look, he's obviously lying. I want Hayes locked up until he decides to cooperate."

"Out of the question."

But Dunwalt was giving Nathan an assessing look. His response sounded less sure.

"I'll take this as high as I have to," Creed warned. "You want disciplinary action, a lawsuit against the department for special treatment of your old school chum? Hell, you want heat for getting in the way of a missing child case? I can handle that."

De Porres intervened again. "Give it one more day, Cap." He lit a cigarette from the one already in his mouth. "I'll order a search for the child, call people in Arizona—"

Creed turned to him. "Marty, you aren't that stupid! There *is* no camping trip. He's done something with Charly himself. You know it, I know it—and I'm advising Mrs. Hayes, as of this moment, to get herself an attorney who will get a court order, forcing him to produce the child."

Nathan was pale. In his eyes was something that might have been panic—or anger. "This is ridiculous. I have all the information at home about where Charly will be staying. They should be at the Grand Canyon by tomorrow evening. I'll call and tell them to put Charly on a plane home, if you insist on making such a big thing of this. She can be here in twenty-four hours."

"Not good enough, Hayes. In less than twenty-four hours I'll have Charly's picture in all the papers, along with the fact that you are being questioned. Your law practice and reputation will be history. They'll never survive the cloud of doubt."

Nathan exploded. "Why are you trying to make me the guilty one here? What about *her*? That card is signed by her!" He pointed a finger at Brooke. "Have you asked her where *she*'s been since yesterday afternoon? Oh, she'll account for some of it, but there will be holes. There always are."

"Hayes—" Creed began.

But everyone else was looking at Brooke. Expectantly.

She licked her lips. "I . . . I was at rehearsals in San Francisco all day. I had dinner with someone . . . well, I was supposed to, but we had an argument, and he left, and then I got the call from Charly and I flew down, came here, and I went to Venice. . . ."

"What time did you arrive in Venice?" de Porres asked thoughtfully.

"A . . . a few minutes after two. I remember looking at the car clock."

He referred to his notes in Brooke's file. "You left here at 12:38. It takes ten, maybe twenty minutes, tops, to get to Venice in the middle of the night. Did you stop somewhere?"

Brooke seemed dazed. "I don't think so, I . . . I don't know."

"You must know if you went straight to Venice from here." Dunwalt's tone was sarcastic. "Did you stop for gas?"

She shook her head.

"To eat?"

Again, no answer.

"Where were you during that hour and a half, Mrs. Hayes?"

"I . . . I may have driven around. . . ."

"But you don't really know."

She slumped into the nearest chair, her expression defeated. "No."

Nathan sighed. "Do you know how many times I've heard those exact words?"

The room was silent, all eyes on Brooke.

"I rest my case," Nathan said.

THE TIDE OF SUSPICION had turned, and in its course it touched on Brooke. But Nathan's accusations, and Brooke's vague answers about the previous night, weren't enough to hold her. There were no fingerprints found on the box, and no one could remember seeing Brooke at the messenger service. She wasn't booked.

To Creed's surprise they seemed to have de Porres' support. He wasn't sure what that was about, though he'd always gotten along with de Porres better than most.

Nathan maintained his story about the camping trip and agreed to call Dunwalt personally within the hour, with the name of the hotel where Charly, her friend, and the friend's parents would be staying in Arizona. Dunwalt would pass the information along to Creed in the morning. In return, Creed would hold off giving the story to the papers until noon the next day.

He wouldn't, however, drop his own search for Charly. "Until we know something firm, we can't let down," he said on the way back to Venice.

"Nathan was so convincing." Brooke's tone was almost hopeful. "That story about the camping trip, and the man who picked up Charly being her friend's father . . ."

"Stick to the facts," Creed said. "I know you want to hope, but the facts begin with Charly's phone call to you. It doesn't fit your ex-husband's story."

She grabbed the edge of the door for balance as they rounded a corner sharply. "You still believe me about the call, then? Nathan didn't raise doubts in your mind . . . even a little?" Her eyes searched his face.

"No."

It was hard to believe. In all the troubles she'd had with Nathan and the police over the past few years, no one had ever believed her. Was Creed different? Or was it that she was now different? Possibly— she thought—a little of both. But she had to ask. "Why?"

"Call it reverse faith if you want," Creed said. "I don't think Nathan's story was convincing at all. He's hiding something. The only question in my mind is what. In the meantime, these are crucial hours if something has happened to Charly. We can't afford to let them slip away."

At midnight Creed and Brooke sat in his living room, surrounded by paperwork, half-empty cartons of yogurt, stale crackers, and stained coffee cups. Neither of them was hungry; they had eaten whatever was at hand, to keep going.

Creed transcribed calls from the answer machine, typing them into the computer, while Brooke went through fax messages, which had earlier appeared on the computer screen and had now been printed out. A separate fax, for hard copy and pictures, trailed several yards of filmy paper along the floor. Some were requests for more information on Charly, others updated Creed's list of known sex offenders. Included was the usual influx of news that he received every day, about children missing elsewhere. While working on the search for Charly, he had to keep up with these, and in the past forty-eight hours, there had been no real sleep, only catnaps along the way. His eyes were gritty with strain. He removed his glasses when the computer screen began to blur, inching forward to squint.

"When the volunteers come in the morning," he said, still typing, "you may want to find another place to stay. There won't be much peace around here."

Brooke looked up from her own pile of paperwork. "You trust me enough to let me out of your sight? After that business at the station?" It hadn't taken her long to realize that part of the reason Creed had wanted her here in the first place was to keep an eye on her, check her out. Decide whether her story was true.

He riffled through stacks of files and loose papers, looking for something. "That business about forgetting some of the things you did last night? It happens, when people are under stress."

"You can't be sure, though."

He sat back, looking at her. "Should I be worried?"

"I don't know. I haven't done that sort of thing since I stopped drinking. There were blackouts, before then."

"Did you ever do anything to hurt Charly during those blackouts?"

She glanced away. "Sometimes I left her alone. At night."

"Purposely?"

She ran a hand through her hair and stood. "Dear God, who knows? I'd start drinking late in the afternoon and somebody would call . . . That might be the last thing I'd remember, until morning. Nathan would be standing over me, shaking me. 'Brooke, goddamn you, wake up! You left Charly alone all night!' "

"What about him? Wasn't he home at night?"

"Sometimes. Sometimes he'd be gone. I never knew where."

"And the housekeeper? Was she there at night?"

"Yes . . . in a room way in the back, though."

"How many times did these blackouts happen?"

"I don't know. That's like asking a blind man to count gnats. You have to see, to have vision." Her tone was one of self-disgust.

"Let's go back to last night, then. Do you think you stopped anywhere—say at a friend's house, or a telephone—and had someone send that package to Nathan today?"

"No." She faced him squarely, hands on her hips. "I do not. In the first place, drunks don't have old friends. They wear everybody out."

"Everybody?"

She smiled. "Anybody I'd still want to be friends with now."

"You did know some unsavory people, though?"

"I guess. They were acquaintances, not friends."

"So the question is, do you think you could have done something like that?" *Something that cruel,* but he didn't say it.

"I . . . maybe, a year ago. I might have done anything, then, I hated Nathan so much. I've changed, though."

Her expression said, *Please God, believe I've changed.*

"What about the lock of hair in the box Nathan got?"

She sighed. "Charly sent me one. Last month." At his upraised brow, she said, "I missed her! She's my little girl! But I didn't stick it in a goddamned box with a doll's hand and send it to Nathan! It's home in my apartment, on my nightstand, in a book."

He went back to typing and let the subject drop.

Brooke poured more coffee for herself and Creed and sat on a canvas chair next to the desk, looking over her cup at him. Finally he leaned back in the swivel chair before the computer, put his feet up on the desk, and rubbed his eyes. "What is it?"

"What has Captain Dunwalt got against you?"

He wondered if she could take hearing it—and wondered, too, if he could say it. It had been a long time since he'd told anyone. And no one talked openly about it these days, except possibly Andy Laskov, the DA. Laskov didn't mince words. He hated Creed and didn't mind telling him why.

"Dunwalt thinks I murdered my son."

He saw the initial shock, then confusion. She sat straight, and her cup thunked on the desk.

"He . . . Why on earth would he think that?"

Creed hesitated, then decided he owed it to her. She had been more than open with him. "Jason—my son—disappeared from our yard in Santa Monica, when he was five. We never found him. There were no witnesses, no one to say he'd been talking to a stranger just before, or any of the usual things. My wife was inside, fixing his lunch. The yard was fenced, he had played out there on his swings alone before . . . but on this particular day, he just . . . disappeared. He had gotten the gate open somehow—" His voice broke, and he stared at the computer screen, blindly.

"I'm sorry. Don't talk about it if you'd rather not." Brooke's hand went out involuntarily, an automatic gesture, but something stopped her. An invisible wall, coming from him. She pulled back. "I don't understand. Why would Dunwalt think that *you* had anything to do with it?"

"Because five years ago—it's different now—children hardly ever disappeared without being seen by someone, somewhere. In a neighborhood like that, where people were home—writers, artists, some older retired people—somebody should have seen him being snatched, or wandering. When no one comes forward like that, you look to the parents. Parents often do things to their children, and then report them missing to cover their guilt."

"Do things. You mean . . ." Her voice lowered. "Kill them?"

"Yes. That, and other things."

"And Dunwalt thought you could do something like that?"

"Well, I never worked under him directly, but I'd given him a lot of trouble over the years. I always figured he was looking for something to nail me with. When Jason disappeared . . ." He let it hang.

"What kind of trouble did you give him?"

"Kid stuff. Adolescent games. I guess I thought I was pretty hot back then, barging into cases where I didn't belong. Other people's turf. I didn't always use accepted means, and to be fair, Dunwalt had good reason not to like me."

"You were violent?"

"Often, in the beginning. I came back from Nam that way." He shrugged. "It worked, then. It doesn't, much, now."

"Why not?"

"I don't know. I guess since Jason disappeared, I haven't had much taste for violence."

She wondered. Creed, in her estimation, had a streak of anger that was like a fire, burning in his gut. He might think he had it banked for now—but she'd seen a small sample of it at Charly's school, when he'd knocked that easel over in front of the children. Add to that his too-often morose moods, and it seemed only a matter of time.

Which didn't make him a child killer.

"They couldn't have had any proof," she said softly.

His smile was thin. "Obviously not."

"Sorry. But your wife—Jason's mother. What happened to her?"

"She's gone. Into a world where things like that don't happen."

"A hospital?"

"Yes."

She sighed. "I don't know what to say."

Brooke sat hunched, holding the coffee cup again, between her knees. Creed knew she was processing what he had told her. He wondered what her judgment would be. It might have been better if he had waited; she had too much to deal with as it was.

"I'm glad you told me," she said finally. "I understand more now."

"Do you?"

"Yes. You're tough on us . . . us parents . . . because you're afraid that if we allow ourselves to weaken, we'll end up like your wife."

CREED THOUGHT ABOUT HER after she went to bed. On the way home from the station earlier, she had said she needed clothes. He had offered to take her to a department store in the morning, but she refused. "I can't think straight. I'd never make it from floor to floor."

So he had pulled up at a small late-hours clothing shop along Main Street, and waited while she ran in. She was back in less than five minutes, her expression weary, carrying a black-and-white plastic bag.

"Find something?" It was the expected male response to these things, he remembered.

Her voice held as little interest as his. "Pants. A couple of shirts. God knows if they'll even fit."

Karen had always spent hours finding the right material, the matching color, the perfect size. Even in her anguish over Jason, she had gone off to the mall for entire days, losing herself in an enchanted forest of clothes, rather than have to think.

He would have to see Karen soon.

BROOKE HAD BEEN ASLEEP for an hour or more in the downstairs bedroom, when Creed heard a noise outside. He was at the computer, lost in thought, so at first he wasn't sure. But there it was again: a grating sound, below, at the gate. And neighborhood dogs were barking. He looked up to see that it was 1:24. Couldn't be Gibbs. Gibbs lived in Santa Monica, only minutes away—but he wouldn't come over at this hour without calling first.

In a bottom desk drawer was a revolver he seldom carried. Creed took it out, a Smith & Wesson 686. He flicked open the cylinder out of habit, knowing it held a full load of forty-fives. Still intact. He snapped it shut. Turning off the desk light, he slid quietly through the sliding doors. Moving against the window rather than out on the deck, he inched over to the stairs. He listened.

Rustling leaves. Ocean. Night noises on the beach.

No footsteps, no stifled breathing. No "sense" that anyone was there.

He swung around the corner of the house, onto the top step, the gun raised in both hands, arms straight.

The stairs were empty. He ran softly down them and nearly tripped over a package on the bottom step.

Christ, he had forgotten to lock the gate again. Ignoring the package for the moment, he wrenched the gate open, looking both ways up and down the alley. No one there—and no parked cars. Even Brooke's rental was now inside his garage; it wasn't smart to leave a car out in this neighborhood at night.

The dogs had quieted, but that didn't mean anything. They usually only barked at the first sign of someone strange to the neighborhood. Then they settled down.

Across the way and a couple of doors from his, a gate stood partly open, still swinging. Creed ran to it, his sneakers silent on the asphalt. Flattening his back against the fence, he listened. A soft clatter, like that of a metal object upended. He took a deep breath, finger on the trigger. Sweat popped out on his forehead. He tensed, then kicked the gate hard, knocking it back with a crack against the inside of the fence while bursting through the opening in a crouch, weapon raised.

A scream, like that of a child in pain. A figure hurtled past his legs. *Holy shit!*

He jerked upright, then felt the held-in breath leave his lungs.

A cat—a cat with its black-and-white fur still on end. It streaked down the alley, already a half block away.

Creed swung back to the yard, which was postage-stamp size. No one here—nowhere to hide. He leaned weakly against the gate, rubbing his brow with the back of his hand.

He could check the other yards, and the street at both ends. But whoever had left the package was gone. Better to get back to the house, see what his visitor had left.

He was pretty sure he knew; these things followed a pattern. It had begun.

Locking his gate, he picked up the brown-wrapped package—carefully, with thumb and middle finger barely touching two corners. Upstairs at his desk again, he turned the light on, up to its fullest wattage. No writing on the outside of the package, no name. He debated waking Brooke, but wanted to see it first.

He removed the brown wrapping, slicing the transparent tape with a penknife, careful not to disturb any prints. The inside box was wrapped in silver foil, tied with a purple ribbon. The card, this time, read the reverse: *From Nathan to Brooke.*

Creed slid the gift paper open with the knife and found a white box, approximately six inches square. He opened it. Nestled in tissue mottled with reddish-orange stains was a doll's severed head with long blond hair and a blue velvet hat. Nails had been driven into its brilliant green eyes.

He heard a gasp and looked up to see Brooke, standing a few feet away. "That's the doll I got Charly for her birthday!" Her eyes were feverishly bright. "Oh, God . . . it was in a closet, in my apartment!"

The phone rang. Creed snatched it up. It was Gibbs.

"We've got another present," Creed said. He told him about it.

"Yeah? Well, I've got one for you," Gibbs answered, "and you won't like it any more than that one. Nathan Hayes is gone."

"Gone? What the hell do you mean, gone?"

"Hell, I don't know how it happened, Keep. I mean he got out somehow—slipped past our people, front and back."

"Shit! How do you know he's not just away for the night again?"

"It gets worse. He never called Dunwalt with that information on the alleged camping trip. Dunwalt is left looking like an ass for trusting his old pal, and he's livid. He roused Judge Peters, got warrants, and ordered a search on the house. We found drawers pulled out, clothes scattered like Hayes had been packing real fast—and there's no sign of that housekeeper Brooke mentioned, either. Both of them are gone."

Chapter 16
THE DISTRICT ATTORNEY

THE DISTRICT ATTORNEY in and for the county and city of Los Angeles was a large, blunt man. Brown hair bluntly cut, simple clothes bluntly worn without thought to style. A thick nose, thick in speech. He came across as a little dumb at times, almost a Columbo kind of guy. (LA being a Hollywood kind of town, its residents were given to hanging stereotypes like that on its cops. The media did nothing to soften the image.)

Underneath all that misleading facade was a man who knew how to tread the tightrope between city politics and city law. He had grown up on the streets, gotten his law degree the hard way—pumping gas at night for tuition—and worked his way up through the ranks. At forty-four, Laskov was the youngest DA Los Angeles County had had in years —maybe ever. But the streets were still there. Andrew Laskov knew about infighting, about backbiting, about winking out the side of his face and still making it seem, when running for election, that he really wanted the good of the people.

In fact, he really did. But it didn't pay to act like that was your agenda, when you had all those billion-dollar corporations out there on your goddamned back.

"You gotta clean up that waste," he'd say confidentially to the president of X, Y, or Z company over drinks in some out-of-the-way bar. "If you don't, I'm gonna have to prosecute on that fraud matter. In the long run, that'll be worse, and hell, you don't want that. Go for the smaller issue. Pinch the wallet a little, instead of a lot."

In that way he'd get a few toxic landfills cleaned up, a few oil spills prevented, and the air over the city he loved was made a few fractions cleaner—which was what he'd wanted all along. Not that it helped much. Hell, LA would never be the county he grew up in, with orange trees on every block and crystal-clear vision all the way from the beach to Big Bear. With all that brown gunk up there, it was like people were shitting into the sky instead of in their toilets. And there wasn't any way it was gonna get better, short of a nuclear bomb hitting the place. Maybe that wouldn't be too bad, in fact. Blow all that crap from here to Mars.

But that would kill his fish. And if there was anything Andy Laskov loved, it was his fish. One fish.

Big Joe.

Big Joe was a trout, living in a two-hundred-gallon tank in Laskov's office. He was only a few inches long when Laskov took office seven years ago. Now he was three feet. Joe used to eat brine shrimp, little squiggly pollywogs. Now he ate guppies, and worms, and full-grown goldfish—

Hell he'd eat Laskov, if he could get close enough. Big Joe was one mean mother.

Andy Laskov held the last of a dozen full-grown guppies over the tank, dangling it. Big Joe broke through the water and went SNAP. Laskov laughed. "You are the greediest, hungriest son of a bitchin' fish in the whole damned world." He dropped the wriggling silver and green victim into Joe's rubbery well of a mouth. It was gone in a gulp. *Like me, if I don't snap fast enough,* Laskov thought.

He was going for the big one this year. State's attorney general.

And he was using, as his major campaign issue, the environmental wins he'd worked so hard for. It was a popular issue in this era, with all the yuppies growing up and the aging flower children already there. If it wasn't for the other thing, Laskov didn't see how he could lose.

The "other thing" was missing kids . . . and all that criticism, ever since he took office as DA, just about, over the snatching of kids in the LA area. Like it was all his fault that the problem got worse during his term.

Hell, Laskov didn't want bad things happening to kids any more than anybody else. He had four of his own, and if anything happened to them, he'd cut the pervert's eyes out, never mind his balls.

But it was getting to be an epidemic out there. A sickness. Some people said there were whole underground movements of perverts, grabbing kids and selling them off all over the country. He hadn't seen any proof of that, though he'd give an arm—and his grandmother's baked lentils and beans—for such proof. Then he could shine on that issue, too.

It was as if some of these kids, when they disappeared, dropped off the face of the earth. A lot of the time, of course, it was the parents that did it, and those were the easiest to prove. The only one over the years that had given him any trouble was—

John Creed.

Just for fun, Laskov threw another couple'a fish into Big Joe's mouth.

God, how he hated John Creed.

A thorn in his side—no, a whole damned tree. Bad enough Creed had been on his back for months to prosecute when Larry Schellenger, the city supervisor, was accused of molesting his little girl. Creed had finally cornered Laskov at a restaurant, where he was having lunch with some friends. Laskov had brushed him off. "You can't go putting a man, a guy whose whole political career is at stake, in jail like that. Hell, if you did that every time some little girl with a complaint against her daddy decides to say he's diddled her, the courts would be backed up for months."

He'd thought for a minute he was a goner then. Creed had knocked him flat, and if it wasn't for a couple of good-sized waiters, hell, he might have been beaten to a pulp. John Creed was like the steam in a pressure cooker, just waiting for the chance to pop. IAD was on his case more than once, over the years, before Creed finally admitted he was out of control and took himself off the force. That was after Creed's own son disappeared.

Laskov knew that Creed had done his own kid. He had an instinct, and there were things in the case that were off, that didn't fit. That wife, for instance—if ever a woman was lying, that was one. Covering up for her husband until she couldn't take it anymore, ending in a nuthouse, finally. While Creed just kept going on.

Well, I've got it all in a file, he thought—*right there in that bottom drawer. No real proof so far, but I'm getting closer. Any day now, I'll have that final piece.*

Just before Creed quit the force, Laskov had gone so far as to talk to the commissioner about him. "The guy's a child killer, I know it in my gut."

The commissioner stood up for Creed. "Bring me proof," the old man rasped. "When you do that, we'll talk."

Laskov never could. The trouble with nailing a cop was that he knew all the angles. He knew how to cover his ass. And Creed had done that, all right. Had even cleaned up his act ever since—or was putting a good face on it, at least.

In the meantime, the fact that LA County *needed* an independent investigator like Creed on missing child crimes, made the DA's office—the whole fuckin' police department, in fact—look bad. The public was yelling for more arrests and more prosecutions, and the mayor had begun yelling too. It didn't look good at the polls. Laskov's anger and frustration had festered over the years, and pussed up into one big boil.

A boil that was sore as hell when the phone rang and changed Andy Laskov's day all around.

"It's your golfing partner," his secretary said, sticking her head in the door. Mary smiled the indulgent kind of smile that only a person who'd been with him twenty years and followed him up the ladder could get away with. "Tell him you've got too much work, you can't go off to the club today."

Laskov picked up. "Nathan?" His voice slid into the educated, oiled-up version he used on important people. Even with friends, it paid to put on the show. "How are things in the world of torts and trespass?"

Laskov listened. He barreled to his feet, planting them firmly on the floor and standing before his window, looking out over downtown LA. "Back in town, is she? I'm sorry to hear that. What can I do?"

As Nathan spoke, the district attorney squared his shoulders. His voice acquired the heavy weight of authority. "Sure. Sure thing, Nate.

I'll talk to the chief. You say she's got John Creed involved? That won't do her reputation any good. Or his, for that matter, getting mixed up with her." A silence as he listened. "Yeah, well, don't worry. The chief owes me one. I'll get him to keep Dunwalt out of your hair. Creed, too. Anything else I can do, you just let me know."

Laskov hung up. He went back to Big Joe and leaned over, putting his big blunt hands on the top of the tank.

The day was looking decidedly brighter. Hell, maybe Creed'd hang himself without any help, messing around with that broad.

He stuck a finger in the water, teasing Big Joe. Big Joe switched his tail and went for it. Laskov yanked back at the last second and laughed.

"SNAP!" he said.

Chapter 17

CHARLY'S ROOM was just as Brooke had remembered, with one addition: the publicity photo she had sent to Charly a few months ago. She had wondered if Nathan would forbid her to hang it.

But it was there, on the wall opposite her daughter's bed. Brooke, standing before it, tried to see what Charly had seen every morning as she opened her eyes. What kind of remembrance was this of an absent mother? She studied the portrait as an actress, a professional, looking for signs of character, strengths, and flaws.

It wasn't a bad face. Firmer now since she had stopped drinking. Not classically beautiful, but even features. Shoulder-length blond hair —glossy and full, for the photo shoot. A face that could be practiced and molded into many images from tomboy to courtesan.

A stupid idea, though, sending Charly this photo. There was very little warmth in it. Better if she'd had someone take a candid shot.

Brooke remembered the photographer who had taken it. Recommended with some hesitation by Leo, because although he was cheap, the man was a sleaze. Leo had warned her: "He puts his hands all over women when he poses them. You might want to carry a hat pin in your bra."

"If he gets fresh, I'll give him one of my best Molly Brown punches," Brooke had answered, laughing. "See this muscle?" She flexed her right arm, baring it above the elbow. It was true—her entire body strength was increasing with every day of rehearsal. "Besides, I've handled sleaze before. The theater is rife with it."

Roger Dorn—or Dickhead Dorn, as Brooke came to think of him from there on out—had a large studio on Baker Street, in Pacific Heights. Just down the street from people like Diane Feinstein, and Danielle Steele. The building was high rent, on a hill surrounded by mansions. It had a sweeping view of the bay, from the city to Marin. Walls were off-white, with vast windows letting in soft light. An elegant placard in gold script on one wall had proclaimed *Roger M. Dorn, Photographer to the Stars*.

Dorn had a background in cinema photography. Brooke wondered if his personal reputation had finally chased him out of Hollywood. He did try to touch her breasts. His fingers wandered uncomfortably low as he adjusted the draped neckline of her black dress. His wavy gray-blond hair, as he bent over her, brushed her cheek. His fingers, Brooke remembered, were stained with a rusty tint. She had asked Dorn about that, while firmly removing a hand from her cleavage and holding it daintily between thumb and index finger—peering at the stains as if curious. If the distraction hadn't worked, she might have resorted to the sock in the jaw—or, more likely, to walking out.

"Those?" Dorn had answered, distracted. "Oh . . . just chemicals. From developing."

He'd had an uneasy way of standing too close and peering at her, also—head to toe, and for long moments. His eyes were too intent, in a slender, ascetic face. While he stared, he would slowly nod—then smack his lips—and move to another angle. Repeating the procedure.

It was the smack of lips that finally made Brooke shudder.

Afterward she had asked Leo, "How could someone with the upkeep of a studio in that area afford to do publicity photos at only forty dollars a sitting?"

"Don't ask me. I heard about him through Derek Johannson. Apparently the guy lives beyond his income—has to rake it in wherever he can. Maybe he does drugs. You know photographers. They're all bizarre."

Brooke started, her reverie broken as Creed spoke from behind her. He stood with thumbs hooked in the pockets of his jeans, chin at an angle, a thoughtful expression on his dark face. "An interesting portrait."

"Dreadful, in a way. He caught all kinds of fears. I look hard."

"But real," Creed said objectively.

"I guess." She rubbed her arms, feeling a chill as her fingers slid over the rayon sleeves of her red blouse. "I just wish now that I hadn't sent this particular shot to Charly."

"Your daughter probably didn't see the hardness. You're her mother, after all. She'd look for the best."

"You think so?"

"Children are remarkably flexible. You can do a lot to them, and they still love you—still see only the good."

"But that's what makes them victims."

"Sometimes. And sometimes it helps them survive."

Brooke turned away, feeling tired. "Where's Gibbs?"

"Downstairs, updating Dunwalt. The captain's taking a real personal interest, now that it looks like he's been duped by your ex-husband. Have you found anything yet that lends a clue? Anything in particular missing, or something that strikes even the faintest warning bell?"

"I don't know. I haven't been here for so long. . . ."

She crossed to the French provincial bureau again, fingering objects on it. Souvenirs from trips taken over the years . . . a porcelain doll in a red- and green-striped Victorian outfit . . . a school photo of Charly's class from last year. Next to it was an autograph book, signed by friends with sentiments like: "Make new friends, but keep the old; the new are silver, the old are gold."

An ancient axiom, written in children's autograph books for years and years. Brooke remembered someone writing it in one of her own, long ago. Odd how each generation perpetuates that sort of thing, she thought. The same way children tell the same jokes, the same rhymes and riddles, decade after decade—with so much pride and gusto. As if they're brand-new.

According to an article she had read in *Psychology Today,* in her shrink's office, the human mind is the world's most efficient generator of electrical energy. It operates somewhat like radio frequencies—thus creating the mass-consciousness effect. Supposedly that explained why people closely connected in some way are often on the same wavelength, down to buying the same clothes, reading the same books, and thinking the same thoughts, without either one knowing—

"Brooke?"

She blinked. Creed was speaking to her from beside Charly's bed. "Sorry. I wander now and then. My shrink says there are empty spaces from all the drugs and alcohol. They act like sponges for random thoughts." Her smile was rueful. "Supposedly it'll get better."

He smiled, too. "I just wondered what this tape is."

She realized there was music playing. Her own voice floated softly across the room, the delivery brash and boyish. "I'm gonna learn to read and write, and find a house with a golden stair. . . ."

The song issued from a tape recorder on a shelf above Charly's bed. Brooke crossed over and sat on the bed, leaning sideways. She touched the EJECT button. A black Memorex tape popped out, labeled UMB in red marker.

"Sounds familiar," Creed said. "What is it?"

"A rehearsal tape from *The Unsinkable Molly Brown.*" Brooke noted it was three-quarters of the way through. "It's the show I'm in. I sent it to Charly a month ago, so she could feel I was close by."

"That's you, singing?"

She nodded. Her fingers stroked the black tape absently. Something—

"Creed, you know that drug slogan, 'Just say no'? The one they also teach children, for when they're approached by an adult who wants them to do something they feel is wrong?"

"Yeah . . . what about it?"

"Charly said that, when she called. She said, 'Say no, Mommy, say no.' "

"You didn't tell me that." His tone was impatient.

"I just remembered."

"What triggered the memory?"

She shoved the tape into her back jeans pocket and rubbed her forehead distractedly. "I'm not sure—"

"Hey, everybody."

Gibbs stood in the doorway. "All clear down there. Captain and crew have bailed for now. Bartles and James are posted outside, just in case somebody comes back."

"B and J? Shit." Creed scowled. Bart Norris and Jimmy Logan: two straight-arrow patrol cops who often got stuck in these kinds of "go-nowhere" assignments. They were pale of face, looked like their pockets were stuffed with hayseed, and drank wine coolers in Melvin Q's Bar while all the tough older cops were knocking back bourbon and beer. The fact that they had been left behind here signaled an almost certainty on Dunwalt's part that Hayes and housekeeper would not return.

"Brooke thinks Charly's suitcases are gone," Creed said. "They could be stored away, but they always used to be kept here in her closet." He motioned with his chin to the large walk-in he had already gone through.

"No suitcases in the attic," Gibbs told him. "I looked before you got here. None in the father's room, either, or the housekeeper's—"

"Look, we all know what's happened here!" Brooke began to pace. "Nathan's hidden her away from me. And the crazy thing is, I should be relieved. If she's with Nathan, instead of . . ." She looked helplessly at Creed.

"We don't know anything yet for sure," he reminded her. The hope that Charly was "safe" with her father needed balance. The only thing Creed was certain of, now, was that Nathan Hayes was somehow involved.

And Brooke was conveniently forgetting Charly's panic when she had called. It hadn't sounded as if the child were safe.

"You coming back to the house?" he asked Gibbs.

"In a little while. I've got to hustle over to the phone company. I'm still trying to get those records of Hayes' phone calls for the past few days."

"They ever come up with anything on Charly's call to Brooke?"

Gibbs shook his head. "It takes a while, when it's direct dial."

"Right. Well, Hayes' calls may be even more important, now, if he does have the child. He's almost certainly been in contact with whoever's taken her underground. Brooke, can you come up with anything at all, anyplace they might be? Does Nathan have a cabin in the mountains or desert—some other house somewhere?"

"There was a cabin up at Big Bear, but he sold it last year. We weren't using it much, between his long hours . . . and my drinking."

"Nothing else? Another house? A beach cottage?"

"Not anymore. This place takes a lot of upkeep, and Nathan wanted to make renovations last year. He sold a lot down in San Diego, and a house somewhere up north—along the coast. Near Big Sur, I think."

"And he has no other family left alive, is that right?"

"No one. Nathan was an only child, and his aunt, one uncle, and both sets of grandparents died several years ago."

"Gibby? Why don't you skip coming back to Venice and start talking to Hayes' friends, old and new? And the neighbors."

"Captain's got people on the neighbors. I should probably start with old school chums. Brooke—?"

She nodded, stopped pacing, and tucked the back of her blouse into her jeans. "We entertained a lot, until the last year or so. I'm sure Mrs. Stinson has guest lists in her office next to the kitchen. All the people Nathan knows well, both business and personal, will be on them. I can go over them with you and underline the ones who know him best."

"Sounds good. Keep?"

"You go ahead. I want to poke around in here a few minutes more. Make sure we haven't overlooked anything."

Brooke gave one more glance around the room, reluctant to leave. She, too, felt there was something they had overlooked—some memory that might unlock everything, if only it would come clear.

"See you downstairs," she said finally to Creed.

He nodded but was already turning away . . . crossing to the closet and standing there, a look of intense concentration on his face.

Chapter 18

THEY STOOD in the circular brick drive, by the Jeep. Creed watched as Brooke turned to look back at the home that she had lived in as Charly's mother and Nathan Hayes' wife for eight years. In the light from old-fashioned posts along the drive, she looked tired and vulnerable—even down to the blond hair that had been pulled back carelessly into a limp ponytail once more.

What was there about her that reminded him of Karen? Was it that kind of whipped-animal look—the one that surfaces with guilt?

And why had that thought even occurred to him?

"Let's go," he said, more abrupt than he'd meant to be. She didn't flinch this time, though, the way she had that first night. Instead, her mood changed—and the corners of her mouth curved slightly as she rolled her eyes.

"Mr. Personality." She slid into the jeep beside him. "Ow! What am I sitting on?" She pulled the *Molly Brown* rehearsal tape from her pocket. Frowning, as if surprised to find it there, she added it to the collection on the dashboard.

Ten minutes later they were on Olympic, heading west toward Venice. They weren't talking. Brooke was pensive, and Creed was thinking of Karen. He was remembering the five-year-old boy with a thick shock of black hair falling over his forehead, and the too-trusting gray eyes.

If only children weren't so damned trusting at that age! Too open, too curious and seeking.

Jason had been in preschool, and after that a private kindergarten, in a good neighborhood. Karen had driven him to school and picked him up every day. He was almost never out of a sheltered environment, so there hadn't seemed to be any need to fill his mind with fears about things that would almost certainly never happen to him. Beyond the usual parental admonition—"Don't speak to strangers, don't go anywhere with anyone, without asking us first"—he and Karen hadn't given Jason a thorough-enough education in self-protection. It was a guilt that haunted him to this day.

With a bitter taste, Creed glanced quickly at Brooke—hoping she wouldn't have to go through the hell he'd been through these past five years.

Traffic in the left lane was slow; cars ahead, waiting to turn at the next light. Creed swerved impatiently into the center lane, tires screeching. The pile of tapes on the dashboard slid crazily, landing on the floor at Brooke's feet. Creed grabbed and caught one cassette midflight, sliding it absently into the tape deck. A strong male voice with orchestral background boomed. "Today is tomorrow, if you want it so. . . ."

Creed flicked a glance at the tape deck. "Your rehearsal tape?"

"Yes. Derek Johannson, the male lead. He plays Johnny, Molly Brown's friend, then husband. He—"

She grabbed his arm. "That's it!" she cried. "That's what Charly was trying to tell me!"

The words from the cassette, now, were: "I'll stay or I'll go, but—"

"*I'll never say no!*" Brooke cried.

She had a death grip on his arm. Creed swung into an empty space at the curb, cutting the motor. He turned in the seat, facing her. "Are you sure?"

"Yes! Charly said that, exactly! 'Say no! Say no, Mommy! Say no!' "

His response was deliberately calm. "Brooke, earlier, you thought it was from the drug slogan. Or the 'safe talks' we give to kids these days."

"No, but I didn't—not really. It reminded me of that, but there was something bothering me—something I couldn't remember. And this was it—I *know* it! Charly must have been listening to this tape while she dressed the other morning, the song must have been fresh in her mind."

Creed searched her face. Brooke seemed certain she was right. And despite his efforts to provide balance, he instinctively knew she was on to something. It was the kind of thing that happened often with mothers of missing children—and the major reason he demanded they stick near him throughout. At any moment, something like this could pop out.

"What do you think it means?" Creed asked. "If Charly was quoting the song, why do you think that might be?"

Impatiently, Brooke rested her head against the back of the seat. "I don't know. I've been singing that song for months."

"Tell me about it. What do the words mean?"

She closed her eyes, letting the verses run through her mind. "It's a love song. Johnny Brown is in love with Molly and wants to marry her. He's telling her that he'll always be true . . . no matter what she ever says, or does. That if she wants him to stay, he will—but if not, he'll go."

Creed reversed the tape to the song's beginning, lowering the volume. Around them traffic sped by, horns blared. Brooke fell silent. She breathed deeply, filling the stomach first, then the diaphragm and the lungs—a technique learned in voice class, for relaxing.

Her mouth moved with the words to Johnny's song. She pictured Molly and Johnny high on a Colorado mountain, Johnny's pledge of love echoing from peak to peak.

It didn't happen quite that way in live theater . . . but that was the way she had always pictured it in rehearsal, to make the scene come alive. She had sent Charly some candid shots of one of the latest rehearsals, with the newly painted mountain backdrop in place. As the song continued, her mind placed Charly in the picture—on the stage, at the foot of a mountain. . . .

Charly reaching out, with mountains behind her, soft and green.
Charly calling—her silky blond hair untended now.

"A rat's nest," Livvy used to say about Brooke's hair when she was a child. "A rat's nest, Brooke-Ann! I'll never get these tangles out! And you— rolling in the grass—behaving like a common hooligan, embarrassing us in front of the neighbors with your skirt over your head, for lordy's sake!"

Charly's blue eyes taking the place of Brooke's own. Becoming superimposed, as in a photograph. Tears in her daughter's eyes. "Say no, Mommy . . . say no!"

And then, more softly, "Mommy, where are you? Please help me. I'm afraid!"

"Here," Creed said. "Brooke, here, take this."

She opened her eyes and realized she was crying. Creed was holding out a bandanna-like kerchief, one that he sometimes used as a headband. She had seen it earlier on the backseat.

She took it and dabbed at her eyes.

"Blow," Creed said firmly. He held it in place.

She blew. Embarrassed. "I feel like a little girl."

"You feel like *your* little girl," he corrected. "Mothers have a way of zeroing in on a missing child's feelings—becoming one with them. What did you think, or see?"

She sniffed. "I saw Charly—at the foot of a mountain. One of the mountains in the backdrop of Molly Brown, when Johnny's singing this song to her. I was remembering it . . . and suddenly Charly was there."

"Anything else?"

"I thought about her hair not being taken care of, and how it must be all tangled and snarled." Her voice caught. "I . . . I remembered my mother calling mine a rat's nest, when it was like that."

"What else?"

"I . . . that's all."

Creed was silent, thinking.

"You say the mountain was from this backdrop?"

"Yes."

"What did it look like?"

"Well, you know, like mountains do in Colorado, snowcapped—"
She leaned forward. "No, wait! They were like that at first, but then,

when Charly was standing there, they were softer, somehow! Maybe . . ." She shook her head. "I don't know . . . green?"

Creed pulled her around to face him. "Have you ever seen mountains like that before? Say the first thing that comes to your mind."

She shook her head. "No. I mean, yes, but it doesn't make sense—"

"*Say* it!"

"Creed, you're hurting me!"

"Say it, Brooke! The first thing that comes."

"All right, goddammit, all right! San Francisco!" Her eyes widened.

Creed dropped his hands and gave a satisfied smile.

"San Francisco . . . ," Brooke said again softly. "Or somewhere near." Her fingers rose to cover her shaking mouth. "Oh, my God. You don't think— No, it was only my mind, after all, making up pictures— linking things that don't have any connection, not really—"

"Maybe. Maybe not." Creed popped the Molly Brown tape out, and placed it in Brooke's lap. "The point is, this is our first possible link. This song—and Charly's message to you—are too close to disregard. Do any of the people you work with in the show know Nathan?"

"Only Sean, who worked down here with me for years—and he's my best friend. Sean *couldn't* be mixed up in this."

Creed twisted the key in the ignition and slammed the jeep into gear. "My volunteer crew should be arriving just about now. I'll need to get them going on the phones and computers, give them all the info they'll need to operate. And I want to talk to Gibby."

Brooke glanced sideways at the hard set of his face. Beneath it lay something she could define only as excitement. "You believe we're on to something, don't you?"

"Let's just say I've got a gut feeling."

"Are you ever wrong?"

"No." Creed gave her a quick, haunted look before he returned his attention to the mounting traffic.

"Well . . . almost never."

Chapter 19

THE VENICE BEACH HOUSE had been taken over by volunteers. Everywhere Brooke turned, there were tables, telephones, stacks of papers, and fliers. Several computer terminals had been brought in, and cables snaked everywhere—along tabletops, taped to table legs, shoved behind chairs and bookcases. All ended at Creed's mainframe computer.

One woman, whose name was Betty and who seemed to be in charge, hefted reams of tractor paper onto the shelf beneath the printer, threading it through. As she did so, she issued instructions to people at three tables, telling them which leads to follow up first. A pencil was shoved through brassy red hair, behind an ear.

Another woman of about thirty removed round wire glasses and rubbed her forehead wearily. "Betty—this guy who keeps calling from Dallas? You think he's for real? He sounds weird."

"Don't dismiss anything. Even weirdos come through for us now and then."

The woman nodded.

Betty finished with the printer and grabbed a bundle of printouts from Creed's desk. "You need a break, Deb? Don't be afraid to ask."

"No. I can go another round." The younger woman frowned at the papers in Betty's arms. They bore heavy notes from a red marker. "But I sure hate office work," she grumbled good-naturedly. "Next time—"

Betty plunked the stack down before her. "Next time, you get office work again. It's what you do best."

The younger woman groaned.

As Creed had warned Brooke earlier, the noise level was high. People talked on phones and to each other. The mood wasn't as somber as Brooke might have expected; rather, it was businesslike. These were people who knew what they were doing—and that was the frightening thing. It was clear they had done this many times before.

Brooke and Creed were waiting for Gibbs, who had called from his car to say he had a possible lead from the phone company and would be there within fifteen minutes. Brooke had tried to help, pouring coffee and making sandwiches . . . but now she was only in the way. Johnny Brown's song kept running through her mind. She stood anxiously looking out through the sliding glass door at a white haze over the ocean. Thinking about the fact that the song might be a clue. But how? And why?

She wished Gibbs would get here. She wished they could *do* something. Standing around was driving her insane.

A man of about twenty, his dark blond hair in a wet ponytail, was at a table next to her, sorting and filing fax papers. He wore flowered beach shorts, a T-shirt, and an earring in his left ear with a silver half-moon and star dangling from it. He smelled, Brooke thought, of fresh salt water—as if he'd just come in off the beach. "Your daughter will be okay," he said, smiling shyly. "Don't worry. We'll find her."

Brooke smiled back. He was trying so hard to be kind.

"My grandson was kidnapped two years ago," one man of perhaps sixty told her a few minutes later, during a coffee break. "He was three. Somebody took him from the Fox Hills Mall." He blinked, and a look of surprise came over his tan, grooved face at the tears that suddenly appeared in his eyes. "Sorry. This happens at the oddest times . . . even now."

He was well-dressed, in the kind of expensive polo shirt and shorts you saw on the Beverly Hills crowd. His silver hair was neatly groomed, as were his nails.

Brooke handed him the cup of coffee she had been pouring. Her hand shook. "I don't know how you can stand it," she said.

"I didn't tell you to distress you, my dear." The man touched her hand. "I just wanted you to know that I'll do everything I possibly can to help you find your little girl. We all will. We do care."

"He owns most of Bradford Studios," Creed told her after the volunteer had returned to his task at manning phones. "At first we thought it was a kidnap for ransom. It might have been better that way. These others, these sickos—"

He broke off as Brooke paled. But the damage had already been done. Brooke escaped to the deck. Creed swore.

He followed her outside and ran into Gibbs coming up the stairs. Gibbs was smiling. The blue cap was perched on the back of his head. He looked like someone who had just won on a Lotto ticket.

"Those phone records, Keep? The calls to and from Hayes' house?"

Brooke turned from the railing to listen.

Gibbs bounced up and down on the balls of his feet, as if ready to run in ten directions at once. He cracked his knuckles. "There have been several calls to San Francisco in the past couple of months."

Brooke interrupted. "That would be Charly, probably, calling me. I don't see—"

"At the theater?"

"At PRG? No. Charly's never called me there."

"Has Nathan ever called you there?"

"Never." She looked bewildered.

"Fantastic," Creed said. He punched Gibbs lightly on the shoulder. "Gibby—you do come through."

"More than you know." Gibbs took Creed aside. They spoke in low tones. Once Creed looked up at her speculatively. Brooke strained to hear, but couldn't.

When they had finished, Creed headed back into the house, moving swiftly. Over his shoulder he said to Brooke, "Pack some clothes."

Inside he spoke to the woman in charge of the volunteers. "Betty —can you get me two tickets on the next shuttle to San Francisco? We'll take any two vacant seats—just get us up there fast."

Gibbs drove them to the airport, a flashing red emergency light slapped onto the top of his unmarked car. They were in the air within the hour.

Chapter 20

THEIR FIRST STOP in San Francisco was Brooke's apartment. "You check in here for those things we talked about," Creed said. He scanned the bedroom from the doorway. "I'll take care of the phone. We'll maximize our time that way."

He had brought several pieces of equipment for the telephone. The first one to be installed was an answering machine. "I can't believe you haven't got one," he had commented on the plane. "Doesn't everyone, in the entertainment industry?"

"I kept meaning to buy one. I should have. I don't know why I put things off so long—"

He had looked up from the list he was making, with a frown. "You don't have to do that with me."

"Do what?" The frown made her cringe.

"Apologize all the time."

Brooke had stared out the window, at the sea. Did she do that? Yes. She did it with a lot of men; always had. With Nathan, for years—and lately with Leo. Not too much with Sean. More with men who were in positions of power—or who had an attitude, at least, of internal power. She didn't know why.

"I . . ." She had been about to say she was sorry. Sorry for saying I'm sorry.

"You don't have to care what I think," Creed said.

"I don't." But she did. Now. She wasn't sure why.

"And don't feel guilty. The chances of your daughter calling again while you were gone are slim. Even slimmer are her chances of having had time to leave a message. I just don't want to overlook anything."

Brooke had glanced out the plane window again, seeing shadows on the sea that in another season might have been whales. Along the coastline were jagged black rocks. *We're somewhere above Carmel and Santa Cruz,* she had guessed. *Near Big Sur.*

"Let me know right away what you find," Creed was saying.

Brooke drew her attention back to the apartment. Creed was already unplugging Sarah Rubin's neon phone, replacing it with a utilitarian black set with buttons and several wires leading into electronic boxes. One was the answering machine; another recorded the telephone numbers of all incoming calls. He had also arranged a tap on the line, from the central Pac Bell office.

Brooke crossed into her large bedroom, which spanned the rear of the apartment and looked down onto a courtyard laced with trees. An ancient oak leaned nearly into the room. On cold winter nights, its dry branches scraped the broad window. Now—in June—dense green leaves closed off the sun. Not that there ever was much sun in San Francisco in June.

Brooke walked deliberately to a large closet, and flicked on a light. She stared up at a top shelf—at an empty space where Charly's birthday present, a Victorian doll in a blue velvet dress, had been.

"Creed?" Her voice was barely audible.

Moments later he stood beside her. "It's gone?"

"Yes."

He rested a hand on her shoulder. "Well, we expected that."

"But to think that someone's been in here . . ." She glanced around nervously. "In my apartment, touching my things . . ."

"What about the lock of hair?"

"It was in a book." She halted midway between the closet and the nightstand by her bed. "The book is gone too." Taking a few more steps, she sank heavily onto the bed.

"You're sure it was there when you left? I saw bookshelves in the living room. Could you have put it there?"

"No. It was *As a Man Thinketh.* I read parts of it every morning, when I first wake up."

Creed stared out the window. "At least we know, now. Question is, how did he get in? Through the door, with a key—or maybe, just maybe—" He ran a finger along the window sills, examining the locks of the double-hung windows for any marks that would show forced entry.

He shrugged. "Nothing. Before we leave here, I'll talk to the neighbors across the way. But I doubt they'd have seen anything. With this tree you don't even need curtains in here, do you?"

"Only in winter," Brooke said. "When the leaves are gone." *Leaves. A leaf. Turn over a new leaf? No, a gold leaf—*

"Brooke?"

She focused on Creed's curious gaze.

"What are you thinking?"

"Nothing helpful." She went back and stood inside the closet. "There is something else, though. Something else missing."

He came up behind her. "What?"

"I'm not sure. . . ." She ran a finger over the shelf above her winter coat and sweaters. "That's odd . . . My Polaroid camera. I wasn't sure, at first, but I do remember putting it away in its box, up here. I hardly ever use it anymore, so I stuffed it alongside . . ." She gave a shiver. "Creed? There was another box here. In it was a negligee, one I never wore because it was just too fancy for my life-style here. Sean gave it to me when I was in the hospital drying out last year. He thought it would cheer me up."

"It's gone?"

"That, and the camera." She turned to him, frightened. "Why would anyone take those things?"

He didn't answer. And she knew what it was he didn't want to say: Only a nut would do any of these things.

Suddenly she wanted to kill Nathan. There was no doubt in her mind that he was behind Charly's disappearance. What she didn't understand was how all this insanity fit in. Was he trying to drive her finally, totally, mad?

"C'mon," Creed was saying. "Let's get over to the theater. Maybe we'll learn something there."

· · ·

THE CAB MANEUVERED through heavy morning traffic along Geary Boulevard. Outside the window was the interminable summer fog. Brooke hated the fog; in LA there might be yellow haze in summer, but at least it was warm.

The theater was on a side street off Geary, on the edge of the Tenderloin. A converted warehouse, it stood close to the sidewalk—not luxurious, just a square old building with a bright new facade. Posters with Brooke's publicity photo and that of her co-star, Derek Johannson, touted the coming opening of "THE UNSINKABLE MOLLY BROWN . . . Produced and directed by Leo Walsh." Beneath that were other names: Sean Murphy and Richard Toskit as Molly's brothers, Danny and Tim . . . Rita Meyers as Mrs. McGlone . . . Art Logan as Monsignor Ryan. . . .

The security guard passed them through the rear stage door without question. "Good to see you back, Ms. Hayes. Hasn't been the same around here without you."

"It's only been a few days, Larry." Brooke smiled.

"Even so." The young guard, no more than twenty-five, blushed to the roots of his reddish-brown hair.

"A conquest?" Creed murmured as they walked down the narrow hall to the backstage area.

"A fan," Brooke answered. "Leo hires these people for their love of theater. It's today's equivalent of the old-time ushers. Larry works the various shows around town—all the theatrical groups."

They circled around to the left side of the stage. Sean and the brothers were stomping through the paces of their one dance piece alone together. They were all over the place, and their energy sucked in the rest of the cast and crew, grabbing them up, commanding attention. Men and women in varied stages of costume stood to the side or sat in the audience seats, watching. Several tapped their feet in time to the music. A few clapped in rhythm as well. Rambunctious orchestral music boomed from a tape.

Sean, his straw-blond hair flying, whirled in a circle on one booted foot. It connected with the seat of his "brother's" pants. The brother tumbled to his knees with a howl. He grabbed Sean's ankle and yanked him down. Sean, despite his slender figure, was strong. He immediately had the upper hand. He straddled the other actor—played "King of the Mountain"—and laughed—a boyish, "I won!" sound.

Brooke laughed with him. She loved Sean—loved the shy, quiet boy whose spirit came alive on stage. Offstage he was her best friend. She had missed being able to talk to him about Charly. Sean was wise beyond his years—which numbered, since his birthday a couple of weeks ago, twenty-eight.

Brooke had tried to call him, twice, from Creed's house in Venice. Both times Sean had still been out of town. She wondered where he had gone; it wasn't like him to leave a production that way. Leo must have been furious, with both of them out.

The dance ended. Sean and the brothers stood panting, wiping sweat from their eyes. Immediately the activity elsewhere became intense. Actors passed by, with greetings to Brooke. "Good to see you back . . . where've you been? . . . we missed you." Stagehands scurried. Extras milled while waiting to rehearse their parts. Music blared discordantly as the technician advanced through tapes, checking out sound levels. The orchestral background was taped for this show, but the actors all sang their parts; no one lip-synced.

Sean spotted Brooke and gave her a quick look of concern. Crossing the stage, he grabbed her up in a warm hug. She smelled his sweat, could feel the dampness of it through his flannel shirt. His thin, wiry arms held her close. Her chin came barely to his shoulder.

"I just heard about Charly," Sean said. "I'm sorry, Brooke. I was out of touch. I didn't know." He held her off, looking at her. "Did you get my message? No, of course, you couldn't have, if you're here." He glanced at Brooke's companion.

"This is John Creed," she said. "He's helping me look for Charly."

"I called your house a little while ago," Sean said, shaking the hand that Creed extended. "Leo gave me the number, and I left a message on your machine. Brooke—" His anxious eyes met hers again. "What can I do?"

"I'm just glad to see you," she said, her mouth trembling. She hated the way even a kind word could trigger tears these days.

But Sean was hugging her again. It was the first time anyone had touched her this way since Charly had disappeared. Brooke sighed. Sean was the kind of friend—always had been, since they'd met three years ago during *A Midsummer Night's Dream*—who could make all your cares go away.

"Where have you been?" she wondered, peering up at him. "Is anything wrong?"

"Not really. I just needed some time away."

"But why?"

Sean dropped his arms. His eyes shifted uneasily. "We can talk about it later. Tell me about Charly now."

"She's still gone," Brooke said quietly. "We don't know, yet, what's happened. We think Nathan may have her—"

"We're up here to talk to people," Creed put in, cutting her off. She glanced at him, surprised at the abruptness.

"Why up here?" Sean asked. "Isn't it more likely she'd be in LA somewhere, if Nathan—" He looked confused. "I mean, they live down there—"

"It's a matter of covering all the angles," Creed said easily. "Speaking of which—nothing personal, but would you mind telling me where, exactly, you've been the past few days?"

Sean blinked. The boyish smile was there, but brief. "Of course not. I was in Carmel. It's a little town south of here, along the coast."

"I've been there," Creed said. "Were you visiting someone?"

"No . . . I was alone."

"You left a show that's about to open, to go on vacation, just like that?"

"Creed—" Brooke put a hand on his arm. "I told you, Sean's my friend—"

Creed gave a casual smile, meeting Sean's eyes. "Sorry. I'm sure you understand."

Sean smiled back, disarmingly. "I do understand. And I'll do anything I can to help. Ask me anything." He ran fingers through his thick, unevenly cut crop of yellow hair. "Damn, this is rotten, Brooke. I never would have believed that Nathan was capable of anything like this."

"You know Nathan Hayes?" Creed asked.

"I've met him a few times. And I know about him, from Brooke."

"When was the last time you saw Hayes?"

"Well . . ." Sean glanced quickly at Brooke, then away. "Before we came up here to work last year, I guess. I'm not sure exactly when."

"You're sure you haven't seen him since you moved to San Francisco?"

"Uh, no . . ."

Creed's voice hardened. "During your trip to Los Angeles in April, for instance. At Moustache restaurant, on Melrose?"

Brooke's bewildered glance swung to Sean. "You saw Nathan in Los Angeles? In April?" She turned back to Creed. "I don't understand. What's this about?"

"Well, it's like this. Gibby found, in checking out Nathan's appointments over the past three months, that your friend, here, met with your ex-husband for lunch in LA a couple of months ago."

Brooke's laugh was uncertain. "You mean, they ran into each other by accident."

"No, I mean the two of them had a cozy lunch . . . according to their waiter, who remembers the incident specifically because Sean went home with him when his shift was over at four o'clock."

"That little bitch," Sean breathed, his face turning red.

"Don't blame him too much. Gibbs can be persuasive."

Brooke stared at Sean, her face pale.

He sighed, rubbing a hand over his face. "He called me. Nathan called and asked me to come down. He said he wanted to help you—and that's the only reason I went, Brooke. Christ it was a big mistake! I knew that five minutes into lunch."

"Why did you go at all?" she said angrily. "And why did he want to see you? What possible purpose—"

"He said you were starting to get too close to Charly. He didn't like it, but he was afraid you'd go off the deep end again if he put a stop to it. He wanted to know how you were really doing now—if Charly was safe around you."

"He wanted something *on* me!" Brooke cried. People passed by, casting curious looks their way. "Did you give it to him, Sean? What in the name of God did you tell him? Is that why he decided to take Charly and run?"

"No! I didn't tell him anything, Brooke, I swear! Hell, there isn't anything to tell. You're clean, you've been clean for months. . . ." He broke off, his facing turning a dull red again. "But you're right. Nathan wanted something on you. I saw that right away. And I got out of there fast."

"Apparently not fast enough," Creed said. "You left a trail a mile wide, with that waiter."

Sean's posture drooped. There were deep circles below his eyes, as if he hadn't slept in days. "I didn't mean any harm. Brooke—"

"Why didn't you just *tell* me? Why did you keep it from me?"

"I didn't want to worry you!"

"You mean, you were afraid I couldn't handle it!"

"You know how you get sometimes. You're so intense, when you're talking about Charly. I guess I just didn't know what you'd do—"

Brooke continued to stare, as if seeing her friend for the first time. "All these years as friends," she said softly. "And you still don't trust me? My God, Sean. I thought I knew you. I thought you knew me."

LEO WAS SITTING in an audience seat, center third row from the front. "Let me handle him first," Brooke said as she moved up the aisle. She slid into a seat beside Leo. Creed sat two seats away, easing low and leaning a foot casually on the chair in front. His attention seemed focused on the activity onstage.

"Hi, Leo," Brooke said.

He raised a hand, delaying conversation. "Hey, Derek—and you, Ronnie! Get that hoe and those corncobs off the stage before somebody trips on them! *Stagehand!* You, too!"

Everyone hopped, both actors and support crew . . . while Leo shouted and rose to his feet, waving his hands frenetically.

Creed leaned over and murmured at Brooke's ear. "Shouldn't the union have something to say about actors doing scut work?"

"Leo claims this all-for-one, one-for-all business promotes camaraderie," she whispered back.

Privately she suspected that Leo's good-buddy system was more about saving money. There were fewer stagehands needed, with everyone pitching in.

Leo kept them on hold a few more minutes before slumping low in his seat with a scowl. "We'll never be ready, never. Opening night will be a disaster—the critics will tear us to pieces. My reputation will be tarnished beyond repair." He frowned at Brooke. "Have you come home to work?"

Brooke waited a deliberate moment before answering. "Thanks for caring, Leo. You might ask how my daughter is."

He flushed. "Sorry. You know how I am when I get in the middle of dress rehearsals. Hell . . . how is she, Brooke?"

"Like I told you on your machine—and that would be the call you never returned, Leo—she's gone. She disappeared from Universal Studios two days ago, and no one's seen her since."

One of Leo's short, stubby hands covered Brooke's. "I got your message, I just haven't had time— Christ, Brooke, I'm sorry. I guess I thought maybe it was all a misunderstanding, something with Nathan, and she'd be home by now."

"We haven't been able to find her. We think Nathan may have taken her somewhere, hidden her away so I can't get joint custody."

Leo stared. He took his hand away. "Then why the hell aren't you down in LA looking for her, instead of up here?"

"Because Charly said something to me on the phone the other day. She said, *'Say no, mommy, say no.'* We think it could be a clue that someone up here is involved."

"You mean, in the company? What the hell kind of clue?"

"From Johnny's song to Molly . . . 'I'll Never Say No.' Charly had my rehearsal tape in her cassette recorder the day she disappeared. She was probably listening to it, and the words are so close—"

"Brooke, you're reaching!" Leo jumped to his feet, impatiently pushing past her to get to the aisle. "What the fuck kind of clue is that?"

Creed intervened, standing and blocking his way. "The tape, and Charly's message, are solid enough for us to have flown here to talk to people. It could be that someone who hangs around here, who's familiar with the show, is involved. Maybe even someone with the show."

"That's crazy!" Leo yelled. "You're going to fuck up the show, just when we're about to open—"

"I'd also like to talk to your sound technicians," Creed went on calmly. "I need to find out how many of these tapes went out and who they went to."

Leo stopped yelling long enough to frown at Creed. "Have we been introduced? Who the fuck are you?"

"This is John Creed," Brooke said quietly, standing. "He works with parents of missing children."

"A cop?"

"Used to be," Creed said. "Not anymore."

Leo's anger dwindled to exasperation. He sighed. "Listen, I've got seven days to opening. I don't need this kind of trouble." At Brooke's expression he shrugged. "I mean, it's not like there's anything I can really do to help. You aren't going to find anybody here that's involved in what's happened to Charly, Brooke—you gotta know that."

"You're probably right," Creed said, his voice still cool, but firm. "Meanwhile, I do want to speak to your sound technician."

Leo ran a hand through his red hair, leaving it on end. Finally, his blunt shoulders went up in an elaborate shrug. "Ellen!" he called out to the rear of the theater. "Can you get up here? Somebody wants to talk to you." He turned back, muttering. "You're both goddamned insane. Why would anyone from here—"

He was interrupted by a short, slim woman with close-cropped black hair. She wore tight faded jeans and a mannish sweat shirt, gray, with a logo over the pocket. The logo was of cupped hands. The hands held figures of a boy and girl. "What now, Leo?" The woman's tone was one of exhausted irritation. "I've got more work than I can handle this week, so I am not scrubbing floors, and I most definitely am not going to suck your cock. Now . . . what else is there?"

Leo's response was more a nonresponse; he appeared to be neither offended nor impressed.

"Ellen Neri . . . meet John Creed. You know Brooke."

The woman narrowed her dark eyes and stuck her chin out at Creed. "I know Brooke, true, but I don't even want to know you. You look like a cop to me."

Creed wondered if "looking like a cop" was something that would follow him around all his days—like a tattoo on his nose. "I'm not here to nail you for anything. I just need your help—"

Ellen Neri sighed. "Like I told Leo, I've got a lot to do. Besides, I don't know anything. About anybody. Zip. Zero. *Nada.* Good-bye."

"A few questions—nothing threatening," Creed insisted.

"Everything is threatening these days. If you're here about my driver's license, I haven't renewed it since 1976 and I don't intend to. If you're here about the census, I don't exist. And my car isn't registered. Neither am I." She began to turn away. "Now, go away and leave me alone."

"It might help save a child's life," Creed said quietly.

The woman halted, then reversed her path—coming back a few paces to face them.

"What's going on, Brooke?"

"My daughter, Charly, has disappeared. There's just a chance that whoever has her is involved with the show, or at least hangs out here at the theater."

The technician gave a speculative look to first Brooke, then Creed, then Leo. Finally she folded her arms and slid into an aisle seat. "Talk to me," she said.

CREED TOLD HER THEIR THEORY. When he had finished, Ellen Neri led them to the back of the theater, where the sound equipment was located in a space behind several rows of seats.

"Let me just turn this off first," she said.

Replacing her headphones, she twisted knobs and pulled levers on a board that glowed with green, red, and white lights. Her eyes darted across the board. Every movement of her slender hands was synchronized and smooth. After a few moments, she flicked a switch, took the headphones off, and rummaged in a cupboard beneath the board. Pulling out a thick blue notebook, she flipped through it.

"Here it is," she said. "A list of everyone I've sent tapes to, and some who have asked for tapes. I haven't had time to send them all out yet."

Creed took the notebook and scanned the two pages of names and addresses. "There aren't many names," he commented, looking up.

"Well, we don't let them out to just anybody. Out-of-town money backers, their accountants, people who have an interest in seeing that the show is actually in production, that it's going on. People *in* the show, like Brooke—"

Creed had seen her name on the list. There was another that was familiar, too: He had to cast back in recent memory to place it, but when he did, he felt a tingle of excitement. He took a pen from his shirt pocket and marked it for later.

"Can you tell me who these other people are?" he asked. "The ones who already have tapes." There were five, besides Brooke and the one he had just recognized.

"This is Larry, the security guard who's on today. He's a real nut about the show—but that's nothing unusual. Most people who work on the periphery of these shows are fans. This one, here, is an accountant for one of our money backers. He's in New York. Leo could tell you more about him. Now, Tom Durston, here, is a hands-on backer. He sent for the tape himself. Likes to keep an eye on his investments."

Neri went down the list, and as she had said, nearly every person to whom a tape had been sent had a valid reason for being in possession of one. The security guard might be a bit iffy. Creed would have a talk with him.

"Anything?" Brooke said, beside him.

"A couple of possibilities. One is an old acquaintance of yours."

"Oh? Who?" She peered over his shoulder.

"Look." He pointed to the marked name.

"My God." She turned the book toward Ellen, pointing to the name in question. "What did he want a rehearsal tape for?"

Ellen shrugged. "All I know is Leo said to give him one."

"Leo?"

"Well, you know SuperDick. He's got a lot of weird friends. Friends who want favors."

"Is there anyone else on the list like that?" Creed asked.

"Some friend of Sean's," Ellen said. "This one." She turned the page. "Sean asked me to send it a month or so ago. Let's see . . . yeah, it's dated April thirtieth. That's the day I sent it out."

"To this address in LA?"

"Right."

He would have Gibby check—but if Creed remembered, the name —Paul Norris—was that of Sean's friend, the waiter. The remainder of the list turned up no further obviously questionable names. "The thing is," Ellen Neri said, "those are the tapes I've actually sent out. But people make copies and pass them around, once they get hold of them. Actors, students, teachers . . . everybody likes to hear rehearsal tapes. They even pay for them."

"She's right," Brooke said. "For every one that went out, there are probably at least five copies out there, floating."

"Somehow, I don't think those are the ones we have to worry about," Creed said. "I'm more interested in our friend, here, for now." He tapped a nail over the marked name near the end of the list. "And why Leo said to give him a tape."

Brooke shoved her hands into her pockets. "Let's ask him, before he disappears in a puff of smoke."

They both thanked Ellen Neri for her help.

"Sure. Just one thing." Neri addressed Creed. "How come you were so certain that knowing about a lost kid would get me to talk?"

"Your logo," Creed said. He motioned to the cupped palms on her T-shirt. "Children of the Night. It's headquartered in LA."

"My one charity," the sound technician said laconically. "Runaway kids. Well, pal, you lucked out."

"If they've got you on their side, so have they," Creed said.

Neri gave him a grudging smile. "Listen, anytime. Let me know if I can help."

LEO EYED THE NAME in Ellen Neri's book. "Roger Dorn. Yeah, the photographer. What do you want to know about him?"

"How did you first hear of him? Has he done work for other people here?"

"All the time. Far as I know, the guy's okay—a sleaze, but he does good work . . . and he's cheap. That's about all our people are looking for."

"Brooke says he lives in a pretty fancy place. You know where he gets the money for it?"

Leo shrugged. "Beats me. Drugs, maybe. Or old family money. There's a lot of that in Pacific Heights."

"You know if he's lived there long?"

"Long as I've been around—" Leo broke off, glaring. "Dusty! Are those script changes ready yet?"

A tall brunette in jeans and a flowered shirt looked up from a card table in front of the stage, near the left aisle. Creed had noticed her earlier, writing on script pages in a blue binder.

"Almost." She removed her glasses and rubbed her eyes.

"Well, hurry it up, will you? We've only got seven days left!"

The woman shot him a look of practiced indifference and went back to writing.

Leo made a production of yanking off his ball cap and pretending to tear at his hair. "Look, I've got to move things along here. How about if we meet for coffee"—he checked a gold Rolex watch—"say, in an hour?"

"Speak to Larry first, will you? Tell him it's okay to talk to us?"

"Larry?"

"The security guard."

"Oh. Yeah, Larry. Go get him, I'll tell him whatever you want."

Leo was already gone, his mind on the script pages in his hand. He was humming—a rumbling, concentrated sound that barely made it out of his head.

THEY STOOD BEHIND THE STAGE, in a narrow hallway beneath a flight of stairs. Creed, having been cleared by Leo, asked the questions.

"Has anyone suspicious been hanging around in the past few weeks, or even months? Anyone who doesn't ordinarily have business here?"

"Sure," the guard answered, chewing on a Snickers bar. "Homeless, looking for a place to sleep. They try to get in all the time. Homeless are mostly why I'm here."

"Anyone else? Somebody ordinary, just hanging around. A fan, say?"

"There's Randy Andy," the guard said. "He's pretty harmless, though."

"Randy Andy?"

"An old vaudeville actor," Brooke interjected. "Randy likes to hang out backstage and ogle the girls while they're changing. He's okay, though."

The guard nodded. "Guy just doesn't have enough to do with his time."

"You know where he lives?" Creed asked.

"Sure. We checked him out a long time ago. It'll be in the files."

"Leo knows," Brooke said. "Randy came in pretty drunk one night. Leo left us all hanging here, to drive him home."

"He left a rehearsal to drive this guy home? Just like that?"

"I guess so. Why? What are you getting at?"

"Seems to me your Super Director wouldn't have much time to look after an old drunk."

"Leo likes Randy. I think he sees some spark in him from the old days, or something."

Creed was silent.

Chapter 21

"ANDY'S OKAY," Leo said to Creed a few minutes later. Cars and buses exhausted the air outside the second-floor windows of the theater office. Brooke stared down into the street, barely hearing.

I was going to bring Charly to that little bakery down there. When she came to live with me.

The coffee Leo had given her was cold. Bitter. She swung her attention back to the conversation. Feeling impatient, wanting to move things along. Every moment that passed . . .

"He's just a street person," Leo said. "Lives in Union Square. But the guy's got a lot of pride, and he doesn't like people to know that, which is why I drove him back there myself."

"Is he drunk like that a lot?"

"Now and then, from what I hear." Leo shrugged. "Doesn't usually show up here that way."

"You know why he did, that day?"

"Something eating at him, I guess." Leo gave a brief laugh. "Shit, maybe somebody stole his cardboard box."

Creed flicked a glance at Brooke. She looked away. There were some things about Leo she never had liked. Certain callous attitudes.

"When exactly was this?" Creed was asking.

"Oh, shit, I don't know. . . ."

"About a month ago," Brooke interjected. "I remember the day."

Leo raised an orange brow, thin and disordered from his constant rubbing at it.

"While you were driving Randy home," Brooke explained, "I took advantage of the time to call Charly. That's when we set up the plans for this weekend." She stared at her hands, which had tightened on the heavy white mug. A thumbnail scratched at a dried line of coffee extending from the mug's lip. "For her birthday."

"What about this photographer?" Creed said. "Dorn? Can you tell me any more about him?"

Leo shook his head. "He's been around the theater scene for years. Older than he looks, probably. Never married. Could be gay, but if he is, I never heard of him being with anyone."

"You've used him a lot for cast publicity photos?"

"I guess you could say that. Why?" Leo's chin stuck out at a defensive angle.

"Just asking. Trying to figure how well you know him."

"Not well at all. I send people to him, that's all. And sometimes I send them to somebody else."

"It's okay, Leo," Brooke said, touching his hand. She felt sorry for him, suddenly. She knew his job wasn't easy. And she hadn't been making it any easier, ducking out like this during the final few days of rehearsals. "Nobody's blaming you for anything."

And there I go again, she thought. Apologizing. She saw Creed looking back at her. He knew.

RANDY ANDY DIDN'T HAVE a cardboard box. His only possession was a scarred brown suitcase, hidden behind an obsolete electrical panel in the parking garage under Union Square.

"So I don't have t'drag it around the City with me all day. See?" Randy Andy darted a canny glance at Brooke, then Creed. "Oh, yes."

They had found Randy up in the park, entertaining a group of homeless with tales of times gone by. Creed had tried asking questions up there, but Randy hadn't been comfortable talking in front of people. "Come on down to my place," he had said slyly. "I'll show you around."

His "place" was this dank, dark corner of the Union Square underground garage. Brooke wondered how he managed to maintain that look of nearly robust corpulence.

Randy was the only overweight bum she had ever seen. Not just pouchy in the belly, from malnutrition, but fat all over. A red flannel shirt, popping buttons, ended in a mound that hung over shiny green pants. Fat ankles bulged over black leather shoes that cracked and peeled but were bizarrely polished to a sheen. A thin layer of yellowish white hair was plastered wetly to a nearly bald head. The red-rimmed eyes were a soft mushy green, like spoiled kiwi fruit.

There was no one in this part of the garage but the three of them. Lights were dim at this end of the lower level. The outdoor fog had seeped in, intensifying an odor of mildew and urine. Water dripped from an overhead pipe, leaving green, oily puddles on the concrete floor.

The aging vaudevillian cast another furtive glance about, then tugged at the brown, smelly dumpster he had brought them to. The dumpster was overloaded. A couple of cartons perched precariously on top fell to the floor. Randy nudged them out of the way. A few moments later he'd uncovered the abandoned electrical panel—well camouflaged by the hieroglyphics of graffiti.

Randy dug a chubby hand into his pants pocket and pulled out a penknife. He stuck it into a nearly invisible crack, wiggling it back and forth until the panel popped open. Revealed was a space of about four by five feet. Into that had been wedged the tattered brown suitcase he had told them about, and a couple of bottles of cheap rum. Old capped wires stuck out from the walls of the plastered gap, on either side.

"I'm surprised you trust us enough to show us this," Creed said.

Randy cast him a shrewd look. "Yeh don't seem like somebody who'd want my case. There's nothin' but mem'ries in there. And it looks to me like yeh've got all yeh need, stored right there inside yer head." A gold tooth glinted. "Bad, bad mem'ries . . . oh, yes."

Creed narrowed his eyes, and Randy gave a raspy belly laugh. "Didn't Leo tell you what I used to do in vaudeville?"

Creed shook his head. Brooke spoke. "Randy was a mind reader."

Randy Andy took a bow, a gold tooth flickering behind a sly smile. "Randolph Andrew Coynes, at your service. Anything yeh'd wanta know about me, yeh can find right here. Right here inside this old bag. I got nothin' t'hide. . . ." Again, the sly grin. "Least, not anymore, not these days, oh, no."

He had been unbuckling the straps that held the suitcase together —almost anxious, Creed thought, to show them his life, his "home." Maybe too anxious.

Creed feigned interest in the more mundane contents—an old-fashioned bottle of Vitalis hair oil, an Old Spice stick deodorant, a worn deck of playing cards. There were age-gray socks, and undershorts with more holes than material left.

What caught Creed's attention were several tiny statues of the Blessed Mother and various saints, only a couple of whom Creed thought he recognized. Joseph, for one—with his carpenter's plane. Saint Francis, with birds on his arm. Reasonably well-known figures to almost anyone who knew about religions—and certainly there was nothing odd in an old-timer carrying around religious figurines. What *was* bizarre was how many there were. Quickly he counted twenty or more. Hard to get a real tally, the way they were scattered.

Randy Andy caught his look. "My spirit guides. Only we called them saints, back then."

"Spirit guides?"

He gave a cunning grin. "The ones who tell me what people are thinking, what they're doing. For the mind reading."

"Oh." Creed picked up a faded plastic statue of a woman in a beige-and-brown nun's habit, with roses in her arms. "You still do this mind reading?"

"Now and then."

"You make money at it?"

The grin widened. "Now and then."

Creed wondered if the man worked now as a street performer. There were street entertainers back home in Venice, who made a small, tax-free fortune that way. They juggled, breathed fire, sang songs, and walked tightropes—all at the tip of a hat. And unless they lived high off the hog, which most didn't, they seldom got caught by the IRS. Many performers were "homeless," with no permanent address. You couldn't get welfare from the government that way—but neither could you be served with Intents to Levy from Uncle Sam.

On the other hand, if Randy Andy had money tucked away—just where was it? Certainly not in this suitcase, which purported to hold all his worldly secrets and goods.

There were more socks—some dirty, smelling of street sweat. Snapshots? No, old publicity photos. Creed picked one up. Randy Andy stared at him from it with a crafty eye.

Well, one eye was crafty, Creed thought. The other was dreamy, almost mystical. The style of the photo had a familiar feel. Creed turned it over. Stamped on the back was: *Roger Dorn, Photographer to the Stars.*

Brooke, from beside him, said, "He keeps popping up, doesn't he?"

Creed glanced at Randy Andy. "When was this taken?"

The soft kiwi eyes stared back, becoming watery. "A thousand years and thirty pounds ago!" Again, the belly laugh. "Oh, yes."

It was true that Randy's face was thinner then—although not by much. Less of a jowl, perhaps. "In what year, exactly, would a thousand years ago put us?" Creed asked.

"Shoot, I don't know . . . nineteen eighty-four, eighty-five?"

"You know this photographer well, then?"

"Not well," he laughed, "just long. Least, not so well yeh'd notice. Saw him down at PRG a month or so ago, and he snubbed me right good. S'pose he's got too many faces in his head to remember us all."

"You saw this guy down at the theater? Recently?" Why hadn't Leo told them that?

"Like I said, a month ago. Maybe more. I don't exactly keep an appointment calendar."

"What was he doing there?"

"Drumming up business, I guess, how would I know?"

"Did you see him talking to anyone?"

Randy glanced away. "I don't exactly remember much. Look . . . that was the day Leo drove me home."

"The day you went to the theater drunk?" Creed asked.

"If that's what yeh wanta call it." Randy's tone was belligerent.

"What would *you* call it?"

His eyes flashed. "In my cups, buddy, in my cups. In the old days, that's what we used to call it—nothin' more. Oh, there were a few

Carrie Nations around, The Women's Christian Temperance Union, yeh know—but not so many dried-up, moralistic alchy's like there are today. Christ, yeh can't even get a little high, now, without somebody lookin' down their noses at yeh. And then there's that no-smokin' business . . . makes yeh feel like a crim'nal, yeh light up a fag around anybody anymore—" He laughed hysterically, his rotund stomach bouncing with every bellow. "Fag! Now, there's a word that's changed meaning over the years! Used to mean a cig. Now yeh don't even dare say it around this town, fer fear a gettin' bushwhacked!"

Randy had taken the deck of playing cards out of their box and was flipping through them excitedly as he talked. His speech had become rapid-fire and rambling.

People who had chemicals running through their veins, Creed knew—whether drugs or alcohol—could maintain conversations only so long. It was much the way Brooke, who was still recovering—still detoxing, in a sense—spaced out now and then, her mind wandering off into dark corners. In ACA they taught you to recognize the pattern. Creed himself had learned it, back in those few final months, when Karen had been drinking.

The problem with Karen was that before she'd had a chance to sober up, she had wandered off for good.

Meanwhile, Randy Andy had slipped out of the groove.

"Let's go," Creed said, taking Brooke's arm. "We've learned all we're going to here."

She nodded. "Thanks, Randy. We appreciate your help."

Randy gave no indication he'd heard. He had the playing cards fanned out on the oily cement floor. "Pick one, anyone," he was saying to himself. His chubby hand hovered, then dived. He glanced at the card and chortled.

"Ace of spades! I did it! Asshole said I'd lost my touch, asshole doesn't know nothin' about nothin'. . . ." He reached inside his "space," and pulled out a half-empty bottle of rum. Uncapping it, he tilted the bottle and took a deep slug. "Know nothin'," he mumbled, wiping his chin where the rum had dribbled. "Know nothin' *asshole*. I still got what it takes . . . oh, yes."

Chapter 22

ROGER M. DORN, PHOTOGRAPHER TO THE STARS, proclaimed the elegant sign in gold script. It was attached to a brick post, by an equally elegant wrought-iron gate.

The mansion was Georgian, huge and sprawling . . . not one of the more familiar single-width Victorians—the "Painted Ladies," as they were called. This type of Pacific Heights mansion was close to the street in front. Along either side ran lush, wide gardens that ended short at a high bank at the rear. The bank was thick with azalea bushes and rimmed at the top with eucalyptus trees. Above them perched other mansions with even better views.

Brooke and Creed followed directions on the discreet iron sign and found themselves at a side entrance—impatiently ringing a discreet, gold-plated bell.

"The rich shall be with us always," Creed muttered.

"What?"

"The rich—"

"No, I mean, wasn't it the poor? That saying. 'The poor shall be with us always.' Or something."

"Whatever. Where you've got poor, you've got rich—feeding off the poor."

"You are one sour customer, John Creed."

A voice issued from the intercom at the side of the wide freshly painted door. "Roger Dorn, here. Who is it?"

Creed pushed a button and identified himself as a former LAPD officer—a ploy that often got him into difficult places. People seldom heard the word "former," so busy were they focusing on the LAPD part.

"I'm with Brooke Hayes, from the Powell Repertory Group. We'd like to ask you some questions, see if you can help us with something." His voice was low and easy.

"Love it," Dorn responded with a lazy drawl. "C'mon up." There was an immediate click, and Creed pushed at the heavy white door. Brooke followed him up stairs that were carpeted in a soft rose plush. Her fingers trailed a mahogany railing, its subtle luster giving off the fresh scent of lemon oil. The walls of the staircase were polar white. At well-spaced intervals were photographs of minor Hollywood stars. Brooke recognized several whose names she didn't know, but whose faces had graced the screens of America for twenty, thirty years or more.

The major stars had positions of more importance in Dorn's studio. They began in a line at the top of the stairs, proceeding along the left wall and ending only when wall ran into window. *Like a parade,* Brooke thought—*consisting of all parade marshalls, each one topping the last.* Lana Turner . . . Glenn Ford . . . Lauren Bacall. A sad shot of Rita Hayworth in her later years; a kind of psychic camera shot—before her death, but capturing its coming like the reading of a palm.

Toward the end of the line were some of the newer stars, in terms of Hollywood old/new: Gene Kelly . . . Cyd Charisse. James Garner. And Steve McQueen.

Roger Dorn was nowhere in sight, but water could be heard running in an adjacent room. "Be right with you," a voice called out. "Look around, if you like."

Brooke stood at the thirty-by-thirty wall of glass, looking out over the city and San Francisco Bay. Creed gave a fleeting glance to the photos of the stars, then crossed to the opposite wall. Here were players of another kind: children and teenagers, the under-twenties—and those who were struggling to appear under twenty. The new, new Hollywood: the bubbleheads, the no-conversation, no-intellect bimbos (both male and female) who had gathered in Hollywood in recent years, seeking fame. Young women and men in their early twenties, vacationing in the offices of plastic surgeons rather than the Bermudas—having the silicone injected, the nose bobbed, the eyes widened, the lips bee stung. All in the name of "art." Or was it money?

God forbid that Hollywood should ever, ever accept people the way they were born. Oh, there were exceptions—the Streeps, and the De Niros, who had proved their worth in any role, any face and form. But the young ones were nothing but meat on a cutting board. They were the tragic ones that, too often, he had seen on the streets. It didn't take long for LA to kill off a dream—or a kid. Take a hundred or so rejections, add a gram or two of coke, a handful of pills. . . .

He had picked up a three-inch-thick portfolio and was thumbing through it. "Sad, aren't they?" Brooke said. She had turned and was watching him.

Each page held an eight-by-ten black-and-white glossy of a child. None looked to be over twelve, despite the bizarre hairstyles. One beautiful young black girl had a side of her head shaved; the other side sported a ponytail. Long, glittering earrings dangled. Her dress, visible from the bust up, was too old, too sophisticated—a black off-the-shoulder affair. Another—a blond, fragile child of certainly no more than seven, had a forties-style upsweep, with loose, sexy curls piled on top, curls that spilled over her forehead above sultry, too-knowing eyes.

Creed stared at the photos, turning pages thoughtfully. At the back was an 8 1/2-by-11 paper with the letterhead, APHRODITE TALENT, INC. A Los Angeles address that Creed recognized as being near Wilshire, in one of the better areas near Beverly Hills. Below were names of the child models in the portfolio. Ages, descriptions, and a code number that he realized, flipping back, related to a like number on each page.

He laid the album down when Roger Dorn entered the room.

"Oh, I see you've found my favorite portfolio," Dorn said. The tone, and the gestures accompanying it, were effeminate. "Aren't they darling?"

That wasn't the word Creed would have chosen.

He eyed the tall, rail-thin man of perhaps sixty. There were fine lines around Dorn's eyes, although on first glance the photographer had looked younger—possibly because of the gray-blond mop of hair with its deep wave over the left temple. "I'm John Creed, I believe you know Brooke Hayes?"

Dorn glanced at Brooke. "Oh, of course," he said after a beat. "I remember. *Molly Brown!* I did your publicity shot a few months ago."

"We'd like to ask you some questions," Brooke said.

Dorn flicked a glance at Creed. "What's up?"

"Mrs. Hayes' daughter is missing." Creed watched for a reaction and was rewarded with only the briefest flicker. "We're talking to anyone who knows Mrs. Hayes, personally or professionally. A shot in the dark—just to see if we can come up with any leads."

Dorn walked casually to his desk and leaned against it, arms folded. His dark green velour shirt was open at the neck, revealing a heavy gold chain with a tiny gold skeleton dangling from it. He fingered the skeleton gently. "I'll help any way I can, but I don't really know Mrs. Hayes." He addressed Brooke. "I've only seen you once, haven't I? When you came for that sitting—"

"But you've been at the theater often?" Creed asked. "At PRG? We hoped that you might have seen something while you were there . . . anything at all. You never know what might help."

"I wouldn't say I've been there *often.*" Dorn's tone was slightly testy. "Good grief, I barely get out of this studio! There's so much to do these days, it seems." He rolled his eyes.

"You haven't been to the theater in the past couple of months, then?"

Dorn opened his mouth, then paused a moment before answering. "I may have been there, a few weeks ago."

"Would you mind telling me what business you had there?"

Dorn's colorless eyes narrowed. "I'm not sure I like the turn this conversation is taking. Surely you don't suspect me of something."

"Of course not," Creed said easily. "But if you remember who you talked to there, that could be just the one person who might have seen someone suspicious at the theater. It's important, in these cases, to cover all the angles."

The photographer leaned back against the desk once more. "Well, I talked to Leo, of course—"

"Anything in particular?"

Dorn smiled, putting an offhand charm into it. "Networking, dear. For future business. God, the payments on this place are *terrible!*"

"You rent?"

"I did, until they converted the mansion into condos, one up, one down. My payments are now five times what they were in 1982! Well, it's like that all over San Francisco. Damn landlords rob you blind."

"So you talked with Leo about future sittings with his actors. Anything else?"

"That's about it," Dorn answered with a shrug.

"Do you remember seeing anyone suspicious hanging around?"

The photographer laughed. "I don't think I'd know if anyone was *suspicious.* I mean, actors are *all* so *weird."* He smiled at Brooke. "Sorry, but I'm sure you know what I mean. There were people running around in all manner of dress and undress . . . yammering at each other, arguing over lines, and Leo's standing there yelling his head off, as usual—"

"You know Leo well?" Creed asked.

Dorn's silver eyes slanted his way. "Leo and I go back. He's sent a lot of work my way."

"That isn't what I was asking."

Roger Dorn straightened. He moved around the desk, busying himself with photos there. The lines around his eyes deepened, extending down the thin cheeks, fanning out as they reached his mouth. "I have a lot of work to do. I really don't see how I can help you any more."

Creed watched him silently a moment. "Just one more question," he finally said. "I understand you asked for, and got, a cassette tape with the rehearsal music on it, from *The Unsinkable Molly Brown."*

"What of it?" Dorn said calmly.

"Mind telling me why you wanted it?"

The photographer shrugged. "Not at all. I glean character details from rehearsal tapes, nuances that help me to understand the parts that the people I photograph are playing. I come up with better portraits that way—at least, for publicity purposes."

"Did you listen to the tape for Brooke's portrait?" Creed asked.

"Of course."

"And what did you glean about her?"

Dorn gave an uneasy glance to Brooke. "Mrs. Hayes . . . is a beautiful woman. But with a hard edge. Not unlike Molly Brown as she grew a bit older, I think—the Molly who saved people on the *Titanic*. I tried to capture that grit."

"Do you feel you succeeded?"

"As I remember," Dorn admitted, "I believed at the time that I failed. The toughness was there, but a certain—oh, levity, I guess—was lacking."

Creed had to give the man points, at least, for creative insight.

"I know I said that was the last question, but I've thought of something else."

Dorn sighed and rolled his eyes. "Go ahead. But then I really must get back to work."

"Do you still work for Hollywood? Do sittings there, I mean?"

"I have occasional jobs in LA," Dorn said. "For private parties. And sometimes for the studios."

"Ever work for Universal?"

Dorn stared. "Yes."

"When?"

"A couple of years ago. I haven't been on the lot since. Now, *if* you don't mind . . ."

Brooke had turned her gaze on Roger Dorn, Photographer to the Stars. Her expression was pale, her features tight. She looked, Creed thought, like a surprised child—one who had just upturned a rock and found beneath it an unexpected slug.

THEY HAD GONE. *Thank God.*

Roger Dorn flipped through a copy of *Beauté,* a hairstyling magazine that was ordinarily found in beauty salons. Dorn paused, tapped with an index finger on the page before him, then picked up the gold-and-white telephone on his ornate French desk. He dialed a number in Hollywood.

"The little girl on page twenty-seven of *Beauté,*" he said, planting his feet lazily on the desk. "The one with all the black eye makeup, à la Madonna. Absolutely decadent, don't you think?" He smiled. "How old is she?" Fingering the page, he drew a line down the child's nose to her mouth, pausing there to outline it gently. "Ten? Perfect. What's her name? Melissa . . . ?" He leaned back in his chair, rolling the name on his tongue. On his face was a look of excitement. Anticipation. "Melisssa. Ah, yes." He sighed with relish. "Perfect. I want her. Get her for me . . . now."

The long, slender fingers of his right hand replaced the receiver on its base. The fingers of his left hand stroked his crotch. His head rolled back, the gray-blond wave at his temple lifting gently in a cool breeze from the one open window. Dorn's eyes closed. His body grew stiff. He began to jerk, to spasm, to moan.

When it was over, there had been no ejaculate. There never was, not since—

Looking around, he reoriented himself to the room. Slowly he rose to his feet, still holding the moments of fantasy close, reluctant to let them drift away. His path through the studio was steady and sure.

In the adjoining darkroom, he went back to work. Developing.

In the red light a child's face appeared. A child of perhaps nine, with long blond curls and haunted eyes. Her face was contorted with fear. Huge tears rolled down her cheeks. Her rigid, open mouth seemed to cry, "Help me! Oh, God, please, somebody, help me!"

Roger Dorn smiled. He was extremely pleased with this work, this piece of art. It had turned out well this time.

Chapter 23

BROOKE STRODE ANGRILY BESIDE CREED, past shops on Union Street. They were looking for a phone. "You heard him. He admitted to a connection with Universal Studios."

"Which could be perfectly innocent."

"Or not."

"I agree—there's something wrong. Certain things don't add up. For one thing, why did he say he was at the theater to network with Leo—that he needed work—yet now he says he's got way too much to do? And there were those photos in the album."

"The children?"

"Yes. The child sophisticates. In my line of work, any situation where children are portrayed, or used, in a way that's much older than their years, rings a warning bell. Of course, it might be only a case of modern life gone bad. But you never know."

A street person, a throwback from the sixties with gray hair to his waist, blocked their way. Creed searched the face automatically, then dropped some change into the man's outstretched hand, barely breaking stride.

"He's gay, isn't he?" Creed asked. "Roger Dorn? I mean, there are outward signs . . . but you said he'd come on to you, made advances during your sitting."

"What he did, to put it more accurately, was try to feel me up.

165

There are a lot of gay men who do that. I don't know what their story is. On the other hand, there are a lot of men in the entertainment or artistic fields who seem effeminate, yet aren't gay at all. It's anybody's guess."

He steered her toward a bank of phones outside a restaurant. "I wonder if he knows your ex-husband."

"I don't see how."

"Dorn's name and address are on the back of that publicity photo of you in Charly's room. That's how I recognized his name on Ellen Neri's list. Surely Nathan's seen it on the back of the portrait, too."

Creed took a calling card from his wallet. "I've got to call Gibbs. Get him on Dorn's tail in LA, see exactly what he does down there these days."

He dialed, then stuck a finger in one ear to shut out traffic noise. The phone was picked up immediately at the beach house, by a volunteer he hadn't yet met. Someone new. As he waited for Gibbs to come on, Creed caught a reflection of himself in the burnished silver plate on the front of the phone.

He looked like a maniac. Along with fog, heavy winds were blowing in through the Golden Gate. The black of his hair was a shade lighter, now, from the summer sun, but it had been growing too fast this past month. It was below his shoulders instead of just grazing them. He had to wear it in a ponytail to keep it out of his eyes. The silver medallion that his mother had given him—a legacy of his Native American grandmother—glinted at his throat. He touched it, reminding himself of his other roots: of Nicholas Allesandro Cristofaro, whose inner strength—and probably pure dumb luck—had gotten him away from the Chicago mob, through historic blizzards, and to a land where he was able to begin a new life.

The challenges are different now, Creed thought. *We're protected from blizzards, for the most part, and some of us are even protected from the mob. It's everyday life that gets us in the end. The little horrors—and the large ones.*

Gibbs came on the line. "Howdy, Keep."

"Anything new at that end?"

"Several sightings. You know the kind—blond hair, blue eyes, about nine, alone with a man in a shopping-center parking lot. Turns out, though, he's her dad, and they're shopping for a new puppy—and/

or a present for Mom—cherry chocolate cheesecake. Whatever." He sighed heavily. "You remember that kid who disappeared in San Antonio last year? Martinez? We just got it through the fax . . . they found him."

"Alive?"

"Sorry. I know how hard you worked on that one."

"Shit! Fucking shit!" Creed slammed a fist on the wall of the phone booth. It had been too damned late when they got the case. The parents had waited too long to report it.

"Keep, don't beat yourself up. There are some things you can do, and some you can't. Listen, what's going on up there?"

Creed brought himself back. He told him about Dorn. "D-O-R-N. Check out the guy's activities down there. Check with the studios, in particular Universal. See if he's got current connections there—although I don't really see how that fits right now. He doesn't match the description of the man Charly was seen to leave there with. Check out this Aphrodite Talent Agency, too. See what they know about him." He broke off suddenly. "Hell, you know the program. Why am I telling you all this?"

"You're getting pretty involved in this one," Gibbs observed dryly. "Maybe that's why."

Creed made a sound of impatience. "Too involved. I can't afford to lose my objectivity."

Gibbs laughed softly. "Too *late*, partner."

Creed stared at the phone, as if a snake had slithered out of it, catching him unaware. Hanging up, he looked over at Brooke. She was facing a shop window, staring blindly. Her shoulders, which were usually squared these days—at least around him—looked frail now. Too frail for carrying such a burden. Creed blinked, seeing the hurt, terrified mother, the one he had tried to close his eyes to for better objectivity.

He realized something in that moment. That no matter how he had been trying to blind himself to it, he had been seeing Brooke Hayes this way all along. From that first night—when she had appeared on his deck, frightened out of her wits beneath the act of bravado she had tried so hard to employ—he had taken on a new role, one he had struggled years to avoid.

Not the role, simply, of cop, or detective, or even child-finder—but that of protector.

It wasn't a revelation that thrilled him.

Holy shit, he thought. *Now what am I going to do?*

THEY WERE AT SFO, waiting for a shuttle back to LA. They stood together at a window, while outside, planes took off and arrived.

"I just don't think we should leave here," Brooke said in a low, hard voice. Her hands were gripping her arms. "I feel closer to Charly up here. It just *feels* right."

Their argument had started in the rental car, coming out 280 to the airport.

"Gibby's hiring someone private here to follow Dorn, anywhere he goes. A PI. He'll also talk to your neighbors and run a check on the security guard at the theater. Leo and Sean I'm not so sure about, but we'll follow up on them too."

"But if we stayed—"

"Brooke, I can't afford to be sidetracked. Bottom line is, there's no real link yet between him and Nathan. And I somehow can't see *any* father getting a person like Dorn involved."

"For God's sake! What if you're wrong? What if Roger Dorn has Charly in that house somewhere? What if she's there right now, and we could have gotten her, what if I could be holding her in my arms—" Tears of frustration and anger formed in her eyes. She brushed them away.

Creed took her shoulders. "She *wasn't there,* Brooke. Dorn was too open, too unafraid. He didn't seem worried about letting us walk around or poke into things. He clearly wasn't worried about our presence at all." He shook her gently. "You've got to trust me. I've been doing this work a long time, and if Charly had been anywhere within a mile of that house, I'd have known it."

"So what the hell are we going to do?" she said despairingly.

He softened his voice. "We're going to keep putting one foot in front of the other—just the way you did when you were getting sober. Remember? One day at a time."

She leaned her forehead against his chest, tiredly. "I don't want to be sober anymore. I want a drink, dammit. I want to forget, the way I always used to. I want to drift away someplace where things like this don't happen."

"I know . . . I know." He awkwardly stroked her hair. "But this will be over soon. We'll find her. I promise."

After a moment, she straightened. He released her, glancing out the window. "Look, the sun is coming out."

Brooke gave a tight smile. "A miracle. This is the meanest, dampest, grayest, coldest city on the face of the planet in summer."

"It just seems that way. Now."

LATER, ON THE PLANE, HE THOUGHT: *Martinez. Danny Martinez.* Gibbs had said he was dead.

Danny was eight when he disappeared. Creed had known, from the first, that they'd never find Danny Martinez alive. But he had gone through the paces, given the parents hope—just in the off chance he was wrong.

The parents were illegal immigrants—afraid they'd be deported while their son was missing, and they'd lose touch with him forever. Non-English speaking, they didn't know where to turn, and thus they waited far too long to report the boy missing.

How were they dealing, now, with the fact that they had, indeed, lost their son forever?

He should have prepared them better.

BROOKE CLOSED A MAGAZINE she had been pretending to read. She slid it back into the pocket of the seat in front of her, and turned to Creed.

"If you honestly believe Nathan's got Charly, why do you look so worried? I mean, if he does have her, that's bad enough—but at least it would mean she's physically safe."

Creed sighed. "Look . . . I don't want to alarm you. But if Nathan does have Charly, the longer he's got to arrange things—to move her around—the greater the chances are he'll take her out of the country. Brooke, the world's a big place. You might never see your daughter again if that happens."

Her fists clenched. "Dammit, Creed! You are so damned hard. I don't need to hear that from you."

"You do," he said just as angrily. "You need to know what the stakes are. This is a dangerous game, and you need to be armed for it. It's the only way to survive."

If they lost Charly, picking up the pieces would be difficult enough. False hope in the meanwhile could only make things worse.

Chapter 24

IT HAD BEEN A LONG, RESTLESS NIGHT, impossible to sleep with the sound of ringing telephones, computers, faxes, and volunteer voices above her bed in Creed's guest room.

To Brooke the hubbub had been more tender than a lullaby, with its implied hope that Charly might soon be found, soon be home.

At eight-forty in the morning the beach was coming alive, and there were hundreds of sailboats offshore. Must be a race. Or maybe the Marina was having a boat parade. They were always having a parade; any excuse would do.

"Here, have some juice," Gibbs said from behind her.

Brooke turned from the railing and accepted the cold glass gratefully. She was beginning to understand that Gibbs took up the slack for Creed—filled in the blanks. Where Creed was blunt and not always thoughtful, Gibbs was the opposite. She wondered if they worked this way together all the time, or if this arrangement had begun with her.

She wondered if Creed would be this distant—and blunt—in a close relationship with a woman.

"How was San Francisco?" Gibbs asked.

"Well, there's a chance that this photographer, Dorn, might be involved."

"That's what Keep said."

"He's been hanging out at the theater, and he has a rehearsal tape, so he'd know the words to that song. But we don't even know if that's what Charly meant by 'say no.' "

She took a deep gulp of the orange juice, then slumped into one of the metal chairs. "On the other hand, Dorn has worked at Universal, so he'd know his way around. I wanted to stay up there and talk to him again."

"But Creed was afraid of losing focus?"

"I suppose. And maybe he's right. But it scares the hell out of me, that we might be passing up a chance to find Charly up there."

Gibbs nodded toward the activity in the living room. "Keep won't overlook anything—in fact, I've never seen him work this hard on a case. Not since Jason disappeared."

Confused, Brooke glanced through the open sliding doors. "Really? But he told me he always brings in the volunteers."

"Sure, that. But I've never known him to fly out of town with a parent before."

Brooke glanced up. "What are you saying?"

"Nothin' much, I guess—if you don't get it." He smiled, pulling the baseball cap over his eyes. "Think I'll take a walk."

She watched him lope down the stairs, then the beach—hands in his pockets, face tilted toward the sun. She could have sworn she heard him whistling. It sounded—although she couldn't be sure, since there were random notes only—a bit like that old Hoagy Carmichael song: "Smoke Gets in Your Eyes."

BROOKE MADE A HUGE URN of coffee, another of hot water for tea, and several dozen sandwiches. After that she was only in the way. There wasn't room to navigate, and hearing some of the calls that came in was too painful. Children lost, children possibly found—

Some dead. None of them Charly. But any call that came *could* be about Charly, and Brooke would listen to this end of the conversation and hold her breath. It was torture, and Creed finally sent her away.

"Take a walk down to the main beach. It'll take your mind out of this awhile. I promise I'll find you if anything turns up here."

She followed the boardwalk—(a misnomer if she'd ever heard one,

for that miles-long narrow strip of concrete)—to the main Venice
Beach area, several blocks away. Lining the walk on the ocean side, at
folding tables, were tarot readers and psychic palm readers, street musicians, a sand sculptor with a hat out for donations, and jewelry vendors.
On the opposite side were tables with socks and T-shirts, others piled
high with "M. C. Hammer" pants, and racks of sunglasses. No prices; it
was expected you'd bargain. "How much is this pair?" . . . "Eight
dollars" . . . "I'll give you five, okay?" A nod and a shrug. "Okay." If
you hung in, Brooke knew, you could get three for a dollar.

In some stores, even the clothes didn't have prices. "How much is
this blouse?" . . . "Twenty-five, but you can have it today for
twenty."

Brooke knew the scam from her years of living in LA. It was an old
scene, on the one hand, out of the seventies or even sixties—yet it
blended well with the new, with the kids on roller blades or skate-
boards, their baseball caps on backwards, long hair flying behind as they
charged by, defying broken limbs and any foolish pedestrian who might
happen in their path.

The sun was brilliant today, the air fresh. Brooke wandered into
The Mystery Annex, an old favorite bookstore. One entire side
was devoted to mysteries, many signed by their authors, and one day
a few years ago, she had found—way on a back shelf—a treasure, a
signed first-edition copy of *The Brass Cupcake,* by John D. MacDon-
ald. She had packed it safely away in her boxes in San Francisco, beside
Livvy's things.

Brooke wondered if she would one day pass her own boxes along
to Charly, and if Charly would then have to lug them around—the way
she had been lugging Livvy's stuff all over the globe. No. She would
never foist that kind of burden upon her child.

Just let her be all right.

The palmist smiled as she passed. He was young, blond, and
cute. He wore a gauzy white shirt over jeans with ragged knees, and
below them, battered Nikes. He flashed her a flirty grin. "Read your
palm?"

She shook her head.

"Oh, come on. Have you ever had your palm read?"

She knew that engaging a "mark" in conversation was part of the scam. People would have to slow down, they'd have to stop and think—and then they could be got.

Even so, she stopped before him, feeling a tug. "Never."

"Well, give it a try. You never know."

"I don't believe in palm reading."

"Hey, it's like God . . . it works whether you believe in it or not."

She smiled. "A psychic palmist, teaching religion?"

He grinned. "It's a big universe. There's room for everything."

She sat in the folding metal chair across from him. "Where did you learn to read palms?" In a college dorm, she suspected—just before dropping out.

"From my Gypsy grandmother," he answered, daring her with his eyes to dispute it. "C'mon, it'll be fun."

Bizarre, more likely. But as Creed had said, she needed to take her mind off things.

"How much?"

"Twenty dollars. But for you—ten."

Brooke tried to remember how much money she had brought. Reaching into her back jean pocket, she came out with a five and several ones. "I can give you eight."

He shrugged. "Okay."

Brooke held out her palm. He took it, his hands warm from the sun and slender, the fingers tan and strong.

Tracing the lines with a fingertip, he said, "You are definitely going to meet a tall dark stranger."

Brooke gave an ironic laugh, thinking of Creed. "I already have."

The young man's eyes twinkled. "And you're going to be rich."

A shadow passed over Brooke's face. "I already was."

He looked up into her eyes. "You're tense. Is it the reading—or is something wrong?"

It seemed that the sun had gone behind a cloud. Brooke's mouth tightened. "Just do your rap, okay? Get it over with."

The kid stared at her palm. He sobered. "There's someone in danger," he said softly. "Someone close to you, someone you care about."

Brooke snatched her hand away. "You can't possibly know that! You're making it up!"

Or, no—Creed had put something in the papers. Was there a picture of her? Had he read about Charly?

The reader's eyes fixed on hers, serious now. His blond hair faded to silver as the sun remained dim. The face was etched with more lines than Brooke had at first thought. He was older—older than the college age she had taken him for. His mouth reflected pain.

"You have to find her," he said. "You have to find her *soon.*"

Brooke was halfway to her feet, words of scorn in her throat. They never surfaced. She sank back down.

"Tell me what you see," she said urgently, holding out her palm again.

The man covered her hand and placed it palm down on the table. Closing his eyes briefly, he remained that way, silent for moments. When he opened his eyes again, they were distant, as if the soul behind them traveled in other worlds. His hand remained over hers, the touch becoming light as air.

"I see a doll," he said dreamily, "with blue clothes. Short, stubby fingers holding it. Something orange . . ."

Brooke froze. Her breath nearly stopped. She leaned forward, forgetting that she didn't believe, forgetting the scam. *"What else?"*

"Water . . . and rocks. Black rocks. Wind."

"Do you see my little girl? *Tell me, for God's sake, tell me!"* She didn't realize she had gripped his hand, her nails biting into it, until his eyes focused, meeting hers in pain.

"It's gone," he said. "I'm sorry."

"No! It can't be! Think, dammit! What do you see?"

The young man shook his head, pulling away. Brooke wanted to scream. She had been within *inches* of Charly, she knew it! Almost able to grab her hand—only to have her snatched away. She could feel her daughter disappearing all over again, being pulled down a long, dark tunnel. She felt herself being sucked into that tunnel, lured away from reality, felt herself falling, falling, falling. . . .

. . .

"STAND BACK, EVERYBODY. Give her room."

A man stood beside her, a large man with an enormous stomach. He was holding her against him, and the stomach felt good, it felt solid and supportive. It helped to make the blackness go away. Everything was sideways, the beach, the vendors, the sunglasses . . . *funny how sunglasses look, sideways. Like a flock of alien creatures—or no, it would be a passel. A covey. A crowd . . . ?*

A crowd had gathered to see the woman who had fainted at the palm reader's table. Anything for a thrill. They would go home, now, to Kansas, or New Jersey, or wherever—probably with pictures (that was a camera clicking, wasn't it?)—or maybe even videotape—"See, Martha? That's that lady who fainted, down at that beach, where was it? Rome?"—

"Venice, George, Venice."

Five minutes of fame for one Brooke Hayes. Playing in living rooms all over America. . . .

Her vision cleared. The man with the large stomach was still holding her propped against it. "You all right, lady?"

She nodded, pulling slightly away. "Thank you. I feel so stupid." She straightened.

He had dark, greasy hair, purple sunglasses, and was smoking a cigar. His pants were dusty and brown, his shirt yellow, with stains that looked like mustard. He had several days' growth of beard, and a sweaty face.

He looked, she thought, like an angel.

Thank you for the use of your stomach, she wanted to say. *I love you,* she wanted to say. *I will never forget you, if I live to be a hundred.*

She was losing it. She squared her shoulders and pulled herself together. "I'm okay now."

She saw then that the palm reader was beside her, too. His grin was quick and relieved. "You had us worried," he said.

In his eyes there was nothing. No acknowledgment of what had passed between them—only the friendly college-boy grin. Even the lines in his face seemed to have faded. The sun was out again, shining brightly.

But the words had been spoken. "A doll . . . rocks . . . water . . . wind. Something orange."

Fighting weakness, Brooke struggled to her feet and raced back to the cottage.

"HE WAS A SCAMMER, a con," Creed argued, playing devil's advocate.

Brooke was pacing, agitated. "Say he's got some real ability, though—even a little. What about the rocks, the water, the wind? It sounds like up north. And you believed it in the jeep the other day, when I imagined Charly up there. I know you did, you were excited about it!"

"You're her mother," Creed said. "Mothers sometimes have psychic links with their children—especially when those children are in trouble. The guy at the beach was strictly carny."

Brooke sighed, rubbing her temples with her fingertips. Her head ached from the ponytail. She yanked the rubber band out impatiently, snapping it between her fingers as she strode from one end of the deck to the other. "What about the doll? He saw the doll. Was that in the news release about Charly's disappearance?"

"No. It wasn't. Brooke, I'll admit there are coincidences here. I'll have Gibbs go over and talk to the guy. He's good with the people down there."

"And if it turns out the kid really is psychic? Couldn't we work with him? The police do it all the time."

"A waste of energy, most of the time. And I told you before, we can't go off half-cocked on this. We have to stay focused."

Brooke faced him accusingly. "You're *afraid!* And dammit, Creed, it's holding us back!"

Creed folded his arms, leaning against the railing. "Afraid?"

"I think you're afraid you made mistakes, looking for your son. And now you hold back—rather than do that again."

Creed's expression was dark, his tone so cutting it was nearly lethal. "You don't know anything about that."

"No? Then how come you're always talking about not making mistakes—about losing focus? How come that's such an issue with you?"

"Oh, and I suppose you see yourself as some kind of psychic, now?"

"It doesn't take a mind reader to see that four years is too long to be carrying around all that guilt and anger!"

"You're overstepping your bounds!"

"For God's sake, Creed, look at yourself! You're even a maniac when you drive. I'm lucky not to be splattered all over three-tenths of LA by now!"

Creed stormed from the deck and into the living room—leaving Brooke behind with a look of determination—and resolve—on her face.

IT WAS THE FOURTH DAY, and the phone calls had become a torment. With each one Brooke was like a woman expecting to hear that the war was over but that her husband (son, lover, brother) had died in action. Desperate to escape, she found Creed talking to a volunteer and asked if he knew of an inexpensive workout gym nearby.

"Excellent idea," he said bluntly. "You need to clear your head."

He sent her to Gold's Gym, where he was a member. "I'll call ahead. You won't have to pay."

She hadn't worked out for a while; there hadn't been time in the past two weeks of rehearsals. She warmed up slowly, not even aware, after the first few minutes, of the others in the room . . . the tight young bodies to whom a workout session every day was more important than reading a book.

That was the thing about these young, single women in LA. They didn't read books. How could they talk about anything? (And if they couldn't talk about anything . . . would they forever be single?)

When her gray sweats were damp and her muscles loose, she began with a step machine, then lifting weights. Finally, a bike with more gadgets and screens on it than her television at home. She ignored them all, thinking about books as she pumped.

What was the last book she had read? *As a Man Thinketh,* that morning . . . that last morning, before Charly disappeared.

Her other, most recent books, had been on codependency. She remembered talking to a nun about codependency a few months ago. The nun—Sister Helen—was a friend from the homeless center in San Francisco, where Brooke did volunteer work twice a month.

"I've been trying to work through the dynamics of my marriage to Nathan," Brooke had said, while sorting donated clothes beside Sister Helen. "Do you think it's codependency when you love someone and want to give everything you have—time, love, and energy—to that person—and don't get your own needs met?"

Sister Helen—a strong, world-wise woman in her forties—responded with: "In my opinion, codependency is bullshit. We used to call it love. And if more people gave of themselves without thought of return, it'd be a better world."

She had winked, then, tossing Brooke a man's frayed-in-the-elbow sweater to add to her pile of clothes. "The martyrs did that, you know."

"The martyrs got burnt at the stake," Brooke replied.

They had both laughed, and Sister Helen had taken her to the convent library afterward. "Try this."

The book she pulled off a lemon-polished mahogany shelf was *Opening Our Hearts to Men;* the author Susan Jeffers. "It's not that codependency is bullshit," Sister Helen had said. "It's that it doesn't go far enough . . . doesn't reach to the higher levels. And Brooke, the dilemma was never male-female. It's *always* been about loving human beings. In my opinion, the goal for all of us should be toward a higher love."

A higher love. The essence of the book Sister Helen had laid in her hands, so far as Brooke could see, was that when women stop blaming men and accept full responsibility for whatever happens in their lives, they will own their own power—and thus be better able not only to love, but to love the right man.

"We cannot blame men for walking all over us. We can only notice that we are not moving out of the way." That was one quote from the book. Another that she had memorized was: *"Pointing a finger is a powerless act —the only real power lies in taking control of our reaction to whatever life hands us."*

And thus do "angels" come into our lives, Brooke thought. Helping spirits, helping hands . . . by way of books given seemingly by coincidence. *"When the student is ready, the teacher appears."* Her therapist had told her that. Her therapist had also told her much of the above —but sometimes things need to be said differently, to be heard.

So . . . she was learning. There had been days when she nearly hit a seven on the scale of personal growth—when she could focus on Nathan's good points as a father and a man and forgive him for not having been the husband she, in her youthful fantasies, had imagined he would be.

At other times, especially since she had begun the joint custody suit, she had hit minus zero.

A couple of lithe bodies, male and female, were "communicating" workout-style on the bikes next to her. Their talk was all about which machines were best, which exercises, whether walking was better than running, whether eggs really are all that bad for the heart—

Well, people have to meet somehow. And everyone wants to be in love.

Brooke wondered if love was like exercise. Amazing, with exercise, how the muscles come back. They can feel slack and unused—but give them a bit of a push, and they come roaring into life again.

With a bit of a push, would her own capacity for love come back —for anyone besides Charly, that is? Her emotional muscles had been dormant for a long time, too.

A glance at the clock on the wall told her an hour had passed. She had to get back. What if they had heard something about Charly?

Chapter 25

"GET ME DUNWALT!" Andy Laskov shouted into the phone. "And Mary, don't let him give you any shit. I want him on my territory—and I want him within the hour. Whatever that takes, get him here!"

Ordering around a captain of police was only one of the perks of a DA's job. Another was getting somebody you didn't like by the balls— and squeezing until it hurts.

The balls to be squeezed today were John Creed's.

"And don't you give me any lip," Laskov growled in the direction of his mammoth fish tank. The water was murky today, the sides green from so much algae he could hardly see in. He'd have to clean it soon— carry buckets of water to the sink, drag that damned garden hose from the men's room down the hall, wash all the shit out of the gravel . . .

"Goddamn fish. More trouble than you're worth."

Big Joe twitched his tail and glided silently to the bottom of the tank—where all was dark and safe.

"I'VE GOT HIM," Laskov announced when an irate Captain Dunwalt stood before him. "I've got John Creed."

"What do you mean, you've 'got' Creed?"

"I mean, I know what he did with his son, and I know how he did it. It's time to pull him in."

The captain ran a finger under his white shirt collar. "Listen, Andy, I know how much you want Creed's ass. But this is crazy. It's been five years since all that happened, and we've never turned anything up—"

The DA lunged to his feet and stomped to the window, rubbing with the side of one fist at imaginary dirt on the pane.

"Besides," the captain continued, "I need him now on the Hayes case—"

"Creed is the last person to be on that case!"

"Because he's on the mother's side? Hell, Andy, I've known Nathan myself, for years. But this doesn't look good. Hayes has skipped, we haven't been able to find him—and the child still hasn't shown up." Dunwalt rose. His back was straight and stiff. "It's beginning to look like a classic case of parental kidnapping, and if Creed can help with that, I intend to use him."

"You aren't listening to me," Laskov said angrily. He faced the captain, pointing a thick finger. "Creed murdered his own son! Getting him on that takes priority here."

Dunwalt shook his head. "I thought you were wrong back then about Creed, and I still think so. If Creed had hurt his own son, we'd have known it at the time. We had good men on that case."

"You had *Gibbs* on that case, goddammit! And he's turned out to be Creed's best buddy. He could have covered up anything he found out."

The captain bristled, rising. "Why don't you just tell me what you've got on Creed? If it holds up, of course we'll pull him in."

"You'll pull him in regardless, if I tell you to."

"Not if I think you've got a personal score to settle and there's no real evidence. Dammit, Andy, I'll go over your head, if I have to."

Andrew Laskov leaned his meaty palms on the desk. His expression was that of a pit bull, prepared for attack.

"I can prove culpability in your department, if you force me to. Bad cops—overlooking evidence five years ago that could have put another bad cop in jail for the murder of his son."

The captain was silent. His eyes narrowed, but his shoulders drooped slightly.

Laskov had him—he knew it. He beamed, sitting at his desk again.

"You're gonna love this. The way Creed did it, I mean. The perfect crime . . . except for one thing."

"The district attorney is issuing a warrant for John Creed's arrest," Dunwalt told Lieutenant Martin de Porres. He leaned against a file cabinet, rubbing his chin thoughtfully.

De Porres gave the Captain a slow, calculating look.

"For the murder of his son," Dunwalt said. "Five years ago."

"I see." De Porres propped a shiny black shoe onto his desk.

"We'll have to send someone to Creed's house in Venice," Dunwalt said without expression. "Pick him up."

"Uh-huh."

"The thing is, it's just too damned bad. If anyone could have helped with the Hayes case, it was Creed."

"That's certainly true, Captain."

"And it comes at a bad time. The department can't afford to lose another of these kidnapping cases—especially not one with such high visibility."

"Right."

"Well . . ." Dunwalt sighed. "I suppose that's life." He glanced at De Porres.

"Yeah . . . life."

"So . . . I guess we'd better do what we have to do."

"What we have to do," De Porres nodded blandly. "Right, Captain."

Dunwalt gave De Porres a strained smile, and left.

"Get Gibbs on the phone," De Porres said urgently. "He may be at his place, or Creed's place in Venice, or maybe in his car. Wherever he is, get him for me fast. And hold any other calls."

De Porres set his phone down gently and sat toying with Old Billy. One dark index finger scratched at a tiny crumb of doughnut that had crusted on the nightstick. He wet the tip of the finger with his tongue and cleaned the sugary substance away. Smiling grimly, he inspected the portion of his face that was reflected in the polished ebony wood.

The phone rang. He snatched it up and spoke quietly. "Gibby?"

"Hey, Marty."

"Shit's comin' down."

"Tell me."

"Not here. Where are you?"

"Pico, headin' east. Just crossed Centinela."

De Porres glanced at his watch. "Fifteen minutes. Meet me in Armstrong's parking lot."

"Check."

De Porres hung up. For the first time in years, he didn't replace Old Billy on the wall. Instead, he picked up his gray suit coat with the silk threads—the one he'd gotten seven years ago at that damned expensive clothier on Wilshire—and shrugged into it. Then, with Old Billy over his shoulder like a shotgun, de Porres glided softly past the outer desks, down the elevator, and across the police parking lot to his car. He slid behind the wheel of his three-year-old gray Hyundai and settled Old Billy beside him on the passenger seat.

"Hang tight, Bill," he said with a grin. "We're back in business again."

Chapter 26

CHARLY HUDDLED IN A CORNER of the bedroom on the Northern California coast. She sucked her thumb. Her blond hair, pulled into an ineffective ponytail, clung to the sides of her face in damp strings. Her cheeks were wet with tears.

She didn't mean not to be brave. Most of the time, in fact, she felt okay—like she could handle just about anything. But then she'd start to think, and it was like somebody hitting her in the stomach, she missed her mother so much.

Her father too, of course.

She didn't understand why no one came to save her. In the fairy tales her mother had read to her years ago, there was always a prince on a white horse. The princess would hang her long blond hair out the window, or something, and he'd climb up it and save her.

Fat chance, she thought, of any prince climbing over those rocks down there on any white horse. And fat chance of her hanging out a rope of hair.

Charly stirred and opened her eyes. The first thing she saw was the deer. That was why she liked this corner. It reminded her of home. The deer, and the trees with gold leaves . . . almost like the painting at home . . .

Not a painting, exactly, her mother had said. A mural. That's what you call something when it's painted on a wall.

She sat up and looked around. Her lunch tray was still on the dresser, still untouched. He'd be mad when he came back. But it didn't help, hiding here in the corner. She stuck her chin up—remembering that her mother did that when she was trying to be brave—and got to her feet. Her left leg was asleep. She must *have been here in the corner a long time. How long had it been since he had brought the tray? And why hadn't he come back yet?*

Usually he came sooner. And if she hadn't eaten, he'd do something awful . . . like that time when he had cut off the doll's hand. She had thought—had thought—

Another time he had cut off the doll's head. Charly had hidden the doll way under the bed, finally, hoping he wouldn't ever find it again. But he had.

"I'm on to your tricks," he had said—with that funny smile, like he was really trying to be kind. "You can't fool me, you know." Then he'd wag his finger, with those funny orange stains.

Classical music rose through the floor, seeming to swell the boards beneath her feet. Charly hated that music now, and once she got out of here, she never wanted to hear it again. Limping to the bed, she covered her ears with her hands.

She must have fallen asleep. In her sleep she had a dream . . . a dream in which she heard her father's voice. At first just hearing it made her feel warm. Charly hugged herself and smiled. She was safe now. Her father was here.

"Daddy!" she cried in the next scene, running through a field of waving orange flowers toward the distant figure. "You came!"

The figure grew closer . . . it was tall, like her father, with blond hair sprinkled with gray . . . and the closer it got, the happier Charly felt. Her father had come! She ran and ran, her legs pumping as hard as her heart, her face breaking into a big wide grin, she was so relieved, and then . . . and then . . .

The figure stooped down and stared right into her face. It was angry. And it wasn't her father at all. It was the man.

"You're going to be punished, Charly," he said.

"But it wasn't my fault! I didn't do anything!"

The figure frowned with disapproval. Charly's eyes flew open. Her heart pounded. She bolted upright, looking wildly around. No more field, no more flowers, no more Daddy. . . .

It was then that she heard it—coming from somewhere on the other side of the bedroom door. Her father's voice. The music had stopped, and she heard it clearly—her father's voice.

But that's crazy!

She couldn't sort it out.

"I'll write down where I'm staying," her father said in that firm, lawyer-

like tone that sometimes made her mother so mad. "Call me there in the morning."

The man answered something that Charly couldn't hear.

"Don't tell her I've been here," her father said.

"Daddy!" Charly screamed it, her heart leaping into her throat.

Silence.

She lunged from the bed and ran to the door, pounding with all her might. "Daddy! Daddy! I'm here, I'm in here!"

She listened for the running footsteps that would tell her that her father was coming to save her.

Nothing.

"Daddy! Daddy, help me! I'm upstairs in the bedroom!" Charly pounded until her knuckles were raw. She yanked and twisted the doorknob and screamed until her voice was no more than a croak. When no answer came, there were long moments of disbelief, then anger, then pain. "Can't you hear me?" she whispered.

It was some time after dark when she woke by the bedroom door—her fingers crusted with dry blood. Her whole body felt bruised; her throat ached as if there were knives in it.

She couldn't have heard what she thought she had heard. Could she?

No. She had to be wrong. If that had been her father's voice, if he had been right here, in this house, so close by—he would have saved her.

Wouldn't he?

Charly squeezed her eyes shut and doubled over, sobbing. A thumb found its way to her mouth again.

Chapter 27

THE APHRODITE TALENT AGENCY was near Santa Monica and La Cienega, in Beverly Hills. It was in a high-rise, high-rent building of bronze and glass. On the same floor were a major insurance company, a small advertising agency, three lawyers, and two architects.

Creed and Brooke stepped out of the elevator and walked down a long hallway, checking numbers on the doors. Brooke smoothed the white cotton blouse she had picked up in Venice to wear with her jeans.

"There's something weird about Aphrodite," Gibbs had said after a visit to the place. "If all the kids in those pictures you told me about are clients of Aphrodite, why aren't there people in the waiting room? Phones ringing? You know how hectic those agency offices are. And get this—the guy who heads it up, at least on paper? His name is 'Arnie Angel.'"

They approached a desultory receptionist reading a copy of *Variety* in an empty room, by a silent phone. Creed moved in with an air of authority, flashing his ID before the bosomy, red-lipped young woman. "Police," he said. "We'd like to talk to Mr. Angel."

"Oh!" The receptionist looked from him to Brooke. Her mouth parted and formed an O like a cherry Life Saver. "I'm sorry. He's not, like, here." Pansy blue eyes widened.

"When will he be in?"

"I'm sure I don't know! I mean, like, he's never here. Well, at least, hardly ever. Mr. Angel works at home, you know, and I'm just here, like, to answer phones." The receptionist rolled the *Variety* between her hands, twisting it. She looked from Creed to Brooke. "I don't think—"

"I'm counting on it," Creed muttered impatiently.

"What?"

Brooke interrupted. Leave this to Mr. Personality, and they'd never get anywhere. "I'm Brooke," she said, sticking out a friendly hand.

"Debbie," the young woman offered. She stared at Brooke's hand, took it with some hesitation, and shook one finger delicately.

"There's a photographer who does work for you sometimes," Creed said, barreling on. "We want—"

"Roger Dorn," Brooke interrupted softly, taking back the reins. "He has a studio in San Francisco."

"Are you a policewoman?" Debbie smiled widely. "I've always wanted to join the police." Her hand went to straighten her mane of blond hair. It was then that Brooke realized the woman bore an amazing resemblance to Angie Dickinson. She had probably grown up watching *Policewoman* in syndication, and all her friends in high school had told her she was a dead ringer for Angie and should go to Hollywood.

Everybody in this damned town was a frustrated actor or scriptwriter.

Well, she could use that to her advantage. "Ahm a deputy," she answered in a western variation of the soft drawl she had worked so hard to overcome since her early Shakespearean days. She gave the receptionist her most open, innocent, Molly Brown smile—the one that had won over most of Molly Brown's enemies. "If y'all could help us out with this, we'd suah as heck appreciate it."

"Of *course*. *Anything*. Just ask me anything at all."

Brooke glanced briefly at Creed. He rolled his eyes.

"The thing is"—her tone was confidential—"this photographah—Rogah Dowern—may be involved in a terrible fraud. There are actually people who paid for sittings and nevah even got their finished photos!"

Debbie nodded eagerly. "I know just what you mean! That happened to me. You wouldn't believe what some of these photographers do."

"Oh, ah'd believe it," Brooke said sympathetically. Inwardly she sighed with relief. It had been a good bet that Debbie—hopeful actress—would have had a bad experience with some screw-up photographer or other. Only the best photographers (and they were expensive) had their business trip together. In that way, they weren't unlike actors, musicians, and writers.

"Y'all understand, then, Debbie, why we'd lahk t'get this horrible man. And it's important he doesn't find out we're askin' questions until we've got the evidence."

"Oh, sure—listen, no problem." Debbie leaned forward eagerly. "What can ah do?"

"We'd like to look at your files on Rogah Dowern."

"Well, ah don't usually go in the files," Debbie said. "They're in Mr. Angel's office"—she nodded toward the door behind her—"and ah don't know much about them."

Creed, standing off to the side with arms folded, could no longer stifle a sound of irritation. But Brooke's tone was reassuring—as if she were talking to a child. "All ya'd have to do is lead us to them, Debbie. We'll do the rest." She grinned conspiratorially.

The receptionist smiled. She gave Brooke a wink, straightened her shoulders, then fluffed her hair. Reaching into the center drawer of her desk, she pulled out a key. "Y'all come along, lahk, with me."

They followed her miniskirted legs—anorexic stilts above four-inch heels—into Mr. Angel's office.

"I CAN'T BELIEVE she actually took on your accent," Creed groaned.

"Actors are all chameleons. If I hang around long enough, I might even become you."

He grimaced. "One of me is enough, don't you think?"

"You said it, pal, not me."

And five minutes later: "Mr. Angel is either a poor businessman, or very clever."

"Pretty skimpy files," Brooke agreed. "Not much here to go on."

They needed names and addresses of Aphrodite clients whose photos Dorn had taken—something that would show who had recommended him to them, or vice versa. They also needed to know if he worked for any other agencies besides Aphrodite, and how often he came down to LA to do that sort of thing. There was nothing in the Aphrodite files to give them that.

"Dorn's name, address, and telephone number in San Francisco— which we already know. His background and credentials—which are all old stuff from twenty years ago. A portfolio of photos of old-time Hollywood stars. Damn!" Creed slammed a file drawer.

"Too bad we don't have the names of those kids whose photos you saw in Dorn's studio. We could look up their files."

"Gibby's got that PI up there, following Dorn. We'll see if he can get into Dorn's studio somehow and get them."

"Creed . . ." Brooke hesitated.

"What?"

"Why do I feel, suddenly, like we're chasing down a dead end here?"

"You're discouraged. That's normal for this phase—"

"This *phase?*" She gave him a dark look. She could do without John Creed's detachment right about now.

He was saved from responding when the office door burst open. They both jumped, dropping files, as Gibbs appeared—with Debbie on his heels.

"I don't know who he is!" she cried. "He just pushed right by me!"

"Gibby? What's wrong?"

"Everything," Gibbs snapped. He crossed to a window and cautiously peered through Levolor blinds. "Look down there."

Creed stood beside him, seeing at first only the parking lot below. Then the three Beverly Hills patrol cars. "What the hell?"

"They're after you."

"What's going on?"

"Laskov ordered Dunwalt to issue a warrant for your arrest. Four cops came to the beach house. Nobody I know all that well. One of the new volunteers, thinking they were just looking for you about the Hayes case, tried to be helpful. Told them you were down here."

Brooke, watching, felt the anger rise in Creed like a monster tide.

"This is about Jason," Creed said. It wasn't a question.

"Yeah."

"So it's happening at last."

"You should know that Marty alerted me about this. He said Dunwalt wanted him to."

"Laskov pushed on him?"

Gibbs nodded. "We've got to get you out of here, Keep. Once the DA's got you behind bars, you won't be getting out."

Brooke remembered the conversation she and Creed had had earlier about his son, and about the old suspicions. "I don't understand," she said anxiously. "Why now?"

"Good question." Creed's voice was tight.

"Listen, I hate to panic anybody," Gibbs said, "but for shit's sake, we've got to get you out of here. I've got one nondescript civilian auto parked down the alley that winds behind this building. Let's *move*."

They moved.

In their dust they left a bewildered Debbie, surveying the open file folders from the vantage point of four-inch stiletto heels.

"Like, they couldn't at least have cleaned up?" she whined.

Chapter 28

THE SUMMER-BROWN HILLS of Santa Maria stretched out on either side of California State Highway 101. Creed cranked up the air-conditioning. He needed to cool off; he needed to think.

Brooke was on her way with Gibbs to the Valley, to stay with a friend of his. Creed didn't want her being picked up for questioning about his whereabouts. Not that there was much she could tell them; she didn't know where he was heading. But they could hold her for twenty-four hours without charges, if they wanted to get sticky about it —make her admit to knowledge of his run. That would make her an accomplice. They could lock her up.

And he wanted Brooke free to help find Charly.

That was the thing he had worked out long ago, when he first got into this work. The kids came first. There were no other priorities, no other rules. You did what you had to do—but if it killed you, you found the kids. And you found them in time.

Goddamn Andy Laskov! What game was he playing now? A variation of "Get Creed off Nathan Hayes' Back?" Or did he really think he'd found out something about Jason's disappearance? Something bad enough to put Creed behind bars?

It had to be something like that. Even Laskov wouldn't issue a warrant for a false arrest. Not in this political year.

Creed's hands tightened on the wheel of the tan Ford Escort Gibbs had borrowed from the same girlfriend who was putting up Brooke. On his head was an LA Dodgers cap. Sunglasses covered his eyes. His long black hair had been pulled back with a rubber band, then shoved up into the cap. He wore a Dodgers workout shirt, borrowed from Gibbs. A glimpse in the rearview mirror told him that he looked—perhaps— like somebody's dad, on his way to a Little League game.

Somebody's dad. Oh, God. What am I going to do? A cry of agony escaped his lips. *If I'd been a better dad . . . better man . . . better husband. It was all my fault!* He pounded the wheel with one fist. Tears formed in his eyes, and he blinked them angrily away.

He had been absent from his marriage at the most critical time. Karen's fear was running high that year—even before Jason disappeared. Three cops had been killed in a shoot-out during a drug arrest, one of them Creed's former partner from the early days. Creed and Karen had attended the formal police department funeral—everyone in dress uniform, banding together to show grief and support of the surviving family. Support for each other, as well: *Don't worry, buddy . . . we'll stand by your family, too, if things go bad for you.*

At home, afterward, Karen had been strangely removed. She had gone to their room and crawled under the covers, fully clothed, refusing to talk. Thinking that by giving her space he was doing her a favor, Creed had left Jason next door with a neighbor who babysat him now and then, and gone in to work. That was his therapy—his antidote to having buried a former partner. Work.

When Karen was still not herself a week later, he began to worry. Too late, he knew now. They should have confronted the issue from the first. Cops' wives always live with fear—but he had closed his eyes to the fact that Karen was running away from hers. It was easier to ignore his own fears, if he didn't acknowledge hers.

The doctors in Santa Maria had helped him to understand all this. But that was long after Karen had escaped into a world where the people you love don't die, and don't disappear.

From one doctor, Liz Storey—a woman with frizzy red hair, a shiny nose, and a soul that seemed to touch his, somehow softening the blow: "Did you know that Karen's older brother ran away when he was fourteen? And that she never saw him again? That was only two years before her father died. Karen's mother was in psychiatric treatment after that for several years, and Karen took over the role of nurturing parent. She was only twelve at the time."

Creed shook his head, bewildered. "I didn't know."

"She never told you?"

"I knew her brother ran away, of course—but the rest? I don't think so." In truth, he wasn't sure. Could it be that he just hadn't heard?

You're so oblivious, sometimes, Karen would often say.

He had denied that, of course.

The doctor was sympathetic. "Information like this is often imparted in the early weeks of a relationship—but at some level we choose not to listen. Troubled pasts are red flags, a sign that there may be serious problems ahead. And when we love, we don't want red flags." She smiled, giving a small shrug. "We want green lights."

"Almost everyone has some kind of trouble in their past, though." Creed was thinking of himself.

"True. But when trouble is acknowledged before you get too deep into the relationship, there are options. You can decide whether to work through the challenges of a life together, or move on to someone with a healthier past and present."

"I don't see how loving Karen, or not loving her, could have been an option."

"Love never is. It's what we do with it that matters."

"You mean we can decide to turn it off—by force of will?"

"Never by force. It's more a letting go—a transcending. You put it on a higher plane, where both partners are set free."

The doctor's words struck a chord with Creed, though it took a while to fully understand their meaning. In recent times he had begun to let go. He would always love Karen—but he had had to move that love to a more distant place in his heart. He didn't yet know about the "transcending" part. He guessed, however, that he was still far from that —if only because there was still pain.

It was four-ten by the Escort's clock. Late afternoon. He'd be at the hospital, in the hills north of Santa Maria, in twenty minutes or so. He didn't know what he felt. But decisions had to be made now—and it wouldn't be easy.

Creed sighed, rolling his shoulders to release tension. *When was anything ever easy?*

"As I TOLD YOU in my last letter," Dr. Storey said, "she hasn't been speaking at all, lately. She seems to hear, and at least some of the time, understand. She follows simple directions. She cooperates in her bathing and feeding. But don't be fooled by that. Karen's emotions are so far buried, and have been for so long, they may never surface again. It's the world's oldest instinct—survival. Karen is protecting herself."

"Don't misunderstand," Creed said hesitantly. "But other people's children disappear. I work with them all the time. It's a terrible time for everyone, and they all have problems recovering. But few do what Karen has done. Why her?"

Liz Storey rounded her desk, standing before him with her hands in her white coat pocket. Beneath the coat she wore a tailored white blouse and dark green pants. When she spoke with patients, Creed knew, she always removed the white coat. "I want them to see me as a friend," she had said during the first session they had had together with Karen, four years ago. "Too many people see doctors as God, and they give their power over to us. My kind of counseling teaches people to believe in themselves. This is the only way to recovery."

"We've talked about your wife's background before," she said now. "There were a lot of losses, and too much early responsibility. That could account for what's happened to her now. We can't know for certain, of course, since we've never really been able to communicate with Karen on a therapeutic level."

"It's just—" Creed shook his head, glancing away.

"Go on," the doctor said softly.

"If there were something—something I could tell you that might explain why Karen withdrew like that— But it might hurt her, if anyone knew—"

He looked at the doctor, asking the favor silently.

"Almost anything you might tell me would be confidential," Liz Storey said.

Creed's smile was grim, acknowledging the way she had covered

her legal ass with the right wording. *Almost anything.* Well, he had often
done the same thing himself in police work. It was standard procedure.

"Why don't we take a walk?" the doctor said gently. "We'll follow
the path to the atrium on the first floor. One of the aides noticed that
your wife's body language is more relaxed when she's around trees and
flowers, so we've been bringing her down there for meals."

"Karen always did love gardens," he said as they walked through
the wide hall to the front door. The hall was paneled in white halfway
up—with wallpaper above that in a soft blue print. He had chosen this
hospital for Karen partly because of its hominess. The cost was higher
than some; he'd had to cut a lot of corners financially to keep Karen
here. But he couldn't bear to think of leaving her in some place that
looked like an institution.

"She was planting a garden," he added, "just before Jason disappeared. An English garden, with roses . . . and those blue flowers that
grow on tall stalks. . . ."

His words trailed off as he remembered finding Karen there one
dreadful, painful day—kneeling in oversized cotton print pants. She had
called to him, "John? Is that you? I'm out here!" Looking up, rubbing
a smudge of dirt from her face, her shoulders bare and tan over a
halter top . . . long brown hair glinting gold, in the late afternoon
sun . . .

He had loved his wife, in that moment, more than life. More than
breath. His love was a terrible physical ache, made worse by the bitter
knowledge he had carried home with him that day.

Now that the time had come to talk to Dr. Storey about it, he
didn't know where to begin.

"Start anywhere," she said when he expressed the thought aloud.
"We can always backtrack if we have to." Her smile relaxed him, as it
was intended to. "Did you know that one of the major causes of misunderstanding between men and women is the way they converse? Men
are by nature linear. It drives them crazy the way we women are all over
the map when we talk. It confuses them."

"I guess you're right," Creed said. "I never thought of it that
way."

They took a path through a grassy lawn. "Women who are known as 'masculine' thinkers are more linear in their conversation too," the doctor said. "But enough chitchat, Mr. Creed. What's going on?"

He sighed. "Nothing, anymore. But something was going on at the time Jason disappeared, something you don't know about. If knowing could help Karen—"

God, what a hypocrite he'd become. He was also thinking of himself; he had to be honest about that. If Andy Laskov was on his back again, he had to settle it once and for all. To do less would be to tie his own hands professionally—to keep him from doing his work.

Unable to breathe naturally, his chest tight, Creed sighed again. "There was a man . . . ," he began.

HIS EYES MET KAREN'S—hers a vacant blue, his gray, with tears in the corners that he tried to hide. As if they were merely an itch, he scratched lightly with a fingernail, easing them away. He had been with Karen for nearly half an hour.

"Just keep holding the spoon to her mouth until she accepts it," the aide had said, in an aside. "It may take a while."

Nearly ten minutes for her to take the first spoonful of applesauce. It broke his heart to see her this way. He gave up on the dinner and took both her hands in his.

"Karen . . . Karen, do you know I'm here at all? Can you hear me? I need to talk to you."

He imagined there was anger, just a flicker—but then it was gone. Funny how the mind plays tricks. And if there was anger, who did his wife think he was? Her husband—or someone else?

"I told Dr. Storey," he said quietly, "about Michael." Creed watched her carefully for some sign of emotion. Nothing.

"I've never told anyone else. Gibby's the only one who knows. It was Gibby who told me."

Karen raised a hand to her hair . . . cut short, now, for easier care. With no expression whatsoever, she smoothed it.

"Honey, I know about that day. . . . I know how Jason disappeared."

He was still holding her hands, and there wasn't a sign that she had heard. No sudden jerk, not even the tiniest spasm. Both slender white hands lay in his, so light that if they did move, he might expect them to disappear like tiny clouds.

"I have to tell them now, Karen. The DA wants to lock me up. He's saying I was responsible for Jason . . . and if I let him lock me up, I won't be able to help find kids anymore."

He had told her, a long time ago, about the work he was doing now. He didn't know if she'd understood or even cared. "Just talk to her," Dr. Storey had said, "the way you would to someone in a coma. We have no idea how much gets through. Tell her everyday things, things that could bring her back to reality."

Reality.

"I promise I'll protect you, Karen. It'll be okay." He wasn't sure about that . . . but oh, God, he hoped it would be okay.

He leaned forward and kissed her gently on the cheek.

That quickly, anger surged through him. It shouldn't have been this way! They had had everything in those early years . . . *everything.* With his lips still on Karen's cheek, he squeezed his eyes closed and smelled her natural fragrance. What was it, back then? Something like vanilla, he remembered. Her skin had smelled like vanilla.

Now it smelled of hospital soap. "My poor baby," he whispered.

Creed stood. Bending over, he hugged his wife and promised to come back soon.

It was a promise, he knew, that he might not be able to keep.

Chapter 29

"THINGS'RE HEATIN' UP, Keep. You need to get back here."

"I'm on my way, Gibby. Just called to let you know. What's up?"

He was standing at a phone booth outside a gas station, still fifty miles north of LA. The temperature was over ninety degrees, and Creed —after identifying himself as an informant over police lines—had waited several minutes for a return call from a safe phone. He was drenched beneath the ball cap and the Dodgers warm-up jacket. He shrugged the jacket off, thinking he must look more suspicious with it, than without.

"Our guy in San Francisco came through on Roger Dorn," Gibbs said. "He called to tell me Dorn was on his way here on a United flight, and I picked up his tail at LAX. Keep? You know that kiddie porn ring we been tryin' to break up, only we can't get the evidence? The one we think steals kids and uses them not just for porn, but every sick way there is?"

"Holy shit. Roger Dorn's involved in that?"

"Well, he's up at that old mansion in Pacific Palisades."

"But Dunwalt already sent men to check that out. It's the first place—"

"The beat cops checked it out, Keep. And we're talkin' the Palisades, here—remember?"

With a sinking heart, Creed remembered. Pacific Palisades was where all the cops near retirement wanted to be. There was so little going on, they could spend their lunch hours swimming on the beach, having lunch at Gladstone's, reading newspapers—

And all too often they got rusty that way. "Goddamn! Why didn't Dunwalt send detectives?"

"Who knows? Maybe it was some internal screwup. Anyway, I just talked to a delivery guy from the local liquor store who says he's seen a blond-haired girl up there. He's not good on ages, but she could be nine, ten. He saw her at an upstairs window yesterday morning."

Creed closed his eyes and leaned back against the booth. It was coming together fast. But it wasn't good news. They had to move.

"Listen, you think we can count on Marty to help?"

"De Porres? Hell, man, he's been crazy for action since they found that offbeat ticker and stuck him in that office. Shoulda seen him when he told me they were after you—never saw a cop with a glow like that."

Privately Creed thought Marty de Porres had some agenda besides boredom going on. But he wasn't about to argue with it. Angels came in strange disguise.

"Okay, listen, Gibby. Call Marty, will you, so I can get back on the road? Set up a meet with him right away, something real private. I think this is what we'll do . . ."

When he climbed back into the Ford Escort a few minutes later, it was with Gibby's response ringing in his ears:

"I love it! It's beautiful!" Then, with a blend of trepidation and excitement: "You know, we could all lose our careers over this one."

Gibby and de Porres could lose their careers, Creed thought. As for himself, he no longer had one. The thing he stood to lose, if tonight went sour, was a child.

"WHERE THE HELL HAVE YOU BEEN?"

Brooke was livid. She hated being cooped up, hated not knowing what was going on. The house in Van Nuys—the fuckin' Valley, for God's sake—was stifling, the heat unbearable. And how far away from the action could they have stuck her? It felt like a prison, a prison with iron bars keeping her from any hope of finding Charly.

"I had to go to Santa Maria."

"Santa Maria? All the way up there? Why? Did you find something out about Charly? Was it a lead?" If that was it, all was forgiven.

"No," Creed said. "I had to see my wife."

Brooke was stunned. "Your wife? You told me you hadn't seen her in months, and you choose this moment, with all that's going on, to pay a sick call?"

"You don't understand—"

"No, dammit, I don't! And I'm beginning to think I need to work on this myself—alone." That was all she'd been thinking about, in fact, for the past several hours—since Gibbs had stuck her here like some kind of goddamned house plant that only needs to be watered now and then. Gibby's friend, a young woman named Anne with a seventies look—faded blue jeans, a shirt with fringe, and long straight hair parted in the middle—had been down in her pottery studio at the back of the lot most of the time. Once she had driven off, then come back with a McDonald's bag full of Big Macs and french fries.

Anne was fine—she was kind and didn't ask questions, but then, she didn't stick around very long either. There hadn't been much of a chance to pry loose information. To the one question Brooke had asked —Do you know where Gibbs went?—the woman had professed ignorance.

"Look, I didn't come here to get into this," Creed said now. "Things are coming together. We may know where Charly is."

Brooke's anger fled. Her knees went weak. She sank onto the worn brown velour sofa and stared. "Thank God."

"We aren't sure," Creed warned, "so don't get your hopes too high. We'll know before the night's over."

He told her about the mansion in Pacific Palisades, and the blond child who had been seen at the window the day before.

"Listen, Creed, you are not going to leave me out of this. I am not going to sit here like some goddamned passive, helpless, little girl, while the big men go out and save the world! Either I go with you tonight— or I go there now, alone, and take care of things myself. I don't intend to sit in this goddamned prison anymore."

Creed sighed. This was the worst parent he had ever had to work with. She was bullheaded and hostile—trouble from the word go. If she didn't mess things up before this was over, it'd be a miracle.

Chapter 30

BELOW THE HILL where they waited, cars threaded by on Pacific Coast Highway, most heading home from the city to Malibu. The hour was late—after nine, and dark—but the commuter hours seemed to stretch out longer and longer with every year. Beyond the chain of headlights lay the Pacific Ocean, dark and silent. There was no moon.

Creed and Brooke sat in the jeep, parked slightly downhill from the huge thirties'-era mansion that had been under investigation by the LAPD for the past three months. The original tip, back then, had come from a "comber"—a twenty-five-year-old whose job it had been to approach street kids and offer them a place to stay. After the tip a brace of detectives was sent to investigate the mansion. But someone had alerted Harold Screer, the mansion's owner and purported head of the operation, and when the detectives arrived, there was nothing to see but an elderly houseman and well-furnished but otherwise empty rooms. It had taken a full afternoon to check out all those rooms; there were thirty-two in the main house, with three cellars below and an attic above full of cubbyholes.

After the detectives' visit, Creed remembered, all activity had ceased. They had kept the informant in place, since he had access to the mansion on a day-by-day basis. He was also motivated. One kid, a twelve-year-old boy he'd pulled in from the streets, had died from injuries sustained during a beating when he had refused to "cooperate." Billy—the informant—didn't exactly get religion. He did get scared.

"Things are weird out there," he had said. "I used to think it was a business, that's all." He had flushed at the investigating detective's sarcastic look. "Hey, I don't care what you think. I just want out. And I'll do anything you want, but you gotta protect me. They'll kill me if they find out I talked."

The mansion had been operating for nearly a year, he had told them. Harold Screer, a nonpracticing lawyer in his midforties, had come from a similar operation on Long Island to establish his new headquarters here on the West Coast.

"It's a nationwide ring," Billy said. "They've got people all over who kidnap children for bucks, and then somebody drives them out here. Some of us just pick up runaways off the streets. We tell them we can get them into homes, get them some food. These kids are pretty desperate after they're on the streets awhile. They think Screer, and guys like him, are their friends. At least, they think that at first."

"They think *you're* their friend, too, don't they Billy?" one of the detectives had said. Creed was in on the talk, and from the way Tom Halley had flexed his fists, Creed thought he was going to beat the informant up. Tom Halley—from day shift. A good man, with a wife and four kids.

There were billions of dollars to be made in child pornography, Creed knew—but porno was only the tip of the iceberg. In this case the Pacific Palisades mansion was frequented by local and visiting pedophiles and operated in much the same way as a whorehouse. The difference was that the "hosts" and "hostesses" were children—both male and female—and by the time they knew what was happening, what was expected of them from their "benefactor," there was no way out.

"If they get caught trying to run," Billy had said, picking nervously at a zit on his chin, "you just never see them again. I don't know what happens to them." Another greasy pimple, this one on his left cheek, claimed attention. The kid was pale and skinny; he had track marks on his arms.

"How many?" Creed had interrupted, trying for control of his voice. "How many have disappeared?"

"Shit, man, I don't know . . . three, four, in the past few months. Maybe more."

Organizations like Children of the Night, Creed knew, tried to get kids off the streets—largely to prevent this sort of thing from happening. But there was only so much you could do. Many kids had run from abusive homes; they were afraid of getting into the "system," afraid they'd be sent home only to be abused again. Anyone who came along and offered a roof and a meal without any apparent strings became an instant friend.

It wasn't that long, Creed thought, since children had been chattel in this country, put to work in mines at the age of seven, treated like beasts of burden. Society hadn't improved all that much, from what he could see.

Brooke, who was visibly strung tighter than a piano wire, interrupted his thoughts. "Where are they, anyway? I can't stand sitting here like this, knowing Charly might be up there."

Creed checked his watch with a penlight he pulled from the dash. "They'll be along any minute. In fact—" He thought he had seen movement behind them in the rearview mirror. Twisting to look back, he confirmed it.

Brooke turned, too, but only a glint on metal—reflected light from the city-lit sky—told her a car was indeed back there. It had crept up silently, without headlights. A few seconds later, Gibbs was at Creed's open window.

"De Porres with you?" Creed asked.

"Uh-huh. And guess who else?"

"Tom Halley."

"Shit! You getting psychic, or what?"

Creed didn't know about that. He did know that the minute he'd started thinking about Halley, he had known Tom would show up. It was Tom's original bust—and Gibby would have remembered that. He would also have remembered how personally determined Tom Halley was to shut down this operation.

"You sure there haven't been any leaks this time?"

"None I could find. And Billy says they're expectin' out-of-town company up there. Word is, there's fresh virgin meat to be had tonight."

Brooke drew in a harsh breath.

"Sorry. But we're not letting that happen, okay?"

"Any other kids up there?" Creed asked.

Gibbs shook his head. "Billy says this is the first since they pulled back after our raid three months ago. They're starting out slow and easy . . . cutting down on the number of kids, but charging more."

"Well, let's get on with it," Creed said, easing out of the jeep. "Brooke?"

He sensed her look of uncertainty. "I thought you said I could come, but I couldn't come in."

"I've changed my mind. If Charly is there, she'll need you."

In truth—now that he'd thought of it—he didn't trust her to stay behind. Better to have her nearby, where he could watch her. "Just stay out of the way," he said, "until we see what's what. And don't ask any questions."

Stepping out, she gave him her best Molly Brown smile across the tattered canvas top of the jeep—the shaky one, the one that said she was trying hard to be brave. He was coming to recognize it.

"Right, Chief," she said.

DE PORRES STOOD TO THE SIDE, gun in hand. Halley banged on the rear delivery door. It was locked, but not as solid an obstacle as the double doors in front.

"Ready?"

They all nodded. Halley kicked the white wood panel. "Shit!" He winced. Kicked again. "Goddammit!"

Creed and Gibbs moved in, lending their weight. Three powerful shoulder lunges, and the lock popped. The door flew back, slamming into a wall. All four men piled through, weapons in hand. Brooke followed, plowing into Gibbs' back. She steadied herself. Raised voices sounded from the front of the house. Overhead, feet pounded.

They ran through the house, down one hallway after another. "This way! Shit, no, to the right!"

"Aren't you gonna yell 'police,' or somethin'?" Gibbs puffed.

"Fuck that," de Porres muttered.

They burst into a wide foyer, skidding to a stop on black-and-white tiles. A tall man in a gray three-piece suit stood in a doorway, face pale, eyes darting right to left. His voice was strained, failing at an attempt to remain calm. "What . . . what's going on?"

De Porres shoved his badge and a folded piece of paper at the man's nose. "LAPD. We've got a warrant to search the premises." He and Tom Halley pushed the man into the living room.

Creed gave a quick glance inside—saw three men in business suits —two Caucasian, one Japanese. One of the men was Roger Dorn. There was a camera on a strap around his neck. In a corner was an elaborate photography setup, furnished with a red velvet chaise . . . candles . . . red light bulbs. On another wall, a fireplace. Liquor bottles and a plush banquet on a side table.

Creed yelled at Brooke and Gibbs and headed up the central hallway stairs. "Let's *go!*"

Taking two at a time, Creed heard noise from above. An oath. A child's cry. On the second landing he halted, feeling out direction. Footsteps pounded on the third floor.

He ran down the hall to the foot of the stairs. The Smith & Wesson glinted in the light from a crystal chandelier. Creed pounded up the stairs. On the top step he halted again, his back against the wall. A door stood open, light spilling from it.

"Get back, Brooke." He held out a hand to check her momentum. The hand was shoved aside. He tried to grab her, but she was already ahead, running toward the open door.

"Brooke, goddammit, wait!"

She didn't listen. Flying toward the door, she yelled, "Charly! Charly, it's me!" Then she was through it.

"Holy shit!" Creed followed. Gibbs broke off, checking out closed doors along the way. Creed piled through the open bedroom door and nearly fell over Brooke, who was standing motionless inside, her back to him.

"She's not here . . . she's not here."

On a bed were child-sized clothes that looked as though they were made for a bride. A lacy white negligee . . . a tiny, lacy white bra, and bikini underpants. The bed was hung with sheer white curtains and surrounded by more cameras, more lights. Candles glowed.

A honeymoon suite.

Creed glanced at the ceiling. "C'mon!" He grabbed Brooke's hand.

The attic stairs were at the opposite end of the hall, he had learned from Tom, down an "L". He pulled Brooke in that direction. She stumbled once on an Oriental throw rug, but righted herself and kept up. They reached the attic door. Creed wrenched it open. This time he filled the stair space, refusing Brooke access. "Stay here! Stay *right here!*" he ordered.

"Police!" he yelled, flattening himself against the wall a few steps up. No response. He inched up a few more, the heavy Smith & Wesson raised in both hands. Swinging his back to the opposite wall, he craned to see around a bend and over the top stair. *"Hold it!"*

A rustle to the left, at the top. "Police!" he called again. "Don't move!" Lowering his voice, he tried to inject calm. "Let the child go. Just let her go. And come down here with your hands behind your head."

Still no response. But he had heard something. He knew it. They were up there with the child.

"Let me make this clear." His voice was deadly. "You have one chance, and one chance only, to come out of this alive. Send the child down. If you don't send her down here within the next fifteen seconds, I'm coming up there. And when I get there, I will tear you apart— starting with your goddamned fucking perverted eyes."

BROOKE, STANDING BELOW, shivered. She had no doubt Creed would do exactly as he said, and even while she was frightened, she wanted to cheer: *Do it, do it! Goddammit, kill them all! Cut out their goddamned eyes!*

Steps sounded on the attic floor. Creed stood back, but never took his eyes, or gun, off the man who descended—pausing only a moment as he inched past Creed on the stair. The man's belt was unbuckled, tie loose, top button of the wrinkled white shirt open. His hands were laced behind his head.

He passed. As he did, Creed raised a foot, shoving the man in the small of his back. He went flying the rest of the way down the stairs, directly into Brooke's path. She jerked back just in time.

The man lay at her feet, doubled over, clutching his head. Blood streamed. The man writhed in pain. Brooke didn't offer help. She was only vaguely aware that Gibbs had appeared. He was hauling the man to his feet, cuffing him, shoving him roughly down the hall.

She heard Creed's voice, soft now: "It's okay. I'm with the police, and I'm coming up. You'll be all right." She saw him move around the bend, out of her sight. She began to follow, her limbs shaky, mouth dry.

"Brooke." She heard Creed call her, his voice heavy. She heard him groan.

"What?" she cried, racing the rest of the way. *"What?"*

She saw him above her then, a child in his arms. The child's long blond hair covered her cheek. Creed's face was a strange blend of fatigue, and grief.

Brooke stopped dead. *"Charly?* Oh my God, Creed, what's wrong?"

"I'm sorry," he said tiredly.

Brooke pulled the hair back from the child's face. Tear-stained eyes met hers.

Thank God, she's alive. That was Brooke's first thought.

Thank God.

But the child wasn't Charly.

Chapter 31

THEY BARELY TALKED on the ride home. A little after midnight, Creed pulled the jeep into an alley several blocks away from the beach house. He let the motor idle. "In the morning I've got to see the police commissioner about this warrant that's out on me. It may be he can help—but for now, I can't go back to the house. I think it'd be all right for you."

Brooke shrugged. She was depressed by the night's outcome. Exhausted. "What are you going to do?"

"It's not too cold tonight. I'll sleep on the beach."

"What about me? You said they'd take me in, ask me questions about you."

"It's late. I don't really think they'll show tonight."

"But you're not taking any chances, yourself."

"No."

"Well, I'm not either. I'll stay with you."

"It could get uncomfortable. This isn't exactly Waikiki."

"And I'm some prima donna, or something?" She glared.

Creed gave a sigh. "Okay. Gibby can get us clean clothes in the morning, and maybe I can get us in the back door at Gold's Gym. We can shower and change there, then plan our next move."

"Whatever." It didn't much matter to her. She supposed she was numbing out. There had been too much—in too short a time. And most of it bad, with not enough good.

Creed drove a few more blocks and pulled in behind a row of new condos on the Marina Peninsula. He checked the rearview mirror, and the vacant lot to his left. It was past midnight, no life on the streets here in this expensive and relatively uncluttered area at the south end of Venice.

They climbed out of the jeep. Creed opened the back and rummaged through it, looking for camping equipment that had been there since his last vacation with Karen, five years ago. He wondered why he still carried it around; there hadn't been much use for it lately.

Pulling a sleeping bag and an old green fishing jacket out, he shut the tailgate quietly. "Here, put this jacket on. We'll cut through the walk street."

Along the walk street—a closed-off "mall" of private homes— were quaint street lamps, shrubs, and large shade trees. Shadows moved. Leaves rustled. Creed walked swiftly, knowing that Westec and other private security companies cruised the neighborhood at night. It would be an inconvenience, and possibly worse, if they were stopped.

Brooke silently brought up the rear.

A couple of blocks over, they came to the beach. Here on the Marina Peninsula, it covered a triangular area the size of several city blocks. Camping wasn't allowed, but now and then a huddled form could be seen. *Huddled masses, yearning to be free.*

But not this free, Creed thought.

Or maybe so. Were these the same men who, at the age of thirty, had always had a pair of track shoes under the bed—ready to run at the first hint of trouble—or commitment? Maybe it was no more than a need to run that had gotten them here. One more form of escape. Not unlike Karen's.

There weren't as many homeless sleeping here as up near Venice Beach. Often these were the "elite" of the homeless—people who had known better times and had too much pride to mingle with what they still saw as riffraff. A similar concept to the AA'ers who lived in Hawthorne but attended meetings in Beverly Hills or the Marina, rather than hang out with "bums."

It was safer here at night than at the main beach, where you could get shot by drug dealers or crazies, just for walking around. Even so, he had brought the Smith & Wesson.

He chose a spot by a lifeguard tower, near the jetty that spanned the Marina's main channel. "We'll be less visible here." He unrolled the sleeping bag.

"There's only one," Brooke said.

"It's a double. Sorry. It's the only one I had."

Brooke stared at the bag. She was so exhausted, she was almost unconscious.

"Just like *For Whom the Bell Tolls,*" she said dully. "All we need now is a raw onion sandwich."

"THE CHILD'S NAME is Heather Leiter," Creed said some time later. They were lying side by side in the sleeping bag, with only their elbows touching. "Ten years old. She was reported missing from her home in Virginia three weeks ago. I recognized her right away."

Brooke shifted. They bumped hips. Her arm rubbed against Creed's shoulder holster. She stiffened and drew away.

"Why did you bring that thing?"

"This?" He touched the Smith & Wesson. "Are you afraid of guns?"

"No. I've used them as props, onstage. I know all about guns. I just don't like what they can do when they're loaded."

Creed sighed. "We're not exactly on Broadway, here. Would you rather I didn't worry about protecting you?"

She had no answer to that.

"They took Heather to Saint John's hospital in Santa Monica," he continued, "for observation. Her parents are coming out on the next flight from Dulles."

"Who was that woman with the curly red hair and freckles?"

"A child-advocate volunteer. She'll stay with Heather in the hospital until the parents arrive."

"There are actually people who volunteer to do that sort of thing?"

"Yes. Connie has three girls of her own at home. She'll try to ease Heather's fears, help her get past the trauma she's been through since the kidnapping."

"*Three weeks,*" Brooke said tightly. "They had her for *three goddamn weeks.*"

"She'll have a period of healing to go through," Creed said. "And she'll never forget. But in time the memories should fade. They won't always be as painful or frightening as they are now."

The LAPD had closed down the mansion. Arrests were being made. People were talking, a nationwide network being revealed. So far, there was no sign of Charly within the network.

It hadn't yet come out that Creed or Brooke had been present at the mansion. Marty de Porres had taken full responsibility. Back at the West LA Division he told them he had acted on a hot tip, and that there hadn't been time to turn it over to the appropriate detectives from Pacific Division.

As things turned out, there wasn't too much for Pacific to complain about, beyond the usual professional jealousies. It was a "good bust," as Creed had said.

Except that it hadn't turned up Charly.

"Are you warm enough?" he asked.

Brooke didn't answer. She didn't trust her voice. *Think what they could do to a child in three weeks.*

"I'm sorry. I never should have built your hopes up."

Brooke stared at the sky. A few stars were visible. A piece of moon, low on the horizon.

"Do you want to talk?"

It took her a while. Her throat was so tight, the words could barely get through. And she didn't know what was worse . . . the anger that suddenly raged through her bones, or the fear. Her body was rigid. "I just want to know why you thought it was so *goddamned important* to go to Santa Maria today, when my daughter is missing and could very well be in the same kind of place as we found that little girl! Goddamn you, Creed! Go*damn!*"

Brooke sat up, pulling out of the sleeping bag and away from him. "You said yourself that the first twenty-four hours are the most important! It's been *four days! Four fucking days!* Unless Nathan's got her, it's too late to hope that she hasn't been harmed!"

Even if Nathan does have her, she thought, *Charly may have been harmed.* And the one man she had trusted to help had gone off and left her today.

"I did what I felt I had to do," Creed said stiffly.

"Well, your mind isn't on business. Maybe if it had been, you wouldn't have gone off to Pacific Palisades like gangbusters tonight, wasting time— Sorry, I know it wasn't a waste, since you found Heather, but dammit, you've got too much on your plate. What the hell do I need with someone—" She jumped to her feet. "I could do this better by myself!"

Shit, her years of drinking had ended up making her strong. She knew, now, how to take care of herself.

What did she need with this man?

Creed swung to his feet, matching her temper. "You are the most—! Look. I went to Santa Maria to see my wife because there's something I've been keeping to myself since our son disappeared, something that could have hurt Karen. But in her condition, I don't see how they can do anything to her, not now, not after all this time. So I told Karen's doctor what I knew. Maybe with this missing piece they'll be able to help her someday. Then I told Karen what I was going to do. I'm not sure if she heard me. They think she does, sometimes. And tomorrow I've got to see the police commissioner, see if there's anything he can do with all this to get the DA, and that arrest warrant, off my back."

He lowered his voice. "And the reason I went to Santa Maria at this particular time is that we can't go on hiding out. It restricts my mobility, and it can only bring you trouble. Once we get Charly back, do you have any idea what Nathan could do to you in a joint custody suit if you're even picked up for questioning about my whereabouts? I'm a fugitive, Brooke."

She tried to see into his eyes, but they were too shadowed. "What if you tell the commissioner, and he can't help?" *What if you're arrested on the spot, and you don't come back?*

"I don't think that'll happen. The timing feels right. But if things go sour, Gibbs will be here to help you."

"Gibbs."

He rubbed his face wearily. "I thought you trusted him."

"I do. But I don't want a substitute, I want you."

"Hell, Gibbs does most of the footwork for me. He's probably better at this than me."

"Even so . . ." She glanced away.

"Sometimes," Creed said, impassively, "there comes a point when you have to go on faith. You have to believe that things will work out."

Faith. It was a lesson she had been trying to learn these past eight months of sobriety. Trying, and failing. When you run into brick walls, the counselor had told her, and can't do any more for yourself—when you lose the people around you that you'd come to love or depended on . . . you have to "turn it over." You have to believe in something —or Someone—higher than yourself.

She had read a ton of books, seeking answers. Some had given the subject another slant—that the "Someone higher than yourself" was, after all, your own Higher Self. That it's all there to draw on, and once aware, you can tap into it. You can do—or become—anything you want.

"I'm sorry about your wife," she said quietly. "I'm sorry if I was unfair."

Creed rubbed the back of his neck and sighed. "Let's get some rest." He held open the sleeping bag. "One way or another, tomorrow will be a busy day."

They crawled in beside each other again. Brooke turned her back and closed her eyes.

AT SOME POINT in the night, she found her face pressed against his shoulder. Opening her eyes, she saw the silver glint of the Smith & Wesson. She shivered.

"Cold?" he murmured.

"Yes."

"Come here." He drew her close, his lips accidentally brushing her cheek. Brooke went rigid. But his arms felt safe . . . and she needed to feel safe. Life had been too frightening of late. She relaxed and inched closer. After several moments, Creed's hand stroked her hair. When she didn't protest, it moved to her breast. His tongue brushed sand from her lips, then pushed between them. She moaned. Her fingers twisted in his hair.

.   .   .

IT WAS ALL ABOUT COMFORT, she thought later. Not passion . . . al-though there had been that, too . . . a quiet passion, an easing of pain.

She looked at Creed, at the hard face, the long black hair with its imprint still on her fingers. From a Native American ancestor, he had told her . . . and an Italian grandfather who'd had the guts, or stupid-ity, to run from the mob. Had all that stoicism come from them, too? There was a gentleness beneath it, though. A sensitivity. Funny what you can learn about a man from the way he makes love. Not the technique, but the tenderness. Where had that other side come from?

Creed shifted . . . sighed . . . and still holding her, he smiled.

"Karen . . . ," he whispered. "Karen."

Chapter 32

GIBBS WAS SHAKING HIM. "KEEP! Wake up. Shit, it took me forever to find you. Listen, you know that photo of Hayes you sent to the newspapers when he disappeared? It's paid off! Take a look."

Creed sat up, instantly awake. Brooke, beside him, rubbed sand from her cheek.

Creed took the fax from Gibbs and scanned it. "From Carmel? Brooke, listen to this. It's a fax from the Carmel PD. A man answering Nathan's description was spotted at a place called the Timber-Inn Motel last night, below Big Sur."

"I checked it out," Gibbs said. "It's back in the mountains— separate cabins, lots of privacy."

"Another motel guest"—Creed continued—"a Donald M. Petrie —was in Carmel for dinner last night and saw Nathan's photo in the news release I sent to the *LA Times,* at a newsstand. He recognized Nathan later at the motel ice machine and called the sheriff in Big Sur. The sheriff didn't know anything about Charly's case, so he contacted the Carmel police. They're hooked into our computer network." Creed gripped the fax, his eyes glowing with elation. "Damn! It's working! I love it when it's working!"

"Ever hear of the Timber-Inn?" Gibbs asked Brooke. "Did you and your ex-husband ever stay there?"

"No. I've never even been to Big Sur. But—"

She drew the green fishing jacket close against an early morning chill. "There's something . . ." She shook her head. "It can't be. Why would Nathan be staying in a motel, if he still owned . . . ? Besides, I *know* he sold it over a year ago. . . ."

"Sold what? Spit it out, Brooke."

"Nathan had a house up north. Remember, I told you that, when you asked me if he had any other houses—a beach cottage, or a cabin in the mountains? He didn't, but his parents owned a place just below Big Sur—on the coast somewhere. Nathan sold it over a year ago, though. He needed the money to do renovations on the Westwood house."

"Do you know where it is?"

"No—we never went up there. Nathan had some sort of bad feeling about the place, and he kept it rented out for years."

"Who managed it? Who collected the rent?"

She ran fingers through her hair, which was matted and full of sand. "I don't know. Maybe there was a caretaker. I think the tenants sent their checks directly to Nathan, though. I remember seeing them now and then on his desk."

"At home?"

"Yes, in his study. He keeps his personal business files there."

Creed looked at Gibbs. "Is the Westwood house still being watched?"

"Not anymore. They pulled B and J off last night."

"Okay, look. I wanted to talk to the commissioner today, about that old business with Karen. But I can't risk it if there's a chance now that we can nail this thing down today."

"You want me to talk to the Old Man? Get him to call off the dogs?"

"At least see if it's possible. Meanwhile, I'll go with Brooke to Westwood—see if we can find those canceled checks. I want that address." Creed stood and straightened his jeans, shoving his shirt inside the waistband. With both hands he smoothed his long hair. "I take it somebody up north is picking Hayes up?"

"I talked to the Carmel PD. They sent a unit along with the sheriff. And the FBI's been notified."

"What are they doing?"

"I think they're sending someone from a local office. Meanwhile, there's been a ton of shit coming in over your hotline. More sightings—all of them in other states. FBI's checking them out."

"Good. That'll keep them busy."

He didn't have anything against the FBI, it was just that he didn't much believe in rescue-by-committee, except in obvious hostage situations, where demands were being made. In parental kidnappings he had always found that one person, working alone or in conjunction with no more than two other trusted people, worked best. Less confusion, less time wasted giving orders or waiting for paperwork to come down.

"Soon as we get that address—"

"Why do we need the address," Brooke interrupted, "if the sheriff is picking Nathan up? Isn't going to Westwood a waste of time?"

"Possibly. But Nathan may already have skipped. And even if he hasn't, there's no reason to think he'll tell us where Charly is . . . not if he's gone to such lengths to hide her."

He turned to Gibbs. "Soon as we've got the address, let's head up there. Can you see about chartering a plane with foundation funds? A Cub, or an Aztec, something small. Get us into the closest available airport."

"Will do."

"And can you bring us some clothes? We'll be at Gold's Gym, in the back."

"Sure." Gibbs checked his watch. "Half hour?"

"That should do it."

Creed glanced at Brooke. "Let's go."

Chapter 33

IT WAS IN NATHAN'S STUDY that all hell broke loose.

They had parked the jeep several blocks away and walked to the Westwood house. There was a back way through the high stucco fence, protected from view by dense hundred-years-old shrubbery. At the rear patio door, Brooke used a key that was still on her key ring, from the time of the divorce.

"I'm not sure that using this isn't illegal, now."

Creed shrugged. "In for a penny, in for a pound."

She lifted a brow.

"My mom used to say that."

Once inside, she moved swiftly to the alarm panel and was relieved to find that the cut-off code hadn't been changed.

In a file cabinet in Nathan's study they found the canceled checks. *Luther Mendelsohn Cain* was the printed name in the upper left-hand corner. Address: 12214 Cliffhouse Road, Seaville, California.

"Seaville," Brooke said. "Isn't that up near Big Sur?"

"Just below it, if memory serves me. That would put it in the same general area as the Timber-Inn Motel." Creed's smile was tight. "I've got a good feeling about this."

"So do I. Let's get out of here."

Nathan's study was raising too many ghosts. His habit during their marriage had been to shut himself off in here after dinner most nights, to work. She didn't mind the work. It was more the endless, nearly robotical routine that had driven her nuts.

"We're different people, Brooke," he would say in that cool, responsible, deliberate way. He would sit behind this desk, wearing those black-rimmed glasses that he barely needed, but that served their purpose in that they provided a barrier from the rest of the world. Nathan had beautiful eyes when he wanted to show them. More often than not —at least around her—he had chosen in latter days to cover them up. Brooke knew that years of practice in a courtroom had taught her husband about protective coloration—and manipulation.

Often she felt that Nathan had deliberately been trying to appear unattractive around her—and those damned glasses were nothing but props. After the first couple of years, it was clear that their sex life had become a dutiful chore to him—a distasteful matter to be dispensed with as quickly as possible. That was why, she knew, he sometimes didn't come to bed. He'd sleep in the little room off this one—no more than a closet behind those country murals over there—on a single-width roll-away bed. "I was too tired to climb the stairs," he would explain the next day.

Too tired for the stairs? Or the wife he would find at the top of them?

But she had sensed Nathan's problems from the beginning: the fear of intimacy, the need to control. "Why do women fall in love with emotionally unavailable men?" she had asked her counselor in recent months. The answer had been that women are often afraid of intimacy themselves—and unavailable men are "safe."

It was as good an answer as any, Brooke supposed. And even aside from having Charly, it hadn't all been a waste. Through her relationship with Nathan, she had learned about her own faults as well. They had held up a mirror to each other. *When you see something negative in another person, it is certain you are seeing that same thing in yourself. When you admire another person, you are becoming the thing you admire. In intimacy, we work these things out.*

She had read that somewhere. It was hard to remember where. So many books . . . trying to pack years and years of growing into the past eight months.

Creed was closing up the file cabinets, putting everything back in order. Brooke paused by the closet door, which was hidden by a floor-to-ceiling mural of a pastoral scene. (Nathan's mother's doing. From the little Brooke had learned, the woman covered up decorating flaws—and emotions—in equal measure. Was it any wonder her son had grown up distant as well?) She pressed on the right side of the gold-leaf frame, midway down, where a handle would ordinarily be. The door swung open, and she stepped in.

The roll-away bed was no longer there. Instead, more file cabinets had taken its place. Well, that told the story. If Nathan no longer needed to sleep down here—

"Brooke." Creed's voice was soft, yet urgent. "Stay where you are. Don't make a sound." The closet door snapped shut, leaving her in the dark.

What the hell? She reached for the light switch, then stopped.

Moments later she heard a voice, not Creed's.

"Oh, shit, man, what'd you have to go and do this for?"

"Hello, Jimmy." Creed sounded casual. "Well . . . we've got a missing child. I needed information. It was worth the risk."

"Yeah, well, man . . . shit. I don't wanta bring you in."

"You could pretend you never saw me, Jimmy."

"You kiddin'? Barty's out there right now, wonderin' why it's takin' me so long. Besides, if it ever came out . . ."

The man is a cop—half of Bartles and James, Brooke remembered.

"Sure. I understand," Creed was saying. "What are you doing here, anyway?"

The other man sighed heavily. "Stupidest thing. Forgot my sunglasses here last night, out in the kitchen. I thought I'd just take one more look around the place while I was at it. Sure never thought I'd find you here, Keep."

"All I need is one more day, Jimmy." Creed's tone was persuasive.

"No way, Keep. No *how.*"

"If it was the other way around, I'd do it for you."

"You think I don't know that? You're making this hard, buddy."

"I hope so."

The other man laughed softly, apologetically. "I'm up for promotion. And I've got three hungry mouths at home to feed. I need the raise in pay."

Brooke could hear Creed's sigh. "I understand. Well, do what you have to do."

Her stomach clutched. She wanted to scream, "No!" Until this moment she had thought Creed would fight being taken in—physically, if necessary. Was he really going to let this happen, now that they were so close?

He was. There were no sounds of scuffle, no more words of protest. She heard a jingle of metal. Handcuffs?

Holy God! She couldn't believe this was happening.

She heard footsteps fading. The front door opened and closed. Silence filled the rest of the house, seeping like a fungus into the dark closet, cutting off her breath. Brooke fumbled with the closet door and stumbled out.

She ran to the front window. Creed was stepping into the back of a police cruiser. A uniformed police officer shut the door behind him and slid into the passenger side.

There was some talk, she could see, between him and the man at the wheel. Then he lifted the car radio and spoke into it. A minute or so passed.

The cruiser pulled away. They were gone.

Brooke turned back, feeling panic. She didn't know what to do. Try to reach Gibbs? But what if they had the phones here tapped? Would they have done that? She couldn't see why, with Nathan gone— But why take chances?

She hadn't brought her purse. No money to get back to the beach house. Not even a quarter to call from a phone booth. And she couldn't remember her calling card number. God-*damn!* She was stuck in god-damned fucking Westwood, knowing where Charly was—*probably was*—and she couldn't even get there. It would take up valuable time, trying to connect again with Gibbs, getting to Venice from here—

She struggled for control. Panic was the old way; she had to remember the new.

First things first. The canceled rent check. It was nowhere in sight. She hadn't memorized the name and address from it; she would have to get another. Yanking open the file cabinet, she rummaged through the alphabetical folders. Always the last place you look . . . should she start at *Z?* No, there they were—under *C.* Cain—Luther Mendelsohn Cain. Her hand dived in—came out with a check—

And the keys to the jeep.

Creed had purposely left her the keys to the jeep! She gripped them in her fist. Relief swept over her. "Thank you, thank you, thank you!"

Slamming the file cabinet shut, she raced through the house and out the back way, the way they had come. She ran through the garden, through the alley, and down the street to the jeep.

Inside the car again, she pored through Creed's glove compartment for maps. She pulled one halfway out. *Los Angeles City.* Damn! Another. *Los Angeles County.* She threw it on the floor.

California State. Brooke yanked at it. Her hand touched something metal below the map, something smooth. She tossed the map on the passenger seat and gripped the metal object.

The Smith & Wesson. Her shaky fingers drew it out. She stroked its silver barrel thoughtfully. A revolver—heavy, and large. She knew about revolvers from using them as props on stage; she knew about pulling back the hammer before each shot. She knew it might have, possibly, eight or nine bullets in it, but the chamber felt as if it were stuck; she couldn't get it open to see.

The gun was loaded, she was sure. It had been loaded last night on the beach—and she had seen Creed put it back in the glove compartment this morning.

It was the first time she had ever held a gun that was loaded with anything other than blanks. A frightening feeling—like holding a deadly snake. The question was, Could she shoot it, if she had to? Would she have the courage to aim at any living thing?

Her shoulders straightened. "Yes," she said aloud. "Yes." For Charly, she could do anything.

"I'm coming, baby. Just hang on."

Chapter 34

CHARLY HAD HEARD her father's voice again. It wasn't a dream . . . and she had not been imagining things. She had pinched herself when she heard it this time—really hard, leaving half-moon cuts on her arm where her nails had dug in.

For a long time she had called out to her father. For a long time she had waited for his answer. It never came.

Charly couldn't think anymore. Yesterday she had had a plan. A plan to get out. But she couldn't work things out now.

This corner of the bedroom had become her "place." She kept coming back here, the way her puppy, Snowflake—the one she had when she was five—used to keep going back to its tiny wicker-basket bed.

"He misses his mom," Brooke had said. "He feels safer in that one place, without too much room to move around. Or maybe he's afraid he'll be hurt if he doesn't hide."

Charly guessed that was why she curled up in a blanket in this corner, her face to the wall. She guessed that was why she kept sucking her thumb. It was red and raw now. She kept telling herself she wouldn't suck it anymore, wouldn't act like a baby, but then she'd find it in her mouth again. Like Snowflake, gnawing on a bone.

He was such a cute puppy . . . all floppy and funny, running into things, and chewing at her shoes. Charly used to take him to bed with her and hold him tight when her mother and father were fighting. Snowflake was the only one she could count on not to be mad, or yell, or hurt anybody at all. She *wished she had him now. But when he was only a few months old, Snowflake had gotten outside alone and been hit by a car.*

Charly huddled into her corner, all too aware of the dangers of venturing forth alone.

Each morning, now, she had to put on a clean dress. Then he would brush her hair. He didn't do a good job, like her mother, but he tried. And he didn't watch her when she was dressing. That was one thing she guessed she was lucky about. She had heard stories at school about what happened to kids who were kidnapped. He hadn't done anything like that to her. Just touching and patting her, sometimes, like after the time he had spanked her, when she tried to run away. But that was almost like he was sorry for the spanking and trying to make up for it. He hadn't done that since.

The worst thing was the doll. She didn't know why he had cut pieces of it off like that. But she thought he was telling her that if she wasn't good, he would do that to her. So every time he came into the room, her stomach would get tight and sick, and her head would go all weird.

That was why she hadn't tried to escape again. But then, yesterday—she thought it was yesterday—she had realized something important. And she had started to think of the plan.

Only now she couldn't remember the plan.

Charly let out a soft sob and turned on the floor, drawing her knees up and scrunching farther into the blanket. Her hair tangled beneath her cheek, and her thumb went back into her mouth.

Sitting in this corner, she saw pictures in her head of the way it used to be with her mother and father. The arguments, her mother crying and her father always so quiet and calm. "You are so damned controlled!" Brooke would yell. "Don't you ever feel anything?" And her father would turn his back and walk away.

Another picture came, of her father sitting on the edge of her bed just a few months ago and telling her, "People have to take charge of their emotions, Charly. If they don't, they're no more than animals."

She thought he was telling her that her mother was no more than an animal. She didn't like him talking about her mother like that, and that was when she began to want to go live with Brooke. Brooke was right—there was something wrong with her father, something not quite right.

"It's like you're unfinished, Nathan," Brooke had said once in an argument. "Like there's a piece missing, and when you find it, you'll be all right.

But I can't wait for that anymore. I can't wait for you to find that piece.'' Her mother's voice had been sad, then—not mad.

Charly wondered why her father had been here, talking to the man. She wondered if her father hated her, now, and why he was doing this to her. She wondered a lot of things.

From somewhere in the house, she heard that song from Molly Brown. *''I'll never say no to you . . .'' She hated the song now. And every time she heard it, she knew that the man was crazy. She knew she had to get away.*

If only she could remember the plan.

LUTHER MENDELSOHN CAIN sat before a massive stone fireplace in an overstuffed rocking chair. Beside him on an antique end table rested a Polaroid camera. Photographs of Charly lay beside it: Charly sleeping, sucking her thumb . . . Charly eating dinner . . . Charly crying for her mother . . .

The selfish bitch. Indulging in excesses, forsaking her marriage, not taking care of her child.

And that father—what a cold fish he was. Hearing Charly cry out for him that way . . . and not a muscle moving in his arrogant face.

Cain sang softly in a thready, off-key tenor. "I'll never say no to you, whatever you say or do . . ." He smiled and rocked, smiled and rocked. Now and then, he would pick up a photograph of Charly and study it. "I'll take care of you," he said.

The fireplace was roaring now. *Good thing,* Cain thought. *It's a very cold night.* He wondered if Charly was warm enough. He would take her another blanket and make sure the heat was turned up.

But first he had to wait for his company. Cain chuckled softly. Nathan Hayes thought he had everything under control. He thought he was doing the right thing. Well, Nathan had some surprises coming.

And so did Brooke. She'd learn what happens to bad mothers.

Neither Brooke Hayes, nor Nathan Hayes, would ever see Charly again.

Chapter 35

THE ROAD WOUND ALONG CLIFFS. Sheer drops on the left side, to the ocean . . . towering mountains to the right. Brooke could see, where the coastline curved to the north, that the mountains grew more majestic, the cliffs several hundred feet high. Must be Big Sur up there. Thank God she didn't have to go that far; this was bad enough.

She flexed her shoulders and rolled the jeep's window down to get more air. Between nerves, the previous night on the beach, and the road with its twists and turns, she was exhausted, worn out.

The large foam cup filled with coffee was cold and bitter now, but it helped. She had bought it at a roadside café more than a hundred miles back. There weren't many conveniences or even towns along this section of Highway 1.

Brooke checked her watch. Eight twenty-three. The sun was slanting in from just above the sea. She had lost time above San Luis Obispo —had gotten onto 101 and gone clear to Paso Robles on it before she realized she should have stayed with Coast Highway 1. At a gas station they told her she'd either have to take 46 across, or stay on 101 to Carmel. That would overshoot her destination; she'd have to backtrack south. She had opted for 46, but ran into construction on the two-lane road and had lost a good two hours.

According to the map, however, and directions back at that café, she should be nearing Seaville soon. "Not much more than a dot on the landscape," the waitress at the café had said.

So—another ten minutes or so, if she had the mileage figured right. When she got there, she'd look for Nathan's former house first thing—the one now belonging to Luther Mendelsohn Cain. God, what a name.

And what was his part in this? Was he working for Nathan? Was he holding her daughter there? Or was this all just one more wild-goose chase, like that fiasco with Roger Dorn?

It couldn't be. It just couldn't. Brooke prayed silently: *If I've ever done anything right—ever in all my life—help me find Charly now.*

A HIGH BRICK FENCE ran along the coastal side of the road. The trunks of large spreading pines, just inside the fence, leaned sideways from years of gusting winds. They overlapped, creating a half arch above the highway. A closed iron gate midcenter protected the drive to the house.

The house where, if all went well, Charly would be found.

Brooke sat in the jeep, its motor idling, on the inland side of the road. *A mansion,* she thought, from what she could see of the house through the gate. Three stories, red brick with white shutters . . . just the kind of house Nathan's parents would have bought in the twenties or thirties. She didn't know how much Nathan had sold it for; he never had talked about business matters to her.

She wondered, suddenly, if he had sold it at all . . . or if the deal had been on paper only, if this Luther Mendelsohn Cain was a paper owner, some kind of tax dodge Nathan had come up with. They must be friends. Otherwise, why would this man be helping Nathan to hide Charly?

It had taken her less than ten minutes to reach Seaville. Another five to locate Cliffhouse Road, a left turn off Highway 1. It then ran parallel to the coast. Approaching it from a rise, Brooke had seen that there were other houses along the coastal side of the road, spaced well apart, all surrounded by fences and trees. This house faced the highway; at the back was a steep cliff with the sea below. It looked wicked and wild—with black jutting rocks and crashing waves. Access from that direction would be difficult without special equipment. Impossible for her, even with it. She was strong . . . but knew virtually nothing about climbing mountains, let alone cliffs.

That front gate would almost certainly be locked. And if she approached it to find out, she would give herself away. For that matter, she had better move on quickly now, before she was spotted by someone in the house.

Beginning a mile or so back, she had looked for a spot to park. But on this side of the road were bare cliffs reaching up the mountainside, while on the other she had seen only centralized cutoffs with clusters of mailboxes, and private driveways.

A decision made, Brooke tapped the accelerator gently and pulled out. A half mile to the north, she found a cutoff with six mailboxes. It was after nine P.M. There would be no more deliveries today.

She parked. Taking out the Smith & Wesson, she shoved it into the leather purse she had been carrying since the night before. She slung the shoulder strap around her neck, testing it for strength. Then she knelt on the seat, rummaging in the back of the jeep for a tackle box she had seen earlier. In it was a piece of fishing wire. She threaded it through the silver loop that held the purse and strap together and attached the other end, tightly, to the belt loop on her jeans.

There. It would be steady enough now for climbing. It wouldn't swing or get in her way.

She waited for the sun to finish its slow, maddening descent into the sea.

HER UPPER BODY STRENGTH was good; Brooke had counted on that. All those long workout and rehearsal hours—wrestling with Sean, fighting with the "brothers," climbing up and down from Molly's cabin roof. Days and nights of carrying heavy scenery, for that matter, along with the rest of the cast and crew—just to keep Leo happy.

Brooke grabbed a drooping limb of one of the pine trees on the road side of the fence. It looked black in the dark night, and sticky sap was beginning to harden from the cold. She hoisted herself onto the wobbly, elastic limb. It sank with her weight, brushing the ground. She pulled herself hand over hand along it, reaching higher and higher, the rough bark cutting into her palms. Long, stiff needles poked her face. Her eyes smarted and teared, but she kept on going. She had to do this quickly, in case anyone at the house was looking. In case there was someone guarding the place.

She had wondered about dogs, too, but in the ten minutes or so that she had crouched outside the fence, listening, she had heard no bark, no sounds at all, other than the roar of waves as they dashed against rocks. And the eerie wailing of the wind.

Electric beams, then? Security alarms? Her only hope was to get in quickly, so that if they discovered security had been breached, she might at least have a chance to hide on the grounds.

Tightening her grip, she swung a leg up as the branch thickened near the main trunk. Wind gusted, nearly shaking her off. Brooke felt the muscles strain in her legs. Cold sweat streamed into her eyes. In a moment she had a secure grip again. She hoisted herself around the branch so she was lying on it, face toward the trunk of the tree, inching forward. Within moments she had cleared the top of the fence. With one powerful leap, she pushed away from the tree and dropped to the ground.

Her knee twisted. *Pain.* A small cry escaped her throat before she could choke it off.

She froze. Had anyone heard? *Be still. Listen.*

No sign of anyone. No guards with flashlights. No dogs.

Odd.

But don't think. Get moving.

She stood and tested the knee. A twinge—but everything worked. Tension moved in waves from her shoulders down her back. Her collarbone ached. It was hard to breathe.

It was then that she saw it. A glimpse, only, through thick shrubbery that swayed with every gust of wind.

Nathan's car. On the drive, illuminated by a porch light.

Maroon, with a black leather fleur-de-lis top. An early Lincoln, heavy as sin . . . an overkill. But there was no mistaking it: a classic, Nathan's pride and joy. Mint condition, low mileage, left to him by his parents, who had bought it in another age and then garaged it, putting it up on blocks.

Brooke had resented that car, and the hours Nathan had spent detailing it on weekends.

Detailing. She had looked it up once in the large leatherbound dictionary with its crisp, unworn pages, in Nathan's study. *Attention to a subject in individual or minute parts.*

Too bad he didn't bother to detail his marriage, she thought.

So Nathan had driven the Lincoln—probably hoping the police wouldn't be looking for it—and she had helped him along. She hadn't even thought to tell anyone about it when Nathan disappeared. She'd forgotten the Lincoln completely.

Brooke wondered who had the Mercedes. Mrs. Stinson, the housekeeper? She had driven it often, taking Charly back and forth to classes, running errands. . . .

Pay attention, Brooke. Think.

She couldn't just go blasting in there, demanding to see her daughter. Not until she knew just how desperate Nathan was to keep them apart. Maybe she could get a glimpse of Charly, though, enough to make sure she was okay. First things first.

There were double-hung windows across the front—four on either side of the door, on the first and second floor. Above them was a steep roof that must be an attic. No windows there, and the second-story ones were dark.

Down here, however, light spilled from those at the left of the front door.

Brooke moved forward quietly, maneuvering around old pines and flower beds. Halfway there her foot caught on something. She started to fall—grabbed an overhanging branch and righted herself. Stickers from overgrown rose bushes pricked her face and hands. She hardly noticed, her focus on one particular window ahead. She could see shadows moving against it, now, through sheer white curtains. At another window the curtains weren't even pulled. *They must be so sure of themselves. So sure they won't be found—*

From six feet away muffled voices could be heard. Brooke stood motionless, straining, but couldn't make out the words. Forgetting caution, she hurried forward, plastering her back against the siding of the house, beside the undraped window. She was exposed here . . . no plants, no trees to hide behind.

Keeping close to the building, Brooke leaned sideways—craning her neck to see through the low window.

They were both there. Nathan and another man. A short man, with thin blond hair. The man who had taken Charly from Universal Studios—she was certain of it. It had to be.

Where was Charly? *Where was she?*

There was no one else in the room—not that she could see. A roaring fire to the left. Good furnishings—antiques, with chintz upholstery. She thought she recognized Nathan's mother's taste; it was that similar to the Westwood house. Eleanor Hayes had been known for her excellent taste—but she seldom took chances, always stuck with the tried and true.

So—had Nathan sold the house furnished? Or had he, in fact, never really sold it at all?

She still couldn't make out what they were saying. But they weren't arguing, that was clear. Both voices sounded reasonable, the tone subdued.

They were making plans, then—plans to move Charly. Creed had said they would do that soon. If only she could hear!

Could she get in a back way? Get closer, from within the house?

She almost started toward the side, to see. But a terrible, wrenching cry stopped her in her tracks.

"Daddy! *Daaaaaddy!*"

Oh, dear God!

Charly!

Charly's voice—coming from somewhere in that house. Brooke began to run. As she ran, she fumbled in the leather purse for the Smith & Wesson. Dragged it out. At the front door she grabbed for the knob. It was locked. She raised the gun to bang on the door. The Smith & Wesson glittered in light that filtered through a narrow pane by the door. Its deadly weight strained the muscles of her hand. *Deadly weight, deadly weight, deadly—*

Her hand fell slowly to her side.

Think, Brooke—for God's sake, think.

You can't go in like this. What if they're armed, too? What if it turns into a mess, and Charly gets hurt? Remember how it was in Pacific Palisades that night, when they rescued that other little girl? Remember how that man took her into the attic, how it took Creed to talk him down, and how anything could have happened?

This isn't the same.

No. But Nathan is desperate. When people are desperate, things get all messed up. You just never know.

Look at you. You're standing outside a strange door in a strange place in the middle of the night, holding a gun in your hands. That was the old Brooke, the one who acted first and thought last. You've got to remember the new.

She stepped back. And saw a figure no more than two feet from her nose, through the thin glass panel beside the door. The knob turned. The door opened.

Nathan's voice said, "I'll be back early in the morning. Meanwhile—"

Brooke turned and ran.

HEADLIGHTS, coming from the direction of Cliffhouse Road . . . fog lights, the kind on the Lincoln. Growing closer. Almost here.

Brooke wrenched the wheel of the jeep, jammed down on the clutch and accelerator, and barreled into the road. Brakes screeched. Rubber burned. Metal struck metal. Her neck snapped as she was thrown against the back of the seat. But the jeep's shoulder harness held. Brooke yanked it free and jumped out, pointing the gun with both hands as Nathan stumbled from behind his wheel, into the road. Momentarily he swayed. Both engines ticked. The front passenger door of the Lincoln had a dent the size of a bathtub.

"What the *hell*? What the goddamned *hell*?"

"Shut up, Nathan. *Shut up, shut up, shut up!* I am going to kill you. I am going to fucking kill you!"

"Brooke!" His mouth worked, then fell into stunned silence.

"Say good-bye, Nathan. It's over, it's all over."

"No . . . Brooke, no!" He raised his hands palm out, defensively.

"You stole my daughter from me!"

"I didn't . . . Brooke, I didn't steal her . . . I didn't."

"I heard her voice, Nathan. I heard her calling you. And you walked out on her. *Damn* you! What have you done to our child?" The gun shook in her hands.

"It's not what you think." Nathan pressed his fingers to the bridge of his nose and slumped heavily against the Lincoln. "Brooke, it's not what you think. I'll tell you about it, I'll tell you everything. Just, for God's sake, put down that gun."

"You always were a good talker, Nathan. A skilled negotiator. Well, I'll give you three minutes. Talk all the hell you want. After that, you'll be dead."

"You wouldn't—"

"You don't know the new me. I'd pull this trigger in a heartbeat. But talk, Nathan. It'll be fun to see you sweat."

Nathan slid to the ground, his back against the front wheel of the Lincoln. His shoulders sagged. One hand passed over his eyes. "God, Brooke, I am so damned tired."

She pulled back the hammer on the gun. A bullet clicked into its chamber.

"Brooke—no!" The hand went out.

"I don't have much time—I have to get Charly. So if you're not talking—"

"Wait! I'll tell you! I just need . . ." He squeezed his eyes shut briefly, shaking his head. "I need to get straight. I've been under terrible stress—"

She moved forward, pointing the gun directly at his head.

"All right, Brooke!" His tone lowered; it became reasoning. "All right . . . all right." He sighed.

"Let me make it easy for you," Brooke said. "I know that house back there is the one you claimed to have sold last year. I know a Luther Mendelsohn Cain lives there now, and I know he's helping you to hide Charly from me." Her voice began to break. "I know I've never really known you, never believed you could do such a horrible thing—"

"I didn't, Brooke, I swear! I wouldn't! You can't think I'd put Charly in danger this way."

"Our child was *screaming* back there!"

There were tears in Nathan's voice. "Don't you think— It was dreadful, to hear her like that. Not just tonight, but before—"

"This has happened *before*? Charly heard you, knew you were there, and she called out to you like she did tonight?" If Charly had been calling out to Nathan, and he didn't answer—

What must she be thinking? Feeling?

Abandoned.

"I was at the foot of the stairs then, too," Nathan said, "by the front door . . . and I heard her call . . ." Tears ran down his face, and he wiped them away. " 'Daddy, help me . . . Daddy, help me,' she said . . ."

"Where is she?" Brooke nearly screamed. "Where was she when I heard her voice?"

"An upstairs bedroom, I think, or the attic. I wanted to just run up those stairs and grab her, get her out of there—"

"For God's sake, Nathan! Why didn't you?"

"Cain said there was someone holding a gun on her. He said she'd be shot if I so much as set foot on the stairs." His eyes pleaded with her to understand, to absolve him of the guilt he had levied upon himself. "I didn't know if that was true—but I couldn't risk it."

"Wait a minute." She braced herself against the jeep, weak suddenly. "Are you saying our daughter . . . that this man kidnapped our daughter? That you didn't take her, that—" The reality of it struck her, then. "Oh my God, Nathan—who is this monster? What is he doing with Charly?"

Nathan leaned his head back and closed his eyes briefly, a look of utter exhaustion on his face. "I've had a private investigator on him almost from the first—Bob Sigart, the best in the whole damned country. He dug up the guy's background, we put two and two together—"

"Just tell me what Cain wants with our *daughter!*"

"He says . . . he says he wants to take care of her. And he wants us to suffer because we've hurt Charly—by neglecting her, giving her grief. The same way his parents hurt him."

"But he—" Brooke was confused. *"He's* hurting Charly."

"He doesn't see it that way."

She gave a low groan. "How did you even find Cain? How did you know he was the kidnapper?"

He didn't answer immediately.

"Nathan?"

He stuttered. "I . . . I've had a tap . . . a tap on your phone the past month. Ever since you started to come down and see Charly again."

"You *what?* Jesus Christ, Nathan, that's low even for you! What in the name of God did you hope to find out with it?"

"I wanted to know how many times you were talking to Charly."

"Why?"

"I guess . . . because I felt I was losing her to you."

Brooke's head moved side to side. She couldn't take it all in.

"Then you've known where Cain was—where Charly was—from the *first?* And you still blamed me? That business at the police station, all those accusations?"

"I wanted you out of the way. I wanted to handle it alone."

The gun, which had begun to lower, came up again. "Well, I can see why! You've done so goddamned *well!*"

Nathan spoke quickly. "Brooke, I was afraid that you and Creed would screw things up. I thought at first I could negotiate on some sane, rational basis—reach Cain with offers of money. And he's been going along with me. But I know now that he's just been playing with me. He doesn't want money. The man is mad—stark, raving mad."

Mad. "What has he done to Charly? Is she hurt? Those dolls—"

"No, Brooke, no! He assured me he hasn't hurt her that way."

"This madman assured you—and you believed him?" She didn't know which was worse—Cain's insanity, or Nathan's. She began to pace. "What do you know about this Cain?"

Nathan ran a hand over his face. He shook his head tiredly. His voice was strained, as if he'd been living alone with the horror too long.

"It's a bizarre story, Brooke. According to a psychiatric report Sigart came up with, Cain's mother was a businesswoman. She and the father were partners. They were on a business trip to Italy when Cain was thirteen, and they were shot by a sniper with a political grudge. He was spraying the street—and the parents got caught in the gunfire."

He sighed. "And this is where it gets really grotesque. It was the same week JFK was shot. We were all glued to our sets, I remember, for days, and they showed the Kennedy tape over and over. Cain was alone in his house at the time; his nanny had to leave to take care of an ill sister in another town. The parents set up an agency babysitter, long distance. But when Kennedy was shot, she was distraught and got mixed up. She thought the nanny was coming back—and she left the job, left Cain alone. That same day the report came over local news that his parents had been shot by a sniper in Italy. It was a small town, and when the film arrived from Italy, local stations began to show it over and over, along with the JFK assassination. The kid saw the tape—saw his parents being mowed down by the sniper. He went running through the house, horror-stricken, looking for the babysitter, and couldn't find her. When the nanny saw the film on TV the next day, and couldn't reach anyone at the house, she went back. She found Cain alone in a dark house, in a state of shock before the television. He had watched it every time it was shown . . . watched his parents being shot, their bodies, the blood, everything."

Dear God. What kind of damage had that done? And this was the man who had Charly?

"Nathan, how do you know all this?" she said suspiciously.

"I told you, Sigart got a psychiatric report."

"Then Cain's been charged before?"

"No."

"Getting a person's psychiatric report isn't easy. In fact, I think it's illegal."

Nathan hesitated. "Andy Laskov helped."

"Laskov? The DA? He knows about this?"

Hayes nodded. "Almost from the first."

Brooke stepped closer, her tone full of anger. "Then why has he been after John Creed? Why hasn't he let him alone, so he could help?"

"I asked Andy to keep people out of the way—and he owes me some favors."

Favors, it's all run by favors. The Old Boys Club.

God-damn!

The only thing you can do is be smarter than them.

Yet there was no denying Nathan's anguish. She remembered the early days, the way he had walked Charly, had fed her and burped her, his soft blond hair falling over his forehead and mingling with her damp curls. She remembered soft lullabies coming out of that tall, rigid frame, the heart that otherwise seemed so cold.

"Nathan," she sighed, "didn't it ever occur to you that there's room for both of us in Charly's life?"

With a wary glance at the gun, Nathan pulled himself to his feet. "Not if it's going to be the way it was," he said stiffly.

"It isn't. Nathan, I've changed. Things could be different now."

"Not according to—"

"What? According to *who?*"

"Leo . . . Leo Walsh."

She couldn't believe it. "Leo has been talking to you behind my back?" Was she surrounded by enemies? Even Leo—a man who only two months ago had asked her to marry him?

"He says you're obsessing on Charly. He's worried about you, and he doesn't want to see you get joint custody right now."

"Leo is jealous, Nathan! Anyway, he's the one who sent me to a lawyer—"

Nathan glanced away.

"Oh, my God. *You* recommended the lawyer. You knew he was inexperienced, that he had no contacts, no network in LA. You figured he'd help me lose."

"This is not important, now, Brooke. We can talk about it later. First, I've got to get Charly away from that madman."

Brooke stepped closer. "Wrong, Nathan. You're the one who's screwed everything up so far, remember? I'm getting Charly out of there—and I'm doing it alone. Now, get back in your car. We're going for a drive."

Nathan looked at Brooke, still holding the gun, as if he'd never known her before. A mixture of emotions crossed his face . . . from anger to sadness, Brooke thought—to despair. She was startled by the heaviness in his voice.

"I never was good enough for you, was I?"

"What are you talking about?"

"No matter what I did, you always wanted something else from me. You couldn't just accept what I had to give."

"You never—"

She broke off. She was about to say, "You never gave." Then she remembered—the thing she had been trying to learn, in recent months, about relationships. *A higher love focuses on what a person has to give, not what he can't give. A man who doesn't remember to call may string a woman's guitar. And a husband who has never learned to show warmth might try to control—in order to protect.*

She stood before Nathan, feeling as if she were on the brink of an important discovery—yet afraid she just might topple over the edge and lose herself in the deep.

Finally she lowered the gun and held out her arms. "Oh, Nathan. What are we going to do?"

He stepped close, awkwardly, and she held him, her face against his shoulder, feeling him tremble.

Chapter 36

IT SHOULD HAVE BEEN WORKABLE after that. *He feels alone,* Brooke thought, following Nathan's car in the jeep. *And he feels afraid. He needs me . . . possibly for the first time.*

But at the Seacrest Motel, a few miles away, it was clear that the moment of trust was gone.

"How long have you been in this place?" Brooke scanned the knotty pine paneling and the wagon-wheel furniture. Nathan's mother would turn over in her grave.

But then, she had probably never seen Nathan in jeans and a red plaid shirt, either—the way he was now.

"I've been here a couple of days," he said.

A lie. And Brooke wasn't sure why, but she didn't tell him that he had been discovered at the Timber-Inn by a guest there the night before, and his whereabouts reported to the police in Carmel.

Trust. An ephemeral thing. She had asked her question knowing the answer, but wanting to see what Nathan's answer would be.

There was a telephone on a sturdy pine bureau, and beside it, a coffeepot. The pot, along with packages of sugar and creamer, were on a black plastic tray. There were several empty packets, a coated spoon, and rings from coffee having been spilled several times as it was poured.

"I'll make fresh," Nathan said. He carried the pot into the bathroom and ran water, coming out a few minutes later with a full pot of water and two clean cups.

It was the first time in all the years Brooke had known him that she had seen him do anything domestic. Coming here, she had expected to find Nathan in a suite of rooms, with Mrs. Stinson, the housekeeper, to look after his needs.

"Where is Mrs. Stinson?" she wondered aloud.

"I . . . uh . . . she's at another motel. An inn."

The Timber-Inn, Brooke thought. *He left her back there, and he's hiding her—that's why he didn't want to tell me where he's been.* "Why did you bring her along?"

"I thought Charly might need her." He shrugged. "Since you left . . ."

"They've been getting closer than ever. Charly told me. I'm glad."

When the coffee was ready, they sat on the low stone hearth of the fireplace. Outside, fog dripped from the eaves of the cabin. Brooke cupped her hot mug of coffee, anxious to get to Charly. But first—

Nathan had built the fire high; it crackled, and smoke rose from kindling and paper. She soon had to shift to prevent her back from burning.

She studied Nathan's face in the firelight. He was exhausted. Only when he was tired or depressed did the horizontal grooves in his forehead show . . . standing out like a relief map, in harsh light. They aged him by ten years, and Brooke remembered that she had always felt more tender toward her husband when he looked vulnerable this way.

"You said you had a plan," she prompted.

"I know you're impatient, Brooke, but—"

"Impatient? You think it's *impatient* to want my child out of that madman's hands? After what you've told me about him?"

"I didn't mean . . . Christ, can't you ever just listen and let me talk?"

"I thought I'd been doing that for years." She bit off the words. She needed Nathan's cooperation now, not his anger. "Sorry. Tell me your plan."

Whatever it was, Nathan would move slowly and deliberately, she knew, giving careful forethought and consideration to every angle.

He finished his coffee in one nervous gulp and stood, crossing to the pot for more. "I think he'll try to move her soon. He's had his fun toying with me—but he knows I'm at the end of my rope. He'll have to be watching his back all the time from now on."

"But if he's crazy, will he even care?"

"Crazy but crafty. And my investigator turned up information that he's got another house, up near Seattle. There was another child, in fact—"

Brooke was only half-aware that her hand had jerked, spilling hot coffee down the front of her shirt. "Another child? You mean, in Seattle? Someone else he did this to?"

"Several, over the past few years, Sigart thinks. Cain has never been arrested or even suspected. But Sigart has a large staff, and working with computers, they put times and places together—child disappearances—and things we know, now, about Cain."

Brooke stared. "What happened to them? What happened to those other little girls?"

Nathan took a gulp of coffee. The cup shook in his hand. "I don't know. That's just it. If only one had been found and had talked—"

Brooke dropped her cup with a thud. "Never found . . ."

Nathan sighed. "That's what I've been trying to tell you, Brooke. There isn't any room for error here."

No room for error.

Brooke trusted Nathan's story—but she didn't trust him not to be too plodding, too slow.

And Creed was in jail.

She could call Gibbs—tell him where she was—but it would take too long, by the time he arrived and she told him everything she had learned from Nathan.

And what could Gibbs do that she couldn't? She had the advantage. She knew about Cain—knew where he was—knew where Charly was.

And she had her own plan.

She splashed cold water on her face and looked into the bathroom mirror at Nathan, standing behind her—the way he had in the old days, looking over her shoulder at himself, and her, with all those questions in his eyes. Those *Who are you, really?* questions. *And why am I with you? What could we possibly be thinking of?*

She dried her face. "Sleep awhile, Nathan," she said softly—playing a role perfected during the old days of marriage and alcohol.

Relax . . . don't worry . . . I won't do anything dumb.

"I'll watch the house, in case Cain tries to leave. We'll take turns."

At his protest she insisted gently. "We can't both be awake twenty-four hours a day. And if he does start to move her, one of us will have to be rested and strong."

"But you had that long drive—"

"And you've been dealing with this longer than I. You're exhausted."

"But what could you do? How could you possibly stop him?"

"I've gotten pretty tough in the past few months." She smiled, showing off the muscle in her upper arm. "Besides, I'll take the Lincoln. You still have the phone in it? I'll call you if he even shows a sign of leaving the house."

Nathan wavered. He could barely keep his eyes open, she knew. His shoulders drooped. He sighed again. "Promise me one thing . . . that you won't do anything rash."

"Of course not," Brooke said. *Relax . . . don't worry. . . .*

She nudged him carefully toward the bed . . . hands on his shoulders, easing him down. She even bent and removed his shoes, the way she had in the early days when he had come home exhausted from work.

A blanket, then—from the end of the bed. Tuck him in. Kiss his cheek.

All is well, Nathan. I won't do anything rash.

He was asleep before she hit the door.

Chapter 37

ONE STOP . . . one stop at the jeep . . . fingers in the glove compartment, closing over cold metal. Silver, gleaming, sliding into her purse.

Grabbing Creed's old green jacket from the back of the jeep. And other things. Putting them in the Lincoln. Climbing in. Hurriedly figuring out the instruments, how they worked.

Driving cautiously along the dark, twisting roads. *Let nothing go wrong. Please, let nothing go wrong.*

At the mailbox cutoff again. Déjà vu, but with a twist: This time she wouldn't fail.

Pulling on Creed's jacket. Twisting her blond hair up and hiding it beneath a fishing cap she had found. Wiping off all remaining makeup. Reaching in the back for Creed's fishing rod and tackle box. Taking the Smith & Wesson from the denim purse. Putting the long, heavy revolver into the box. *It would show through any pocket.* Stepping outside the jeep with the box and bending down. Rubbing her fingers in dirt, smudging her face. Walking along the road, openly, to the house.

She rang the bell at the gate and stood looking into the lens of the security camera.

Several moments passed. Finally, a squawk, a rattle of static.

"Yes . . . who is it?" A thready male voice.

"Lu-Ellen Cole," Brooke said, retrieving and thickening the Georgia accent. She cleared her throat. "Y'all don't know me, but ah've

245

been fishin' down below, an' mah jeep broke down. Hate t'bothah y'all at this hou-ah, but ah haven't been able to raise anothah livin' soul. Can ah use yoah phone to call fuh help?"

A long silence.

" 'Lo? Y'all they-ah?" What was happening? Had she overdone it? Had he already guessed who she was?

"Are you alone?" said the voice.

"Lahk a dyin' man with no rel'tives." She affected a swagger with her chin and shoulder posture. "Out he-ah from West Vahginia, campin'. A fine ol' jeep, had it fuh yea-ahs, but lahk as not the cross-country trip did 'er in."

"You should go back and wait. The highway patrol will come along."

"Well, now, ah did put a help sign on the thing, but it seems lahk ah been waitin' yea-ahs. Ah reckon' those ol' boys're off havin' a party somewheah t'night."

"I still think you should go back. Tell me where you're parked, and I'll call someone for you."

Brooke sighed. "Ah'd suah appreciate that. Only thing is, to tell th' truth, I gotta real bad need to use the facil'ties. Ah wouldn't bothah y'all . . . just in 'n out."

Another silence after that. *He's not going for it. Damn!* Was he afraid Charly might call out for help again? It was Brooke's fear, too, but for another reason. If Charly recognized her voice, even with the accent, and called out for her—it would end everything.

Well, she had an alternative pl—

A buzzing sound emanated from the gate. It swung open slightly. Brooke stared as if the thing had come alive and might swallow her whole if she walked through.

She stepped forward. Pushed on the gate. Entered the grounds. She was in.

THERE WAS A CAMERA at the front door too. Brooke pulled the fishing cap down farther over her forehead and affected the jutting chin, the tomboy swagger, as she rang the bell and waited.

The slight blond man she had seen with Nathan earlier opened the door. He smiled. "I'm sorry to have been so difficult, but this happens quite frequently around here. It gets irksome, especially so late at night."

The door widened, and Brooke stepped inside. She heard Cain's words through a haze of emotion. *I'm in. I'm in the same house with Charly!* It took enormous effort not to run up that oversized staircase and scream for her daughter.

She tried not to meet Cain's eyes, but was drawn to them. This was the monster who had stolen Charly—and, if Nathan was right, other people's daughters. He had sent those mutilated dolls and done God knows what—

But he looked so gentle, so insignificant. Frail—as if the breeze from a raised voice might lift him away. His hair was wispy, with a slightly damp lock in front. Brooke was sure, suddenly, that Cain had licked his fingers and straightened that lock before opening the door. It was frighteningly easy to picture the young boy, lost and alone in some big house—watching that Italian news film over and over—his parents being murdered before his eyes, blood in the streets, no one to talk to about it—

Stop it, Brooke. This is a beast, a creature of evil. He may have killed those other little girls. He could kill you—and Charly. You can't afford to feel sorry for him.

Glancing around the enormous hallway, she said, "People break dowahn heah all the tahm?"

"That, or they get lost."

"Well, as ah said, ah do rightly appreciate this." She reached back and set the fishing rod beside the front door, but hefted the tackle box. "Got a few things in heah to freshen up, if y'don't mind."

"Not at all. The bathroom is right through there." Cain gestured to a door off the center hall. His eyes, a pale gray-blue behind round glasses, smiled gently. "Take your time."

Brooke nodded her thanks. On the way to the bathroom she had to pass the bottom of the stairs. *Was she doing the right thing? Or should she just run up there, right now, yelling?*

But Cain had told Nathan that someone had a gun on Charly. And there was no telling how long it would take to get to her. She needed to know more—and she wanted the Smith & Wesson in her hands, pointed at Cain, before she made her move.

She flicked on the bathroom light and locked the door behind her. A fiery glow came from gold wallpaper, flecked with red velvet. Brooke set the tackle box on a marble vanity around the sink. For a moment she simply stood, staring at her reflection in the mirror. Her mouth was dry, her hands ice-cold and shaky. Her eyes were too large, too green, too dark—like someone on uppers. Absolute terror. Another alternative to drugs.

Running hot water, she warmed her hands. Dried them on a tiny red linen guest towel. Then she flushed the toilet.

Chin up. Shoulders back. That's right. Now get out there. Play the role. And remember—you're tough. You can do it.

As quietly as possible, she snapped open the green metal catches of the tackle box. The Smith & Wesson gleamed among hooks, lures, and fishing wire. It looked reassuring. Substantial. She hefted its weight, then turned the gold-plated knob of the bathroom door. Opening it slightly, she gripped the gun in both hands and pushed the door open the rest of the way with her toe. Stepping out, she turned to the front.

A shadow passed over her eyes. Heavy blows rained around her shoulders. Brooke fell.

Pain!

Oh, God, what is it? What had he hit her with? What was he doing to her legs?

She tried to swing onto her back, but there was something heavy pinning her down. She felt heat. Flashing lights. Agony around the waist and hips. Classical music blasted her eardrums. Nervous laughter sang a counterpoint.

The Smith & Wesson gleamed dully, uselessly, from beside her face. Her hands were nowhere near it. She couldn't feel them, didn't know where they had gone.

The floor darkened, wavered . . . disappeared.

Chapter 38

"WHAT DO YOU MEAN, Creed is gone?" Andy Laskov raged into the phone. "You telling me you never even charged him?"

"Commissioner's orders," de Porres said laconically. "You'll have to take it up with him."

"The PC interfered? Dammit, what is this between him and Creed? The old man's gone too far this time, Marty. I'll have his ass, and Creed's too."

"Whatever you say," de Porres intoned. "Sorry, Andy. But, well, you know, when the old man speaks . . ."

Laskov bellowed on. "Don't give me that shit! You've been cozy with Creed from the first. You and that asshole Gibbs, and Dunwalt—"

De Porres turned the speaker button off, hanging up. Captain Dunwalt, across from him, nodded with satisfaction and stood. Gibbs, off to the side, tugged at his blue cap and gave a smile. He began to follow Dunwalt out, but at the door he turned.

"What's your part in this all about, Marty? Boredom? Just askin'."

De Porres smiled. On the desk before him, Old Billy acted as a paperweight for a folder from Hawaiian Airlines. Inside were round-trip tickets for next month. "Not for much longer, Gibby. Not much longer at all."

Dancing girls . . . swaying palms and steel guitars . . . leis and mango cream . . .

A great fantasy. And a pretty decent vacation plan, too.

But hell, he could never actually live like that. Sitting around on hot sand all day? He'd go nuts.

And now he wouldn't have to. Once this case was over, the PC had promised him a spot in Special Investigations.

No more desk work—and no more bum ticker. The commissioner's own doctor would issue a new certificate, stating the irregular beats had been temporary; too much coffee, something to be watched, but certainly no reason to worry.

"In appreciation of your cooperation," the old man had wheezed. "The department needs more men like you. If you had gone ahead and charged Creed, let it get into the machinery, instead of calling me—well, you never know, a child's life could have been lost. Of course, we can't be sure, even now. But at least we've got a chance."

"Thank you, sir. I can't tell you how much—" De Porres had given him a curious look. "I don't understand how the doctor—how he could take a chance, lying like that."

The commissioner had laughed—a heavy, rasping snort. "It's done all the time, Marty. How do you think I've managed to stay in my job all these years?"

Marty brought his attention back. Gibbs was talking to him.

"What did you think of Keep's story about his wife? And Michael Stossell—that artist she was with when Jason disappeared?"

"I think you've known about it all along," de Porres said blandly. "I think you found out she was in bed with that guy instead of watching the kid, and you kept it to yourself."

Gibbs shrugged. "For a while. I confronted her with it first, and she begged me not to tell Keep. She really loved him, you know. That Michael guy, he was somebody to talk to, to be with when Keep was never around, and it just sort of got out of hand."

"Hard thing, being married to a cop," de Porres agreed. "One of the reasons I've never married. What made you finally spill the beans, back then, to Creed?"

"When I saw the DA had it in for him, I had to tell him. I thought he'd use it to protect himself. But that was long after Karen was up in Santa Maria—and Keep couldn't bring himself to expose her like that."

"Well . . . they probably won't charge her with neglect now, not in her condition. If you've got proof, though . . ."

"I've got Stossell's admission. Whether Keep will ever let me use it is something else."

"Depends, I guess, on whether Laskov drops his vendetta once he has the facts."

"You think he will?"

"Andy? I think he's as mean as that old trout swimmin' around in his office. Still, he's not stupid. He'll have to patch things up with the commissioner, it bein' an election year . . . and it looks like that means he'll have to nigga-lick Creed, too."

Gibbs gave a grin and a snort. "Nigga-lick? What the hell kind of term is that, Marty . . . nigga-lick?"

"Caribbean," de Porres said with an answering grin. "Or maybe I made it up. Hell, I don't know. All I know's I've been doin' it since I hit this desk a year ago—and I don't fuckin' plan to do it anymore."

He gave a firm rap on the desk with Old Billy, issuing Gibbs out the door.

Chapter 39

IT WAS THE LONG WAY AROUND, but the only safe approach—Creed was sure of that now. His hiking boots slipped on wet rocks as he scrambled down them toward the sea. It had been a long time since he'd done any rock climbing; since the camping trips with Karen, and they had lasted only until she was pregnant with Jason.

Spray from pounding waves reached upward to drench his face, his clothes. Around his shoulder, and fastened to his waist, was a coil of rope—a dim white oval against black: black shirt, black jeans, black boots and headband. . . .

Creed raised his face to the sky. That too was black—as dense and inky as the Dakotas at midnight.

He couldn't see his watch and wondered how long it had been since he had left the rental jeep along that mountain trail. A half hour? He guessed it had been a total of four hours since he had chartered the Piper Cub to Monterey. From there he had rented the Cherokee. The clothes and climbing equipment had come from an all-night army surplus store. That was after midnight. It should be close to two A.M. by now.

Too late. *It had taken too long.* Would Charly still be here, or had Nathan already removed her to another place? Creed had seen lights on in the house, from the front—but that didn't necessarily mean anything.

He stepped up his pace, feeling his way along the slippery rocks—

not daring to use the flashlight attached to his belt. Even a pinpoint of light might be spotted immediately in this near-total darkness.

The winds had picked up in the past few minutes. Below, waves crashed. Tidepools became whirlpools. He could just make out their light foam. Over his head, twisted pine trees moaned and complained.

He was glad he didn't have Brooke to look after; this would be tough enough alone. He was glad, too, that she was safe in Venice. At least he had to assume she had made it from the Westwood house to the jeep, and then back to the beach house okay. He hadn't taken time to call but had hustled to the airport the minute de Porres had turned him loose. He wanted to be well out of town before Andy Laskov realized he was gone. If there was any way possible, Laskov would throw a monkey wrench into things.

He wondered where Gibbs had been when de Porres released him. Well, he could trust Gibby to look after things. To look after Brooke.

He could see the house above him now, although still a few hundred yards to the left. The pines grew thicker there. That would help his climb over the cliff when he neared the top.

The problem would be getting across the next thirty feet or so. He had made it to a huge boulder, sharp and dark, like an iceberg jutting out of the sea. Between this and the next, which was almost a twin, stood perhaps thirty feet of arctic temperature water. Waves . . . gusting wind. And no telling how deep. He might have to swim, with only the rope as an umbilical cord to dry land.

With spray coating his eyelashes, he stood wedged between rocks, his back to one, feet against another. Below was a deep crevice and angry sea. He took the rope from his shoulder, feeling along the rock to his right for any kind of indentation, something to cleave the rope to. Usually—near the bottom, where the erosion of years of high tides had taken place—

Yes, there it was. A long, uneven groove—a chink, a fissure. He looped the rope around it and tied a knot, leaving several feet to pay out. The next step would be the most difficult—descending into that frigid, violent sea. He could lose his balance, strike his head, never come up for air. . . .

He'd better not think of that. Instead, he thought of the anger he had been nursing all the way up here. He wanted his hands on Nathan Hayes—and on his cohort, Luther Mendelsohn Cain. This whole case had been too queer from the beginning. The mutilated doll, the phone call from Charly to Brooke—Hayes' story about the camping trip. All of it bizarre for a parental kidnapping. Yet there was no doubt Hayes was involved. De Porres had verified Nathan's stay at that motel, the Timber-Inn. Hayes had checked out, though, de Porres had learned. Early that morning.

One thing—they had found the housekeeper there. Mrs. Stinson. Her presence confirmed even further that Charly was in the area. The housekeeper had been picked up, but so far, she wasn't talking.

His foot slipped. Creed grabbed for a hold in the rock, found none, slipped farther into a wall of ice water and felt his breath explode—

He was up to his neck, and only the rope had broken his fall. No bottom—his feet hadn't touched.

He felt his blood freeze, his pulse slow. Hypothermia? Was that what they called it when the body froze, shut down, when you couldn't function anymore? Creed wondered, briefly, if he was too over the hill to manage this—if it was stupid to even consider it. Would his muscle strength, kept in shape only by running and a now-and-then trip to Gold's Gym, hold up? Would it get him out of this in time?

He struck out in the direction he believed to be the next boulder. He couldn't actually see it anymore.

Christ, he thought, *the tide's even stronger than I figured it would be. These boots are cement blocks.*

Don't think. Don't think about the cold, about the fact that you can't feel your own tail. Holy shit, keep moving. Move fast.

Where? Which direction? The waves are too high, can't see above them. No direction—don't know which way to go. Arms so heavy . . .

Light. Light from the house? Or something else? A boat? Couldn't be, not on a night like this. Had to be the house. Swim to the right. Doesn't feel right, though—should be left. Do it anyway. Follow your instinct. Your head's not worth a damn, it's too numb.

But the light's getting farther away. Am I being pulled out to sea? Chest burning, lungs straining—have to swim against it though, swim against the tide. Can't let down for a second. Thirty feet—thirty lousy feet, that's all.

Or was it more than forty, now? How far have I drifted from that other boulder, and the safety of those rocks?

Push. Push toward the light. No, two lights. Two lights, bobbing. Moving swiftly, now, several yards away. Oh, God . . . a boat, after all? A fishing boat, coming home? No engine sound . . . but then, the waves are too loud.

Doesn't matter. The light is gone.

Where the hell have I drifted to?

Follow your instinct—swim to the left. That's it. A denser blackness ahead. The boulder? Yes!

Arms nearly useless, though, from the cold. Lungs too stretched . . . they aren't expanding anymore.

Waves, swamping . . . pulling everything down. A sharp pain in the chest, ribs . . .

Going under.

Numb. Everything numb. Can't hold on.

Brooke was right. I put things off too long. I was afraid of failing— and what one fears nearly always manifests.

Someone had told him that. Who?

His mom.

Chapter 40

SOMEONE WAS TALKING—but the sounds were muted, as if they came through a sieve. Brooke opened her eyes.

Light—too bright. Too white. It hurts.

She crawled back into darkness. It was safer there.

But the voice continued. *Charly,* it was saying.

Charly.

Try again.

Squinting against the light. *Cameras. Some kind of room, with cameras on tripods.*

Brooke moved her head sideways. *Him . . . it's him.*

Who is he talking to?

". . . a complication. I'll have to rethink this, decide how best to make you disappear. Well, you are good at disappearing, aren't you Brooke? Isn't that what you did to Charly . . . the day you moved to San Francisco?"

Her. He was talking to her. While she was unconscious? Had he been talking to her all this time?

How much time? How long had she been out?

Brooke raised her head. It was all the movement she could manage. Her hands were tied painfully behind her back, her legs trussed. Some kind of wire. It glistened in the kinetic light.

She looked to the other side. A woman, lying beside her in a

256

negligee. Short black hair and a lifeless face, molded and shiny. A corpse. Eyes staring at the ceiling out of deep sockets. Too-long lashes. Too-painted cheeks.

Not a corpse. A mannequin. A store mannequin . . . in the negligee that Sean had given her, the one taken from her closet in San Francisco.

And photographs all over white walls. School photos, class pictures. Hundreds of them.

"You like my gallery?" Cain asked.

He stood above her in black pants and a lime green shirt. The style of both was old-fashioned, out of date. The shirt was too tight, the pants too short. Black socks sagged around the ankles. Thin blond hair needed trimming. Brooke saw every detail through a mist, thinking: Nothing fits. It's too pathetic. This can't be a monster. It can't.

She saw the cameras again and realized there were four, and that they surrounded her. Intense heat from klieg lights fanned her face. Beneath her lower back was some kind of lump, something hard.

"Where . . . is my daughter?" Her voice was rough and halting. "Is Charly all right?"

Cain smiled. "A most excellent model, Charly. A mobile face, great expression, good form—"

"Model?" Had he done things—

Brooke wrenched her head and shoulders up, trying to get to him. Her stomach muscles spasmed. She groaned and fell back. Her head thudded against the polished wooden floor, and the lump beneath her back dug into her flesh.

Cain said patiently, "You're wasting strength, Brooke. Save it for when we leave here."

"I want my daughter!"

He didn't answer.

"Where are you taking us?"

"It's a secret," Cain said. "A secret." He gave a gleeful chuckle and clapped his hands. A tiny jump made the socks sag even farther.

Mad. He's totally mad. My God, what has he done to Charly?

But Nathan will wake up, he'll try to reach me on the car phone. When he can't . . .

She remembered then that she had purposely turned off the alarm clock in the motel room. And Nathan had always been the kind to sleep forever, if no one woke him up. She had counted on that.

Think. Keep him talking . . . play for time.

"Who's this?" Her head motioned to the mannequin.

"Do you like her? She's very pretty, isn't she?"

"Why is she wearing my negligee?"

"Isn't that what faithless mothers do?"

"I . . . I don't know." Her mind reeled. But she had to keep him talking. "What are all those pictures?" She looked at the class photos on the wall.

"A hobby. I like still pictures. You can move people around . . . make them do anything you want."

She risked it. "You mean like those films of your parents being shot? You must have wished you could turn them around, make them come out differently."

His face screwed up with pain. He stamped a foot, like a child. "Don't talk about that!"

A damaged child. A madman.

Then she remembered. There had been class pictures on Charly's dresser, in her room. The entire class, together—and a duplicate of the wallet-sized photo Charly had sent to Brooke.

"Are you the photographer who took Charly's class pictures this year?"

"This year, *and* last," Cain said proudly. "It takes a while to learn about the families. It wouldn't do, after all, to free a child who came from a happy home. There would be no point."

Brooke tried to shift position. The lump beneath her waist had begun to hurt. She couldn't seem to move enough to get away from it.

"I don't understand. How did you get a job like that?"

"It's simple." Cain smiled. "I submit bids to school districts all over the country. It's a most excellent way to meet children, to get to know who their families are. They pay with checks, or credit cards, and since I'm listed as a business, I have access to their credit histories. I know everyone they owe money to, how they live, where they travel, and how often. I even learn their social security numbers. A credit history is an excellent contemporary portrait of a person's life . . . don't you agree?"

She ignored the question. "How did you end up with Nathan's house?"

"Oh, I do extensive research. I knew when he was merely *thinking* about selling it. Then, when he advertised, I bought the house."

"But why? You didn't have to live here, to do this."

His smile grew broader. "Well, but don't you see how perfect it was? Bringing Charly to a house her father owned, but that she never saw because her father was too busy—and her mother too drunk?"

Brooke flexed her wrists, trying to loosen whatever it was that bound them. Not wire, she didn't think . . . that would cut into her flesh more. Rope, then. Thin rope. It might stretch, if she worked it enough.

But the more she tried, the more that hard protrusion pressed into her lower back.

"There is something in the eyes when a child is unhappy," Cain was saying. "There was something in Charly's eyes when I found her this past spring . . . but it took a while to research everything, of course."

That word again. "Research?"

"Well, you see, I first have to find out who the problem parent is —in this case, you or your husband. For the punishment."

Punishment.

Cain spoke gently. "Poor Charly . . . poor unlucky child. She had a drunk for a mother, and an absentee father. It was necessary to plan suitable discipline for you both."

"Discipline," Brooke whispered.

Cain adjusted the position of one camera, then pulled a light meter from his pocket. He peered at it, nodded, and picked up a cord with a switch at one end. "Smile, Mother. You, too, Brooke. *Look this way!*"

Involuntarily Brooke's eyes flicked to the camera. Pain shot up her right leg. It ran through her lower back like a hot poker. She yelled. Her whole body arched, twisted, jerked. Shutters clicked.

"Lovely," Cain said softly. He smiled again. "That was truly lovely."

Brooke lay panting, drenched with sweat. She let out a sob. *Dear God. It was that thing, below my back. Something electrical. Connected to the wire around my legs.*

She must have bitten her tongue; she tasted blood.

"You were trying to distract me with conversation, weren't you, Brooke?" Cain nodded slowly. "But I think I've won this round."

"You won't win forever," Brooke said through gritted teeth. "Nathan will come. He'll bring the police." *And Creed. Creed will catch him.*

But Creed was in jail.

Why hadn't she brought Gibbs along? Dear God, she had been so stupid, coming here like this.

"The gates are all locked, now," Cain said, "and you don't seriously believe that Nathan will climb that wall—the way you did, earlier?"

He seemed pleased at her surprise. "You thought you were so clever. But, you see . . . it was *my* trap, all along."

"You . . . you wanted me here? Why?"

"For the punishment, of course."

"Oh, right . . . the punishment." She tasted bile, the taste of fear. It burned her throat and lungs.

"This is special for you, Brooke. Some mothers just go away. They go on business trips, or vacations, and leave their children with sitters. But you . . . you went away for good. You never came back. Why didn't you come back?" Cain's finger moved on the switch again.

Brooke's neck snapped. Her head flew back. Excruciating pain surged down her spine. "Stop it! *Stop it!*" she screamed.

"Mommeeee!"

Every cell in Brooke's body seemed to explode, as if the pain in that voice were too much to bear and keep on living. For a split second she couldn't make a sound. Then it tumbled out, along with tears. *"Charly!* Oh, Charly, honey, oh, God, *where are you?"* She began to flail with all her strength against the wires around her legs.

"Mommeee! I'm upstairs! I'm upstairs, here!"

"Honey, I'm coming! I'm coming, hang on!"

But she wasn't coming, she wasn't going anywhere. She couldn't get free—

Then everything went haywire. There was a deafening crash. She saw Cain look up to a window, saw his face pale, saw the absolute bewilderment. He dropped the electrical switch. Glass flew around him in a diamond spray. In the next second, Cain was on the floor, a large dark figure on top of him. The figure had its hands around Cain's throat. It was squeezing, squeezing. It banged Cain's head, over and over, against the hard wooden floor.

Creed! She couldn't believe it.

It was Creed.

Cain's face was nearly black. Creed was killing him. He was unconscious, or dead, slack, his tongue lolling from his mouth, his pale, pathetic body rising, then thudding—and still Creed kept at him.

"Creed, stop! Oh, God, stop!"

He didn't hear her. She yelled again. "Stop it! Let him be! We've got to get to Charly!"

Creed's head snapped up. His eyes were glazed. She saw that he was drenched . . . clothes, hair, boots. His mouth twisted. "I'm going to kill this son of a bitch!"

"No! Get me out of this first. What if somebody's up there with Charly?"

Creed shook his head, as if clearing it. He rocked back on his heels. "Charly." He began to focus. "Where is she?"

"Upstairs! Dammit, Creed! Help me!"

He dropped his hold on Cain. The man's inert body fell like a bundle of sticks. Creed stumbled over to Brooke. He started on the wires around her legs.

"Be careful, it's some kind of electrical wire."

His eyes flicked to hers as he worked at it. "It's twisted around you. Here, turn." He unwrapped it, like knitting yarn. "Again . . ."

She felt her legs go free. He held out a hand. "Let's go!"

She pushed to her feet. "Charly! Charly, where are you? We're coming!" They raced into the center hall and up the stairs. The way they had gone after the little girl in Pacific Palisades . . .

But this time—this time—it would be all right. Charly was here. She had to be all right.

They halted a split second at the top of the second-floor landing, throwing open doors—three on the left, three on the right. No one.

Nothing. They raced to the third. Here there was only one door. Brooke rushed headlong toward it, sailing ahead of Creed. She yanked at the knob, but the door was locked.

A key. A key, hanging on a hook beside the door.

She grabbed it and shoved it into the lock. It turned. She wrenched the door open. "Charly!"

There was a bed. A bed, and a portrait of her—Brooke—on the wall. Dolls on a bed.

"Charly!" She didn't see her. Didn't see her anywhere. Brooke whirled around to Creed. "Where *is* she?"

He was heading for another door. "Bathroom. She must be hiding."

Brooke followed Creed into the room.

Tiles. Gold fixtures. A dripping faucet. They checked the tub, the cupboards below the sink. Any possible hiding place. But the bathroom was empty.

"Creed, she's gone!" Brooke cried. There was pain, confusion, and fear in her voice. "My God, how could she—Charly's gone!"

Chapter 41

IN A ROOM BELOW, Luther Mendelsohn Cain stirred. His mottled face slowly regained color. He coughed, choked, then coughed again. His breath came through damaged vocal cords—a labored hiss. Eyes fluttered open. Thin fingers with orange stains rose, shaking, to a bruised throat. Cain's arm flung out as he tried to raise himself. A camera fell, the tripod hitting his chest. He turned on his side, shoving it away. It took every ounce of strength to get to his knees. His legs were weak. His chest hurt. His throat felt as if he had swallowed raw chunks of steel and glass.

"I have to save her," he mouthed. There was spittle on his chin. It shimmered in the dazzle of remaining klieg lights. "I can't let them hurt her."

His foot struck something. He looked down. "Mother." He stifled a sob. In the struggle moments before, his mother's new nightgown had gotten dirty. It was covered with bits of shattered glass from the broken window. Her face was coated with it, jagged shards that poked at her vacant eyes, her perfect nose, her silent mouth. He knelt and picked them carefully away. Pieces of glass dug into his bony knees. He hardly noticed.

"I'm sorry, Mother. I did my best to save her. But they know me now. They'll come after me. They won't let me keep her." He cocked his head, placing an ear at the mannequin's mouth. Listening. Tears fell against the mannequin's marble-like cheek.

"I know, Mother. I'll have to kill her. It's really the only way now."

Chapter 42

CHARLY SQUEEZED HERSELF into a tiny ball, in a hiding place beneath the drooping branches of a pine tree. She didn't know how far she had run, and she didn't know where to go for help. There weren't any other houses that she could see. No houses, no cars, no people.

She didn't even know where she was. She remembered finding the door that was in her bedroom all along—except that she had been too stupid to see it —then racing down steps that opened into a tiny hallway that had stacks of firewood along it. She remembered how it felt, seeing that outside door. Not even believing when it was unlocked, not even believing the fresh, wet air on her face, the night sky, the strong smell of damp earth.

She had run like crazy through a garden, but the wrong way, and nearly fallen over cliffs into the ocean. Then she'd had to run back the same way, all the while thinking that he must be right behind her, that he knew she had gotten away, and he'd kill her now if he caught her. She had run smack into a wall, and for a minute she thought she'd never get away. It was too high, no gate, no time to look for a way out. But there were trees, lots of them, and she had shinnied up one, the way she and her friend Becky had at home so many times, just for fun. She remembered reaching the top of the wall and letting go, scared to death (it was so far down!) but letting herself fall. She had scraped a knee, but picked herself up, then run across a road, up a hill, following a dirt path through woods. Wet branches had whipped her face, and she had fallen twice and cut her knees again. All the while she was looking for other houses, for a light some-where in a window.

Nothing. It was like those movies on TV at night, where there had been a nuclear war, and one or two people woke up to find themselves on a planet all alone.

Finally she had stopped to catch her breath. And she had found this tree. It was real old, she knew, with these big heavy branches, and a good hiding place. When she played with Becky in the garden at home, she was always good at finding hiding places. Her favorite was an old weeping willow—

But why had it taken her so long to find that door? She was stupid! She should have known it was there. She just didn't think—

Something cracked nearby. A branch? Somebody there? Her stomach twisted into painful knots. Charly tried real hard not to breathe. Fog dripped from the tree. It was all over, now, long skinny trails of it between the hills.

She was glad. It might help her hide.

No more sounds. There were probably a lot of animals, here. Maybe foxes, or even wolves. She hoped there weren't bears.

For a while she had thought that her mother would be able to save her. But then there was that awful crash, and her mother screaming, "No, stop it, no!" and she knew that something awful was happening downstairs. She wanted to run down there and help her mother, and she almost did, but then she thought that if her mother was in trouble, there was only herself left to stop the man from hurting everybody. And what could a kid like her do, all alone, and without any gun or anything? She had to get the police or something.

That was when her mind had cleared, and she'd thought about the panel. The panel with the deer and things.

Another crack of twigs nearby. Charly stiffened. What was it? Another animal? Maybe it was her mother—

"Charly?" *a soft voice called.*

She held her breath, not daring to make a sound.

"Charly," *the voice whispered again,* "come out, come out, wherever you are . . ."

Oh, God, it was him! *He knew she was here! How could he know? She had to run.*

She saw a shadow move, no more than a few feet away. And remembered reading somewhere that when you're hiding, you shouldn't look at the person who is looking for you. Because they feel it, and they know where you are.

Charly scrinched her eyes shut as tight as she could.

"Your mother is gone, now, Charly. I'm the only one left to take care of *you. But you were very clever to have gotten out. I didn't even know about the door."*

 It was like the one in my father's study at home, Charly almost said aloud. I just thought those deer and things were only decoration this time.

 "I suppose the back stairs were always there," Cain said conversationally. "Your grandparents must have disguised the door when they remodeled. The one at the bottom too, hiding it behind that wall." His voice lowered, becoming gentle. "You never knew your grandparents, did you? I didn't know mine, either. But grandmothers and grandfathers are supposed to be good to children. They're never supposed to say no." A soft whisper. "Charly, I'll never say no to you."

 She felt her knees and stomach shake as the thin voice began to sing. ". . . whatever you say or do . . ."

 The voice rose. It bounced off walls of fog and echoed eerily through the hills. "Today is tomorrow, if you want it so . . ."

 Charly shivered. *He's crazy. He's so crazy.*

 "Hello, Charly," Cain said. His hand touched her shoulder. "I knew I'd find you here."

 She screamed.

BROOKE HALTED in the middle of the road in front of Cain's house. "Creed!" She grabbed his arm.

 "It came from up there." He motioned to a point way above the steep bank before them—to a copse of trees in the fold between two hills. Only the tops of the trees could be seen, as darkness against fog that wound through them. "There's got to be a path. C'mon."

 "Charly!" Brooke yelled. "Charly, we're here! It's all right! We're coming!"

 She bit back a sob and followed Creed along the road. Cain was on the loose. He had disappeared. And they hadn't been able to find Creed's gun.

Chapter 43

It was worse than they could have imagined.

Cain stood pinned within the circle of Creed's flashlight—one arm around Charly's neck, near the top of a precipice. Creed and Brooke had followed his voice—calling to them, teasing them, luring them on. Now they faced him from several feet away. Behind Cain the sheer, vertical cliff fell several hundred feet to where the mountain curved inward away from the sea. Cain held the Smith & Wesson to Charly's throat. There was blood on her knees, and her face was stained with tears. But her chin was high. She was trying hard to be brave.

"You can't have her," Cain said. His voice shook. "I can't let you have her."

Brooke was crazy with hate. She wished Creed had killed this madman. She wished she could kill him herself, now, with her bare hands.

"Just put the gun down," Creed said reasonably. "That way, no one will get hurt."

Hysterical laughter echoed around the hills. "No, you don't understand. If Charly goes back to her mother and father, she *will* be hurt. I can't let that happen."

"I'll see that Charly is taken care of," Creed promised.

"You?" Cain's voice was full of scorn. "You couldn't even protect your own child."

He knows who I am, Creed thought with despair. *How can he know so much?* "I tried," he said quietly. "I did my best."

"You let him be stolen!"

"I thought he was being watched!" The words, so long held back, were wrenched out like a bad tooth that had festered for years. Creed steadied himself. "I thought he was being watched."

"Your wife," Cain said shrewdly. "What was she doing when your little boy disappeared?"

"She was lonely," Creed said protectively. "It wasn't her fault . . . it was mine."

"That's exactly it," Cain said. "Isn't that what I said? *Your fault.*"

"We never would have hurt Jason. We didn't know . . ."

The answering voice was hopeless. *Destiny,* it said. "Who ever knows?"

Cain moved closer to the edge of the cliff, still holding Charly within the crook of one arm. He pointed the gun at Creed and Brooke. His hand shook. "It will all be over in a moment. She won't feel anything."

Creed jerked forward, then stopped. He drew in a soft, almost inaudible breath. Brooke, too, nearly stopped breathing as she looked to the far right and saw what he had seen. Just outside the circle of light.

She glanced at Creed, then began to plead earnestly with Cain. "I promise I'll take better care of Charly, if you'll just let her go. I'll do anything you say. Just let me have her. Things will be better, you'll see."

"Faithless woman! I can't trust you. You lie."

"No!" she said desperately. "I promise, I'll do anything! You can watch me, keep an eye on me, make sure I do it!"

Cain inched backward. "Too late. It's just too late."

"No!" Brooke yelled.

There were still ten feet of solid ground left behind Cain when Nathan Hayes spoke. "Let her go. Let her go, Cain!" He stood directly behind Cain and Charly now.

Cain swung around, leveling the gun. But Nathan was holding a sharp rock the size of a softball. He swung it with all his might, striking Cain's head. At the same time, he grabbed Charly's arm. Cain, blood streaming from his temple, toppled toward the edge of the cliff. He swung his arms out for balance, and Charly was free. She tumbled into

Nathan's arms. Creed rushed forward and grabbed Cain, but the momentum took him over the edge. Creed was on his belly, his top half out of sight.

Brooke screamed. She ran, her hands outstretched, grabbing him around the waist. "Creed!"

He was slipping, his weight pulling her over. She saw that he had grabbed Cain, had hold of his arms. Brooke's fingers grabbed his belt, then slid to the last hold, his legs. She was losing him! Her arms felt pulled from their sockets, screaming pain along them, pain in her hands, her fingers, her chest. She heard sobs coming from somewhere, and Charly screaming, "Mommy! Mommy!"

Brooke was slipping, along with Creed. She could see the rocks, now, several hundred feet below. "Creed, let go of him, let go!" she cried. But she saw that Creed no longer had a grip on Cain's arms, and it was Cain now who held him, held him by the wrists. And she was hearing the same words, "Let go, let go!" but they were coming from Nathan, "Brooke, let go!" She felt hands at her waist, tugging. Nathan's voice, shouting at her to let go of Creed.

The weight on her arms eased abruptly. For a moment she thought she had lost Creed, and her heart slammed into her throat. But then she heard the scream, and looking down, she saw Cain's light body falling like a rag doll, drifting slowly, twisting and turning, becoming smaller and smaller, his blue shirt flapping, *like a doll, like a doll, like a doll. . . .*

EPILOGUE

A HOT EVENING SUN STREAKED THE SKY with shades of gold and salmon over the Pacific Ocean. From Creed's deck Brooke watched Charly walking with Gibbs along the sand. It had been two weeks since Charly had been found.

"I'll admit Roger Dorn's presence in this case confused things," Creed said. "But I always have to look at the possibility that child pornographers might be involved. The problem is too widespread these days to overlook."

"Nobody's blaming you," Brooke said. "You came through for me, and I'll never forget that. I guess I didn't understand, at first, that it happens so much—the child pornography, I mean. Who *are* these animals?"

"Well, there are the child marketeers—the ones who furnish kids to purveyors of porn. Kids are either kidnapped or recruited off the streets and sold back and forth between the marketeers and the pornographers. They're even sold between private parties, through classified ads. The ads list the kid's age, price, what countries he or she will be in, and what dates they'll be there. Then there are people who don't directly touch children, but publish the magazines that show them in sexual situations. Some of the people who buy them look at the pictures, but never touch. Some go out and find children in the neighborhood to molest."

2 7 0

He leaned his elbows against the railing. Charly, in jeans rolled to her knees, was running through the water now. Gibbs was chasing her with something that looked like a crab. She was laughing, her long blond curls glinting red from the setting sun.

"And then there are the photographers, like Dorn, for instance, whose motives are mixed. They get off on taking the photos—as well as on looking at them. That's the main reason he worked for Aphrodite. Agencies like that cater to the child sophisticate market. It's not open porn—but portraying little girls as sexpots has its dangers. It encourages people to think of children as sex objects."

Brooke gave a shudder. "Charly says Cain didn't do anything like that to her. Do you think that's true, or is she blanking it out—or afraid to talk?"

"I suspect it's true. The pictures he took of Charly weren't sexual. He had those shots of her crying, the ones you saw—and ones of her eating, doing ordinary things. I think he wanted photos of her being taken care of—or at least what passed for that, in his warped mind. They found a lot of the same kind of thing in his Seattle house."

"Those other little girls . . . Does anyone know yet who they were, or where they are now? If they're even alive?"

"The FBI is working on it. They've matched photos with one missing child from Nevada, but they haven't found her yet."

"Do you think he . . . killed them?"

"I don't know. And unless they turn up, we may never know, now that Cain's dead. They could have escaped and found their way to one of the underground networks that protects kids who are afraid, or ashamed, to go home." It was what he still hoped, after all these years, had happened to Jason—although in his most rational moments, he saw that hope for the futile fantasy it was.

"I still don't understand," Brooke said, "how he had those doll packages delivered down here, if he was up there with Charly all the time. I mean, I guess he could have driven to my apartment in San Francisco, that's not so far. But would he have left Charly long enough to come down here?"

"Not at all. You remember the photographer at Universal Studios?"

"That nice man? He didn't! Not him."

"No, it was his assistant, that young kid, Felipe. Cain 'researched' him, apparently, and approached him long before he took Charly. He offered him money to deliver the boxes and threatened to report him to Immigration if he didn't. Felipe didn't know what was in the boxes—he just dropped the one off at the messenger service, and the other at my house. After we were at Universal that day, though, the boy started thinking. He has younger brothers and sisters back in Mexico, and he said he wouldn't want anything like that to happen to them. He told his boss—Arnott, the photographer—who looked for me, couldn't find me, and ended up with de Porres. He told Marty about it."

"Will Felipe be picked up by Immigration now?"

Creed smiled, his eyes on Gibbs at the water's edge. "If they can find him. It seems he's disappeared."

Brooke's gaze rested on Gibbs, too. His jeans were wet to the knees, and he was kicking water back at Charly, who had started a water fight. They were both laughing. "He's such a kid," Brooke said.

"And old as the hills. A strange dichotomy."

"Jiminy Cricket."

"Hmmm?"

"Your conscience—isn't he? A little?"

Creed laughed softly. "You noticed."

"Shall we take some sandwiches down there? I'm getting hungry."

"Sure." They went inside, to the kitchen. "By the way, how's the show going?"

It was a Monday, the theater was dark, and Brooke was staying in Los Angeles for the night. "Leo was pretty good about letting me off the hook those first few nights." She got mayonnaise and cold chicken out of the fridge, while Creed reached into a cupboard for bread. "I think he felt guilty for his part in my problems with Nathan. But my stand-in, I hear, was great."

Brooke, Nathan, and Charly had flown directly to Los Angeles after the rescue. They had stayed together for three days and nights at the Westwood house. Since then, Brooke had flown each evening to San Francisco to be in *Molly Brown*. Days, she flew back to LA to be with Charly. The three of them, Nathan, Brooke, and Charly, were seeing a psychologist and a trauma expert together. Until today Creed hadn't seen them since that night in Seaville.

He filled a thermos with iced tea, while Brooke sprinkled salt and pepper on the chicken sandwiches. "How has it been with Charly?" *And with Nathan?* he wondered, but didn't want to ask.

"Both strained and wonderful. Charly had nightmares at first. She woke up crying, and Nathan and I were up nearly every night, all night, just sitting with her." She licked mayonnaise from a finger. Creed thought she had never looked so good. Her hair was shiny and pale, and her legs beneath the white shorts were becoming tan.

"Having her back—I just can't thank you enough."

"You don't have to."

"But if it hadn't been for you—"

Creed shrugged. "It's my job."

"Right." She studied him silently over the counter.

He busied himself with wiping up spots of tea. But he felt her eyes on him. They had never once talked about the night, together, on the beach. He had no idea what she felt about it—or even if she remembered it.

Finally he had to ask. "Are you going back to him?"

Brooke smiled as if surprised. "To Nathan? No. Why would you think that?"

"You seemed to be getting along well, that night after we got Charly. And you've been together a lot since."

"Well, Nathan really came through, didn't he? It feels good that after so many misunderstandings, so many bad years, we can talk now, and that we can help Charly together. But Nathan and I never should have been married in the first place. We were all wrong for each other. We still are."

Creed thought about that as he rinsed out the rag he had used on the counter. "You said earlier that you're moving back to LA. What about the show?"

"Molly Brown? I'll do it another month, then Leo's promised to replace me with my understudy. I've had an offer for a part in a new show down here—a revival of *Pajama Game*—and I've decided to take it."

"Are you doing this to be near Charly?"

"Absolutely." She wrapped the sandwiches and stuck them in a paper bag. "It wouldn't be fair to move her between cities all the time, for visits, and I can't continue to fly back and forth each day the way I've been doing."

"Will Nathan cooperate in your visitations now?"

"Better than that. He's writing up a joint-custody agreement himself. I'll have representation, too, of course, but the fact that he's willing to do this is a major step forward."

They took the steps down to the beach. The sand was cooling off, and a light breeze had come up. Charly and Gibbs were sitting, now, on dry sand, their legs crossed, talking quietly. Gibbs was good with kids. He knew how to talk *to* them, rather than down to them. If Creed guessed right, Gibbs was probably drawing Charly out, getting her to talk about her fears.

"Did you ever hear the whole story about your friend, Sean?" he asked Brooke.

"Yes. The waiter he was with when he was down here in April had recently learned he has AIDS. Sean went to Carmel to meet him and talk about it. It just happened to be at the same time that Charly disappeared."

"Has Sean been tested?"

"Yes. For now, at least, he's okay. But he could still test positive in the future."

"I'm sorry."

"Me too. I'm hoping he'll come back here to work. He needs friends right now. Listen— Would you like to go for coffee, after I take Charly back to Westwood?"

"Sure. But didn't I hear Nathan invite you to dinner, when he dropped Charly off?"

She glanced up at him. "I'd rather go someplace with you."

Creed grinned. "Okay."

They reached the water's edge and headed up the beach toward Gibbs and Charly.

"You know, Creed, I didn't like you much at first."

"You didn't?"

"No. I thought you were kind of unfriendly—maybe even a little mean."

"Well, you were probably right."

"And that business with Cain, at the house. I thought sure you were going to kill him."

"I was."

"You're really angry, still, aren't you? About your life?"

"I'm working on it. I've spent a lot of energy, the past four years, building myself a house of cards. Now I need to remodel. Make it into something more substantial."

"Well, I'm pretty handy with a hammer," Brooke said. "If you need an extra hand."

Creed laughed. "I may take you up on that."

"Have you seen Karen lately?"

"I went up to Santa Maria last weekend. I took her some soap."

Brooke glanced at him curiously. "Soap?"

"Caswell, vanilla. A personal thing." *So she won't have to smell like a hospital anymore.*

"How is she?"

"Unchanged. I thought that when I talked to her that day, told her I knew what had really happened, that she was with someone when Jason—" He had told Brooke about this earlier, explained what really had happened the day Jason disappeared. "Well, I thought that might jolt her out of it. But the doctors think she's been gone too long. They don't expect any miracles."

"But you can't be sure."

"No. And meanwhile . . . I'm having trouble with that final step."

"Divorce?"

"Yes."

I can't promise you anything.

He wanted to say the words, but thought maybe it was too soon for that.

Brooke heard them anyway. She squinted into the distance. "You know what I think the best kind of commitment is? It's when two people agree to be exclusive to each other, and to treat each other unselfishly, and with love. It's a kind of ethical declaration—involving loyalty and trust. Does that strike you as anything that's workable, Creed?"

He squinted into the distance, too. Then he took her hand. "It does."

"Well, then, that's enough for me. I don't want more—not right now, anyway. I've still got some growing to do."

They could hear Charly and Gibbs talking now. Charly was nodding, and they looked like a couple of wizened gurus, their faces screwed up so seriously—discussing the environment, the state of Planet Earth.

It was a good day. The air was warm and promised a good night. Boats were headed south, back to the Marina, their sails snapping in a golden breeze. Scents filled the air, of beans cooking, of hamburgers, hot dogs, fried potatoes, and strong coffee.

The homeless were still here. But even they seemed gentled by the perfect sunset, by thoughts of a mild night, and the coming sleep.

This is as good as it gets, Creed thought. And he should know. He had known the best and the worst that life had to offer, and this moment was by far the best in a long, long time. He had found a child.

It doesn't get any better, Brooke thought as Charly came running, tumbling into her outstretched arms and laughing. *I'm one of the lucky ones. My little girl is home.*